DIARY OF A
SMALL
FISH

Published by
Peter B. Morin
Boston MA
2011

For Betsy, Kate and Will

Chapter 1

Unexpected Company, Muckraking and Junk Mail

I used to play an obscene amount of golf at the exclusive Hyannisport Club. I knew at the time it was irresponsible and overindulgent, but I never thought it was a federal crime.

At the beginning of a perfectly glorious Labor Day weekend, I sat on the back deck of my Cotuit home, cleaning my Pings, preparing for the typical holiday Friday afternoon: eighteen holes, a few martinis and a well-aged New York strip.

Life was good. Then the doorbell rang.

When I opened the door, a massive United States Marshal glared at me with a stone face. He wore a black suit with a badge the size of a pastrami sandwich. His jacket was pulled back on the side to display a gun on his hip.

"Paul B. Forté?" he said in a gravelly voice, deep and mean.

I felt the skin of my face go cold. "Yes?"

He reached inside his suit coat and withdrew a piece of paper.

"You are hereby served." He shoved the paper in my chest.

Stunned, I took the document.

"Have a nice day," he said. He turned, marched to the black sedan idling in the driveway, and got in. I watched as it roared backward into the street, slinging the white clamshells onto my lawn, shifted into drive and squealed rubber.

My throat fought to swallow, but it was dry as gin. "Thank you," I croaked.

I looked down at the document quaking in my hand. It was folded in thirds, the outside with large block letters:

UNITED STATES DISTRICT COURT
DISTRICT OF MASSACHUSETTS
SUBPOENA TO TESTIFY BEFORE A GRAND JURY

Subpoena.

I sat on my front step, stared at the heading for a minute or so until I mustered the courage to open it.

TO: PAUL B. FORTÉ
300 OCEAN AVENUE
COTUIT, MA, 02635

You are COMMANDED to appear in this United States District Court at One Post Office Square, Boston, Massachusetts, on Thursday, September 30, 1993 at one-thirty in the afternoon (1:30 P.M.) to give evidence in the matter of United States of America versus Raymond L. Stackhouse, U.S.D.C. No. GJ1993-0427. If you fail to appear, a warrant may issue for your arrest.

My friend, my golf buddy, the target of indictment. And I, a witness against him. I stared at the words as they swam around on the page. Shit! If what Ray had done was a crime, could I be charged too? Should I testify? What about the Fifth? Would my answers to their questions incriminate *me*? What was the crime in playing golf, for crissakes?

I needed to hire a good criminal lawyer, and fast.

I struggled to my feet, my knees—my whole body—wobbled

as I stumbled through the house, back to the deck where my clubs leaned against the railing, all in a nice, neat row and glistening in the sun. I remembered the first time I walked the fairway of the local municipal course with Dad and Mom. Dad explained how golf was a game of honor and I must know the rules and always play by them. I thought I'd done that—in golf and everything else.

I walked to the railing, leaned against it, and threw up on the azalea below.

How did it ever come to this?

The Hyannisport Club is a breathtaking ocean side masterpiece overlooking Nantucket Sound, just up the hill from the famous Kennedy compound. That might sound like an ad for the place, but they're not the type to advertise. They much prefer their "well-kept secret."

My membership made me very popular on Beacon Hill—at the time, at least. I'd hosted senators, fellow representatives, trade association counsel, lobbyists, and practically anyone else who asked. They were all astonished by the panoramic ocean views and the pristine condition of the course. Who wouldn't be? But what attracted them most was its connection to the whole Camelot thing. Jack Kennedy had played here! The resilient Kennedy mystique coursed through the place. Fame and power. I was far from a person of fame or power, but I had a knack for golf, joke-telling and holding my liquor—all traits I inherited from my father. I also had a knack for slicing my tee shot on eighteen into Arnold Schwarzenegger's tennis court. That always cracked them up.

Ray was one of my regular guests. A real class act, a generous man, and the chief legislative counsel for the Providential Bank Holding Company. Coincidentally, I'd been a member of the Massachusetts House of Representatives. So let's just say that Ray's generosity to me was subject to misinterpretation. I wouldn't expect robust debate on that.

But it couldn't possibly be a federal crime. Could it?

At 5:00 the morning after a sleepless night, I stood in shorts and flip-flops at the end of my driveway, reading the dew-dampened front page of the Boston Globe.

GRAND JURY INVESTIGATES LOBBYIST GIFTS TO POLS

Providential Records Show
Extensive Gifts To Bevy of Reps

BOSTON – While the Providential Bank Holding Company was busy fighting for legislative approval to enter into the life insurance and financial services businesses, its lobbyist Raymond L. Stackhouse was spending lavishly on gifts for a long list of state legislators. The favors included rounds of golf, expensive dinners and eye-popping bar tabs at some of the poshest resorts and private golf clubs in the United States.

Expense records provided to the Globe by Providential officials show that Stackhouse spent nearly $150,000 over a three-year period on rounds of golf at Innisbruck Golf Resort in Florida, Casa de Campo in the Dominican Republic, Doral Resort in Miami, Pebble Beach in California and the Hyannisport Club on Cape Cod.

The poshest private golf clubs. Hyannisport? That just wasn't fair. Sure, it's a spectacular course and the food's better than average. Yes, there was the Kennedy connection, and the Shrivers, and now Schwarzenegger. Granted, technically it was still owned by Mayflower descendants. Hyannisport village was thick with old money and locked jaws. But still. I joined the place for two hundred fifty bucks and half the members were tradesmen. If they let me in for that kind of chump change, how posh could it be?

God, I hated the press, and experience told me they were just getting started.

I finished the story and threw the paper in the trash—a practice I started when I was married to Kate, to protect her peace of mind. I had pretty thick skin about a bad story. It came with the territory. But she was a worrier. She used to lose sleep over a bad news article. She felt the scowls of people in the supermarket. *There goes the poor wife of that political hack*, they must have thought. It's not like she actually came to see it like them, she assured me, but she really came apart when she saw that picture of me and Ralph Michaels on the seventeenth hole at Casa del Sol Golf Club on the front page of the Herald. Ralph was another golf nut who Ray had introduced me to. The lobbyist for the Massachusetts Bankers Association. Those telephoto shots across all that open territory were very grainy. They made me look like a gangster, especially with the sunglasses and the cigar. That story got the snowball rolling, but none of us were too worried about it. It was just a goddamn game of golf. Or maybe more than my skin was thick.

Now the snowball was an avalanche.

It was already 5:30 A.M., and I had to get to my office in Boston as the general counsel of the MBTA, greater Boston's public transportation system. I had a little game going with my rivals about who gets to the office first and leaves last. It wasn't a "friendly" game either, but I was ahead and intent on keeping it that way. Even if I was sleepwalking and struggling not to puke.

During the ride to Boston, I tried to concentrate on the positive side of things. Christ, it could have been me. If I had been appointed Banking Commissioner as the Governor originally planned, I'd be indicted myself.

It's pretty sick that a man's freedom could depend on his job title, but that is the nature of politics. And at that moment, I was reminded how much politics sucked.

After a week or so, my sleep improved, although my appetite wasn't what it had been. The sudden, fleeting panic attacks came less frequently. I'd thought through my situation and felt a weak confidence that this whole thing wasn't as big as I'd feared. I kept thinking of Dad's words and telling myself you can't get in trouble for following the rules.

I also focused on my work, and that helped. At least I began to get some of my sense of humor back.

Then I received a certified letter from the Massachusetts State Ethics Commission. It began, "You are hereby notified," which is never a good start. It informed me that I was the subject of an investigation regarding the unlawful receipt of lobbyist gifts and the failure to report them.

The letter contained a subpoena, summoning me to be deposed the following October 7th and "commanding" me to produce a list of seven described categories of documents, each one of which began with the words "any and all."

"Any and all documents evidencing communications between you and Raymond L. Stackhouse," for instance. This is why people hate lawyers. What the hell does "any and all" mean? Doesn't either word cover it? This kind of excessive lawyering drove Dad berserk. I wondered what he'd say to me now.

I made a bunch of calls around the State House and was relieved to learn that I was nothing special. Dozens of others got the same letter, with the same subpoena for the same itemized list of documents.

Aha, I thought, but did you guys get a grand jury subpoena?

I hoped my gallows humor would come in handy.

Chapter 2
Facing the Music, Privileged Information and Suing for the King

On the morning of an Indian summer day that golfers die for, I entered the federal building in Post Office Square with my lawyer, Alan Croston, at my side. I called Al the day after I got the subpoena because he was a pal of Governor Floyd Williams and served on the Yale Law Journal and in the Justice Department with the United States Attorney for Massachusetts, Bernard Kilroy. Made perfect sense.

We were meeting with one of Kilroy's deputies to negotiate a proffer agreement, something I knew nothing about until I first met with Al two weeks before. As he explained then, yes, I could assert my Fifth Amendment privilege against self-incrimination, and thereby guarantee that they would train their sights on me.

"For what, Al? Since when is playing golf a federal offense," I pleaded.

"At the end of the day, you accepted a gift from a lobbyist. You're the ham sandwich. They squeeze you until you agree to cooperate. You've told me everything?"

"Absolutely."

"Then believe me, you don't want to be squeezed."

I'd have preferred my crash course in white-collar crime from more of a distance, but Al didn't have to work hard to convince me that it is always better to cooperate with prosecutors. I just hoped I was up to the task.

Walking into that building after one hour of sleep, I wasn't sure.

Assistant U.S. Attorney Boertz was a humorless law and order type with greasy hair, pursed lips and wire-rimmed glasses. I sat in his office with a woozy head while Al and he volleyed back and forth about the scope of my testimony. The tone was serious and tense, and I could see Al's foot wiggling. I tried not to be nervous—after all, if I just told the truth, I couldn't get in trouble—but that simple axiom just seemed more dubious than it should have.

They finally hammered out the language of this proffer letter, and I signed it with Al's nod of assurance. Then Boertz began his "interview," so to speak. I followed Al's instructions the best I could.

Think about the question before answering.

Think about the answer before answering.

Answer the question only.

Answer the question simply.

Boertz asked me questions, showed me documents and asked me more questions for some amount of time, I had no idea how long. At one point in the midst of it all, I felt as if I were dreaming. Then we were done.

When Al walked me out the front door of the building at lunchtime, I asked him how I did.

"Well, you don't follow directions particularly well, but don't feel too bad. Most people in your situation don't." When he saw me blanch, he clapped my shoulder and chuckled. "You did fine, Paul. You did fine. You can never get in trouble for telling the truth."

That was faintly reassuring, but it wasn't going to help me sleep that night.

I sleepwalked back to my office, feeling numb and not a little bit helpless, but damn it, I had work to do. I picked up a "vente" iced coffee from Starbucks and went to my office on 7. I still had whole afternoon to get lost in my work, so I lugged a pile of official documents to my desk to perform my twice-weekly ritual of signing—actually stamping—my name.

It is the practice of public agencies that the general counsel must "approved as to form" every contract document before the authorized executive will execute it. I had this nifty signature stamp to save time and prevent carpal tunnel syndrome. I kept it locked in my desk, because this was a public agency and there were too many nefarious uses for it.

Even though I was pretty sure the practice was bureaucratic mumbo jumbo, I went through each document with care, because the MBTA is, well, a cesspool, and I didn't want to get shit on my shoes. It was the two or three page consulting agreements you needed to watch for. The ones with no term, no maximum contract limit, no specified scope of work. All left to the discretion of the General Manager. Very loosey goosey, to use legal terminology.

There I sat, thumbing through the pile that morning when one of those loosey gooseys looked back at me.

A two-page letter agreement, drafted for the General Manager's signature, addressed to Vincent J. Erichetti, President of Epsilon Environmental Consultants, Flagstaff, Arizona. It set forth a "memorandum of understanding" that Epsilon would assess the possible extent of environmental contamination on all MBTA property, with the purpose of structuring a program of insurance to protect the Authority against liability for environmental clean-up costs or damages. The investigation had no fixed price. It was to be done on an hourly basis, with no description of the hourly rates or the number of people assigned to the project. Just that a "report" would be provided to the General Manager within six months.

Nobody could be that incompetent by accident.

I penned a note to Jack Halsey, the GM:

> *Jack, this letter agreement is unacceptable. It has no scope of work or not-to-exceed price cap. It has no hourly rates or staffing limits. This letter leaves you open to an expense that you cannot foresee. I will not approve it in its current form. Please let me know if you would like me to redraft it for you.*
>
> *PBF*

I would have preferred to call it a "piece of shit," but I made my point. Besides, the note wasn't for his eyes. I attached the note to the letter agreement, made copies of both for myself, put them in an envelope, and walked it down to the GM's office where Halsey's secretary, Betty, sat at her desk. I handed her the envelope and told her, "Hand this directly to Jack, and Jack only."

"Will do," she said.

Late in the afternoon, I was sitting in my office when Billy Cruddy strode briskly through my door, gripping a document in his hand. He didn't knock, just barged in.

"Hey Billy, what's up?"

"This is what's up," he said, as he threw my note and the

letter agreement on my desk.

"What about it?"

"Sign that fucking thing right now," he said, stabbing the air with his stubby finger, looming over the desk. My adrenaline surged and I worked to control my breathing.

"Billy, who the fuck are you? I wrote that note to the GM. I'll speak to him about it. You can go fuck yourself. And get away from my desk."

Cruddy took a step back, but he still wasn't taking no for an answer. "Halsey is on a plane to Washington right now. He won't be back until Monday. I'm acting General Manager in his absence, and I want this signed right now." He had the mien of a guy who was just barely in control, like if you nudged him an inch he'd explode. I could almost see his heart beating through his shirt.

"Billy, if you want that to go out as is before I speak to Halsey about it, then you sign it and send it out without my approval. I am telling you right now, I will not approve that piece of shit, so maybe we ought to walk it down the hall to the Chairman and see if he'll order me to." When I said it, I had no reason to think the Chairman wouldn't, but I was pretty sure the bluff would work.

Cruddy stared at me, his dull wheels turning. Then he swiped the letter off of my desk and stormed out of the office.

I sat there for a good half-hour while my heart slowed, running over the entire incident from the discovery of the letter to Cruddy's heavy-handed visit. I called down to Betty's desk.

"General Manager's office."

"Betty, it's Paul Forté."

"I didn't give that envelope to Cruddy, Paul. He saw it, asked what it was, and took it."

"I believe you. I just wanted to confirm it."

"I swear," she said.

"No problem, Betty."

"Thanks. Sorry."

I called the General Manager's cell phone. He answered, in the middle of an airport, or so it sounded.

"Hey Jack, sorry to bother you. I have a problem with this Epsilon letter agreement. You mind if it holds till we can talk about it?"

Jack didn't answer right away. "Doesn't sound familiar, Paul. What's it about?"

"Never mind Jack, we'll talk when you get back. Sorry to bother you."

I took a piece of paper out of my desk and wrote a memory dump of everything that had happened, and attached it to the copies of the note and letter. Then I called my pal, Rex.

"Data Quest Investigations," said a pretty voice.

"Hi Rachel, it's Paul."

"Hey Paul, how's it goin'?" Good ol' Rachel.

"Goin' good. Your dad still around?"

"Hold on. You gonna come visit?"

"Maybe immediately."

"Thanks for the warning," she said, and she transferred me to Rex. It rang twice and a recorded voice came on. *Please state your name at the sound of the tone.*

"Harold Stassen," I said after the beep. Rex picked up the phone and chuckled.

"This is Tom Dewey, how can I help you?" he said.

"Sorry, I can't resist."

"You're not the only one who does that."

"My names are better," I said. "Your work day over yet?"

"Not if you say so. I'll buy you a drink."

"I'll be over in ten minutes."

As I hung up, my secretary tapped on the door. "You have a 5:30 with the trial department," she said.

"Sorry Cindy, I have to run to something more important. Set it up for tomorrow instead?"

I grabbed the papers I had clipped together and headed for the door with my coat.

I hustled out the building and walked a brisk pace across Park Square, over Arlington and up Boylston Street to the Trinity Church and crossed over to the building with the black marble façade. Data Quest Investigations occupied the third floor. You can take the elevator to it, but then you have to call ahead and punch in a special code or the elevator won't stop there. The product of a seriously dissatisfied spouse of a divorce client who barged in and shot the place up, personal property damage only, thank the good Lord. I don't use it, just in case. I go up the back staircase, which has a door into the office that is right across from Rachel's desk. I have been entrusted with the secret knock: short, long, long, short, short, short. Morse Code for "PI." Very clever.

I went through the secret knock twice, and lacking any response, pounded on the door with a ham fist. Rachel opened the door.

"Hey stranger," she said with her beautiful smile.

"What's the point of having a secret knock if nobody answers it?"

"Sorry," she said. "Girl's room."

"I forgive you. Where's your dad?"

"He's in his office. Let me tell him you're here." She rang him on the intercom, and told me to go on down to his office.

"Say Rache, what do you say you and I go over to the Gardner Museum some Saturday afternoon?"

"Think my dad will approve," she asked, thinking, I believe, that Rex would say no way. She was only about ten years younger than me, but her father was my friend. No harm in a little teasing, though.

"Tell me something, Rache," I said. "If I wasn't your father's friend, would you be interested in me?"

She bit her lower lip. "Well, I do like older men," she said.

I walked down to the end of the hall, knocked on the only door there, and walked in. Rex sat at his desk staring at a computer screen full of numbers.

"Pimlico results?"

"Cayman bank account records."

Rex was the genuine article. Green Beret in Vietnam. U. S. Treasury agent, specialist in cyber-related financial crime. Retired with a bullet hole in his shoulder, courtesy of a member of the Russian mafia. Now he runs this hot little boutique PI firm, finding things no one else can find, and at exorbitant rates. He has about a hundred agents in the field, based out of three offices in Boston, Los Angeles and London. On the side, he writes screenplays of the crime spree/thriller variety. A real Damon Runyon character. Big stocky guy, very good shape, thick Gordon Liddy-type mustache and eyebrows. Hard eyes that make you nervous.

"What can I do for you today?" he asked. He likes doing things for me. I feed him a good deal of business referrals from lobbyists, fellow golfers, people along the way who might want to find out if their wives are actually taking tennis lessons on their feet. He reached into his desk and brought out a bottle of Johnny Walker Blue and a couple of Waterford snifters, poured two fingers into each and slid one across the desk to me.

"Now you're talking."

"Just a wee taste," he said, putting the glass to his nose and barely wetting his lips with the brown liquor.

I reached into my suit coat, pulled out the papers and tossed them to him. "I need to look into this Epsilon outfit a little bit."

Rex examined the documents and my handwritten notes.

"What do you want to know?"

"I want to know why a public transit authority in Massachusetts wants to give an open-ended consulting contract to an Arizona company. Who is this guy Erichetti, where's he from, who are his company's clients, and who are his subcontractors."

Rex chuckled. "That's some inquiry. What do you anticipate the answers to be?"

I took a sip of the brown stuff and swirled it around in my mouth. "This stuff is good. I have no idea what the answers are. But most of the environmental clean-up work that the MBTA needs done is funded with federal money. You know what that means."

"Another qui tam."

"Qui tam pro domino rege quam pro se ipso," I intoned.

"Law school latin. I'm not impressed."

"Could be quite a bit in it."

"As good as the $11 million I got for the Aerotex fraud on the Navy?"

"Might come close."

"Or the six point five I got for the Comdex FDA contract."

"Then again, could be more."

Rex sat silent for a minute, thinking.

"Where did you get this information?"

"Never mind," I said. He stared at me. "It's a public document," I said.

"Okay, whose case is it?"

"Yours, Rex. You do with it what you want."

He thought some more. "Here's the problem," Rex said.

"I know the problem. In order for the case to be worth a reward, you have to wait until a fraud has been committed. If I have information that a fraud has been committed, or is about to be committed, I have a responsibility to the client. That's why it's your case, Rex."

"You don't want to hear a word about it."

"Not one. At this point, my notion is just rank speculation."

"So whatever I find out, it's my business."

"Right."

"You have nothing to do with it."

"Not one iota."

With a refill, we discussed nonsense like the Red Sox and the British Open. Rex then kicked me out of his office, I went by Rachel with the sad dog look, and she laughed and said "You're cute." That was the best I would ever do with her, and it was plenty.

The following day, I wrestled with the mumbo jumbo until mid-afternoon and then took a breather. I put my feet up on the desk and drew on my Romeo & Juliet, all chocolaty and spicy, a thin line of smoke dripping from my lips. Staring at the wall photos: the State House, me with Dad and Tip O'Neill, me with Dad and Daniel Patrick Moynihan. Dad and President Nixon, President Reagan, President Bush. Me and the Governor. Me and the Speaker. Me and the Senate President. The dad pictures were still a bit awkward for me, like I was a little leaguer standing next to Babe Ruth. But they lent an interesting context, and I loved the idea of having him close, in case I needed his advice.

I asked him, "What do you say, pal?" But I didn't get an answer.

I was about to knock off and head home when I got a call from one of my old House colleagues, another golf nut, even if his game was atrocious. He'd done his share of gallivanting also, and now ran the lobbyist registration desk in the Secretary of State's office.

"Hey Birdie," he said.

Birdie. A stupid nickname, but not as stupid as his. "Hey Snowman."

"Hey, c'mon, my game's getting better."

"Couldn't get worse. What's going on?"

"Just a heads up. I received a request for public documents that's a little different."

"Oh?"

"Yah. All expense records for the past eight years for twelve specific lobbyists."

"So?"

"All twelve of them were our golf hosts."

A jolt zagged through my chest. Then I thought for a moment. "They won't show much, will they? Those guy never expensed that stuff."

He'd certainly checked. "Nah, they don't show anything. But someone's lookin'."

"Who's it from?"

"The Department of Justice."

At times like this I really missed the Old Man.

Chapter 3
Meeting My Peers

On the appointed day, ten minutes before the appointed hour, Al joined his sleepless client outside the federal building. He obviously had something on his mind, because he didn't even say "how are you doing?" Perhaps the answer appeared too obvious.

"I've learned that Bernard Kilroy himself will be conducting the grand jury examination."

"So?"

"Well," he said, his eyebrows jumping, "his handling of the questioning of a grand jury witness is quite unprecedented. Very rare."

"Even for a guy who's talking about running for Attorney General?"

"Yes. This is not explainable by ordinary assumptions. Do you know this man?"

"I've never met him. Who is he?"

"Bernard Kilroy is a shrewd, ruthless prosecutor who will stop at nothing to get a conviction." That is not the type of guy you want questioning you.

"Any advice?"

"Yeah. Whatever you do, don't call him 'Bernie.'"

"Why not?"

Al rolled his eyes. "Don't really know, but he's maniacal about it."

"Sounds like a well-grounded fella."

"Look, I'm telling you. Just keep your testimony truthful and within the bounds of your proffer letter—Stackhouse and Stackhouse only—and you've got immunity. And don't make any wisecracks. Floyd told me about you."

I'd never had much cause to contemplate the meaning of "immunity," but I decided that it was a fine word indeed. The rest of what he said, I didn't hear.

We took the elevator to the twelfth floor, followed a barren hallway to Courtroom 17, and sat on a shopworn bench outside the courtroom.

"Remember, you're going in alone, but if you want to talk to me for any reason, you can demand to see me."

"That's comforting, Al. But I think I'll be okay."

"Just remember to keep your testimony within the four corners of your proffer letter. Don't be volunteering any new information."

"You're making me nervous. You can leave if you want."

"I'm going nowhere until you walk out of there."

"Suit yourself, counselor. I know you don't need the billable hours."

I picked up one of the stray Globe Metro sections that littered the bench. On the front page above the fold, I read the following:

FEDERAL GRAND JURY
CONTINUES WITH STACKHOUSE CASE

BOSTON – As many as a dozen former legislators

are expected to be questioned today before a federal grand jury hearing evidence against former Providential banking lobbyist Raymond L. Stackhouse.

The ex-reps are accused of receiving free gifts from Stackhouse over the course of more than seven years, from rounds of golf and expensive meals at posh resorts to sets of golf clubs, Super Bowl tickets and free passes to theater shows and concerts. According to knowledgeable sources who spoke on condition of anonymity, all of the witnesses have received immunity in exchange for their testimony.

There's that word again. Posh. I finished reading the article, handed it to Al, and stared at the floor.

How could treating your friends to golf and dinner be a federal felony? Stackhouse hadn't done anything different than other lobbyists. They all gave out dinners, drinks, Red Sox tickets and a lot more, to probably half the legislature. It wasn't fair that he was singled out, and especially not by a federal prosecutor. This was state misdemeanor stuff, tops.

I asked Ray once, long before any of this came out, "Your boss ever ask you why you spend all this time with a back bencher with no power?"

He said, "Nope."

"So why do you?"

He sighed. "You're the only guy I know that understands what golf is. The honor of it. The character required to be good at it. The pure ecstasy of spending time in such a pristine environment, cared for so zealously by men devoted to turf. You get it."

He was right. Ray and I were aficionados. Just as others derived a physiological pleasure from watching bullfights, our narcotic was golf. We had a weak spot, a profound vulnerability for something that produces endorphins that arrest reason and restraint. Tempted by lure of a round of golf, we would cancel appointments, call in sick, invent the passing of a distant relative. We were addicts.

But we weren't criminals.

The doors opened, and I looked up.

"Mr. Forté?" asked a grim, tense-looking man. Round, slightly puffy red face. A drinker. Gray pinstripe suit.

"Yes, sir," I said, rising.

"Bernard Kilroy," he said, giving me a perfunctory handshake. "Follow me, please."

All business.

When I showed up, I thought was ready. Following that guy into the room, I wanted to go to the bathroom, lock myself in a stall and cry for my deceased mother.

The room was narrow, with a low, water-stained ceiling and a threadbare carpet with duct tape patching seams and tears. I was led to a witness box with its heavy oak chair. And no cushion.

The other half of the room held several rows of benches. There were a couple dozen people sitting there. I thought they were spectators, but then remembered that grand juries are secret. I looked around the rest of the room. A court officer. A stenographer. Kilroy. Me. Not even a judge.

So that was the grand jury? All of them in common, casual street clothes. Three were reading what looked like novels. One read the Boston Herald. One had a Wall Street Journal. Another had a crossword puzzle. The rest lounged, like they were used to sitting for extended periods without fear of anyone criticizing their posture. It was demoralizing, yet I felt a sense of optimism and had no idea why.

"Could you state your name and address for the record, please," Kilroy started.

"Paul G. Forté, 300 Ocean Avenue, Cotuit, Massachusetts." The same numbness that I'd felt during the proffer conference returned to my head. Like it was stuffed with cotton.

"Mr. Forté, are you here under a subpoena?"

"Yes, I am."

"And have you agreed to testify here today under a grant of immunity from prosecution?"

"Yes, I have."

"Directing your attention to the period of January 1986 to January 1989, what was your occupation?"

"I was a member of the Massachusetts Legislature."

"What is your current occupation?"

"I am General Counsel of the Massachusetts Bay Transportation Authority."

"Were you selected and recommended for that position by the Governor?" he asked, voice sterner.

"He asked me if I was interested in it, sure," I said. It wasn't a nationwide search, in other words.

"Was that the original position he had in mind for you?"

"I don't know what he had in his mind," I said. Really, if what I thought he had in mind was correct, I'd have been the Banking Commissioner. Kilroy didn't ask it the way Boertz had.

"Mr. Forté, were you not originally intended to become the Banking Commissioner?"

"Oh," I said, "I see what you mean. Yes, I guess so."

"And this was because of concern in the Governor's office that you were too close to the banking industry."

Well, Jesus Christ, how could he ask that kind of question, I thought. This wasn't what I'd gone through with Boertz. Then I remembered. "Well, I recall reading something in the Boston Globe about that, but that story came from 'an administration source who asked not to be named.' I guess that person preferred that I read it in the Globe."

Kilroy smiled. I hoped he understood that if he gave me a little slack, I would give him everything he asked for, but still be able to preserve my own dignity, after a fashion. Perhaps I gave the man more credit than he deserved.

"Do you know what the basis of that concern was?"

What was he talking about? The man either hadn't talked to Boertz or was on a different mission. Should I let him lead me where he wants to go, or stick to the truth, I thought. I followed my lawyer's advice.

"As it might pertain to Ray Stackhouse? No."

"No?" Kilroy spun around, a hint of anger in his surprise.

"No. My relationship with Ray Stackhouse could not possibly have been the basis for the anonymous concerns in the Governor's office." Boertz hadn't gone there at all. Kilroy was freewheeling it, and I had no control. I couldn't afford to let him crash.

"But you did have a relationship with Raymond Stackhouse." *Raymond*.

"I did and still do, yes. But the Governor's office didn't know about my relationship with him." I hoped he'd take the hint.

"Is it fair to say your relationship with Mr. Stackhouse was indicative of your close relationship to the banking industry?"

"I'm sorry, I don't know what 'close relationship to the banking industry' means, Mr. Kilroy."

He jammed his hands into both suit pockets and stiffened his shoulders. "You've played quite a bit of golf with Mr. Stackhouse?" he asked.

"Oh, yes. Still do," I said. The grand jurors lowered their papers and began to listen with a collective lassitude. I noticed one in particular. A real stunner. Short jet-black hair. Dark eyes. A delicate nose. Pretty, thin lips. She smiled back. She looked like a wise guy.

"Dined with him on occasion?"

"Oh definitely," I said, "A number of times. Still do." Okay, we were back on the script, so to speak.

Kilroy led me through the minutiae of the wheres and whens that made up my allegedly illicit relationship with Mr. Raymond L. Stackhouse.

"I show you a copy of a document and ask you if you have seen this before," he said. The restaurant tab at The Impudent Oyster, from three years earlier. Six pages, maybe $2,000, covering dinner for fourteen.

"Yes, I have," I said.

I looked over at the black-haired lady. She had on some sort of corduroy jacket and a tee top. She was definitely paying attention now. Wicked smile, too.

"What is this document, if you know?"

Boertz had shown it to me. "It's a dinner tab from the Impudent Oyster, one of our Fourth of July events," I said.

"Now let's be clear, sir. You don't know this for certain to be the actual bill, do you?"

"Not for certain, no."

"But why do you believe it to be from this particular dinner?"

"Well, the date is right around July fourth, the number of people in the party is pretty much in line with the group we had, and for that particular night, I remember what I ordered."

"What did you order?"

"A lot of martinis and osso buco."

"How do you know?"

"The Impudent Oyster is the only place on the Cape that has osso buco on the menu. And I drink martinis."

"And you see those on the bill?"

"I do. A lot of martinis…"

"What is 'osso buco'?"

"Braised veal shank. It's a northern Italian staple. Delicious."

Kilroy looked like he was sorry he asked. "And these Fourth of July events also included golf, correct?"

"Oh, yes," I said. The initial panic of the event had worn off. I knew the truth of my words, and felt a warmth to them, because they were my path to safety. I was smiling at the front row of the jurors, some of whom returned the smile. Perhaps they'd never seen a politician tell the truth so unselfconsciously. What the hell did I have to feel guilty about?

"Please explain what you mean by 'Fourth of July event.'"

"For the past several years, Ray and I and a few House members got together on the Cape for golf and dinner. I hosted them at Hyannisport, and Ray was the dinner host."

"Did he always pay for dinner?"

Oh no, more improvising. "I am not sure, but I recall once the others played a game of liar's poker for the tab, and they laughed at Ray, because he was such an honest guy, he couldn't cheat at the game and he lost."

Kilroy stiffened again. "Is it your testimony that Stackhouse paid for dinner because he was a lousy poker player?"

"Well, I know this. He paid that tab, and they played liar's poker. I don't gamble, but the others said Ray lost. I just drank my port and talked to the wives." Just what I explained to Boertz.

And it was true, every word of it. But I didn't think Kilroy was concerned with the accuracy of my answers.

He turned to the jurors. "Ladies and gentlemen, the witness and I are going to take a brief recess to the next room. Please excuse us for a few minutes." He turned to me and made a sharp gesture with his hand, and he strode to the door briskly. I followed him.

Oh-oh.

As the door behind me closed, he spun around and pointed his finger in my face.

"Listen to me, Forté. You've got a proffer letter in your pocket because Al Croston's your attorney. But I promise you, if you keep fucking with me, I will crush you like a bug."

I was nearly catatonic, but I knew what I'd told Boertz and I was determined to obey my lawyer's advice. No one was going to force false testimony from me. I boiled inside, my heart making a racket against my ribs.

"I discussed with Mr. Boertz the information that I would testify to. We did not discuss a script, particularly not a script I haven't seen."

"You are playing a dangerous game, Forté."

"Listen, Bernie." Oh, shit. "I'm telling the truth, and it's one hundred percent consistent with what I told Mr. Boertz before."

My anger with this man grew with every word I spoke.

"You're trying to make a federal felony out of a common, petty offense—and I'm not going to help you at the expense of my friend, who is a decent and honest man."

Kilroy's red face seemed to puff out along with his eyes. "Look, fuck face, if you want to examine the propriety of your behavior and my prosecution, we can do it in front of another grand jury. Just answer the goddamn questions and quit playing games, or you'll learn the hard way how the federal system works."

We stood and stared at one another for a moment.

"Understood?"

"Understood," I said. I understood perfectly well: No way in hell should this guy be Attorney General.

We re-entered the grand jury room and I resumed my spot on the witness stand. The jurors seemed uniformly focused on our entry.

"Mr. Forté, once again, I ask you. To your knowledge, did Mr. Stackhouse pay for the dinners you enjoyed at The Impudent Oyster?"

I tightened my face. "I never saw him pay the bill, but I assume he did," I said, looking at the hands in my lap. That was the best I could do.

"Who were the participants in your golf outings?"

"Me, Stackhouse, James May and Augustus Mannion."

"Yes."

"The Chairman and Vice Chairman of the Committee on Banking?"

"One and the same."

"How often did this golf event take place?"

"I'd say from 1985 to 1990."

"And Mannion was always present?"

Kilroy paused, flipping through papers on his desk. I looked at the lady. She examined my taciturn demeanor. I frowned, glancing at Kilroy, slumping my shoulders. She stifled a chuckle, furrowed her brow and frowned back. She had a good shape. Real angular.

"Did you have any arrangement with Mr. Stackhouse regarding the cost of the golf portion of these events?"

"He told me to mail him my club bill when I got it and he would reimburse me for the cost."

"And did you do that?"

"Yes I did—eventually."

With that Kilroy pulled a few photocopies out of a file and put them before me, and I identified my club bills and the several checks drawn on Ray Stackhouse's personal account that reimbursed me for the greens fees, snacks and beers that I had bought for everyone.

"One final question, Mr. Forté," he said, turning his back to me and facing the grand jurors. "When you were drinking all those martinis and eating your osso buco with Mr. Stackhouse and your colleagues, did it occur to you that what you were doing was against the law?" Freewheeling again, up on his soap box, the shit.

"You mean eating and drinking?"

Several of the jurors guffawed, led by the cutie.

Kilroy turned to me and narrowed his eyes to slits. "I mean, Mr. Forté, against the law governing your receipt of items of value from a registered lobbyist."

"No," I said.

"You didn't believe in your heart what you were doing was illegal?"

"Illegal, no."

"Would you care to elaborate?"

I knew what I'd done wasn't entirely ethical, even if it was innocent. But he didn't ask me that. "The statute forbidding gifts from lobbyists says that the gift cannot be given to a public official 'for or on account of his official act.' I don't believe Mr. Stackhouse included me in the festivities because I could do anything to help him. In fact, I never did do anything for him. He knew better than to ask."

"You never took any official action on behalf of Mr. Stackhouse?"

"For him or anyone else."

"Are you certain of that?"

"Yes, as certain as I am that you're tie is fuchsia."

He smirked. "Why do you think Mr. Stackhouse invited you?"

"Because he wanted to play at Hyannisport."

"Nothing to do with him being the chief lobbyist for the

banking industry and you being a member of the Banking Committee?"

"No. He didn't need me."

"But he always brought along May and Mannion," he said.

"On these occasions, yes."

"I admire your candor, Mr. Forté," he said. "Are you presently the subject of an investigation by the State Ethics Commission?"

"Yes, I am," I answered.

"Thank you very much." Kilroy turned to the members of the grand jury. "Do any members of the Grand Jury wish to ask Mr. Forté any questions?"

Twenty-three dead faces looked back at him. The lady with the smile raised her hand.

"Yes, ma'am."

She stood slowly and ran her hand along the back of the bench in front of her. She was definitely angular, and God was she pretty.

"Did you say your dinners were always at The Impudent Oyster?" she asked.

"Yes."

"How's the osso buco?"

Sometime after two-thirty, I walked out of the grand jury room. I didn't think the inquisition was that hard on me, but then I realized that the shirt under my suit coat was soaked. Croston was sitting there shooting the shit with some guy with a clip-on tie. He excused himself and began to lead me down the corridor past the elevators.

"That guy wearing a clip-on?"

"That's Magnuson from Treasury. He's doing a counterfeiting trial."

"Where are you taking me?"

"The back staircase. The press are outside the front door downstairs."

"Good idea."

Croston walked me down thirteen flights of stairs to the service entrance.

"Don't talk to anyone about your testimony," he reminded me for the hundredth time, and gave me a slap on the shoulder. "Don't worry about this, it'll be over soon."

"Not soon enough," I said, and slipped out the door, past the dumpsters and onto Devonshire Street.

It was mid-afternoon, but even in the flat September light it still felt summer warm. I was wound up tight and in no mood to return to my office yet, so I went around the corner and crossed Congress Street to Post Office Square Park. I had my pick of benches, so I decided to spy on the press for a bit. I picked a bench that faced across Congress to the entrance of the building I had just escaped. There were a bunch of reporters hanging around. Good thing none of them knew who the hell I was. That was one of the advantages of being a back-bencher. You didn't matter to the press. Unless you had plans for higher office. Then they played with you until you became viable. Then they got together and assassinated you. It was a favorite Boston sport.

So I was watching them idly smoking their butts and loitering when out the front door walked the juror with the mouth. As she strode past the reporters, they all paused their yammering and looked at her ass. Pavlovian! She went to the crosswalk and pushed the pedestrian crossing button. So few people do that anymore. While she waited for the WALK light, she looked across the street and saw me sitting on the bench, looking back at her.

Caught.

She crossed the street and strolled toward where I was sitting. God what a lovely walk, long legs moving in those jeans and boots, swinging her arms in that corduroy jacket over a funky olive green tee.

"Walk me to the T?" she said.

"Why not, nice day like this."

We strolled along the promenade, underneath the trellis of wisteria to the stone benches at Franklin Street, where she sat, took a box of Marlboro reds from her hip pocket and lit one.

"I'm Shannon," she said, sticking out her hand.

"Well, you already know my name," I said, taking her hand. She had a good firm grip.

"First time you've done that, I take it," she said.

"And last, I hope."

"How'd you think it went?"

"I dunno," I said. "I didn't like how cocky the guy was. Like he knew a lot more about me than I did, you know?"

She peered at me through a cloud of smoke. "Yeah, I got that, too."

It was humid, and the sun wasn't making my already soaked shirt any more comfortable, so I thought a little air-conditioned environment would be in order. Like a tavern.

"Say," I said. "Should we get a beer or something?"

"I have an appointment I gotta get to."

"Shit, then I'll have to go back to the office."

She looked at her watch. "Almost three. Isn't it quittin' time at the T?"

"Nah, I got stuff to do. Maybe a rain check, though?"

"Sure, deal. I know where to find you."

"Deal. See you later."

She took a drag from her cigarette, threw it down and

stomped on it as she rose, gave me a wave and walked down Franklin Street toward Batterymarch.

You know how a guy checks out a woman while he's talking to her? It's a skill you acquire and never lose, although I had been somewhat out of practice until lately. But I exercised that skill during that little exchange, and I was impressed. Now, with her walking away from me, I got the impression she knew exactly what I was looking at.

Chapter 4
A Moonlight Sonata and a Latte

The following Monday morning promptly at 6:30, I pulled into the parking lot of Poopsie's Grille & Pub in Pembroke to meet Hargood Kensington III. He was the Governor's lawyer, and every once in a while he gave me a ride to town, just so we could keep track of things. I also liked to ride with him because his huge Mercedes sedan cost about one year of my salary and had a ridiculous sound system. But it was too big and too heavy. I hate Mercedes. I preferred my old Saab.

"Goody, you sure you don't want to ride in my car?" I asked him out the window.

He laughed. "You're quite a joker."

I parked, climbed into the chariot and we were back on the highway in a jiffy. The sumptuous sound of classical piano enveloped me.

"Beautiful sound. Beethoven?"

"*Moonlight Sonata*. Vladimir Horowitz at the Vienna Opera House." His eyes fixed ahead, he was still engrossed, until the movement ended, and he emerged from his trance.

"So," he said, "what's going on? Anything I should know about?"

"Are we dispensing with my duty of confidentiality in the usual manner?"

Horowitz's fingers danced. I had confidences to keep, and talking to Goody wasn't keeping them. There were political considerations.

"Let's just say I am your legal counsel—now I can't disclose what you tell me, even if you're violating your confidence."

"How efficient."

Goody piloted his Mercedes up the passing lane of Route 3 at an exhilarating speed, one my Saab would not recognize. Horowitz reached a feverish pace to match.

"Okay then," I said, feeling like I was on a carnival ride. I told him about the Epsilon agreement, my note to the GM and Billy Cruddy's reaction to it.

Horowitz's fingers played mischief.

"Stupid bullshit," Goody said.

"So far, yes."

"You have a hard job."

"Yeah, thanks. I know that. So what do you think?"

"Well, I oughtn't suggest anything overtly at this point, because you understand that, while you are my client for the purpose of this conversation, my primary client is the Governor, and what I advise you might not be consistent with his interests."

"You live in a complicated world, Goody."

"What would you like to do?"

"I'd like to kick Cruddy in the balls."

Goody laughed. "You have larceny in your heart."

"I'm having a friend of mine who knows about these things check out the vendor."

"As long as you don't share the contract document with him, I don't see any problem with that."

"Why not share the document?"

"Because you have no right to disclose its existence."

"Even if it's a public document?"

"No. If someone asks for public documents they must be disclosed, but someone has to ask first."

"What a stupid rule."

"It is what it is, Paul." Horowitz got gentle again. "Listen. I don't need to tell you that you cannot trust the Chairman."

"I know—he told me that himself. One of the first things he said to me."

"He's a charming fellow."

"His two sidekicks are rotten."

"Cruddy and Fetore, you mean."

"Them. They fire people for sport."

"What?"

"For sport, they fire people. They thrive on watching people shit their pants. They call these emergency meetings, summon a bunch of people into a conference room, and then call me in to sit there silently. These people don't know why they're sitting there, but every one of them is terrified he'll be leaving with his stuff in a box."

"Jesus."

"I told Cruddy once he was bad for morale."

"What'd he say?"

"He said, 'morale is an overrated commodity.' No shit. I told him morale is no commodity at all when there isn't any. He called me a wise prick."

"You are a wise prick."

"Thank you, coming from you, that's a fabulous compliment."

"Don't mention it. So listen. Whatever you think is going on, you're probably underestimating."

"That a fact?"

"And I and the Governor are particularly sensitive to the path that led you to where you are, you know that, right?"

"Well, no one ever assured me of that fact, but I appreciate it." Apparently, he didn't know about my appointment with the Grand Jury. No point in spoiling a good apology though.

By then, Horowitz was wrapping it up, we were at the tail end of the Expressway, and Goody jumped off at the South Station exit to leave me at the corner of Kneeland Street. Before I got out, he touched my arm and said, "Just understand that we are aware of the position we have put you in, and we'll protect you. You know what the right thing is and how to do it. I know you're a smart ass, but you've got good ethics and you've got balls too. Just don't get too cocky, and take the Chairman's advice."

"Which advice?"

"Don't trust him."

"Aye aye captain."

"Call me if you need to chat."

"Will do." I shut the door of his Big Mercedes and it roared off.

During the brisk walk through Chinatown to the office, I thought about what Goody had said.

It was indeed my responsibility to keep the Chairman and members of the Board of Directors out of trouble. That came straight from the mouth of Governor Floyd Williams, the man responsible for my current occupation.

He told me, after apologizing for his people throwing me under the bus on the Banking Commissioner thing, "Go on over to the T, you'll make more money and get less press—but you have to keep my buddy Jay out of trouble." His "buddy" Jay was John Liguotomo, the hard-nosed Chairman of the Massachusetts Bay Transportation Authority. The guy was a smart dude. Smart and mean.

The day of my formal appointment, he summoned me to his office for our introductory meeting. He told me that he had no idea who I was and he had someone else in mind for the job until the Governor called him. "So I just want you to know how good a friend the Governor is to you right now." What the fuck does "right now" mean?

"Well, that's very good to know, Mr. Chairman," I said.

"Just remember that," he said. "And let me give you this piece of advice too: Don't trust anyone."

"Anyone."

"Anyone," he said, "including me." He had these dark, beady eyes set under bushy eyebrows, and he grinned when he said it.

"That's a helluva way to begin an attorney-client relationship, Mr. Chairman."

"It is, isn't it?" he said.

And that was it, end of meeting. As I walked out of his office and headed back to the Cape to catch a tee time at The Port, I wondered if I'd made a big mistake.

By the time I walked into the transportation building, I'd worked up a sweat, so I stopped into Starbucks for an iced coffee. Lou Fetore came in behind me.

Lou has a problem with aggression. He's also as dumb as a bag of hammers. So, one might think, he would be a threat to my peace of mind. Goody assured me I had protection. So this was a good way to face one's nemesis, except the dude still scared the shit out of me.

It was like waiting for the subway, deep underground late at night, and there's a psychotic homeless guy ranting on a nearby bench. You're concerned he might snap and come at you wielding the lid of a tuna can. You have to calm yourself on the outside. Play the nonchalant, just-minding-my-own-business-and-nothing-intimidates-me role. Same thing with being threatened by a rabid dog. Avoid eye contact. Stand very still and don't make any sudden moves. Eventually he'll go away. So what did I do?

"Hey there Lou, what's crackin'?" I asked the dull-witted man, and looked him right in the eyes.

He hung his head between his shoulders like his neck was broken. A bushy unibrow dangled over eyes that were too close together. He had a shiny bald spot, and grinned like he was on lithium. And he swaggered. A real ass-back-and-forth swagger.

So he turned his swaggering ass, and seeing me, he said, "You're in a little late this morning." Like it was his business.

"Lou, when you wheeled your state-issued American sedan into the garage this morning, I'd already eaten breakfast at my desk," I lied.

He grinned, the ugly goon. "Your car isn't even in the garage."

"You sleeping in the garage these days, Lou? Wife put you out?"

"What'd you have for breakfast?"

"Pussy. I had pussy for breakfast, Lou. Breakfast of champions."

He laughed at that. "You think you're a tough guy, don't you."

"I know I'm a tough guy, Lou. My name, Forté. Tough, *en Français*."

The dope wouldn't ever know it meant strong, not tough, but you can have fun like that with an idiot.

"*On Fron-say,*" he mimicked me. "You faggot." I laughed at him. "Listen to me, faggot, if you ever again refuse to do what me or Cruddy tell you to do, I'll rip your fucking head off."

"Cruddy or I. Speak English."

"Fuck you. Cruddy told me you refused to approve the Epsilon agreement. Stupid move," he said with a sneer.

"You don't have to convince me you know about stupidity. Get your latte and go waste some tax money."

The baristas witnessed this exchange with a mixture of horror and amusement, it seemed, and after Fetore moved on with a final, vicious "fuck you," my server raised her eyebrows.

"Be safe out there," she said, handing me change.

I went up to my office and killed paper for a few hours, distracted by the fact that Fetore knew about the Epsilon bullshit.

As I suspected, Cruddy didn't wait for Halsey to get back. As soon as I left the building, he went to my deputy, who I'd deliberately not briefed before leaving that night. He didn't deserve to be put in that position, but if he were, abject ignorance was his best defense—a luxury I didn't enjoy. So in a way, his unwitting approval of that piece of crap agreement would do both of us a lot of good. Halsey and I were blameless, at least as far as the record.

The question was, did I owe it to the Chairman or the other Board members to inform them of the possibility that one of the Chairman's chief assistants might be involved in something nefarious. I convinced myself that I had no reason to inform anyone of anything.

Yeah, that's the ticket.

Mid-morning I got a strange call from Jackie Delaney, one of my old lobbyist pals. He'd been subpoenaed to testify at the Stackhouse grand jury, too. No surprise there.

"So how'd it go?" I asked.

"Kinda weird," he said. "Out of the blue, this Kilroy bird asked me if I'd ever played golf at Hyannisport."

"You told him the truth."

"Of course. I been there, what, a half dozen times?"

"So why you think he asked you that?"

"I got no idea. Just thought you should know."

"Huh. Well, thanks, Jackie."

"We didn't have this conversation, right?"

"No problem."

Weird is right, I thought. The guy must have had a proffer agreement that gave him immunity for his testimony as it related to Stackhouse. Just like me. Any questions about anyone else would be outside the scope of the proffer, and would have been improper to ask. So Kilroy just slipped a question in about a place, not a person. The weasel.

Still, why Hyannisport? And what about the records request to Snowman?

When Halsey returned from Washington in the afternoon, he called me down to his office. I told him about the letter agreement, but only enough that he understood that it was just one of those typical loose agreements that get shuffled around every day. He knew, as I did, that the boys in the Chairman's office were occasionally going to take care of some friend in the business, and he ordinarily wouldn't waste political capital on what, on its face, represented nothing but a potential embarrassment. Halsey wasn't wrong in that assessment. Too many times, people in a position like his regard their lawyer's warning as hand-wringing nonsense. No sense in my trying to convince him at that point. I wouldn't have been the first boy to cry wolf in that building.

After I finished my explanation, Jack remained silent.

"What's wrong," I asked him.

He had his face scrunched up, like he smelled something foul. "Why would Cruddy be so worked up over you wanting to wait until I returned?"

"Why would he wait until you were out of town, and then sign it himself?"

We looked at each other. Then he shrugged.

"Do I want to know what develops with this?"

I gave that a moment's thought. "I don't think so. Not yet. If I find anything you should know about, I'll let you know. Okay?"

"Fine with me," he shrugged. "Just keep me out of the zone of impact."

The Ethics Commission deposition was a pointless exercise. I should have taken it more seriously, and I might have, if the Commission's staff lawyer, Todd somebody, had had the sense to shave the peach fuzz from his insubstantial upper lip. He had coke bottle glasses and almost no chin, and he was more nervous than I should have been. Maybe it was just that the threat of a little fine paled in comparison to a federal prison.

Al was gracious with the guy, bordering on patronizing. Every time he tried to flex his muscles, Al dismissed him with a pleasant wave of his hand, reminding him that the U.S. Attorney's office was involved, and I would plead the 5th to any question he intended to ask. This appeared to frustrate him greatly, like it was his first Big Case and he wasn't taking no for an answer.

"Look, Todd. Why don't you just write up a proposed disposition agreement that contains all of the facts you think you need and imposes a fine that's in line with the dozens of other miscreants you folks are persecuting, and send it over. I'm sure we can find a way to dispose of this matter without any needless saber rattling."

Todd grumbled something about this being a "grave matter" but acknowledged the futility of continuing.

Chapter 5
Ale and Reds

To my delight, Shannon what's-her-name hadn't wasted any time before calling the office. She left a message with my secretary that "Ms. McGonigle was confirming her appointment at 'Mr. Brandipete's' on Thursday the sixteenth at two P.M." That telephone message gave me a buzz, and not just because I finally had a last name.

The place was still bustling with the tail end of the lunch crowd when I walked in.

Brandy Pete's is an institution in downtown eating and drinking establishments. Originally located in an ancient brick building two blocks down on Broad Street, its sawdust floors, franks and beans, yesterday's meatloaf, and the sardonic humor of its owner, Pete Colacello, had been the staple of financial district denizens for twenty-five years. In the eighties, Colacello retired and his son, Pete Jr., sold the place to some yuppie named Farthington. Franks and beans were replaced by "bangers and mash," the clam roll was jettisoned for crab cakes á la Meuniere. But Farthington apparently had a knack, because the crowds grew, and Pete's became downtown's favored after-work bar, not least because Pete, being an avid smoker, brazenly flouted the City's anti-smoking ordinance, and Farthington knew how to keep his customers. The food was okay too, even if it was too expensive. I mean, $13.50 for Fish and Chips?

I scanned the crowd and didn't see her at first, so I headed toward the barstools nearest the kitchen door, the spot where you can see everyone coming in or out, and you could avoid being seen if you wanted to. I knew, because that was my spot. And Shannon was right there, sitting on my regular stool.

Shannon had slung her corduroy jacket onto the backrest. She was in another one of those tee shirts. I'd never seen one look so good. The bartender threw napkins down in front of me.

I looked at her glass. "Harpoon, please," I said. She drank ale with attitude. To match the mouth.

She fished the Marlboro reds out of her hip pocket, took one out and flicked her wrist that way smoking women do to signal a gentleman's job. I took the matches off the bar and lit her cigarette. Isn't that great the way a lady can do that? It's all in the flick of the wrist.

"It occurred to me on the walk over," I said. "Are you allowed to fraternize with a witness outside of the Grand Jury?"

"Fraternize? Sounds dirty."

"Converse? Socialize?"

"I don't know—I didn't pay much attention," she said, raising an eyebrow, inhaling smog and blowing up and out of the corner of her mouth, crooked face, clever smile. On so many people it would have looked goofy—but not on her. Gotta love a woman who can be gorgeous and goofy at the same time. She had these very dark eyebrows that danced over her eyes.

"Well, I'd hate to cause you trouble being seen with me," I said.

She flashed me a gimme-a-freakin-break look.

"My problem is I tend to ignore some rules I maybe shouldn't," I said.

"Rules are for people who don't need them. Good people don't need them. Crooks find ways to break them. It's a game to them."

"Some would say that without rules we would have anarchy."

"That's because the world is full of crooks," she said, her voice halfway down her throat, as in ya knowudimean? "Let's make it simple—let's not discuss anything about ol' Ray."

"Good deal," I said.

I watched her. She dragged on her cig, flicked an ash. She inspected the pictures behind the bar, and I followed her eyes—Babe Ruth, Ted Williams, James Michael Curley, Leverett Saltonstall, Milt Schmidt. The usual—politicos and local sports celebrities. She checked out the other people scattered down the bar and my eyes followed hers. Two guys in suits drinking Coors Light and smoking cigars, a fifty-something couple sharing a Cobb salad and some chardonnay, and three scruffy post-college types with boilermakers watching the rerun of the Sox-Twins on cable.

"So what do you do when you're not a grand juror?"

She chuckled. "I'm a painter." She flicked an ash with a click of her thumbnail. Long, thin, delicate fingers, no polish, nails short but not chewed.

"What medium?"

"Oil."

"Messy," I said.

"But the fumes make you happy."

"Where do you sell your work?"

"All over the place. I did a chest of drawers for a Cincinnati family last month."

"How much is your painting on a chest of drawers worth?"

She raised her eyebrows. "Isn't that a little personal?"

"Maybe. I'm just wondering about the art market in general."

"Thirty grand," she said, grinning with a twitch of one eyebrow.

Jesus. Thirty grand for a chest of drawers.

"How often do you pull that off?"

She glanced over and looked back down at the bar. "As often as I want."

We talked through a stream of Harpoons, burning through her pack of Marlboros and into another, talking about everything else but the story that had brought us together. The bar went from almost full to dead empty to shoulder-to-shoulder as the after-work crowd jammed in for their couple of shooters before the commute to the suburbs. Mostly stock brokers, bond traders, a lot of nifty striped ties and matching suspenders.

"You sound like you grew up around here," I said.

"Hey, what the fuck? Did I say 'beah' or something? You look like you grew up in Weston or Carlisle or someplace."

"Close."

"Prep school, right?"

"Guilty."

"I am so not in that world."

"Tell me more."

She grew up in Savin Hill—or 'Savage Kill,' as they called it. Her father was a public servant in the City of Boston, one of Mayor John Hynes' precinct captains for sixteen years. She and her friends passed out campaign literature and held signs at the T stations. After Hynes retired, Senator Finnerty got her father a job at the MBTA, where he was the shop steward for the Carmen's Union. They were always involved in some sort of chicanery. He'd let one guy clock in for another guy if the wife was sick or he was visiting his mother an extra day down in Delray Beach. They were looking out for their own.

"People say it's a dirty business," she said, "and it is. But it's a people business, and it's just a plain fact that people are dirty."

"I find your lack of idealism disappointing," I said.

"You should be talking," she shot back. "At least his kind of corruption helped somebody who needed it."

"That make it okay?"

"Better'n influence peddling."

"There are degrees of corruption?"

"Maybe."

"Do you think a lobbyist treating a legislator to a round of golf or a dinner is corrupt in itself?"

She made slits of her eyes. "Depends on his purpose. If he spends a bundle on dozens of politicians, I assume he's buying influence."

"Buying influence? Is that corrupt?"

She looked at me wide-eyed. "Do you think it isn't?"

"What does buying influence mean? Are we talking about trading a gift for an act, creating a sense of obligation? Or are we talking about developing relationships? The mere appearance of impropriety?"

"What's the difference?"

"The former is a problem. The latter is bullshit."

"What's wrong with avoiding the appearance of impropriety?"

"Appearance to whom? I'll tell you who. Your political enemy, that's who. The major daily newspaper that doesn't like your politics. That's what's wrong with it. Your political enemy wants to make you look like a crook," I said. "When the rules let you ruin a reputation without evidence, that corrupts the system a lot more than any game of golf ever will. Anyone can perceive an appearance of impropriety."

"Don't you think that most of your colleagues are susceptible to influence?"

"What the hell is influence? What does that mean?"

She looked at me, the slit eyes again saying 'you're shitting me, right?' She slid her beer glass around in little circles, looking at it. "It means that most of them are walking idiots, they'll vote however the last guy asks because they couldn't care less, and for a nice meal or a round of golf, they'd put on fishnet stockings and bark like a dog in the middle of Filene's Basement."

I had to laugh at that. "You know, you're goddamn right."

"Damn straight…but I agree with you."

"Yeah?"

"Yeah," she said, screwing her face up like she smelled bad Chinese food. "How do I know how something's going to look to someone else? People's sensibilities are so goddamn touchy these days."

"No foolin."

The bartender passed by, and Shannon asked him for potato skins and fried calamari.

"The thing is," I said, "a politician is going to raise money for his campaign. He's going to remember the ones who contribute, if he's smart. He's going to take their calls. But he's going to take everyone else's call too. And if he's got an ounce of integrity, he's not going to act any differently for those people than he would for the lobbyist who buys him lunch or a round of golf. As a matter of fact, he may be more inclined to say no to his golf host than the roomful of contributors."

"Why?"

"Because it's a lot easier to say 'no can do' to a guy you play golf with."

She looked skeptically at me. "It's also easier to say 'you're full of shit' to someone you're drinking with."

"Hah hah, funny broad. But you're right."

"You know it."

As we gabbed on, the crowd slowly thinned. She was alternately cynical, sarcastic, and naïve, empathetic. Philosophical about the inane, inane about the philosophical. Completely unpredictable. And what an edge on her humor.

At some point—we weren't really paying attention to the clock—it got dark, and the after-work crowd had transformed to a couple dozen of the regulars who would stay for dinner and catch a late train out of North Station.

"You married?" she asked.

"Divorced, almost a year."

"Kids?"

"Nope."

"That's good. Did your wife like politics?"

"No."

She looked like she expected more, but I wasn't biting.

"No? And?" she said, voice rising, looking at me with this comical, stunning smile and raised eyebrows.

"She never said she didn't, but she's got nerves, she worries about everything. But she's not with me anymore, so…"

"Why'd you get into it?"

I wasn't eager to explain, but I took a breath and tried to let it all flow.

"I had it in my blood."

"Yah? How?"

"My father was a big shot in Washington." I found myself fiddling with the Bass Ale coaster.

"How big?"

"Big," now peeling away the edges of the cardboard.

"He famous? Like Edward Bennett Williams or Clark Clifford?"

I winced. "He was the biggest shot you never heard of. But everyone who mattered revered him."

"D'you matter?"

I choked up. "I did."

"Where's he now?"

"Our Lady of Peace Cemetery, in West Palm Beach."

Her jaunty look dissolved. "I'm sorry."

"No problem, it was a few years ago. He and my mother died in an auto accident on a country road in Ireland."

"That's terrible."

"Yah, well, if you're going to go out, you know?"

Killed the subject. Not that I ever planned it that way, but the truth is the truth.

"You got any siblings?"

"Nope. Just me. I'm all alone."

We sat in silence for a while, surveying the room, listening to snippets of conversation, watching people stir drinks, looking over shoulders. I had the thought, looking around, that there must be at least a few adulterers, tax cheats, a stock manipulator.

Usually I'd be relieved not to talk about the end of my marriage. Who likes talking about their failures? But this was a lady whose whole demeanor said "dish," and for the first time in months, I wanted to.

"So anyway, we'd just gotten married when the local rep retired and left the seat open. I asked Kate what she thought, and she asked me what my father thought. He said he'd raise a bunch of money for me, make sure the bills were paid at home. My wife adored my father. She was awed by him, like most people were. She said he was a gentle man with a fierce intellect and steely judgment. She always thought I should take his advice."

"Did you?"

"As often as I could."

"So she signed off?"

"Something like that."

She leaned on the bar, chin on her fist, peering at me like she was trying to read my mind, and then shifted, and said, "Can I ask you a personal question?"

"Why not."

"Did you ever cheat on her?"

I looked up, a little surprised. "Why do you ask me that?"

"I'll tell you after you answer."

"No. Never."

"Never?" she said with disbelief.

"Thought never occurred to me."

"Pffffft," she spat, "liar."

"I beg your pardon? Do you know me?"

"Hey relax, cowboy," she said. "I ain't that old, but I never met a married man wasn't tempted," rolling her eyes.

She was right, I had had plenty of thoughts of roaming. But only thoughts. There were a few times when women had thrown themselves at me, and I'd politely declined. It wasn't even hard. And I never went looking. I wouldn't have done that to Kate.

"You're charming, smart and funny," she said. "If you wanted to, you'd have your hands full." She gave me another of her crooked smiles, one eyebrow raised. This woman was playing me like a Stradivarius. "Never thought of it, huh?" she said.

"Maybe I did think of it, but what the hell, it's all moot now."

She stared right into me with a bright, amused smile.

"So why'd you ask me that?"

She swirled her glass on the bar. "I'm a nosy lady."

"I'll say."

"I wanted to see how firm your ethics were. You know, a man can pontificate all he wants about honesty and impropriety, but if he cheats on his wife, his word is shit."

"Yah, well, we all have weaknesses. Some are just weaker than others."

She raised her eyebrows and nodded. "So why'd it end?"

My throat was parched. If I had to answer that question, I was afraid I'd break the golden rule of bachelorhood. Women don't like criers.

"I'm not entirely sure right now," I said, tight in the chest.

"You want my take," she asked me, chuckling again.

"Why not," I said, exhaling. The first few words she said I barely heard through the ringing in my ears.

"My take is this. After you got elected, at some point you became a politician. When you got to the State House, you found the adulation people gave you was easy to come by. Pretty soon, you began to think that things like free golf, and dinners and drinks were perks of the job, and you convinced yourself that there was nothing wrong with it. How am I doing?"

I smiled. "Not until you're done." She was dead on.

"You picked up a sort of swagger that your wife didn't recognize." She paused for a swig of Harpoon and a new smoke. "At some point, you weren't sure she still loved you, and you were afraid to make the effort to find out. You were hungry for affection, but you resisted the temptation to get it elsewhere, and you called this fidelity. But when you were lying in bed at night and thought of sex to get to sleep, you were not thinking of her, but maybe one of the chicks prowling the State House that smiled or winked at you."

She met my eyes with a look of arrogance and mischief, and kept them there, a glaze now in them. I stared back, and she didn't flinch except for a moment to flick an ash, black eyebrow twisting for a moment in that way, crooked smile even more crooked, very vexing and sexy.

"You know about those women? The ones that wink at you?"

"I know them all right," she said, shrugging.

"Sounds to me like you know that world pretty well."

"I should," she said, "I'm an orphan of it." With that, the wry smile dissolved, eyebrows dropped to her cigarette, and the corners of her mouth dipped for an instant. She shook it off with a wide toss of her head, billowing smoke straight toward the ceiling fan, and caught the bartender's eye for another Harpoon.

I looked at my watch.

"What are you looking at? You can't leave till you grade me."

I signaled the bartender for one more.

"Okay," I said, took a sip on the Harpoon glass and lit one more Marlboro, the last, I promised myself. "You get a C minus."

She erupted. "C minus, come on, I did better than that."

"You got almost everything wrong. I give you the C minus because of your true read of the typical politician. But I, my friend, was not the typical politician."

"You're full of shit," she growled.

I gasped surprise. "Woman, you hurt my feelings. We're being honest, aren't we?"

"Okay, okay," she said. "I'm sorry. But you gotta admit, you've got your share of hubris."

"Thank you," I said, and stifling a laugh, "I accept your apology, and I admit that I do," and I couldn't keep the laugh in, and she began laughing with me.

"It's just that I don't know any politicians worthy of respect."

"Neither do I."

She stubbed out her butt. "So how'd she leave you?"

"Are you asking for a description of her last goodbye? You don't seem like the sentimental type."

"Oh I'm unbearably sentimental," she insisted. "I'm an artist. I feel. I emote. I wear my heart on my sleeve." She sat up straight, one elbow on the bar and facing me straight on. For a half dozen Harpoons, she had great posture when she wanted to. I thought she deserved an answer, so I took a breath, stubbed out the last smoke I hoped to have and tried to begin.

"All right," I started, feeling suddenly unsteady on the stool. "It's pretty simple. We agreed it was best."

"But?"

I knew she deserved more, but my mind would not feed my mouth any words. It happens with an excess of poisons in your system.

"It's too soon," I said, almost whispering to hide the tremble.

Shannon looked at me for a long time, slit eyes again, a frown of discernment fixed on her face. She reached out and gave my hand a squeeze, and said, "I can see that. Will you take me home?"

There is no describing the sensations that go on inside a man when a woman who has captivated his soul asks him to take her home. We just can't help wondering what's in store. But then follows the cold sorrow that she might just be asking for a ride.

"Sure," I said.

Shannon waved off my cash and settled up with the bartender, and we walked the two blocks to my aging Saab that I'd dumped in a lot on Broad Street. She climbed in the passenger seat, turned on the radio and spun the knob to the Emerson College FM station.

"Farragut Street, Southie," she ordered, cranked down her window, opened my sunroof, and drummed the dashboard to Buddy Guy's "Damn Right I Got the Blues" as I drove slowly up Congress Street. By L Street, she was singing "You're My Thrill" along with Billie Holiday, directing me over toward Castle Island, up the hill and around the corner to a renovated triple-decker on Farragut Street across from the beach, where I pulled up and stopped as Dan Hicks began to sing "I Scare Myself."

There are not many who have ever heard of Dan Hicks, much less know his music. But that song was one of my favorites, and so when I slowed to a stop in front of her building, I sat back and listened, as the intro to the song ran full circle and Hicks began to sing.

It occurred to me that I was singing the song softly, and so was Shannon. She was leaning forward with her forehead on the dash, eyes closed, lips moving.

The tune faded out, and she opened her eye, peeked back at me and rolled her eyes. She turned her body full to me.

"Some kind of voodoo," she said.

"Who do voodoo?"

"You do."

We cracked up and got quiet again.

"You mind if I ask you a personal question?"

I laughed. "What, you mean, like 'did you cheat on your wife?'"

"Okay, I'm a nosy bitch, I admit it."

"Go ahead. Ask me anything you want."

"I'm just curious. Your father was a big shot Washington lawyer. Your parents died, you're an only child. You must be loaded. But you work at the MBTA and you drive a shit box car."

"So?"

"Well?" She had her nose turned up, that wrinkled brow again.

"Maybe I already spent it all and I'm broke."

"Nah, you're not the type."

"Maybe my father had huge gambling debts that wiped out the estate."

"Not likely either."

"Maybe I'm just a cheap Yankee."

"You're French."

"You're pretty analytical for a painter."

She maintained her look, waiting.

"Spending money doesn't heal a broken heart," I said. "Besides, I like this car."

She smiled and patted the dashboard. "So do I. You're a good man, I can tell that," she said, reaching for the door handle. "But you can't come in."

I told her it was all right, and she put her hand to my cheek, gave me a quick, hard kiss, opened the door and was gone. There was no "call me." There didn't have to be.

I watched her go up the walk and into her building. The dim moonlight and a distant streetlight accented the outline of her form. She moved like a dancer. I watched her until the door closed behind her, and I looked up and examined the black steel and glass building. As I surveyed it, a light went on across the entire glass front of the fourth floor, and I saw her pull the curtains.

Looked like a nice crib for an artist chick who couldn't get out of jury duty.

Chapter 6

Bad News in Small Bites

The newspaper delivered another panic attack. It sat on the passenger seat as I sped up Route 3 from the Cape to Boston. I glanced at the article as I drove.

"LOBBYIST INDICTED," the headline screamed, a picture of the spectacled, Ivy League Ray Stackhouse beneath it.

"…indicted on fifteen counts of mail fraud and nine counts of wire fraud in connection with…"

I glanced back at the road, then down again.

"…thirteen legislators and former legislators testified under grant of immunity…

"Said Stackhouse's lawyer, Bud Galvin, 'I am supremely confident that my client will be vindicated'…"

They're always confident. I put the paper down so I didn't end up in the North River and flicked on the radio for the news, but decided it would only agitate me. So I switched over to WGBH and listened to Mahler's "Resurrection," performed by the New York Philharmonic with Leonard Bernstein conducting. He was way overdoing it, as usual.

Anyway, I had something (or someone) else on my mind. And she was pretty stubborn about staying there. Over and over, I recounted every word that had been said between us. I felt like a high school sophomore after a spring dance.

But I had a lot of other stuff on my mind too, and thinking on how my approach to life had almost ruined Kate, I decided it wasn't fair to get someone else involved in my mess, especially that exquisite woman. So I decided that I'd just bury myself in my work at the T and hope Ray's situation didn't drag me to my death.

I hadn't spoken to Al since I met the grand jury, so after I got settled in the office and had my coffee, I called him to check in. "Please hold," his secretary said. That's usually good for a two-minute wait, but he picked right up.

"What the hell did you say to Kilroy?"

"Good morning, Al."

"Good morning, Paul. What did you say to him," he said again, a bit louder.

"I didn't do anything but answer his questions. Why do you ask in that fashion?"

"Kilroy called me this morning. He's bullshit at you. A full week after you testify, and he's still furious. I need to know why."

"I have no clue, Al. I gave him all of the testimony I had discussed with Boertz. But he went off on his own a little bit and I gave him truthful answers that maybe didn't help him out. But that's his mistake, not mine."

"Did you give any testimony that caused the grand jurors to laugh?"

"Are you asking me if I was a smart ass, Al?"

"If you want to put it that way, yes. Were you a smart ass?"

"On the whole, no. But he did feed me a big slow-moving softball, and I couldn't resist swinging. What did he say to you,

Al? I mean, I made one pretty good wise crack, but it wasn't out of line."

"Did you make the grand jurors laugh at his expense?"

"Is that what he told you?"

"That's exactly what he said. And he followed that with 'your client didn't appreciate the narrow scope of his proffer agreement.'"

"What the hell does that mean?"

"It means, Paul, that Bernard Kilroy may well hunt you down for anything that took place outside of your activities with Stackhouse."

"Al, that doesn't change anything."

"But you've given him the motivation now. You've created enmity. I don't know how, but you have. I only hope you didn't say anything else you weren't supposed to."

I had no reply to that.

"You didn't call him 'Bernie,' did you?"

"I might have, yeah."

"You bird brain."

"Hey, sorry, but it just sort of slipped out. What did he tell you I said, anyway?"

"He started ranting at me the minute I took his call. He mentioned the phrase 'insult me' and 'fail to appreciate the severity of his risk.' He said you 'lacked respect for the process.'"

"What else?"

"At the end of his rant, he mentioned something about 'osso buco.' I have no idea what that was about."

Oh-oh.

The panic attacks returned with Kilroy's enmity. I sensed a sort of violence in the man, and I had no control over what he did with the resources of the federal government. Dad had once begun to explain to me the "art of conciliation," but I probably wasn't listening as well as I should have.

For a few more days, I watched the sun rise and set from my office on the seventh floor of the Transportation Building. I stayed at my desk late into the night, wading through tall stacks of files and documents dealing with railroad law, federal transportation funding, construction contracts, real estate development, employment discrimination, labor negotiations, public bidding law, even the First Amendment. It was fast-paced and exhilarating, and it took my mind off Kilroy, but not Shannon's "osso buco" remark.

Or her eyebrows, or her smile, or her shoulders and jean jacket, or any other random detail about a woman that an infatuated mind would conjure.

There was an ever-present pall hanging over the T, cast by the two goons, Cruddy and Fetore. "Pit bulls," the Chairman called them, with affection. They ran roughshod over everyone they came across. I hated to pay either of them a compliment, but they were pretty good at it. Every one of the senior managers seemed to suffer from some sort of physical ailment brought about by the anxiety of not knowing if, or why, they might get fired. Every one but me, who had taken to calling the two of them "Mutt and Jeff." They heard about that and put a big target on my back. I could be such an idiot sometimes.

But hey, what's the point of doing your job if you can't have a sense of humor too?

So I just put my head down and kept on working. And thinking about that woman. Christ, hadn't I given her enough time to take the first step?

• • •

After months of agonizing about it, I decided to put the Cape house on the market and get a place in the city. The drive back and forth wasn't doing my back any good, and as often as the solitude was comforting, it was depressing. So I'd sell the place and give the dough to Kate. Since Mom and Dad died, I sure didn't need the money. Then I'd buy a condo in the South End or someplace.

With the grinding passage of a few more days of no bad news, I'd managed to put Kilroy out of my mind, for the most part. I'd even entertained the thought that it had blown over. Then one day I met Al for a cocktail at the back bar at Locke-Ober, and while I was sipping a nice cup of loud mouth soup, he delivered a real zinger.

"Congratulations," he said, laden with sarcasm.

"What?" I asked, sipping frigid gin.

"I've just received word from a source inside the Justice Department that you are the target of a grand jury."

Cold gin hit my windpipe, and I gagged and gasped, spraying the gin across the bar table. It took me a few minutes to stop hacking, but after a few sips of water and drying the tears from my eyes, I recovered sufficiently. "Target? What about the Goddamn proffer agreement?"

Al took a breath and a sip of his Manhattan. "We talked, if you remember, about the scope of that proffer, and about how it only covered your testimony as it related to Stackhouse."

"I remember well. And that's all I testified to." I slugged down the remainder of my Sapphire and waved for another.

"Not according to Kilroy, from what I'm told."

"What the hell is he talking about? What's the transcript say?"

"We're not entitled to a copy of any transcript. And as the target of a grand jury, you're not allowed to know anything about what's going on."

My cheeks burned. I felt an urge to hurl the lead crystal goblet of melted ice against the bar mirror. "What country do we live in here, Al? The United States or Russia?"

The suited gentlemen milling around the bar eyed me over their shoulders like I was a madman, and they weren't far from right.

"Your rights as an accused only vest when you are indicted."

"Some fucking system. So what were you told?"

Al twirled his glass. "Apparently, there is some part of your testimony that Kilroy believes was untruthful, or some part of it that did not relate exclusively to Stackhouse. Did you tell the complete truth, Paul?"

"Absolutely. No fucking doubt about it. Not even close."

"Well, they're looking at perjury, so you might want to reflect on it and see if you come up with something."

"What, you think I'm one of those accused criminals that talks himself into his innocence? Can't see his own guilt staring at him? Al, I did nothing wrong. I accepted dinner from a friend and did nothing in return for it. For him or any of the others."

Al's fingers froze on his glass. "Any of the others? What 'others,' Paul? What did you say about 'others?'"

I felt the blood drain out of my face. "He asked me if I'd ever done anything in return for Ray's generosity. I said no. He said 'are you certain,' and I said 'not for him or anyone else.'"

Al stared at me with a still, blank face, as grave as if he'd just learned his mother was dead. "This is a problem," he said, shifting his gaze to the drink in his hand.

"Why's that, Al?"

He stared at his glass some more.

"Why's that, Al?"

"Because you opened the door with the 'anyone else' remark. He must believe you've performed an official act for one of your many hosts."

The next two Sapphires dulled the panic, but on the ride home, I did contemplate the bridge abutment in a different way. How could I possibly be accused of a crime? And what did this Kilroy guy have against me?

Ray's indictment dripped stories in the paper every day, each one of them like a drop of acid in my stomach. There might be a rule about grand jury testimony being "secret," but that didn't stop people from blabbing. I got a couple of updates from my old State House friend, Francis X. Shakerman. Shakey was the only Jew I ever met who was named after a Roman Catholic missionary. He'd spent thirty-five years in the House Clerk's office, his last six during my own tenure. He was one of the first guys I got to know, just as Dad had suggested. *Make friends with the clerk's office staff,* he said. *Ask about their families. Get to know them. Bring the secretaries flowers on Secretaries' Day. Shoot the breeze with the lawyers.*

Shakey was the First Assistant Clerk back then, and I probably played a thousand games of backgammon with him. He spent his retirement years monitoring the trial calendars of the Suffolk Superior and Federal District courts. He called me at my office late one November afternoon.

"What's up, Rep?" These old State House guys. They just can't break the habit.

"Howyadoin, Shakey? How you think Ray's holding up?"

"The man's tie couldn't be blown out of place by a Nor'easter. He's cool as Elvis."

"What's your prediction?"

Shakey personified the ham and egg lawyer. Got his degree

from Suffolk while working in the State House, never practiced in the private sector. A creature of government, canny and streetwise. "The prosecutor will lay out a typical government case. A lot of documents—receipts, canceled checks. And enough witnesses to establish time and place. Very methodical. And dull. The jury's gonna snooze. Then Kelly's gonna ask every witness the same question on cross-examination."

"What?"

"Something like this: 'Did Mr. Stackhouse ever ask you to do any official act in exchange for his hospitality?'"

"What's your take on that?"

"People don't like lobbyists much, Rep. Might be good enough, all those bar tabs and greens fees. I hear he's expanding his investigation to include other lobbyists. You hear about Delaney's testimony?"

My heart was pounding to get out of my chest. "Yup," I said, about all I could get out.

"And the document subpoena to the Secretary of State?"

"Yup."

"More bodies are coming."

I thought of telling him I might be one of them.

"Any idea who's in their sights?"

"My guess? Someone who's elected."

I almost fessed up again. Christ, lying was harder for me than it used to be.

"Shakey, you been around a long time. If a lobbyist buys me a round of golf, and never asks me for anything, but I vote my conscience, have I broken the law?"

I could hear Shakey breathing, a slight rumble in his throat. "Is voting an 'act' or a form of 'speech?'"

"I have no clue, Shakey. How's the missus?"

"Still puttin' up with me."

"Piece of cake."

"See you later, Rep."

On the ride home, I considered visiting a doctor for some sleeping pills. But they'd mean I'd have to cut back on gin, and that wasn't a fair trade.

One afternoon just before the Thanksgiving holiday, Cindy tapped on my office door.

"There's someone holding on the telephone who refuses to give her name but says you'd better speak to her or there'd be hell to pay." I figured it was some nut job calling to report that she had her pocket picked or something. But I was in the mood for some wacky diversion, so I told Cindy to put her through, and I picked up my receiver.

"Paul Forté."

"Yes," the voice began, nasal and screeching, "I am calling to complain."

"I'm sorry ma'am, but this is the general counsel's office—we don't deal with customer complaints, let me give you that number…"

"No, this is not a service complaint," the voice screeched, "I'm calling to complain about the general counsel."

Just as I thought. Some disgruntled patron, looking to score some easy money without having to hire a lawyer. "Ma'am, are you represented by counsel in a matter involving the MBTA?"

There was silence for a few moments. "Well," the voice said, "yes and no."

My patience began to wane. "What is the yes part?"

"I am associated with counsel who is engaged in matters with the MBTA, and I am dissatisfied with that engagement." The nasality of the voice had abated, and I smelled a prank.

"What is the nature of your dissatisfaction, madam?" I asked.

"I haven't seen the guy in weeks," now with the true voice of the speaker.

I felt my insides being tickled.

"How the hell are you?" I asked her, laughing.

Shannon had a laugh of her own. "I got you, didn't I?" Of course she had.

"I've been waiting for your call daily," I said to her. Ten seconds of silence. "I've thought of calling you daily."

"It's great to hear your voice," I said, relieved and happier than I had been since I watched her curtain close.

She laughed again. "Well, it's great to let you hear it. I guess I forgot to tell you that I travel a lot for my work. Most of it I do at the client's house. Right after you left, I went to Jackson Hole. I got hired by the wife of a hedge fund manager to paint a mural of Cypress Point's sixteenth hole on the wall of a ballroom. You should see the joint. It's got to be ten thousand square feet."

"Cypress Point, huh?" My mouth salivated.

"Yeah, some fancy place in California. Very exclusive. 'We're *members* there, you *know*,' the lady says to me, with this affected drawl. So I threw out a ridiculous number and she didn't even flinch."

"You are a true native of Savin Hill. So it takes you two weeks to paint one wall? How many coats?"

"Hey, they had a cocktail party, and all their friends saw the work-in-progress, and before I knew it, I was the *dame célèbre* in Jackson. People throwing money at me to paint their hallways and bathrooms."

"So you telling me you're hanging out in bathrooms? Some dame célèbre."

She laughed. "These rich people are very strange. This lady is paying me two thousand dollars just to paint an image of someone peering through a peephole in the bathroom."

"That's sick."

So it went, like we were sitting in the corner at Pete's again. The only thing missing was I couldn't light her butts. At some point, we had a nice comfortable silence and I sat there with a big smile.

She asked me, "So, you surviving okay?"

I thought of telling her about my worsening situation, but didn't want to spoil it.

"Yeah, I'm surviving fine. You?"

"Yeah," she said. "I'm coming home for Thanksgiving. Then I have to go back."

"I'm glad to hear it. We can spend some time together then?"

"I'd like to see you. I'll call you when I get back. We can make some plans."

"Okay then," I said, "how would it be if I closed this customer complaint call with 'problem solved'?"

"That would be accurate," she said, "Talk to you soon."

As soon as I'd begun to look for a one-bedroom in the city, a cozy place off Columbus Avenue dropped into my lap. It never hit the market, and was owned by an architect and his designer wife who were moving to Seattle. They wanted seven-fifty for it, furnished. I closed on it three days later and brought clothes up from the Cape a bit at a time. I wasn't in a hurry to sell the place down there, and the market was on the upswing.

The day before Thanksgiving, Al and I met for breakfast in a back booth at the Hungry Eye. Mine was two soft-boiled eggs on a toasted corn muffin. I was hopeful I could keep it down.

"What's the good word?"

"I have the names of a few of the lobbyists who've testified to the grand jury. Linnehan, Cheever, Delaney?"

"That's Brae Burn, Winchester and Charles River."

Al chuckled. "You remember them all?"

"I have no present recollection. Just guessing. What'd they have to say?"

"They all admitted to treating you, but claimed it had nothing to do with legislative business."

A waitress served our plates. I broke the yolk on one egg and watched it run into the cornbread.

"Any bad news?"

"Kilroy's focusing on the numbers. Greens fees, lunches and drinks. There may be a lot of others."

I broke up the corn muffin, chopped the egg and mixed them together into a yellow and white mash.

"You didn't happen to report all this largesse as income on your tax return."

"Not much chance of that."

"Then we can add tax evasion to your list of worries."

The eggs crept up my throat. I pushed the plate away. It was the first corn muffin I never finished. "Let's look down the road at the worst. Say I'm indicted. What happens then?"

He nibbled at his grapefruit. "I expect Kilroy's going to want to get before a jury as soon as possible. In this case, the soonest would be six months, if we wanted it. But I'd want to drag it out."

"Why? Why give him more time? Isn't that what the speedy trial is all about?"

Al patted his mouth with a napkin. "This case is more political than legal, Paul. His trial schedule is part of his campaign for Attorney General. He doesn't want to let this drag on because it delays his announcement. If we can hold out for the next U.S. Attorney, we might find out that the Justice Department hierarchy isn't as hot on this case as Kilroy is."

"Al, that election is two years away."

His lips cracked up at the corners. "Yes, it is. You'll be amazed how fast it goes by."

The yolk-soaked cornbread sat forlorn. "I don't relish the idea of having this hang over me for the next year."

He laid his napkin on the table. "Think of it this way. If you think the wait will drive you crazy, it'll give Kilroy apoplexy."

"It will, huh?"

"Absolutely."

"I suppose I could live with that."

Al threw a twenty on the table next to the bill. "You're a stalwart man, Forté."

"For a corrupt politician and tax cheat, you mean. You have no idea how I get by, Al."

"To the contrary, I have a pretty good idea."

"Don't give away my secret. Thanks for breakfast."

Chapter 7
Gourmet Blubbering, Gourmet Delight

I went back to the office and wasted an entire workday staring at the pictures on the wall. By late in the afternoon, I'd imagined myself in each of the pictures wearing prison orange. It was just the sort of mood to be in when having dinner with an ex-wife. It had been more than a year since our divorce, and title to the Cape house was still in "Paul and Katherine Forté, husband and wife as tenants by the entirety," which says a lot about how ambivalent our break-up was. I'd gotten a sweet offer for the place, and needed to get Kate's signature on the purchase and sale agreement, so we were meeting for some northern Italian at Al Forno in Federal Hill.

She looked fabulous, as usual, and despite both of our efforts to keep it cheery, it was a pretty sad date. She signed the P&S, just to get it out of the way, and in the midst of a nice bottle of Brunello di Montalcino, we had a good cry together. The truth was, we were tragically fond of each other, but we were just a disaster together, and there's nothing worse than behaving badly with someone you think you're nuts about. It was all very maudlin and sentimental and entailed too much public blubbering, which is not all that out of place in an Italian ristorante.

But the veal was out of this world, and once we got past all the mushy stuff and into an absolutely sublime tiramisu with Vin Santo Fiore, it was sort of like the old days before we got married. She told me about her new business, more animated than I had seen her in years. She even confided with a mischievous smile that she was dating someone, which made me happy, honestly. I didn't ask for details, and she didn't offer any, but I could tell that she had found a spark, and she deserved that. Then she said something strange.

"I think we were supposed to be together, just not intimate."

I gave her a puzzled look.

"I always felt a kinship with you, but when we got sexually involved, I felt as if we were doing something wrong. Sometimes I think we were brother and sister in a previous life, and our intimacy was a sort of incest."

"That would explain your getting dressed in the closet, then," I said, winking at her.

"Yeah, I guess it would."

She asked me how my legal problems were going. I lied and assured her that they were nothing, I was a bit player of no importance and it would all come out all right in the end. I didn't see any reason to tell her I was going to be indicted, and if she found out, she'd understand why I'd fibbed. I'd been hiding that kind of thing from her forever.

As we finished the dessert wine and I paid the check, she said, "I worry about you," and she launched into a soliloquy about how she always worried about the controversies and the press and my reputation and how she never wanted to talk to me about her fears, and then she veered off and confided that she always believed that I must have been screwing those State

House women because we didn't have enough intimacy and that was her fault and I must have felt unsatisfied and sexually abandoned and she started to cry again and said she was sorry she failed me as a wife.

Things could have careened out of control, me on the edge of becoming pathetic myself. But I bucked up, patted her on the arm and told her it was not her fault, communication failure is always two-way, and the important thing was to not look backward and to move on.

"One thing you need to do, Kate—don't worry about everything. Worrying is bad for your health. It weakens the body. I worry about what worrying will do to your health."

"I understand that, but the doctors want me to take pills for anxiety and depression, and I hate taking pills. I tried a few and they make me feel so strange and loopy."

"Let's get the hell out of here," I said, and while I walked her to her car, assuring her that she hadn't failed me but we just weren't made to be together, she blurted out, "you did sleep with some of those women, didn't you?" It wasn't in an accusatory way, but seemed almost voyeuristic. We stood at her car in the cold air and I just hugged her and told her the truth—that I hadn't ever cheated on her, even if I did feel a little lonely once in a while, and she hugged me back and said she believed me, and thanked me for that.

She said, "We can stay in touch, can't we?" I told her nothing would make me happier. I told her I loved her, put her in her car and walked off. Then I cried like a baby all the way back to Boston.

God, the heart is a vicious organ.

I got back to my place about 9:30, found a message from Shannon on my voice mail and called her back. She'd just gotten in from Jackson, she said, and her body clock was three hours behind.

"I'm starving and I've got no food in my place."

"So go get a meatball sub."

"Buy me dinner."

"I'll be right over."

When I pulled up to her place, she stood outside waiting with a ciggie in her mouth and hands in her pockets. It was a little raw out, what you might expect for Thanksgiving, but she looked like some sort of Eskimo, with a fluffy fur collar on a hooded parka. She jumped into the car quickly.

"Woo, Jesus it's cold out there. Does the heat work in your shit box?" She looked at me with a cheery smile. I could have died.

"Is that what I get after weeks? You insult my car?"

She came close and kissed my cheek. "I'm starving, Paul."

The Saab rolled off Farragut and back down to Broadway. "What're you so cold for? You've been in the Grant Tetons for months."

"Different kind of cold. And I don't go out much. My little hovel is miles from town and I don't have a car unless I borrow one of the three Land Rovers."

We drove down Broadway and across Herald Street into the South End. I turned onto Tremont Street and found a parking spot in front of Hammersley's Bistro. More karma.

"Come on, I'll feed you some yuppie food."

"Do they have osso buco?"

"You are such a smart ass," I said. We got out and hustled through the chilly air to the door.

At ten P.M. the place was jamming, packed with upscale urbanites, their voices and the clink and clatter of plates echoing in the high ceilings. At the Maître d' station, I gave my name to a haughty young man named Carmen. He gave me a why-are-you-bothering-me look, but when his eyes landed on Shannon, the brows over them rose with his smile. Over the hissing of the grill from the open kitchen, I heard him say "no problem" in a sing-songy voice, and he led us to a cozy deuce along the back wall, a little close to the restrooms, but who'd complain? Carmen pulled out the table for Shannon to slip in, slid it back in place, laid our menus down like they were wounded birds and swooshed off, saying "Enjoy!"

"Old school chum, I guess."

"You know how it is with gay waiters and short-haired women."

Another handsome, slim fellow arrived, introduced himself in a contralto as Rinaldo and took our drink orders, lavishing attention on Shannon and practically ignoring me. He swished off.

"What is it about gay guys and their lack of manners to us straight men?"

"They say the same thing about getting the shit beat out of them by jocks from Eastie."

"Well, I was a tailback at prep school. They should love me."

"They would if they got to know you."

Rinaldo came back with the drinks—a Sidecar for Shannon and Sapphire for me—described the specials for us, and slinked off to give us time.

"You're eating alone, by the way. I had dinner with my ex-wife down in Providence earlier."

Shannon frowned at me. "Aww! Why didn't you say so? We could have done this another night."

"Are you serious? I've been dying to see you for months. I'd have met you at a laundromat." I reached out and patted her hand, and she turned it over and gave me a squeeze. And the smile, too.

"So what's up with your ex? Can I call her Kate? Is that okay?"

"It is certainly okay."

Rinaldo delivered our drinks and took Shannon's order, mushroom risotto and a tomato and mozzarella salad, frowned at me for passing, and slid away. "I needed her to sign some papers on the Cape house, so we had dinner."

"Was it all right?"

What does a man say to a woman he's sure to be falling for when she asks him how his meeting with his ex-wife went? Is frankness called for? A complete answer? One line? A ten minute exposition? These questions might have occurred to a calculating man, to one deliberate in the practice of contrivances. They did not occur to me, and I was glad. I would not make the same mistake again as I made with Kate, where inner thoughts were guarded, or worse, dressed in gaudy disguises.

I gave Shannon a complete account, eyes on my glass, watching my fingers twirl it on the napkin, occasionally glancing at her. She had her chin on her fist, elbow on the table, staring intently at my face, so I was sure she discerned every twitch of my eyes and mouth that must have shown everything.

As I came to the end of my soliloquy, I looked at Shannon's face with eyebrows raised and saw in it no hint of cynicism or whisper of jealousy, but just empathy, and I would have guessed as much for Kate as me.

She held my gaze inscrutably, narrowed her eyes, picked up her glass and took a long slow sip of her Sidecar. "Do you want to tell me about the failure of your marriage, Paul?"

"Which would you prefer first, my marriage failure or my looming indictment?"

The color left her face, but she was still inscrutable. "I'll take the marriage first," she said, as though she was choosing a menu item. She lifted her hand, extended two fingers for the split second it took Rinaldo to notice, and wiggled them.

"Okay. When I met Kate, she was an artist and a free spirit who had to drop out of college to help support her parents."

"I like her already."

"I met her when I walked into a Newbury Street store and saw her behind the counter. I asked her if she would be my date for a New Year's Eve Party."

"How spontaneous of you."

"Well, I needed a date—but she just did something to me. Sort of like you."

"Don't be going there, chief. You're talking about a divorce here."

"True. Anyway, we had a fabulous time at this party, and afterward, we ended up back at her apartment. We smoked some dope and we got nekkid and got to playing around with her oil paints, but she wouldn't let me paint her nipples blue."

"Sounds like a smashing first date."

"The next day we drove to the Berkshires and stayed in bed for three days."

"Is this technically still the first date, or do you have to go to a second date when it's the next day?"

"Why do you ask?"

"Because I'm trying to determine how much of a slut you were."

"Fuck off."

"No, that's what you were doing. Three days in the sack. You stud."

"We slept a fair amount."

"Aren't you proud of yourself, then?"

"Do you mind?"

Rinaldo delivered the drinks and the tomato and mozzarella

salad. "Your risotto will be right out. Would you like some wine that that?" She waved him off with insufficient attention, I thought.

"Sorry. Please continue," she said, raising her fork and knife to the tomatoes.

"After a few years…"

"In the sack?" she said, mouth full of tomato.

"Will you please shut up?"

"Well?"

"Okay, I'm trying to get to the important stuff here."

"Hey buster, three days in the sack is important. God, I'm starving." She attacked the mozzarella.

"You seem to be focused on sex."

"Well, champ, isn't that where your little narrative is going to end up?"

"How do you know that?"

She rolled her eyes. "Paul, it's behind every marriage break-up. It's behind most family break-ups. It's behind practically every scandal and tragedy in the history of mankind." She shook her head and raised another forkful of red and white to her mouth.

I pondered that. "Well, yes and no. It wasn't the sex life that broke us up. It was the complete failure of communication— and that led to the problems with sex and everything else."

"You haven't stumbled upon any great revelations there either, lover boy. Communication failure is the mother's milk of cultural corrosion," another forkful following.

"Jesus, when was the last time you ate?"

She sniggered through the mouthful but waved it off. "Let me ask you a question."

"Shoot."

"How well did you know Kate when you married her?"

"We lived together for three years."

"That's not what I asked you."

"How well did I know her?"

She rolled her eyes again, like she was dealing with an idiot.

"For example," she said, pausing to swallow. "Did you ever describe your first sexual experience to Kate?"

"No."

"Did you describe any of your previous sexual experiences to her?"

"Jesus—no."

"Why not?"

"Is it your understanding that women care to hear about the sexual exploits of their future husbands?" I assumed the question was rhetorical.

"Well, they certainly ought to," she stated. "Why would a woman not want to hear about them?"

"Jealousy, duh…"

She gave me the *you're-shitting-me* stare.

"What's she got to be jealous about? That her future husband isn't a fucking virgin?"

"That's a non sequitur."

"What?"

"Fucking virgin. It's a non sequitur."

Rinaldo arrived at the table with Shannon's risotto, just in time to hear my last line. He smirked. Shannon caught it and looked up at him. "What red do you recommend with this?"

"People seem to like the Pinot Noir," he said, a little huffy maybe.

"Have the Barbera, it goes better with the mushroom."

Rinaldo wanted to stab me with my own fork. Shannon went for the Pinot, perhaps to make him feel better. He twirled on his heel and pranced away.

"So, you guys didn't talk about the secrets you had before you married."

"I guess not. Eventually, we didn't talk about much of anything meaningful. I mean, I felt like I wanted to, but neither one of us could find words. We became miserable in our silence."

She paid attention to her risotto for a bit. "So tell me about the last time you were intimate with Kate."

Even with all I had revealed to her, the request startled me. "Why?"

"Call me a shameless voyeur. Pretend I'm drunk."

"That's good enough for me."

"It'll have to be."

"Okay, so, at some point, our sex life dropped off to practically nothing and she began to get dressed in the closet."

"Excuse me?"

"You heard it."

"How'd that make you feel?"

"Pffff, how do you think? I really resented it, although I didn't say anything. I did begin to parade naked in front of her, just to let her know—I don't know what. But I don't think she even once stole a glance at me, which can damage a man's ego. You know you've got a serious problem when you drop your towel and your wife averts her eyes."

"Yah, that's pretty debilitating, I bet," she said.

"So she'd been doing that for months, but once in a while she'd be able to shed her shell. The last time we were intimate, she said to me in the middle of some very awkward foreplay, 'I feel like I'm about to fuck a complete stranger.'"

"Jesus."

"Yah, really."

"How did you react?"

"I reacted a bit roughly, and she seemed to respond, so

things sort of escalated into this vigorous and sweaty fucking that involved a lot of vulgarity—something you'd see in a cheap porn flick at a frat party."

"Yikes."

"Yah, that sort of signaled the end of our viability. It scarred both of us."

"No, Paul."

"No?"

"Sounds like you were doomed from the beginning. You were two strangers who just thought you were close because you didn't know any better—which is no different from most marriages these days."

She was absolutely right. There was so much I never shared with Kate. She probably held back herself. No wonder she hid her body, if she was hiding her thoughts too.

Shannon leaned back in her chair, staring up at the Art Deco. "It's terrifying to put it all out there and leave yourself naked. It's a huge gamble, you know?" She fell silent and her gaze dropped to the risotto as she fiddled with her fork. "When I first began to paint, my work was very intimate. I felt like I had stripped myself naked on the canvas. It took a long time to gather the courage to show them to anyone. One day, my teacher asked my permission to show a couple of them to a gallery owner, and she begged me to let her show my stuff. But I just couldn't do it.

"A while later, a lady stopped into the studio at the end of class. She was a beautiful and gentle lady who owned a boutique gallery on Newbury Street, and she convinced me to loan her a few pieces to show anonymously, just hang them and see what the reaction was. I felt like I could trust her, I don't know exactly why."

"What happened?"

Rinaldo paid us a visit, cleared Shannon's clean plate, coaxed us into sharing some black forest cake and Fonseca twenty year-old and bustled away.

"After a few weeks, she called me and asked if it was okay to sell the pieces. I said, 'you mean someone wants to pay money for them?' and she said 'fifteen thousand for the two.'"

"Holy shit."

"No foolin'. That was more money than I'd ever seen at one time. So I sold them and gave her a few more. When perfect strangers looked at my work, I felt unbearably vulnerable. I couldn't even attend my own show."

She sat lost in thought for a moment, and then with a sudden, fierce intensity she continued, "You have to learn to feel that way about everything you do. Especially with love. When you are fearless about sharing anything in your heart, you are truly in love." The fingertips of her hand clutched together upturned, her delicate chin leading the rest of her body pressing forward toward me.

Her words made my heart quicken and thump against my sternum. A racket of clacking plates and laughter and chatter caromed off the stark marble walls and as I stared at her the noises seemed to come together to form a crystalline bubble around us. I must have been looking at her oddly.

"What the fuck did I say?"

"I felt like we were on our own planet for a second."

She guffawed at that—I don't know why—and I could hear her laughter echo off the walls. I scanned the crowd to see many eyes cast her way and felt proud to be with her.

Rinaldo showed up at the wrong time again, using cake and port as his weapons. But even he couldn't break the spell. Shannon paid him no mind and he flounced off.

"We can never come back here again, you know."

She flicked her fork into the cake, slipped it under a morsel of black gooiness and slid it between her lips. "He'll get over it."

"Tell me about Jackson."

Our forks skirmished over the cake and we sipped the Fonseca while she told me about Jackson Hole and the roster of projects that would keep her busy until she didn't quite know when. Late Spring, maybe. That left my heart on the floor, but I hid it well.

"What's going on with Stackhouse?"

Her eloquent speech about honesty shamed me out of fibbing. "There's a new grand jury."

"Who's the target?"

"Me, I'm afraid." I couldn't keep my face from sagging, especially when I saw the hurt look in her face.

I gave her the cold hard facts as best I could without losing it, and she was sweet enough to caress my hands while I did, which inclined me to consider making some stuff up that would maybe get me hugs or better.

"At the end of the day, I just have to recognize that I followed the rules. I played by the rules. I don't know what this Kilroy guy thinks, but I can't control that."

I looked in her eyes and felt her caressing hands in mine. I saw in those eyes an empathy I'd missed for a long time, and a hint of something else I couldn't quite identify. I was just hoping it wasn't pity.

"Enough of that or I won't be able to sleep."

Rinaldo visited, and I think he rejoiced over Shannon's grabbing the check.

If he ever knew how hard I fought her to tip twenty percent. But I failed and threw a ten on the table on the way out, which neither of them noticed.

Like our first time, Emerson College radio blues filled the car on the ride back to Farragut Street. I was overcome with the urge to take one hand off the wheel and put it someplace, but I resisted it. When I pulled up in front of her place, there were no parking places to be had, which blew my primary excuse to park and walk her up. I idled for a bit while a song ended, and before I could make a move, she beat me to it.

She turned and put her hand on my cheek. "Paul, I'm developing strong feelings for you. I miss you when you're not with me. I want you to know that. But there's a lot about me I can't tell you yet, and it's why we can't be intimate. Can you accept that?"

I took a moment to get the tennis ball out of my throat. "I can."

"Can you trust me?"

"I can."

"Will you let me be with you through your legal problems?"

"I will."

"There's so much to say, it's…"

"Don't worry about it, darling."

Her face froze and she practically sneered at me. "Did you just call me 'darling?'"

Only one way to respond to that. "Goddamn right I did. Deal with it."

She smiled. "I'm pretty sure I'm falling in love with you."

I would not be manipulated by such ham-handed tactics. "Get the hell out of my car."

She did, with a kiss on the lips and a big honking wink that made me roll my eyes and wonder what the hell I'd gotten myself into.

Chapter 8
Masters at Work, a Secret Admirer

Early on Tuesday morning after the Thanksgiving break, before the law department was fully populated, with my signature stamp poised, I ran across a contract that had a couple of extra zeroes. I called down to the general manager's office to ask Halsey if it was a big deal to hold it for a day. Betty answered the phone.

"Hey Betty, can I speak to Jack?"

"Sorry Paul, he's not in until later this afternoon."

"What about Cruddy, he around?"

"No, he's on vacation this week."

"Really? Where'd he go?"

"Flagstaff, Arizona."

"When'd he leave?"

"Day before Thanksgiving."

"Thanks, Betty. See you later."

"Okay, Paul."

I went to the conference room and called Rex—or rather, Senator Packwood called him.

"Your friend Cruddy flew to Flagstaff last week."

"I know."

"You know?"

"Yes, I know."

"Do I want to know?"

"No."

"Goodbye, Rex."

"Goodbye, Senator."

Later in the afternoon, Cindy tapped on my door.

"The Chairman's office just called. He would like to see you right away."

"Call him back and tell him he can kiss my ass," I said, real serious.

Cindy blanched until I smiled, then she sighed relief. "Don't do that."

I put on my suit coat and hustled down about three hundred yards of bland hallways until I reached the impressive facade of the Executive Offices. Liguotomo's personal secretary regarded me without the slightest sign of amity and commanded me to sit. After a good ten minutes, the door opened rapidly and Fetore left the office. He looked at me and smirked as he passed.

The Chairman came to the door and waved me in. I obeyed. He went past the couch and easy chair, and sat behind his desk, pointing me to the two wooden armchairs.

"Sit down, Paul." I obeyed again.

He sat looking at me for a very uncomfortable minute.

"Do you know why you're here?"

"Because you summoned me."

"Do you know why I summoned you?"

"I presume because my client had something he wanted to discuss with me."

"Is that what I am? Your client?"

"According to statute, that's what you are, sir."

"Wouldn't that mean that you have an obligation to tell me things I ought to know?"

"Anything pertaining to my representation of the T that I thought you should know and didn't already know, yes, sir."

"How would you know if I didn't know something?"

"I don't believe there's much that goes on in this building that you don't know, Mr. Chairman."

He smiled with his eyes tightly closed. "That's generally correct." It seemed he enjoyed this cat and mouse game.

"Is there something in particular that you think I should have told you and didn't? Since there's so little you don't know?" I thought that deserved another smile, but I didn't get one. He just stared at me blankly, like his mind was elsewhere. Or perhaps he was annoyed that I was having as much fun as him.

"What is your rule of thumb?" he asked.

"My rule of thumb?"

"Yes, for deciding when to tell me something you think I should know but might not know?"

"Well, I can think of two rules."

"What are they?"

"First, if you've done something that might get you in trouble. Like when you voted to award a contract to a company you have a financial interest in. But you knew that, so I didn't have to tell you that. I just fixed the problem."

"What's the second rule," he asked, with a hint of impatience.

"When your two goons are up to something that I think you should know about. Like when I called you to tell you they were going about fixing your vote problem all wrong. But then, I assume that you are aware of everything they are up to."

He looked at me sharply. "Why do you think that?"

"Because you're too smart to let them act independently."

"You think so?"

"Yes, I do, sir."

"I don't think you should assume that I know everything they're up to."

"Are you saying that you don't trust your own guys?"

He looked at his hand as it played with an elastic band. "What did I tell you before you took this job?"

"Trust no one."

"That's right."

"Even you."

"That's right."

I looked him in the eye with a tense smile for as long as I thought it would take to tell him that I wasn't afraid of him and wasn't hiding anything from him. "So, have we taken care of the reason for my visit?"

"I don't know. Have we?"

"I don't know. But I have an idea."

"I'm all ears."

"If there's something you want to ask me about, why not call me on the phone and say, 'Paul, what do you know about so-and-so.'"

"Let's try that. Paul, what do you know about an outfit called Epsilon?"

I'm pretty good at maintaining a calm exterior, but only a sociopath can keep the blood from running out of his face.

"I know that some piece of shit consulting agreement came to me for approval, I wasn't willing to approve it as it was, but your boy there jammed it through without my help."

"That's all?"

"Mr. Chairman, it's not like it's the only shitty contract that goes through here. I just object to having to attest that its form satisfies me. I'm not a contract cop, I'm just trying to do my job."

"Sometimes we think maybe you're trying to do it a little too well."

"It would seem to me that you'd prefer that rather than the opposite."

"Don't be so sure," he said. His hand fiddled with an elastic band as he looked at me.

"What's this I hear about a possible indictment?"

"Don't know a thing about it," I said.

"Is that something you think I should know about?"

"You mean would it be, if it were true?"

"Whatever," he said. He seemed to be tiring of the game.

"Since the target of a grand jury is not supposed to know anything, I don't know how he could possibly know what to tell, if it were his employer's business to ask. It's a scary idea, your actions being examined and having no knowledge of it, don't you think?"

"Do you think a general counsel of a public agency could do his job if he were facing a criminal trial in his future?"

"Hypothetically?"

"Yes."

"I think that would be a matter for the agency's Board of Directors to consider, were that to occur. Hypothetically."

"Well, perhaps we'll revisit this topic again."

"Maybe we should do this every week or so, keep in closer contact?"

"I'll think about that. You can leave now."

I did. And I'd be lying if I said I didn't look over my shoulder a couple of times on the walk back to my office.

• • •

About mid-morning, one of my contract lawyers came in to give me a heads up. He was working on a case involving an old trolley car graveyard that we had sold to another agency. The clean-up company had just put through a change order for its contract on the job. The original contract price had been $7.5 million. They had discovered seventeen more trolley cars buried in the muck. The change order request was for another $7.1 million, and he had been told to authorize it by the general manager's office.

"Doesn't this have to go to the Board of Directors for a vote?"

"No," he said. "This is covered by insurance."

"Says who?"

"The project manager says it's covered by a contamination policy."

"Do you have any reason to doubt the legitimacy of the job?"

"I know the project manager who's supposed to be watching the contractor."

"Tell the project manager on the job to make an extra copy of the cargo manifests of the material leaving the job site."

"You want them?"

"Yes."

He looked at me puzzled, and left.

Cindy tapped on my door. "There's a 'Charles Manson' on the phone," she said, looking at me like it just might be him.

I picked up the phone, as Cindy stood glued to the door. "Hey Charlie," I said, "how's the chow there at San Quentin?"

"Your phone safe," Rex asked.

"Yes, it is."

Cindy stood in the doorway, expecting something.

"You can go, Cindy—this is attorney-client communication," I said, and she flounced out.

"I've been busy. Very worthwhile," he said.

"Okay," I said. "What next?"

"Now that we've got a line on them, we'll just keep tabs."

"Speak to me generally about how this sort of scam might work—not specifically here, but in broad terms," I said.

"Okay," Rex said, "no harm in that. This type of consultant would be retained to evaluate a client's potential liability for environmental clean up, or damage to another's property, and then evaluate the client's insurance coverage against that risk. If it's insufficient, they'd structure a new insurance program, put it out to bid among the insurers and bind the coverage. The trick is that the client is not competent to evaluate the consultant's opinion or the need for the coverage. So if the relationship between the consultant and the carrier isn't strictly arms-length, the client could end up buying much more coverage than it needs for too high a price. The consultant is paid by the client for the work, and gets a cut of the premium from the insurer on the other end."

"Is that ethical?" I asked.

"This is the insurance business," he said. I guessed that was a joke. "It might not be ethical, but it's not illegal, taking the commission split. It is if the product they're selling you is bogus."

"That's just garden variety fraud."

"A very expensive garden."

A thought occurred to me. "Rex, if the client were currently engaged in an environmental liability case, wouldn't that case be something that the consultant would look into, in the normal course of its due diligence?"

"Absolutely. They would have to pretty much examine all of

the client's real estate, what activity has been conducted on the property before and during its ownership, and what sort of limitations, if any, there are on liability."

"Before its ownership?"

"Yes," he said, "under the federal law, the property owner can be liable for contamination that occurred before he bought the property. 'Innocent owner liability,' it's called."

"Isn't that un-American?"

"Hey, Congress enacted it."

"That's exactly what I mean," I said. "There's something like that going on right now with one of our properties."

"The graveyard. I know about it. Don't say a word."

"Anything more about Epsilon and our fellas, beyond Cruddy's trip to Flagstaff?

"He didn't buy his plane ticket with his own credit card and has no hotel reservation."

"Maybe he believes in cash and sleeps at the Y."

"Maybe. Or maybe he's using an alias and someone else's credit card."

"Sounds more like Cruddy. Thanks Rex. Tell Rachel she lost her chance. I'm a committed man."

"Poor lady."

"Bye Rex." Click. I just love a guy who knows how to take a joke.

I went back to returning phone calls, typical bullshit. A couple of my claim investigators came in for a smoke and we chewed the fat while they each sucked down a couple of Pall Malls. These were the guys who take the calls that come in from people claiming they have been injured. Slipping on a subway platform, falling down stairs, getting their clothes caught in an escalator. They take a statement, find out when and where the mishap occurred, then they go out on the street and investigate the claim. It's a dirty business.

They told me about this man who claimed he slipped and fell down the staircase at South Station, broke up his knee. He had a heavy Haitian patois, Jamie said, and claimed he was a preacher. Jamie ran the guy's name through our national anti-fraud computer database. Turns out the guy had filed seven claims in seven cities from Boston to Kansas City, for the same day. So we'd play the guy out, pretend to settle the case, then have the feds bust him for fraud. The piece of shit.

So pardon us if we get all jaded and rude with some of the alleged victims of urban injustice.

I was tidying up my desk before leaving for the night when my desk phone rang. Cindy had left promptly at 5:00, so I answered it myself.

"General Counsel's office."

"Paul Forté?" asked a man's voice.

"Speaking. What can I do for you?"

"What can you do for me?"

"That's what I said, yes."

"You can pack a toothbrush and study how to live in confinement."

My heart jumped into double time. "Who is this?"

No answer, but he hadn't hung up. "This is your conscience calling."

"Who the fuck is this!"

"Your handicap's gonna suffer, pal."

I slammed the phone down on the cradle.

More sleepless nights ahead.

Chapter 9
Dropping Shoes

Historically, I have been at my nadir during the period between Thanksgiving and Christmas. I hated shopping, all the commercial crap made me ill, and the parties were all with people you didn't really want to see. This year, I had no one to give a gift to. Or at least no one who was around to share it with. And I was facing the possibility of jail.

It was exactly 4:57 P.M. on Tuesday, December 7th when Al called me. I was in the middle of a cheeseburger and diet coke.

"I heard from Kilroy's office. The grand jury has returned an indictment on one count of perjury and sixteen counts of mail fraud and conspiracy. I've read the indictment and it's on its way to you right now by messenger."

The contents of my stomach rose as adrenaline coursed through me and my heart thrashed around in my chest. I knew this was coming—I *knew* it—and yet my throat constricted, the breath rushed out of me, and no matter how hard I tried, my eyes teared. There was just no way to prepare for it emotionally.

Perjury. For telling the truth! I'd never done anything for any of them, except made birdie when I had to. They never asked, I never offered. I know the rules! I followed the rules!

"I'm sorry, Paul." Al's voice snapped me back.

"Okay." I gulped before continuing. "What hap—"

Cindy tapped on the door and tiptoed in with a manila envelope in her hand. She laid it on my desk and slipped out, closing the door behind her. I tore the envelope open and saw this:

United States of America
District Court of Massachusetts

United States of America v. Paul B. Forté
Violations:
18 U.S.C. 371 Conspiracy
18 U.S.C. 1341 and 1346 – Mail Fraud
18 U.S.C. 1343 and 1346 – Wire Fraud
18 U.S.C. 2 – Aiding and Abetting
Indictment
The Grand Jury charges that:
General Allegations
At all times relevant to the indictment:

1. Defendant Paul B. Forté was a duly elected member of the Massachusetts House of Representatives.

That's as far as I got. I dropped the phone on the desk, grabbed the wastebasket, put it in between my knees and upchucked the cheeseburger. I must have made some pretty horrid noise, because Cindy opened the door and gasped at the spectacle of her boss ralphing into a trash receptacle. I waved her out and hurled again. The nausea passed, leaving a cool sweat on my face. I picked up the phone.

"Al?" I could hear him talking to someone. "Al?"

"Are you alright? Let's talk about this later, Paul. Get a good night's sleep tonight, if you can. We'll talk first thing in the morning."

"Good idea. Will they arrest me at my home in the morning?"

"I've arranged your surrender. I booked you a room at the Four Seasons, if you want it. It's comped. I can pick you up in the morning."

"I don't have any clothes here. Besides, I don't want to sleep in a hotel bed. I'm going home. I'll drive up to your office in the morning."

"There might be press hanging around your house."

"I'll take my chances. I can't stand the idea of a hotel—not even the Four Seasons."

"Suit yourself. Remember, driver's license and passport only. Empty pockets."

"Empty pockets," I peeped.

He instructed me to leave my best suit at home and dress like "the regular guy that you are," whatever that meant.

Pizza and red wine was the perfect meal to wash down an indictment. In light of my initial reaction to the document, I might have thought oatmeal was more prudent, but for some weird reason, on the ride back to the Cape my taste buds screamed for smoked sausage and artichoke hearts, and Ramone's had just the ticket. So I settled down in my kitchen to read the government's allegations, with a ten-inch pie and a bottle of South African Merlot for company.

I stared at my name just below a big "V" for a good minute. United States of America versus Paul B. Forté. Me against the greatest power in the Western World. Two hundred fifty million to one. Hardly seemed like a fair fight. After a page or two of legal mumbo jumbo, I got to the meat of it. If the pizza was going to start a jig in my belly, it would be now.

This was what the government alleged:

23. At all times material herein, Stuart Winship Pierce was a registered legislative and executive agent for the Massachusetts Savings Bank Action League, whose membership is composed of state-chartered savings banks whose ownership is limited to Massachusetts residents.

24. As a registered legislative and executive agent, Pierce was subject to the prohibitions and limitations on gift giving contained in G.L. c. 268B.

25. As a member of the Massachusetts General Court, Forté was subject to the restrictions and limitations contained in G.L. c. 268A, specifically as it pertains to receipt of items of substantial value as that term is defined.

No quarrel so far.

26. On or about July 17, 1989, Forté was a guest of Pierce at The Country Club of Brookline, during which time he consumed a meal and played 18 holes of golf with Pierce and unnamed others. Pierce's hospitality to Forté constituted an "item of substantial value" under state law.

27. On or about August 6, 1989, Forté was a guest of Pierce at Kittansett Golf Club in Marion, Massachusetts, during which time he consumed a meal, played 18 holes of golf and consumed alcoholic beverages with Pierce and unnamed others. Pierce's hospitality to Forté constituted an "item of substantial value" under state law.

28. On or about August 22, 1989, Forté was a guest of Pierce at The Country Club of Brookline,

during which time he consumed a meal, played 18 holes of golf and consumed alcoholic beverages with Pierce and unnamed others. Pierce's hospitality to Forté constituted an "item of substantial value" under state law.

29. On or about September 6, 1989, Forté was a guest of Pierce at Kittansett Golf Club in Marion, Massachusetts, during which time he consumed a meal, played 18 holes of golf and consumed alcoholic beverages with Pierce and unnamed others. Pierce's hospitality to Forté constituted an "item of substantial value" under state law.

Funny. I had no idea we'd gotten to playing together that often, but we sure were having fun. In that gale at Kittansett. I'd had to hit a driver on a 170-yard par three. And I was short.

30. On or about October 16, 1989, in his official capacity as an elected member of the House of Representatives, Forté sponsored an amendment to House Bill 2696, An Act Relative to Interstate Banking, which amendment was requested by, and redounded to the benefit of, Stuart Pierce and his client.

The pizza and wine made it to my Adam's apple. *Sponsored an amendment? What the fuck?*

A call to Al's house yielded his voicemail, into which I hollered a profanity-laced tirade. Then I stared at that sentence in between fresh pours, as if, maybe, one more glass of wine would erase it from the page. But the Merlot wouldn't do it, or the Cab that followed.

Sponsored an amendment.

The Cab was gone by midnight. Sleep was only a vague possibility, but I gave it a try.

I watched Larry King interview Pamela Anderson, clicked over to WWF where some guy in a mask with a bull neck got KO'ed by a fellow in dungaree overalls. I thought about Shannon and whether to put any of this burden on her. It was only eleven P.M. in Idaho, maybe she'd still be awake. Which suit should I wear tomorrow? What does a "regular guy" wears to a federal arraignment hearing, besides handcuffs? Should I try to think about sex? No, she said she wasn't ready. Wonder if Fetore's wife really did kick him out. He's a stupid thug. I'd like to bury my elbow in his eye socket. Trust nobody, not even me. I wonder if she's that beautiful naked. Must be some imperfection, a scar somewhere. The greens at Kittansett are worth a year at Allentown, easy. They have a golf course. Won't be so bad, will it?

What fucking amendment? What did I forget?

And who was that asshole that told me to pack my toothbrush?

By 4:00 A.M., the electricity of panic had left me. There remained the dull exhaustion of fear, sadness and worry that suppressed a rage that screamed "this can't be happening to me!" As the dawn light winked under the lip of my window shade, I'd decided I had no right to dump this on Shannon, I settled on what to wear, and dropped off.

The alarm went off about twenty-seven minutes later. At least now I'd have the dark circles under my eyes, maybe look a little sympathetic.

I met Al in front of his office at 8:00 sharp, and we began a slow walk toward the FBI office at Center Plaza. It was an unusually mild December morning. We both wore trench coats, but mine was open. I don't know if it was nerves or what, but I was sweating underneath.

"So, how'd you sleep?"

"Not bad. Got two hours at least, but I did a lot of productive thinking."

"Really?"

I almost pushed him into traffic. "No, Al." I think it was the first time in his life he'd felt stupid. "What is this amendment thing all about?"

"I was going to ask you the same thing," he said.

I stepped off the curb at Congress and Milk, and he grabbed my coat and yanked me back as an MBTA bus roared by.

"Beats me, Al. I mean, I have a hard and fast rule. I don't conduct official business on behalf of golf partners. I have well-defined limits and I live within them."

The pedestrian sign blinked "WALK," and others did, but Al kept his hand on my arm as they funneled around us.

"Are you sure?"

"Am I sure of what? That I did nothing for Pierce? That I have well-defined limits? That I live within them? Be precise, for crissakes."

Al pursed his lips and led me into the crosswalk behind the crowd. "You know, Paul, the memory tends to do unpredictable things to someone charged with a crime. Despite my experience, I have yet to perfect the method of yanking the truth out of my own clients. It's disconcerting how often I am surprised."

"How considerate of you to think of me, Al. I don't remember doing anything for Stuart Pierce or anyone else. I vote and debate according to my conscience and nothing else.

"Unless those are official acts, I have no idea what they're talking about."

"I'll get the House Journal for the day in question, but I'll need to get the actual amendment document they're referring to. If you have some 'unofficial' means to get it faster, I'd encourage you to use it. I'll ask for it through discovery anyway, but I prefer the belt and suspenders approach."

"Sure thing, Al. Don't want my pants falling down."

We finished the walk to Three Center Plaza in silence and rode the elevator up to the sixth floor, where the door opened into a plain, cream-colored hallway with carpeting that should have been replaced long ago. Still not as bad as the grand jury room, though.

At the end of the hallway was a glass door with a big government seal with "Federal Bureau of Investigation" emblazoned on it. On the other side of the glass I could see a metal detector and another glass window with two female clerks sitting behind it. Al led me through the glass door into the small waiting room, and went to the window.

"Attorney Croston here with Paul Forté for surrender."

"Who is the case agent?" the lady behind the glass said through the voice box.

"Hartfield."

"I'll let him know you're here."

"I'll turn you over to Mr. Hartfield and then you'll see me when you get into the courtroom. Try to relax. This is routine for them, even if it isn't for you. They're all professionals here." Easy for him to say. I felt a little better, except for the hissing in my ears and a slight weakness in my knees.

A door opened and a tall guy with sharp features, maybe forty, stepped out. He wore a white shirt and black tie with gray flannel dress pants.

Agent Hartfield introduced himself to Al, quickly mentioning that he was aware of Al's prior service. They had a brief, cordial chat that mentioned several people they both seemed to know. Al introduced me, and the agent stuck out his hand. When I shook it, I noticed mine was cool and damp. Hartfield's piercing blue eyes bore into me, like he was assessing my every mannerism, but he didn't have the face of a malicious man. He was all business, for sure.

As Al prepared to leave, Hartfield said, "You might want to give Mr. Croston your coat. You won't need it. He can give it to you in the courtroom."

I looked at Al and he nodded. I removed my trench coat and Al slung it over his arm and said goodbye.

Hartfield escorted me through the door into a maze of hallways to a stark white-walled room where he searched, fingerprinted and photographed me and catalogued my personal belongings—a driver's license. He led me out of the white room, down another maze of hallways into an open office area filled with cubicles. It wasn't shabby, but it wasn't government chic either. Spartan, clean.

At the end of a row, he directed me into the corner cubicle and pointed to an empty chair. He sat behind his desk, pulled his keyboard forward and peered at the computer screen. I took a quick look around the cubicle. A couple of family pictures. Summer at the Cape, maybe. Some official-looking shoulder patches tacked on a cork board. And a picture of Hartfield and three other guys in golf attire, standing on a tee someplace. I took solace in that.

"Mr. Forté, do you know who I am?"

"You're the guy who's been investigating me for perjury, I'm guessing."

"Yes I am, sir. I am the case agent." Maybe it was just that my senses were out of whack, but he sounded almost apologetic about it.

Well, what the hell, I wasn't going to take it personally. The man was just doing his job. "Did you draw the long straw or the short one?"

Hartfield winced and smiled. "I try not to compare them, but..."

He didn't finish, but I had nothing to say, so I kept quiet, see if maybe he'd go on and say something. And he did.

"Let's just say the FBI doesn't choose which cases to bring."

"I understand. It's business."

"It's business," he said, exhaling.

"Well, then, Agent Hartfield, let's do the business we gotta do and I won't hold it against you."

I'm in federal custody, there are probably a hundred weapons within fifty feet of me, and I'm telling him that. And he must have appreciated it, or thought I was a damn fool, because he chuckled. Then he got down to his business, asking me a series of questions, all the usual personal information, was I married, have kids, where did I work.

When I confirmed that I was general counsel of the T, he glanced up from the computer screen.

"You work for Liguotomo."

"For the time being anyway. You know the man?"

He looked back at the screen. "Yah, we know him."

We know him. He continued with the questions.

"Family?"

"None."

Again he looked up. "Parents?"

"Deceased."

"My sympathies. You're too young to lose both of them."

"You don't get a choice, I guess."

"Their names?"

"Charles Forté and Margaret O'Reilly Forté."

Hartfield halted his typing again and turned to face me directly.

"Your father was Charles Forté? The lawyer?"

"You knew him?"

"No, I never had the pleasure. But my father did."

"No kidding."

He sat back in his swivel chair with his hands resting on his thighs. "My father was a lawyer at the SEC. Head of enforcement. He spoke very highly of your father."

"Small world."

"Small world." He nodded as he went back to his keyboard.

Hartfield finished with the questions—names, addresses and telephone numbers of all living direct friends and business associates. Did I have any alcohol or chemical dependencies? Did I have any friends or relatives living outside the United States?

While Hartfield typed, I looked at the photo of him and his pals on the golf course.

"That picture at Doral?"

He glanced over at the picture without his fingers pausing.

"Yah, last spring. Agent's annual meeting in Miami Beach." He kept on typing, focused on the computer screen.

I looked closer at the picture. I could see the clubhouse in the background.

"That's the Blue Monster first tee."

Agent Hartfield stopped typing and looked at me. "Yeah, you played it?"

He actually smiled at me, this federal agent.

"Hey, Agent Hartfield. I have a right to remain silent."

He chuckled. "No crime in asking."

"You of all people oughtta know the answer to your own question." Another chuckle. The guy had a sense of humor, anyway.

He stared at his screen and tapped. "Mr. Hartfield, you mind if I ask you a question?"

"Can't promise I'll answer it, but sure, go ahead."

"What the hell is this business with an amendment?"

He sat still for a moment, like he was thinking maybe he might answer. "Sorry, Mr. Forté, I am not at liberty to speak with you about details of the case. But I'm sure your lawyer will be able to obtain that information in due course."

"Figures. No harm in asking."

"None at all."

He went back to tapping, finally finished his report, and while the printer whirred, he seemed to consider something for a moment, then spoke.

"My father," he said. "He didn't talk about his work. Once in a while, he'd tell me a story or two about your father."

What did I say to Agent Hartfield? "He was a good guy." I'd been hearing stuff like this my whole life. "I wonder what he'd think of my predicament."

"I don't doubt that you do. I'm betting he'd think it was a bunch of bullshit."

I heard a hammer drop. "Why do you say that?"

Hartfield stared at the Doral picture, then over to his family. "Mr. Forté, there are times when a man says to himself 'this is not what I signed up for.'"

"I guess we all have a job to do. But I appreciate your frankness, and mum's the word. Is your father still with us?"

"He's in a nursing home in Newton. He'll get a kick out of hearing about this." He stood. "Time to go."

I stood with him, and he led me back through the white

maze to the reception area where we'd first met.

"This is Marshal Dawkins. He'll take you to the courthouse. Good luck, Mr. Forté," he said as I shook the hand he extended.

"Thanks Agent Hartfield."

Marshal Frank Dawkins stepped forward. He reached to his belt and produced a pair of handcuffs.

"Please place your hands together in front of you, sir," he said with a formality that was as intimidating as the cuffs. The jolt inside me returned, seeing the cuffs, hearing his instruction. My throat closed, my heart quickened, and I could feel the trembling begin in my hands and legs. I told myself to suck it up and took a few deep breaths that Dawkins noticed.

"Try to relax," he said as he handcuffed me. "Procedure says to cuff behind you, but we've got discretion."

I wondered what caused him to exercise this discretion. He led me to the elevator, where he turned a key in a special lock and we descended. The door opened into a sally port area where a black Crown Victoria idled.

"Crown Vic, huh?"

"Fed's Special."

He led me to the passenger side, opened the back door and helped me in, placing his hand on the top of my head.

"Watch your head."

Another marshal sat in the driver's seat, looking straight ahead. Dawkins went around to the other side, got in next to me, reached in front of me, pulled the seatbelt around me and secured it.

The driver pressed the button on a squawk box outside of the driver's window.

"Prisoner secure," he said to the box. The steel door of the sally port opened and the driver pulled the Crown Vic out onto

Pemberton Square and on toward the federal courthouse.

Once in the car, my heart quieted down and I took a few deep breaths. "You play golf, Marshal Dawkins?"

"Nah."

"No?"

"Not my bag," he said.

"Was that a joke?"

Dawkins looked at me, and chuckled. "No, not a joke."

"I do," the driver said.

"Yah?"

"That's Marshal Tucker," Dawkins said. "This is Mr. Forté."

Tucker nodded his head and glanced at me in the rear view mirror.

"Howyadoin," Tucker said.

"How do I look?"

He glanced over his shoulder and gave me the once over. "Better than most."

"That's some consolation, I guess. Where you play golf?"

"Walpole."

"Another Donald Ross," I said. "Seems all my troubles started on Donald Ross courses." Tucker sat in the driver's seat, but he wasn't driving. Traffic stood still, but I was in no hurry.

"You play it?" Tucker asked.

"Sure."

"With who?"

"Tony Shambo, the utility lobbyist."

"Good guy."

"Yah."

I looked at Dawkins. "So, what's your bag?"

"Fishing."

"Fishing, huh?"

"Yeah," he said, drawing it out, like he wasn't sure it was a blessing or a curse. Tucker worked the Vic through the city traffic, the occasional pothole jostling us.

"Sounds like you're pretty avid, the way you say that."

"Avid is right. My wife calls herself a fish widow. But she knows what it means to me, so she don't mind."

I nodded to him. "The peace of mind, you mean. The sense of calm, camaraderie."

"That's right."

"Fish widow."

"Yes, sir."

"Never heard that before. I've heard golf widow plenty. Not fish."

Dawkins nodded. "Yeah, lot of golf widows out there. You fish?"

"Not much, no. I've been called a fish, but I don't fish."

"You been called a fish?"

"A small fish, marshal. I'm a small fish."

He seemed to consider that but didn't respond.

The Vic bumped off Devonshire onto a drive at the back of the courthouse and halted. A throng of news cameras, microphones on the end of long booms, on-the-scene talking heads, scribes with pads—clamored for a word from the now-infamous former pol.

Tucker lowered his window and shouted, "prisoner arrival" into a squawk box as the throng attempted to shout questions through the open window.

"What's your handicap," some joker yelled.

The steel door slowly rose and Tucker pulled the Vic into the sally port and stopped. We sat in the car while the door cranked shut, finally cutting off the cacophonous inquisition.

"How'd the press know I going to be here?"

"Prosecutor's office tips them off," said Dawkins.

"Where we going now?"

"See the judge," said Tucker.

"Here come da judge," said Dawkins. "You remember that? 'Here come da judge'?"

"Flip Wilson, Laugh In," I said. Dawkins smiled.

Tucker got out and walked over to a bank of small steel lockers on the wall, opened one, took his weapon out of his belt holster, put it in the locker and shut it. He came back to Dawkins' door and opened it. Dawkins got out, shut the door and did the same thing while Tucker stood by. They both walked around the back of the vehicle and opened my door.

"Swing your feet out first," Dawkins said.

I swung both feet out and scootched sideways until my feet reached the concrete floor. Dawkins grabbed my upper arm by the armpit.

"Lean forward and come to me on three. One, two, three."

I lunged forward as Dawkins pulled me up while Tucker put his hand over my head to guard against me hitting it on the roof, and I stood.

"Nice work, counselor."

We stood in a barren garage of white cinder blocks. Besides the steel lockers on the driver's-side wall, there was only a white steel door ahead and a camera in the corner above it. They led me to the door and Dawkins pressed a red button below an intercom.

"Prisoner secure."

The steel door clicked, Tucker pulled it open, and Dawkins led me into a narrow, barren corridor of more white cinder blocks. One wall of the corridor was lined with five steel doors, each labeled with a large black number above it.

He led me down the hallway, the steel doors on my right, into a narrow room opposite where three men in blue blazers and wide ties sat behind an elbow-high counter. Behind them on the wall a bank of television screens displayed images of empty cells and hallways. On my side of the counter, a computer terminal sat at standing height and a digital camera pointed at a dark green screen on the facing wall. Dawkins led me to the counter and removed my handcuffs.

He instructed me to empty my pockets, and when I'd produced just my driver's license, he patted me down.

"You get many guys carrying stuff they shouldn't?" I asked.

Dawkins and the others chuckled. "No accounting for how stupid some people can be."

"Even white collar guys in suits?"

"Lawyer brought in here last week dropped a bag of dope on the counter."

"I guess he was arrested by surprise?"

"No, he turned himself in," said one of the three men.

"This gentleman is Deputy Marshal Garcia," Dawkins said, nodding to the speaker. "He'll be getting some information from you, he'll take your picture and fingerprints, take a few minutes."

I stood at the counter as Dawkins withdrew into the hallway, leaving the door open.

"You like to sit?" Garcia asked.

"I'm good."

"Nervous?"

"Petrified."

"That's natural. Try to relax."

"Easier said than done."

"Sitting's better."

I figured he knew, so I sat in one of the metal chairs along the wall. I could still see his head above the top of the counter.

Garcia asked me all the personal information I'd already

given the FBI—addresses for the past ten years, employment history, social security number, family members, did I own a firearm.

"Are you on any drugs?"

"You mean prescription medication?"

"Anything."

"No."

"Any health condition that we should be aware of? Diabetes? Epilepsy? Seizure disorders? Heart condition?"

"Nope."

"Do you have any distinguishing marks on your body?"

"Like what?"

"Like tattoos, moles, scars."

"No. What do you do when there are?"

"Take pictures of them. Do you have any enemies or people who may wish to do you harm?"

Wow. "Yes."

"Name?"

"Bernard Kilroy."

Garcia laughed out loud. "That's good. That's a good one," he said, shaking his head as he typed, still smiling. "I don't blame you."

"What, his rep get all the way down here?"

Garcia looked at me seriously. "There isn't a person in the building doesn't know about Mr. Kilroy."

"What is the purpose of that question, anyway?"

"Gang members. Lot of rivalries."

"Ah."

Garcia finished his interview, stood me up in front of the green screen, snapped my picture and pressed my fingers one at a time on a blue pad at the computer. The screen flashed up my mug shot, with name and federal ID number at the bottom and my digital fingerprints along the left side. The sight of it made me light-headed.

"Oh God," I muttered, reaching out to hold the counter. Garcia put his hands against my back to steady me.

"I got you, don't worry. It'll pass in a second." He was right, I recovered shortly.

"Sorry, it just came rushing up on me."

"Don't worry about it. Happens fairly often. Seeing the mug shot sometimes brings it home. Some guys even puke."

Dawkins walked in. "What's the matter, Mr. Forté get the perp rush?"

"Not too bad," Garcia said. "Least he didn't puke."

"You need to puke, Paul?"

"No, sir." I flashed back to Cindy's face.

Dawkins looked at Garcia. "I'll take him to number five."

Garcia nodded. "We're done, Mr. Forté. Good luck to you, sir."

"Thank you, Mr. Garcia."

Dawkins led me out and down the corridor to the steel door with a "5" stenciled above.

"What's this?" I asked Dawkins as he fished a key from his belt.

"Holding cell. We have to process you before you go upstairs."

"'Process,' huh? What does 'process' mean?" Another rush of anxiety. Something about the cold white walls and the heavy steel doors.

He swung the door open with a hard tug and led me forward into a holding area that had five jail cells along the left wall. "It's not too bad, just try to relax. Everyone goes through it. Everyone."

He led me along the corridor, and I looked into each of the

cells as I passed. They were identical. Shiny plastic benches on each side, and a steel toilet tucked behind a short privacy wall at the back. There were no prisoners, but one of the cells contained some personal belongings.

At the last cell, he stopped me, tugged opened the door and led me in. It was identical to the others, except for a privacy curtain on wheels sitting in the middle of the cell and a box of rubber gloves on the bench.

"What's the drill?" My stomach fluttered.

"Step behind the screen and remove all of your clothing except your shorts," Dawkins said.

I froze and looked at the rubber gloves. "A strip search?" A shot of panic erupted from my chest and zapped my arms and legs. As I said it, my hands began to loosen my necktie. I'm too respectful of authority.

I stepped behind the screen and took off my suit coat as Dawkins sat on the bench on the other side of the screen.

"Nobody gets treated different on this procedure," he said. "This is for our safety as well as your own."

The cell was cool, so I decided to leave my shirt until the end, slipped the suit pants off, folded them and laid them on the bench. "You've had problems with lawyers in suits before?"

"You wouldn't believe what lawyers in suits have had on their person coming in here."

"What're they here for? Embezzlement? Fraud? Do I need to take my socks off?"

"Socks off too, sorry counselor. Mostly drugs."

I was down to my boxers now. "What next?"

Dawkins came around the screen and patted down the clothing. "Okay," he said, "drop your shorts." I turned around and looked at him. He shrugged. "Everyone, I promise."

So I obeyed orders and slid my boxers down to the floor.

"Now what?"

"Spread your feet apart, squat down and cough."

I looked again at the box of rubber gloves.

Dawkins smiled. "Don't worry about it, that's not what the gloves are for."

I did as instructed, praying that my nerves would not cause some embarrassing rectal malfunction. Even under those circumstances, it's important to preserve a shred of dignity.

"You can get dressed," he said.

I obeyed. "So what's the deal with that," I asked him as I sat on the bench to pull my suit pants on.

"We've had people hiding weapons. Drugs, poisons. Nobody gets to the courtroom without a complete search."

I wondered what kind of weapon someone could hide in that fashion. Like what, a dart? Then my morbid curiosity got the better of me.

"But that wasn't a complete search."

Dawkins gave me an amused look. "I don't get many prisoners complaining about not being anally probed."

"I ain't complaining, Marshal."

He explained that the squat-and-cough method was effective at revealing the presence of hidden items. "They can make it through places standing up, but when they squat and cough, it seems to be more than the anus can handle."

"Thank you for that, Marshal."

"Call me Frank."

"Okay, Frank. What next?"

"Get your suit on straight, and we'll take you next door to see the pre-trial services person."

I followed instructions again, and Dawkins—Frank—led me out of the cell, through the steel door, and along the corridor to another steel door. He opened that door, and I saw a small closet-sized room with a metal chair and a steel mesh screen on the opposite wall. On the other side of the screen sat a lady in a dark jacket and blouse.

"This is Ms. Gianferrante, from pre-trial services. She'll ask you some questions and when she's done, I'll be right outside."

Ms. Gianferrante must have been used to the look I had on my face.

"Have a seat, Mr. Forté. A lot of my questions you've already answered, but we keep the records separate deliberately. I just need some information about your current living situation, employment, family, that kind of thing. You don't have to answer any questions you don't want, but nothing you tell me here is admissible. The information is used only to assist the judge-magistrate to determine appropriate pre-trial release conditions."

Dawkins gave me a reassuring nod, and I stepped into the room and sat in the chair as he closed the door with a soft clank. That Dawkins, he was a cool dude.

I looked through the screen at Ms. Gianferrante. She looked like a pretty rough broad, but she had kind eyes and long dark hair and a nice modulated voice. She introduced herself again, and explained that the purpose of her questions was to provide the court with information that would assist it in determining whether I was a flight risk, a threat to others, or a subject of any threats from others.

She asked previous addresses during the past ten years, which got me explaining about my divorce and my ex-wife and whether or not there was any animosity there.

"Does she have any siblings who might wish to do you harm?"

"No, no, she has no siblings. We were both only children, and our parents have all passed away." Ms. Gianferrante glanced up at me.

She asked me about assets, and I told her that I owned my South End condo by myself, with a small amount of debt, I had a retirement account and personal bank and investment accounts holding about three million dollars, and that I'd never held a U.S. passport.

"You've never left this country?"

"Why would anyone want to?"

This answer seemed to confound her.

"Tell me about your friends and family in the area," she said, and then she caught her blunder. "I'm sorry, I mean friends." She gave me a sad look. "Sorry, you get into a pattern here, you know?"

"No problem. Maybe if I had a first name, this would go easier."

"Gina."

"Gina Gianferrante. Very alliterative."

She shrugged. "Ah, I got used to it in grade school."

"That's not your married name?"

"I'm not married. And I'm asking the questions here."

"Sorry. What else?"

"Friends."

"What kind of friends?"

"What kind you got?"

"I got asshole buddies, drinkin' buddies, golfin' buddies, casual friends, and a million of that kind of friend who're your best friend until you need them and then don't answer the phone. And I got an ex-wife and a girlfriend."

Gina raised her eyebrow and smiled. "Any of the aforementioned friends liable to agree to be responsible for your appearance in court should the government see fit to release you on unsecured bond?"

"Sure. The ex-wife, my lawyer, my private investigator

and the girlfriend."

"Can you give me their names please?"

"Sure. Kate Swan Forté, Albert Croston, Rex Barkley and Shannon McGonigle."

Gina copied down these names on a form and looked up. I might have caught a fleck of amusement in her eyes. "Any of those names a problem?"

She looked back down at the form and didn't look up again. "No, no problem." She shuffled her papers together. "I think that's all I need at the moment, Mr. Forté. I appreciate your cooperation, and I will make a note on my report to that effect."

"Does that make a difference?"

"For some, yes, it does," she said, rising from her seat with a demure smile. She pushed a red button on the wall next to her seat and almost immediately, the steel door behind me clanked and Dawkins appeared once again at my side.

"Good luck, Mr. Forté. I'll see you in my office after your arraignment." She looked at Dawkins as he stepped in, and I saw that hint of amusement again.

Dawkins led me back to cell block number 5 and ushered me into one of the other vacant cells.

"What's the drill now?"

"Have a seat, try to relax. We'll take you up to the courtroom in a few minutes, when the clerk calls down."

"Okay then."

Dawkins went away and came back a few minutes later.

"Time to go," he said, and opened the cell door. He brought me out into the corridor and down to the end to another steel door that had an "E" above it. He unlocked the door and opened it, revealing an elevator with a jail cell in the back half of the car.

"What's this?"

"I call it the 'jailevator.'"

"I like it."

He led me in and closed the outer door, opened the jail door, I stepped into the cell and he closed that door. He pushed "5" and the elevator began to move.

"So this is all about golf, huh?"

"Tell you the truth, Marshal, I think it's more about politics."

He laughed. "You got that right. Seems like a lot of trouble to get into, for playing golf."

"You said you don't golf, but you got friends that do, right?"

"Oh sure."

"Any of them ever tell you they go out and play golf, the wife doesn't know about it, and she finds out?"

"Sure have."

"Would you rather have that trouble or this trouble?"

"Tough call."

The elevator stopped on five and Dawkins touched a red button and waited.

"Door has to be opened from the outside," he explained.

"Smart."

Dawkins unlocked my cell door, directed me out and shut the door. The outer door clicked, and opened to show the inside of the courtroom. Dawkins and the Marshal who opened the door led me from the back of the courtroom past the judge's bench to the first table where Al had risen from his seat, and removed my cuffs.

Behind Al was another table where a young woman in a plain blue suit looked at me gravely. She had close-cropped black hair and granny glasses. Behind her an oak railing separated the courtroom from a row of benches that were now crammed with the prodigious posteriors of the motley

Fourth Estate.

That railing, "the bar," as it is called, signified the separation of the lawyers from the non-lawyers. Hence the expression "pass the bar," "bar exam," "member of the bar" and all that mumbo jumbo. I'd always wondered if it was there to protect the lawyers from the public or vice versa.

Al gave my hand a shake and I sat down next to him. My coat was draped over the chair next to him.

"How're you holding up?"

"Okay, I guess. The strip search was a bit of a shocker, but the marshals are gentlemen."

Al began to respond when a door opened out of the woodwork of the back corner of the courtroom, a Marshal called out, "All rise!" and the courtroom snapped to attention. A stocky, somber man with curly black hair walked briskly through the door, bounded onto the raised bench in his black robe, and rapped a wooden gavel as he sat.

"Please be seated."

A clerk sitting behind a large desk below him spoke.

"United States of America versus Paul G. Forté, case number one-nine-nine-four-dash-one-one-two-six, before the Honorable Charles Boose Wheeler, for arraignment, on the charges of mail fraud, conspiracy and tax evasion," the man read.

Judge Wheeler spoke. "Counsel introduce themselves for the record."

"Good morning, your honor, Albert Croston for the defendant, Mr. Forté."

"Frances Holloway, Assistant U.S. Attorney, for the United States."

"Thank you, counsel. Mr. Forté, would you stand please?"

When I heard those words, I felt waves of heat wash up

from my chest, spreading over my neck and into my face. As I stood, my ears began to hiss again and my head became light. My legs quivered. Oh, shit, I thought, not again. Don't faint, you idiot. I struggled against my knees buckling, and I barely made it to my feet, leaning my hands on the table until the rush passed.

The clerk rose and spoke. "Mr. Forté, you are charged with violations of title eighteen section thirteen forty-one and thirteen forty-six of the United States Code, theft of honest services, mail fraud, Title Eighteen, section 1343 and 1346, wire fraud, and Title Eighteen, section 371, conspiracy to commit those offenses. How do you plead?"

"Not guilty," I said. Not, not guilty *goddammit*, how I'd dreamt it. Not in the dramatic way that innocent people do when they're falsely accused of criminal conduct. That's the way I'd planned it, but at the moment, I just didn't want to throw up in open court.

"Raise your right hand, sir."

I did.

"Do you solemnly swear that the answers you are about to give are the truth, the whole truth and nothing but the truth?"

"I do."

"Mr. Forté, my name is Charles Wheeler. I am a federal judge of the United States District Court. I am going to ask you some questions that pertain to the information you gave to the probation department. These questions are relevant only to the issue of bail, but nevertheless, you have a right to remain silent, and you do not have to answer. Has your counsel advised you of your rights under this proceeding?"

"Yes, he has, your Honor."

"Do you wish to exercise your Fifth Amendment right?"

"No, your Honor, I'll answer the questions."

"Okay then. Have you had an opportunity to review the report prepared by the pre-trial services office of the Probation Department?"

Al rose to his feet. "Your honor, I have just been handed a copy moments ago. If we could have a moment to review it?"

"You may."

Al and I looked it over. Gina did good work. I stopped reading and looked up at the judge.

"Have you had a chance to read it, Mr. Forté?"

"Yes, I have."

"Is the information in that report consistent with the answers that you gave to the probation department when you were interviewed?"

"Yes, it is."

"And is that information true, to the best of your knowledge?"

"Yes, it is."

"Thank you, Mr. Forté, you may sit down." He looked to the prosecutor. "Ms. Holloway, what are the maximum sentences for each offense?"

Frances Holloway stood. She was a rail thin woman, about my age. She had a gaunt face and bony fingers. "The mail fraud counts are up to seven years. Conspiracy is five years. Perjury is three."

"Do you have any objection to his release on unsecured bond?"

"Your honor, Mr. Forté faces a lengthy prison sentence, he has the means and motivation to flee the jurisdiction. We'd ask for detention without bail."

I gasped, along with the rest of the courtroom. Who the fuck was this lady?

The judge was equally incredulous. "You're asking for

detention without bail? On what basis do you consider Mr. Forté a flight risk?"

Holloway stammered. "Your honor, the government is entitled to a three-day continuance—"

Judge Wheeler cut her off. "I know what the government is entitled to, Ms. Holloway. And I know that it's Wednesday, and this is the government's little trick to keep someone they don't like in jail over the weekend. I've been at this a bit longer than you. I am asking you the basis for the government's position that there are no conditions that will secure the defendant's appearance. By my reading of the indictment, the defendant is accused of lying about his golf game. Do you suggest that he is that bad a golfer that he would represent a danger to the public?"

The rabble murmured.

Ms. Holloway suffered from an abject lack of presence. If she wasn't advocating my incarceration, I might have felt sorry for her. But at the moment I wouldn't have minded if she'd had an aneurysm.

She stood uncertainly, finally opening her mouth. "The government would request that the defendant's passport be surrendered."

Croston was ready. "Your Honor, as the Pretrial Services report plainly states, Mr. Forté does not have a passport."

Judge Wheeler looked at the lady. "Ms. Holloway? Any further objection to allowing Mr. Forté to roam freely?"

"No, your Honor."

"Good. Let's talk scheduling."

Holloway jumped up. "Your Honor, we request the next available trial date."

Al glanced at me and winked.

"Mr. Croston?"

Al rose. "Your Honor, the right to a speedy trial belongs to the defendant. I suggest we settle on the discovery schedule and a time for pre-trial motions and look at a trial date in twelve to fifteen months."

Holloway's gasp was audible. "Your Honor! There's no reason for this case to languish—"

Wheeler peered over the tops of his half-rims and held up his hand. "Ms. Holloway, I appreciate your concern for the administration of this courtroom, but frankly, it's none of your business." He looked over the bench at the clerk below him. "Mr. Ficker, let's have dates for pre-trial motions and pre-trial conference in, oh…September of next year."

The clerk looked at the screen in front of him. "September 7th and September 23rd."

"When do I return from France?"

"You return on Friday the 4th."

Wheeler addressed Al. "Mr. Croston, does your client have any reservations about facing a judge with jet lag?"

"None whatsoever, your Honor."

"September 7th for pre-trial motions, September 23rd for final pre-trial conference. Mr. Ficker, let's plan to find time for this trial to commence in late November, early December. Ms. Holloway, how many days does Justice estimate the trial will take?"

Poor Ms. Holloway. "I'm not sure, your Honor. I'm covering this for Mr. Kilroy, but I would anticipate that question will be addressed in the joint pre-trial memorandum."

Wheeler did not hide his annoyance. "Thank you, Ms. Holloway, so would I. I ask so that we might have as much consideration for other litigants looking to schedule a trial in December. And Ms. Holloway, please convey to Mr. Kilroy my displeasure with his having sent substitute counsel who is so unprepared. Mr. Croston? Do you have any idea?"

"Your Honor, the government's witness list may be extensive. I anticipate that we will be calling approximately forty-seven witnesses ourselves, maybe more. I expect that the government will have an extensive list of documents to admit, and I believe we will be able to stipulate to most of them. I estimate that the trial will go at least six weeks."

"Forty-seven witnesses, Mr. Croston?"

Al glanced at Holloway. "Yes, your Honor. At least. Most of those witnesses will be the government's grand jury witnesses, and we will call them if the government doesn't. Unless, of course, the government wants to stipulate to the testimony they are going to offer."

Wheeler looked at Holloway. "I would encourage the government to do just that."

Wheeler spoke down to the clerk below him and the clerk nodded. "All pre-trial motions to be filed by September 7th. Final pre-trial conference on September 23rd. Ms. Holloway, will Mr. Kilroy be trying this case?"

"He will, your honor."

"Mr. Forté should be so lucky. Mr. Forté, you are released on fifty thousand dollar unsecured bond. Court is adjourned."

We rose as the judge departed.

Ms. Holloway slapped her briefcase shut and looked at Al.

"Say hello to Mike," Al said with a tight grin.

"There's only a slight chance I might." She proceeded up the aisle, lowered her head and barged through the pressmen hounding her for comment.

"Now what?" I asked Al. He looked at the disheveled wags waiting for us.

"Do you want me to make a statement?"

"Definitely."

Al handed me my coat and went to the end of the bar that separates the gallery from the lawyers' tables. A dozen men and women shoved recording devices toward his mouth. All of them asked him different questions at once. He ignored their questions and raised his voice over them.

"This case is about an overzealous prosecutor trying to turn a game of golf into a federal crime. It will become clear soon enough that the only reason Mr. Forté is here at all is that he declined the prosecutor's offer to dismiss all of the charges against him in exchange for his complicity in the prosecutor's baseless and politically motivated campaign. Mr. Forté is a man of honor who has always played by the rules. He will not be bullied into aiding in the prosecutor's campaign for Attorney General. Thank you."

Al turned from the babbling crowd and I followed him to the rear door where the marshals were waiting.

"Gee Al, you read my mind."

"You think that might make him lose some sleep?"

"That would be justice. Good job."

Dawkins, Al and I crowded into the jailevator and rode it down to one. We did a bit of closing business where the marshals checked for arrest warrants, and finding none, they told me I was done.

"That's it then?" I asked Dawkins.

"You're free to go, Paul."

"Thank you, Marshal Dawkins. I appreciate your professionalism."

"And we yours, sir. Sorry for your troubles." Dawkins extended his hand, I grasped it, and he gave me a vigorous shake.

"Good luck to you," he said.

I expelled a lungful of emotion. That Dawkins. Good man. And Garcia, too.

Dawkins led Al and I to the door at the opposite end of the corridor from where I'd entered through the sally port. It opened into the lobby of the office of the Marshal's Service. It had carpets and muted tan walls and pictures and furniture with upholstery. It was federal institutional chic, but it was beautiful. Al led me out into the courthouse lobby, all marble and shiny. It looked so luxurious and free. I'd been in it dozens of times, but never appreciated it as much as that moment.

I followed Al along the edge of the lobby to another corridor that led to the Office of Probation Services. I was soon ushered into Gina Gianferrante's office, and this time she got up from her desk to meet me, shook my hand, and gave Al a polite hug. She and Al exchanged a terse banter about my probationary obligations, which I pretended to listen to, Al handed her a check, the amount of which I could have cared less about, and she looked at me and asked, "Is there anything you want to ask me before you leave?"

"Yes," I said. "Is it permissible for the accused to have a drink?"

Chapter 10
A Working Lunch and an Ink-stained Ally

I walked with Al back to his office building. The wind had picked up and I now had the trench coat buttoned to the neck.

"Are you in the mood for some preparation work right now, or would you prefer to give it a day or so?"

"Let's go with Plan B, Al. I'm wiped out. I'll call you in a couple of days."

"I understand."

I walked with Al as far as Post Office Square and then moved on, not knowing quite where I would go next. I only knew I wasn't eager to go back to the T and have people staring at me.

I was all keyed up and hadn't eaten since the day before. I took a long walk up town to Rex's office, figuring I could buy him lunch and filch some of his good scotch in the process. I took the private stairs up the back, and miraculously, the secret knock worked. Rache opened the door and gave me a big sad pity-smile.

"I see you've heard the news," I said, patting her shoulder.

"I'm sorry to hear about your troubles," she said, like she'd speak to a pet.

"Yeah, well…it'll all come out all right. Your dad in?"

"He's on the phone, I'll tell him you're here." She went down the hall and returned shortly. "He told me he'll be a few minutes, but he wants you to wait."

"You mean out here? With you?"

Rache giggled. "You're so funny. So dad tells me you've got a honey."

"I do. I was holding a candle for you, but Rex is overprotective."

She blushed. "Awww…truth is, she's a lucky woman," looking quickly away.

"Thanks, Rache, I appreciate it. I know why Rex is proud of you."

We sat in an awkward silence for a moment.

"So, if you don't mind telling me, what is this all about," she asked. "You played a bunch of golf with lobbyists and that's a federal crime?"

"Don't you think playing golf with lobbyists is a jailable offense?"

"You? No, I don't, but that's beside the point, I guess."

"I guess it is, yes."

"But would it be any different if you were playing a weekly poker game with them, or palling around in a way that didn't involve gifts?" Rache is a smart lady.

"You've got a point, Rache. I'm going to suggest to my lawyer that your approach be explored."

Rache's intercom buzzed, and she picked up the phone and listened for a bit. "You can go on down now. We're getting deli if you want a sandwich."

"Corned beef on a Kaiser roll, muenster cheese, hot mustard and pickle."

"You got it."

"Thanks, honey."

"You're welcome, darling."

By the time I got to Rex's office door, he had poured two fingers into the crystal glasses. He handed me one, we clinked and sipped.

"Congratulations on your recent change in status. First retired, then indicted. You follow in the footsteps of many formerly esteemed Massachusetts pols."

"Not the legacy I sought, Rex." I slugged the scotch down and tapped the empty glass on his desk. "More, please." Rex obliged with two more fingers. "Atta boy. So how's the weather in Flagstaff?"

Rex raised his eyebrows. "We're putting together a hell of a dossier."

"Do tell."

"Epsilon has quite a business operation. They've got a sales force in the ten largest public transportation marketplaces, they're doing business with the four largest surplus lines insurers in the world, and they've got a half dozen subcontractors who actually do pretty good work in testing and remediation."

"You mean the MBTA isn't their only victim?"

"Not by a long shot," he said as he swirled his glass. "They've placed close to a billion in coverage during the past two years."

"This is going to make you a rich man, Rex."

"If I pursue it."

"What the hell do you mean, if you pursue it? That was our deal."

Rex shook his head. "Our deal was it's my case to do with as I wish. We made it before you got arrested."

"What has my arrest got to do with it?"

Rex looked at me inscrutably. "For a smart guy, you say some stupid things."

I met his stare until I cracked and smiled. "Okay, I know what it has to do with it, but I won't allow it."

Rex smiled back and shook his head. "You have no choice, counselor."

"Don't act rashly, inspector. I'm not due to go to trial until next year. You've got plenty of time to reconsider."

"Yes, I do. I've also got plenty of time to figure out how to achieve both objectives." He pantomimed a twirl of the mustache and changed the subject.

We shot the breeze, had some laughs and eventually devoured two mountainous corned beef sandwiches, a couple of bags of chips and a quart of Pepsi until Rex's wall clock read three.

"Please get out of here so I can earn an honest living," he said.

I obeyed, gave Rache a smooch and walked through Copley Square toward the South End. I turned the corner from Dartmouth onto Columbus and spotted a small crew of news rats milling about. There was one guy with a video camera, probably from local cable news. I ducked into Clery's Bar to elude them and think. How the hell did they figure out where I lived? Did I want to talk to them, and what should I say? If I didn't, should I refuse to say anything and let them film me barging past them? Could I get to my car around the corner and beat it before they saw me? Or should I just hop a cab and go see Shannon?

I took a seat at the empty bar and waited for a bartender to show. The local cable news program showed on the television screen, muted. A very attractive young lady with short blonde hair and perfect teeth stared at the camera as she spoke. Her lips moved, but every feature of her face and body remained still. She could have been a cyborg. I don't know what she was talking about, and I had absolutely no idea how she felt about it.

A freakishly tall man with long hair and a beard came out of the door in the back of the bar.

"Sorry to keep you waiting, man. We don't have much business before four, trying to get the crock bites breaded."

"No problem. I'll take a twenty ounce Long Trail."

"Comin' right up."

"You mind if I ask how tall you are?"

"Six ten."

"Ever play ball?"

"Nah, can't jump."

"You look like someone I've seen before."

"Mick Fleetwood," he said, telling not asking. "I get it all the time."

"That's it, yes. Mick Fleetwood. Before the Christine McVie and Lindsey Buckingham days."

"Yeah, when they were still a blues band. With Peter Green."

"Yeah, and Jeremy Spencer. I saw them at the Boston Tea Party on Lansdowne."

"I remember that place."

A guy walked in from the street and sat two stools down. He had a plaid shirt and a windbreaker, khakis and Hushpuppies, and he carried one of those notepads with the spiral at the top. The kind that reporters use. He saw the tall guy pouring and asked for the same. The tall guy delivered our beers.

"You guys all set for a bit, I'll go finish up the crock bites. Need anything, holler."

"What's your name?"

The guy chuckled. "Sampson."

"Figures."

The other fella looked at me talking to Sampson. When Sampson left, he still looked at me.

"Do I know you?" I asked.

"Nope, but I think I know you."

"You're a reporter."

"Yeah, I was stakin' out your joint around the corner."

"Yeah, I know. That's why I'm in here. I have no comment on anything. Interview over."

The guy shoved his pad aside and put his hands up. "Nah, relax. I'm off duty," he said, raising his huge glass to salute. So I did the same.

"There's no such thing as an off-duty reporter."

He laughed. "Yeah, I guess not."

"Who you work for?"

"Boston Phoenix."

"Oh, Christ, then I definitely don't have anything to say."

"Why's that?"

"I've been reading the Phoenix for twenty years, and it's never had one good word to say about a Republican."

He laughed, "Yeah, I suppose that's true. But we've also never had anything good to say about Bernie Kilroy, either."

"Who's Bernie Kilroy?"

The guy smiled. "Some fucking putz, that's who."

"What's your name?"

"Cory Fitzpatrick."

I shook Cory Fitzpatrick's hand. He had kind of a dead fish, but his hand was rough as a carpenter's.

"You mind telling me what your angle is, Cory?"

"Usually I'm the one asks the questions."

"This is hardly usual."

Cory took a long pull off the tall glass and wiped his upper lip.

"The Phoenix isn't interested in your golfing habits. We're interested in Bernard Kilroy's political ambitions."

"That's very interesting, Cory. Why?"

Cory hemmed. "It's like this. You ever hear the old saying about fighting with someone who buys ink by the barrel?"

"I've known that one for a while, but usually fail to heed it."

Cory laughed. "Yeah, you're not alone."

"So am I to understand that Kilroy is in some sort of pissing contest with the Boston Phoenix?"

"Not with the Phoenix per se."

"No?"

"No." He drank again. "We're doing a story on politics in the U. S. Attorney's office. Kilroy's ambitions are not popular. He's obviously using Stackhouse and you for political gain, and some question the use of the federal Justice Department for that purpose."

I watched Cory Fitzpatrick drink again, and waited till he looked at me. "I don't believe you."

"I didn't tell you why *we're* doing the story."

"You're doing the story because Kilroy has had some issues with a certain federal judge who happens to be married to the publisher of your newspaper."

Cory stared at his glass. "Perhaps. I don't know. That knowledge is above my pay grade."

"Bullshit. Do you play golf, Cory?"

He nodded. "I did the Hyannisport CYO caddie camp in the late 70's, the last year they ran it. I was Greater Boston Schoolboy Champ in 1981 out of St. John's Prep. I went to U. Conn on a golf scholarship. Then I broke my collarbone and lost my scholarship." He moved the corner of his plaid shirt aside to show me the bump.

"What're you now?"

"I'm a 3.3 at Presidents in Quincy. I begged my editor for this story."

I liked Cory, would have played golf with him that moment if asked.

"What do you want from me?"

He shrugged like it was a stupid question. "Information."

"What information?"

"Whatever you want to share."

"How about we'll give you what we can, if it'll help us."

He paused a second and chuckled. "I don't suppose you'd give me anything that hurt you."

"There's that St. John's Prep training."

I clinked his glass, drained the last of my Long Trail, and took the card he held out to me.

"See you later, Cory."

"Hey let's tee it up sometime, huh?"

I managed to get back to my car undetected by the jackals and decided to head for the Cape. I wouldn't have the place for much longer, and solitude is better by the seashore. As I walked into my house a little after six, the phone rang. It was Al.

"What's up?"

"Stackhouse accepted a plea. Guilty on seventeen counts of mail fraud in exchange for his cooperation."

"Cooperation, huh? What's that code for?" I feared I knew the answer.

"We're going to find out. I've got to get a hold of a copy of that amendment of yours," Al said. "I don't want to wait for discovery."

"Don't call it *my* amendment. I don't know a fucking thing

about any amendment."

"Okay then, the *alleged Forté amendment*."

"That's better, but don't worry about it. I think I've got it covered."

I agreed to meet Al later on in the week and said goodbye.

I called Shakey after pouring myself four fingers of Johnny Walker.

"Heard about Ray," I said.

"Goddammit, I hate being scooped. I was about to call you."

"If I were paying you what I'm paying Al Croston, you would have called me first, too."

"Good bet there. I did call Chairman Mannion first."

"And well you should have. So what's your take?"

"My take is your golf partner is singing like Maria Callas."

My mouth went dry. "He's cut a deal to help them get me."

"Or others. I'm sure he's got more to tell them about Mannion than you. Still."

The racket in my chest started up. "Fuck."

"I know. It's not good."

I sat in silence. What about Pierce? Why not Pierce? Why me?

"Anything I can do for your situation?" he asked, but I didn't hear the words. "Paul?"

I snapped out of it. "As a matter of fact there is. Did you read my indictment?"

"You insult me. Of course I did."

"Save me $1,000 in legal fees and get a hold of a copy of the original amendment they say I proposed. Your contacts in the clerk's office still good enough to do that?"

"That's two insults. Give me till the end of the day."

"You're a mensch. Happy Hanukkah, Francis."

"Merry Christmas, Rep."

Some timing for a holiday.

A little pizza, a little wine, some soft music and six months of exhaustion, I would have thought I'd sleep okay without a pill. And I would have if the goddamn phone hadn't rung ten minutes after I dropped off.

"Hello."

"Forté." The same voice as before.

"Lurch," I said.

"Can you survive time in prison?"

I was just tired enough. I had no more adrenaline. My stomach was through puking. I was tired of being tired. Tired of being worried. Tired of this *fuck* believing he could get into my head.

"Can you kiss my ass?"

Chapter 11
Shop Talk, Evading Temptation

After a restless weekend of ducking the phone calls from a few dozen intrepid gents who call themselves journalists, I returned to my office Monday. The place was like a morgue all morning, all the lawyers and staff not knowing what the hell to say. So I told Cindy to order a bunch of sandwiches and got everyone into the conference room for lunch. Half of them looked like they were at a wake, the other half like maybe I was contagious. I put on the brave face and cracked a few jokes, but I seemed to be the only one in the mood. So I gave them all a pep talk, told them to do their jobs and I wasn't going anywhere. I don't think I convinced them. Truth was, I don't know if I had convinced myself.

After lunch I made a million telephone calls, employed the stamp a couple hundred times, and the moment the clock said five-thirty, I hustled to the bar at Biba to meet my old school chums, Dan and Scott, for a few cocktails on our way to the Speaker's Ritz-Carlton "holiday party." Okay, it was a mammoth fundraiser, no "Christmas" decorations allowed. I could always count on my pals to write a check for a fundraiser, provided it included a half-dozen martinis at a decent bar and a night on the town away from their wives. And maybe I'd be able to get a word in private with the Speaker about my infamous amendment.

When I arrived, the bar was crowded and noisy, but I quickly saw the fellas, both with bright red Christmas ties, holding half-empty glasses and chatting away with a very attractive lady. No surprises there.

"Monsieur Forté," yelled Dan when he spied me, hand waving over the crowd in a flourish. "Come and meet our new friend, Stacey!"

Scott chimed in, "Si, Señor Fortissimo, help us explain to this woman what 'arbitrage' means." From their exuberant demeanor, I deduced that they had arrived well ahead of our appointed time.

Stacey was a knockout in a spaghetti strapped dress, jade green that matched her eyes. She had strawberry blonde hair, thick to the shoulders. She had a tiny nose and freckled cheekbones. Killer smile, perfect teeth, but a tiny gap, like Lauren Hutton. She looked vaguely familiar.

"Hello, Stacey," I said, "Are you so desperate that you must endure the conduct of these boors?"

"I've nevah been desperate for anything," she said. She had just the hint of a Boston accent.

We were clowning our way through a drink when Stacey said to me, "Dan and Scott have done their best to explain what arbitrage means, but now you tell me what you do."

"I am a lawyer that never lies," I said. "I play by the rules and always tell the truth."

"Funny," she said, scanning me up and down, "you don't look broke."

Dan and Scott hooted. They were big fans of this Stacey, and I kind of liked her myself.

"I'm the General Counsel of the MBTA."

"The T?? You're the General Counsel of the fuckin' T?" The true sign of a Boston native.

"You are familiar with it?"

"You could say so. My father ran the Southie bus maintenance facility till he retired, and my brother's the shop steward at the Readville yahd."

"No fooling. Where do you work, Stacey?"

She took a belt from her cosmopolitan. "Compliance officer at Morgan Stanley."

"Does that make you the black sheep of the family?"

"What do you mean?"

"Are you the first member of the family not to work for the MBTA?"

She laughed. "You know the culture, don't you?"

"Indeed I do. So do you generally get compliance at Morgan Stanley?"

She laughed again. Man, she had a nice laugh. "People are used to doing what I tell them."

"We could use a gal like you at the T," I said.

Dan stood with a silly grin, enjoying his booze. "Paul's just been indicted!" he said, like I'd won a lottery prize.

Stacey didn't miss a beat. "Really, how exciting. What's the rap?" She had a gorgeous smile.

"Someone's jealous of my two handicap."

"He has expensive tastes in wine," Scott said.

"Hangs out with sandbaggers," Dan said.

Stacey liked our answers, but she kept looking at me, expecting an answer.

"I played golf with a few lobbyists."

"A few?"

"More than a few."

She looked at her watch. "Hope it was worth it. I gotta go." She drained her cosmo and began to gather her coat off the barstool.

"Awww Stacey, you're not leaving now, are you?" Dan asked.

"I'm goin' across the street to Kevin Flannery's fundraiser," she said.

"What a coincidence, so are we."

"Then settle up and let's go," she said.

"Danny boy, take care of the bartender, will you?"

We walked briskly the half-block to the Ritz-Carlton, hustling along, faces into a crisp breeze, maintaining a patter of glib bons mots. I glanced sidelong at Stacey, trying to figure out where I'd seen her before. Had she been one of the regular State House crowd, a committee staffer who I'd seen around the building? Nah, I'd definitely have remembered her. I just couldn't place her.

We reached the Ritz in minutes and found our way to the check-in table at the Mezzanine. Stacey went off to the powder room, so Danny and Scott and I checked in and found our way to the bar where a wavy-haired Greek made us three Sapphire martinis. I took the guys to a spot where I could survey the room, see who was there.

Everybody, that's who.

The ballroom was crammed with pols, lobbyists, staffers, coatholders, bagmen, drivers, Secretaries, Assistant Secretaries, Deputy Assistant Secretaries, commissioners, assistant commissioners, first deputy assistant commissioners. A bunch of people who'd perfected the art of the job title, and usually, the longer the title the more useless the title holder.

There were half a dozen guys in the room who'd done time, a few more who'd narrowly escaped it and another handful whose charmed lives had the risk of jail in their future. Bid rigging, conflict of interest, contract padding or maybe just some run-of-the-mill influence peddling. It was how business was done, simple. They lived in a world where ethics, morals and conscience had their own parochial definitions. They were the fourth generation in a culture where the spoils of government were harvested like potatoes. Some of them were insulated from risk by the simple accident of the block or housing project they were raised in. They had a *patron*, someone who could make a few calls, let the right person know they were dealing with a *good guy*.

And most of them were, in the context of their culture. They hustled to make money for their families, to get their kids out of the rancid city schools and into B.C. High or St. John's Prep or Xaverian Brothers, and then into Boston College or Holy Cross or maybe even Harvard if they were good enough students or athletes. They went to church on Sundays and didn't cheat on their wives, who often were their high school sweethearts. They raised their kids to respect authority, to play by the rules—at least in sports—to do their homework and obey the Golden Rule. But when their kids reached working age, they would be first in line for the T or Turnpike summer "jobs," during which they would be paid a good salary to do work that was unnecessary or even counterproductive. The goal was to ensure their children did better than them. Who could fault a parent for that?

And woe to the man who threatened to take a morsel of bread from their table.

I moved Dan and Scott around the room, said some hellos to old colleagues and some of the lobbyists who weren't golfers. They were all cordial enough, but they had that look in their eye. Like I was a dead man walking. Some of them weren't squeaky clean, but they'd also never been caught. Maybe they just looked at me differently. See how I wore my ill repute. Maybe it was a sort of respect. Like I used to be just some nobody from the Cape, an amateur who didn't know the game. Now I'd made my bones. Facing time in the joint, I was still out on the town, looking good in my dark suit. Bullet proof, afraid of nothing.

Yeah, right. What an idiot.

You could tell the pols from the lobbyists just by the quality and fit of the suits. The reps helped themselves to the free booze and food, in that order. The lobbyists nursed a drink, had nothing to eat and spoke in quiet tones, furtive glances over the shoulder to keep tabs on who was with whom. They knew the first rule of lobbying. Be the last guy to talk to the rep before the vote.

There were two kinds of lobbyists: in-house and freelance. The in-house were graduates of top law schools, technicians who knew how to draft, did their homework, wore sharp new suits and carried filofaxes and those new PDA things and sent reports to corporate. The freelancers were graduates of Suffolk or New England, went to night school while on the payroll at the State House. They knew every nook and cranny of the building and were childhood friends with a Speaker or Ways and Means chairman. They took amendments drafted by their client and got them tacked onto a bill in the dark of night. They made more money than they'd ever dreamed of back in the projects, and if you ever tried to fuck with them, you'd be dead. But they were the "good guys," and they were a hell of a lot of fun, too.

It was a rotten business, and I was relieved to be out of it.

"Jesus," Dan said, "I'd better keep my hands in my pockets." He was right. The place was a rogues' gallery.

"See that guy over there?" I nodded toward an Italian guy, black hair slicked back. "That's Bobby Bodigliano—'Bo Bo,' they call him. He's a firefighter from Chicopee, serves in the House too. He collects two checks, even though he hasn't been out on a fire drill in fifteen years. He goes home to the firehouse every night, sleeps there. And when he leaves here, his arms are full."

"Full of what?" Dan asked.

"Whatever they might need at the fire house. Copier toner, pens, whiteout, napkins. I don't think the City of Chicopee Fire Department has spent a dime on toilet paper since Bo Bo got here."

"If that's the small time stuff, what's the worst you've heard of?"

"Dan, the worst I've heard of would curl your hair. But it's all rumor, and it's so dirty I don't even want to think it's true."

"How do they get away with that crap?"

"They regulate themselves, Scott. The Attorney General didn't get elected without their support. They're colleagues. If something pokes above the surface, someone says 'cool it,' and things quiet down for a while. Once every decade or so, someone goes too far, and he'll get thrown under the bus just so the others won't take casual fire. But even then, the sentence is pretty light and the guy's back on the street with a new job."

We went over to the smoked salmon and I introduced Dan and Scott to Rep. Sal Baglio. "Bags" has lifetime tenure on the seat from East Boston by virtue of his ability to stymie any attempt to improve the facilities at Logan International Airport. As a result, Logan is one of the worst airports in the country to travel through. Way to go, Bags. But the meatballs over in Eastie love him for it, and he eats on the house at every restaurant in Eastie. They're all subway folks over there. Bags' accent-infused jabbering amused Dan, a Yale man.

After a few words with Bags, I pulled Dan and Scott away, and we went through another half-dozen or so hihowayas with my old colleagues. They all gave me a pat on the back and condolences, as though my dog had died. And although I'd been out of the House now for three years, they all said the same thing. "How's the golf game?" Thanks for asking, fellas.

Eventually, we made it around to the clutch of people surrounding the Speaker, and the procession of prostrators and sycophants moved along until I got to Flannery. He gave me his Perfect Smile and a vigorous clap on the shoulder to go with the "Paulie howaya pal? How's life treatin' ya?"

The guy knew how to make you look good in front of your clients and friends. He was a smooth dude, and he looked it, with his tortoise shell glasses and salt-and-pepper hair. Plus the Christmas tie. I introduced him to Dan and Scott, and he did the same act with them.

Then he said to me, "Paulie, how's your golf game?"

"Not too bad."

Flannery said to the boys, "This guy can play golf, you know."

"Mr. Speaker," I said, "I think everyone in America is aware of my golf game right now."

Flannery laughed. "Ah, baloney, Paul! Nobody reads that shit. The only thing I hold against you is that you took my money in a Nassau once."

He was right, I had. Ancient history, but a city guy's got a long memory when it comes to losing money in a game of skill.

In fact, that golf game was the first time I received an allegedly illegal gift from a lobbyist. At the end of that round, I tried to give our host a hundred bucks cash for my greens fee, but he waved it off, wouldn't take it. I asked Flannery about it the next day.

"This is the way it is," he said. "The best you can do is offer. You have to strike a balance between the letter of the law and social convention."

It seemed like fair advice at the time. It was either that or avoid golf entirely, and public service was enough of a sacrifice. That would be going overboard. I shared this with Dad once, and he concurred. "Reciprocation is the best form of recompense," he'd said. "Just be sure it's on a golf course, not in the State House." One might be inclined to criticize his advice or my lack of circumspection, but hindsight is twenty-twenty.

"I see you've kept your Irish memory," I said.

"Paulie, you're a talented kid and a good guy. You'll be fine," he said, putting his hand on my shoulder and, pulling me in closer, he whispered, "Your indictment is bullshit. Fight like a bastard. Keep your wits and trust your friends."

"That's good advice, but how do I tell my friends from my enemies?"

"There's only one enemy. Kilroy."

"Since you mentioned it, the problem seems to be an amendment that the Journal says had my name on it, only, you know, that would be highly unusual for a man in my position."

Flannery's hand remained on my shoulder as he stood pensively. "Doesn't ring a bell, Paulie." He shrugged. "Maybe we were just throwing the Republican a bone, you know what I mean?"

Hah. "Sure, I know what you mean. Let's hope I don't choke on it."

By then, the next clutch of prostrators had queued up for their hihowaya, so we said our goodbyes and moved along.

"He seems like a regular guy," Dan said.

"He always treated me well, despite my meager status."

"Aren't the feds looking at him for something now?" asked Scott.

"One of his lobbyist pals loaned him his Cape house for a week. He didn't declare the value of the free rental as income on his taxes."

Dan blanched. "You mean the feds are prosecuting people for the value of a vacation week?"

"Apparently if you're the Speaker of the House, yeah."

"Jesus Christ," they said in unison.

"Remember, the government never got Al Capone for racketeering. They got him for tax evasion." I took the boys around the room for another hour or so, and they had their fun goofing on the Bagses of the world.

Ten o'clock arrived. Dan and Scott were ready to head back to the 'burbs to nudge the wives and see what happened, so they said goodbyes. So I shoved them toward the stairs and headed across the room to check out what this gal Stacey was all about. Something I just couldn't finger about her.

Before I could locate her, though, I saw Stuart Pierce heading toward the bar. He moved like a marionette, his eyes darting casually from side to side, a nod here and there. His eyes settled on me and they smiled along with his thin lips. I didn't know if it was prudent to speak with him, but at the moment, I didn't care, I was as loose as a goose.

Pierce was a guy I'd never figured out. He didn't say much. He represented a small group of state-chartered savings banks (I think they were all family owned). Didn't hang around with the other lobbyists. When one of his bills was on the House calendar, he'd just stand around outside the Chamber, lurking. He wore linen suits that draped off his thin frame as he slouched against the same Doric column, day after day. He had an aquiline nose and a sharp, piercing eyes that seemed to regard everything and nothing. In the entire ensemble, he resembled a vulture.

Still, despite his taciturn demeanor, he had a dry wit and exquisite timing, so we got along pretty well. More important, he was at the end of a long line of Brahmins, which came with membership at both The Country Club and Kittansett. Needless to say, my golfing history with Stuart Pierce was extensive, and about to become notorious; and yet, despite my repeated efforts, he'd never found the opportunity to accept my reciprocal offers at Hyannisport. He suggested once that it might be his aversion to the idea of stepping foot on Kennedy soil.

I joined him.

"Hello, Paul," he said, bony hand sliding from the navy linen suit coat pocket.

"Whaddaya say, Stuart? What's new?" As if we didn't know.

His eyes darted about as he sidled up to the bar and ordered himself a vodka and soda. "Bar vodka," he specified.

"Bar vodka? Come on Stuart, you're still clipping coupons on your great grandfather's Union Pacific bonds, for God's sake. Live a little."

He chuckled gruffly. "When you're born thrifty, you can't shake it no matter how much money you've got."

The bartender delivered his drink, which he accepted without gratuity.

"I'm glad to see you here. Have you got a moment?" he asked me.

I tossed a buck on the bar and followed him to the corner of the room.

Pierce shifted. "I'm very sorry about the trouble I've caused you, sorry about this whole mess. I hope you'll understand that it's simply business and that I have no personal agenda that concerns you."

"Oh. Well, I've only read the indictment, so I don't know what you actually told the grand jury. To tell you the truth, I don't know when I've ever done anything to help you, except to sink a putt. You've never asked me for anything, that's for sure. I don't know what this so-called amendment business is all about."

"I didn't either. Then Kilroy showed me the House Journal."

"What did it say?"

"There was an amendment that exempted state-chartered savings banks from the capital gains tax on earnings from foreign states. The House Journal for that day attributes the amendment to you."

I felt my shirt collar tightening.

"Perhaps it is a matter so insignificant that it slipped your memory, Paul. When you were on your way into the Chamber during the debate, I asked you to deliver an amendment to the Speaker. You took the amendment from me, and I presume you handed it over to the Speaker and told him it was from me. He probably handed it to the Clerk and the Clerk scribbled your name on it."

My heart stopped, then resumed double-time. I vaguely recalled his description. "You mean I was a delivery boy? Like one of the House pages?"

"Something like that, yes."

"Did you use the word 'amendment' or the word 'document?'"

He shifted. "I don't recall what word I used. I just asked you to deliver it to the rostrum."

"So what if it was an amendment. Why would the Clerk put my name on it?"

He shrugged. "I don't know. I left the name blank; they usually put the committee chairman's name on it. Maybe you were the only committee member in the chamber at the moment."

"So what's Kilroy want from you?"

"He's going to ask me about the golf at The Country Club and Kittansett, and your little errand on my behalf."

"My 'little errand?' Stuart, you could have given that amendment to one of the goddamn pages to deliver. You didn't need me."

"We both realize that now, Paul. But at the time I don't think either of us considered the implication of your involvement."

"Jesus H. Christ, Stuart, that implication might send me to fucking prison."

"There's another thing." Stuart took a tiny sip of his vodka and tonic.

"What is it?"

"I told him about your reciprocal invitation to Hyannisport and the fact that I'd never taken advantage of it but that as far as I'm concerned, it still stands."

"What's the problem with that? It's the goddamn truth."

"The problem with it is, he suggested that it would go better for me if I didn't recall that part."

"You mean he's encouraging you to perjure yourself?" I felt my pulse in my fingertips.

"He doesn't see things in such black and white terms," he said, lips barely moving.

"Well that's what he's doing!" I glanced around and a few heads turned. "Listen Stuart, I don't know what he's got over your head, and I know he's willing to do anything to squeeze you, but I expect you to do the right thing." I realized when I said it that I was pointing my finger at his heart. He realized it too.

"Hey, we're all under pressure here, Paul. In the heat of the moment, sometimes it's not so easy to know what the right thing is. I hope you appreciate my position too."

"I'll appreciate your position when I hear your testimony under cross-examination."

"I can't fault you for that. I'll tell the truth," he said, far too casually. He drained his drink and turned back to the bartender. "Another bar vodka, please."

I left Stuart waiting for his cheap vodka and walked to the other side of the room where Stacey stood with two other ladies, all sipping their cosmopolitans and laughing about something. So I wiped the scowl off my face, put on the Big Grin and slid into their little pow-wow, sidling up beside Stacey. "State House shop talk?"

They obviously weren't on their first cosmo. Stacey introduced me around—although she did ask my name again. Maybe I wasn't quite as notorious as I'd feared.

The brunette named Maggie looked at me curiously. "I remember when you were in the building." The Building. That's what career State House employees called it. Sort of like the way parolees call prison The Joint.

She continued to look at me. "You used to be a rep from the Cape."

"That's right."

"You just got indicted for playing golf."

The others inspected me.

"I did indeed."

"Sorry to hear that, Paul."

The perky little blonde named Amy chimed in, "Yeah, sorry to hear that, Paul. I remember you too—we voted you hottest freshman in your class." They laughed at my expense, but they sure knew how to steer clear of a lousy subject.

Maggie piled on. "You know how many women in that building wanted to jump your bones?"

"Yah," Amy said, "like, us." Honest to God, this was a well-timed ribbing.

"I was married at the time, so I guess I didn't notice."

"At the time?" Amy asked.

"Yeah, I guess politics didn't agree with my wife." I hadn't been alone for that long, and I really was out of practice. That and, well, I just wasn't ready to share my marriage failure with three women.

"It sure agreed with you," Amy said, practically purring. *Jeez,* I thought, *down* girl.

Maggie jumped in. "I remember, you spent a lot of time debating on the floor."

"I did—one of the highlights of the job."

"You were really good at it," she said. "You should be in television."

"How long you been divorced," Stacey asked.

"I've been on my own about a year."

"Looks like that agrees with you too," Maggie said.

"I haven't figured that out yet."

"Let me know if you need any help," said Amy.

I began to think I should take some drastic action here before these women cut the small talk and got nasty. Not that I didn't have fleeting visions of a foursome at the Hilton, but I hadn't had sex of any kind for well over a year (like a guy doesn't count?), and this sort of raw libidinousness was nerve-wracking.

"You have no idea how much I appreciate the offer, but I'm still licking my wounds..." to which they woo-hooed like a road crew at a short skirt. I felt violated. Well, not really.

"Poor choice of words," I muttered.

I think finally the girls were getting the point that their fresh meat was a wounded soul, so they softened up and gave me gentler treatment.

"Okay, let's not humor the condemned man. Tell me what's going on in the building."

The place was abuzz with Stackhouse's plea, my indictment, and certain unidentified other investigations going on. Maggie and Amy had been working inside the State House for at least eight years. They were legislative aides who took care of all the constituent work, logged and returned phone calls and letters, kept the schedule, babysat, and sometimes even drove their inebriated bosses home. Both of them worked for reps who were under investigation by the State Ethics Commission and might even have been called before my grand jury.

They gossiped about what they'd heard, while Stacey stood by, tight-lipped. When Stackhouse was indicted, everybody had assumed Mannion would be next, but it was me instead, and that started the building buzzing.

The big difference between Stackhouse and the other lobbyists was that Stackhouse kept meticulous records that he submitted to his employer for reimbursement, under the company's own direction, since its chief counsel had opined that Stackhouse's schmoozing was within the letter of the state gift statute. But when Kilroy decided to use a federal law against Ray, his employer turned over all of his records to the feds and the Boston Globe. In the prosecution business, that's called the "woo-hoo moment." The rest of the sane world calls it throwing a good man under the bus, and Providential had paid for their treachery dearly in the ensuing few years. The other lobbyists did not itemize these expenditures, and being independent consultants, they simply built the cost of "doing business" into their $10,000 monthly fees. So the only evidence of their so-called wrongdoing was eyewitness testimony, which regulators couldn't find. Then I opened my Big Mouth, and they decided to cast a net and see what kind of fish surfaced.

Word was that when they went after me instead of Mannion, he wanted to cut a deal but the feds wouldn't accept anything that didn't include jail time.

Besides him, there were literally dozens of other reps who'd become targets of investigation by the Ethics Commission because they attended one or more legislative conference where dinners were bought or golf was played. They were all accused of illegally accepting gifts solely because of their status as elected officials, which was not what the statute said, but the Ethics Commission didn't care about that. In fact, there were so many of them that the Commission staff was overwhelmed. To cut through the caseload, they offered settlements that required an admission of culpability and the payment of a fine. Compared to the cost of fighting the winning battle, it was an easy choice. People were caving all over the place. As much as it offended my sense of justice, I'd already been among the first.

Some of the settlements were grotesquely unfair. Amy had worked for the very unfortunate Emilio Giglio, who picked that year to retire. "Gigs" had played two rounds of golf in his life, both of them atrociously, but when he retired, a bunch of lobbyists gave him a little retirement gift—a complete set of top-of-the-line Ping Eye 2 golf clubs, with the bag and all. Knowing his game the way they did, it was as much a gag gift as one of true sentiment. When the Commission discovered the gift and cited him, he agreed to a settlement that included a $6,000 fine. Gigs was a good sport about it, though—he donated the clubs and bag to the Speaker's annual charity auction, where they were auctioned off to a raucous crowd as "the most expensive golf clubs in the history of the Massachusetts politics."

This was a singular focus of the State Ethics commission at the present time. Tagging ex-reps for their gag retirement gifts and free meals. But it was nothing compared to what Kilroy was doing—turning those state misdemeanors into federal felonies.

"It seems that the guardians of the public morality are focused on some fetid corruption here," I said.

"Hey," Maggie said, "most of the guys with real stuff to hide are pretty damn good at covering their tracks. What they really need around here is a couple dozen Staceys—"

Stacey interrupted. "No thanks! My job is hard enough at Morgan." The girls looked at her.

The sophistication of their understanding of the particulars impressed me—you hang around that building long enough, there's no telling what you can learn through osmosis. To say nothing of good old-fashioned eavesdropping.

Stacey asked me, "Paul, why do you think the U.S. Attorney chose to go after you?"

"Beats me. I was just a small fish up here."

"You don't become general counsel of the T if you're a small fish, Paul. I think you're understating your significance."

"I certainly hope not, but someone else knows better than me."

They stood around for a few moments, eyeing one another, and I thought it was time for me to scram, so I started to say goodbye, but Stacey and Maggie cut me off, insisting that they had to go but Amy wanted to stick around for one more and I couldn't leave her by herself, so I really had to stay. That sort of deft teamwork usually takes a rehearsal, but they had those grins that you can't hide. They both gave me a nice kiss full on the lips and a "see ya honey," like we'd all been old pals. I like that about brassy women. And then I stood there with Amy, who looked like a cat with a canary.

I felt trapped and ambivalent. I mean, I wasn't looking for

this, I never did. I'd planned to jump on over to Blues Alley and catch the last set of the Chuck Morris Band. But my reticence just seemed to melt away as I looked at this gorgeous lady with the blonde hair and fulsome cleavage. It had been a long, long time. Chuck Morris wasn't leaving town anyway.

"You're about as subtle as a rock band, you know," I said.

She broke out in a grin. "What's so good about subtle?"

"You want to go downstairs to the bar where it's quieter?"

"I live three blocks from here, it's much quieter there."

And so she took my hand and led me out of there like the fire alarm had just gone off. In fact, I thought I heard one ringing in my ears. Maybe it was the burn of Shannon's glare.

When you're in your mid-30's and you've been with only one woman for ten years, you think you might forget what wicked sex was like. You forget the first time clothing was stripped away and you felt fingers touching your skin in secret places. There is a high voltage electricity to it that few couples can maintain. Kate and I were not among them. It was frightening to me that what had started out so passionate and free had so quickly withered. It had to do with silence and sadness and worry and anxiety and vulnerability—all the things that make the job of living with a person forever so goddamn terrifying.

These were the things that bombarded my brain as Amy pulled me down the stairs of the Mezzanine toward the exit of the Ritz onto Arlington Street. And when the cold air hit my face, the reticence that had almost given way to lust returned, and by the middle of the next block, in the mall of Commonwealth Avenue, I hauled her up to a stop and sat her down on a bench.

"I can imagine how much fun it would be to let this play out," I said, "but it's not something I can do right now."

I feared she might be one of those hotheaded Irish girls and get all huffy, being turned down, but she turned out to be a good sport.

"Awww, rats," she said, "We all knew you were hands-off when you were in the building, but when Maggie and I heard you were divorced, we were sort of making a sport out of who got you first."

"That was pretty obvious."

She smiled, "Yah, I'm sorry, I get a little overenthusiastic sometimes."

"I give you an A for effort, and I am flattered by your attraction."

I asked her if she wanted to see the last set of Chuck Morris, and she said no, but she'd take a walk to her building instead. She asked me for a kiss, and she kept it honest, and I thanked her for understanding.

"I don't know who it is, but she's a lucky gal."

"Well, she doesn't even know yet, so I don't even know if it'll come to anything."

She gave me a vote of complete confidence and insisted that if it didn't work out, I would come right to her.

I lied and promised I would.

Chapter 12

Chinese Christmas and a Missing Document

The dreadful Holiday Season was near its zenith with the arrival of Christmas Eve.

It used to be bearable for me, when I could accompany Kate to her folks in rural Connecticut, just the four of us cozied up in a charming old farmhouse, Bing Crosby's *White Christmas* and all that. But then they died too. Cancer, within a year of each other. Not as bad as a freak car accident on an Irish country road. Or maybe worse. It depends on your perspective. It occurred to me when her mother went that perhaps only children shouldn't be allowed to marry their own kind. Now that we're no longer together, it's moot. We can't even be alone together.

I accepted a few party invitations, visited with some old classmates, had some laughs, a bit too much to drink and eat, the sort of thing that's expected this time of year. Another time, they might have been a howl. But holiday parties are no less depressing than the holidays themselves. Except Halloween. Properly planned, a Halloween party is the nuts, although facing criminal prosecution tends to dampen one's frivolity.

And this Shannon lady. Man! Talk about playing hard to get.

I drove by her place three nights in a row, never once were the lights on. I'd have thought she'd come home for Christmas.

On Christmas Eve, I found myself at the St. Botolph bar. I'd drunk too much, but there was a party of revelers whooping it up, also with no better place to be, so I kept pace with them until my first slurred word and then headed for home. I called Kate to wish her well, see if maybe she wanted some company, just to not be alone, but I got her answering machine. Good thing, because I was in no shape to drive to Providence.

I was damned if I would spend the rest of Christmas eve drunk and alone in my condo, so I walked over to Copley Square, thinking I might osmose the Christmas spirit from the lights adorning the trees in the plaza of Trinity Church. The night was unusually warm for December. A thin fog enshrouded the plaza like dishwater in the air. The lights glowed dully as people trickled into the church. The old clock on the Boston Public Library said 11:52, and I wondered if they were having a midnight service, so I teetered across the plaza to investigate. As I approached the front of the church, the sonorous bass of the pipe organ came to life, soon met by a melodious treble and the sweet, radiant harmony of young choir voices. I broke out in goose bumps.

I followed the people slowly through the vestibule into the cavernous nave and slipped into the back pew as the organ quieted. In a moment, it piped again as the procession of robes entered the apse and moved toward the altar. The choir voices began O Holy Night, a song my father had sung to me as a child, with his classical guitar.

Long lay the world in sin and error, longing
For His appearance, then the Spirit felt its worth.
A thrill of hope; the weary world rejoices,
For yonder breaks a new and glorious morn.

Soon I knelt (maybe it was the choir singing "fall on your knees"), head buried in my hands, humming through the tennis ball in my throat and sobbing like a fool, attracting furtive glances from even the street people who had advanced beyond the last row that I alone occupied.

What kind of mess have I made? I'm a goddamn criminal. I've ruined my life. All for a few meals and golf games I could easily afford. Dad would have been mortified, his only son tried in a federal courtroom. How badly he would regret ever teaching me how to play golf. I've failed them. I failed at my marriage. I have no one.

This pathetic maudlin sentiment would not do, I thought. I was the fortunate recipient of a superb education, but no one ever taught me how to grieve. I got up and left the church as the choir reached its crescendo.

He knows our need, our weakness never lasting,
Behold your King! By Him, let Earth accord!
Behold your King! By Him, let Earth accord!

I huddled in my coat and marched down St. James Street through the mist. I didn't stop until I was in Chinatown, which I noticed when the smells of egg rolls and dumplings reminded me I hadn't eaten since morning. A little dim sum was what the doctor ordered! I stumbled into The Dynasty, a ballroom-sized place with gaudy glass chandeliers and faded carpeting. It was nearly deserted except for a large round table at the front. It was occupied by a large Chinese family—a very old man and woman; a younger man and woman; and two young teenage girls. They all drank tea and ate from heaping platters on the table.

The younger man rose. "We close now." He had smooth skin, kind eyes and shiny black hair. The old woman jabbered at him, waving her hand and pointing outside. His mien softened.

"I would like some dim sum," I managed to say. The teenagers tittered and the old man regarded me blankly. The old lady continued to jabber at the younger man. He waved his arms and spoke to the girls, who promptly rose from their seats and cleared the empty plates from the table, taking them through a swinging door. The man waved his arm toward me and gestured to the vacated seats. I sat, and the old man passed me an empty plate and slid the platter over. He said something to the younger man, and they all tittered.

I smiled stupidly and looked around at them all, shrugged and asked, "What'd I do?"

The younger man said, "You drink too maah," nodded and smiled. He didn't look much older than me.

I nodded my head vigorously. "Yes, I did!" They all laughed and jabbered to each other.

The man poured tea into a tiny ornate cup and slid it to me. "Gree tea." I drank, but it was insipid, tasteless. "Good fo you." I toasted him and the others as the old woman pushed a platter of chicken feet toward the man and gestured while she jabbered at him. "She say, you heart weak."

"I'm sorry?"

"You heart weak," he said, pointing to his temple. I thought perhaps he meant I was crazy, which I could understand. He reached over and pointed to the few white hairs that salted my temples. "You get gray. Young man, gray hair. Heart weak." He pushed the chicken feet toward me. "Eat." I popped a chicken foot into my mouth, sucked off the skin and gristle and spit the bones and nails delicately onto my plate. They were tasty, if you didn't think about it. Like chocolate covered ants. I looked down at the plate. I could see how each of the bones fit together to form the foot.

I ate more, some dumplings and whatever else the young girls pushed my way at their mother's command.

"You say my heart is weak," I asked the man.

"Weak, yah."

"Is that the same word as broken?"

"No, different. You heart broken too?"

"Yes."

"Ohhhhh, very bad," he said. "You eat chicken feet every day. I give you herbs for cooking. And gree tea. Drink gree tea. You feel bettah."

"Okay. Will you be my doctor?"

"I am doctor. Chinese medicine. Chinese remedies three thousand yeah old."

"How long have you been a doctor?"

"Thirty-fi yeah."

"You must have started when you were ten."

He chuckled, his shoulders bobbing. "I sixty-fi."

I looked over at the old man. He must be a hundred and fifty then. "I want what you're taking."

The doctor went into the back and emerged with a bag full of herbs, roots, legumes and a bottle with tiny pills that looked like 4-12 shot. I looked at the ingredients on the bottle and noticed one: "penis sheep," it said. I didn't ask. The doctor took each item from the bag and explained to me how to make his turkey soup. I tried to pay him, but the whole family jabbered in unison and he shooed me out the door, bowing several times, and I heard the door lock behind me.

I walked back to my condo with renewed sobriety, and immediately set about making a pot of soup with all of the doctor's weird ingredients. I had to substitute two Cornish game hens, what I had available at one-thirty on Christmas morning.

Perhaps it was the soup, but I muddled through Christmas day without once entertaining the thought of jumping off the roof. It's so obvious why people do that sort of thing at this time of year.

On New Year's Eve, I received a plain white envelope in the mail. It contained a small handwritten, unsigned note that said "Happy New Year!" and a copy of the Boston Globe article from the day after Ray's plea. As if I hadn't already read it.

LOBBYIST PLEADS GUILTY
TO INFLUENCE PEDDLING

Stackhouse Ready to Cooperate
Trial of Legislators to Follow

BOSTON – Former Providential Banking lobbyist Raymond Stackhouse has agreed to plead guilty to thirteen counts of honest services fraud in connection with expensive meals, gifts and golf bought for dozens of Massachusetts legislators.

The plea ends months of speculation about Stackhouse's involvement in purchasing trips to Puerto Rican resorts for legislative conferences, first-class travel to the Super Bowl, the Mardi Gras and other lavish events, and rounds of golf at America's poshest clubs for some of Massachusetts' most influential legislators.

According to sources, Stackhouse's plea deal requires him to testify in future cases rumored to implicate more than a dozen current and former members of the Massachusetts Legislature, several of whom are expected to face charges.

Stackhouse's conviction is a huge blow to former Republican representative Paul Forté, whose indictment had courthouse wags scratching their heads. Then it was revealed Saturday that Forté had conducted legislative business on behalf of one of his many golf hosts, domestic bank lobbyist Stuart Pierce. Investigators are now combing the records of Forté's legislative activity, which appears initially to be sparse, anonymous sources said.

The conviction is also expected to increase political pressure on House Speaker Kevin Flannery to resign, as nervous legislators look to avoid collateral damage as the next election cycle approaches. Flannery, who more than two years ago was photographed alongside Stackhouse on a beach in Puerto Rico with a dozen other Democratic leaders, is under investigation for tax evasion and influence peddling, and is said to be negotiating a plea.

The postmark was the Boston postal annex, within five blocks of countless people who might be diabolical enough to rattle my cage. The U.S. Attorney's office was one of them. Or maybe I just had concerned neighbors.

Forté's legislative activity, which appears initially to be sparse.

Assholes.

I got a call from Shakey the first week after New Years.

"What's up, Francis?"

"Tried to get that amendment, but it isn't in the file."

"Nothing?"

"Oh no, not nothing. There's a document indicating that an FBI agent, William Hartfield, removed a copy of the amendment."

"Is that normal, for someone to do that?"

"It's not necessary. It's a public document, anyone's entitled to a copy of it. I've never seen something like this."

"Well, he doesn't take the only copy, does he? He's got to

leave a copy behind, wouldn't you think? How's the goddamn system supposed to work, anyway?"

"Every piece of legislation has its own file. The original documents are preserved and archived. Sooner or later they'll do it digitally, but for now, the papers are held together in brown accordion files. If someone wants examine a file, he signs a register and the file is reviewed right in the office. If he wants a copy of something, the copy is made and the original is kept in the file. Simple as that."

"Who else has had access to the file?"

"According to the House Clerk, only the clerk's office staff."

"Who on the staff?"

"No way to tell. Only people outside the staff are required to sign in. The only outsider to do so was this Hartfield."

"Would he take an original?"

"Not unless he's dirty."

I couldn't believe that.

Chapter 13
A Life in Boxes, Tromp l'oeil and a Rooftop Eden

Like most public servants, I look forward to the long weekend of a national holiday, especially George Washington's. This one, not so much.

Shannon's prolonged absence, and her ineptness with the telephone, were more debilitating than I could have imagined. My plan to start packing up the Cape house backfired when a Nor'easter brought sheets of rain and sleet and the glumness that accompanies it. With the sale of the house scheduled for the end of the March, I began to pay the price for being a bit of a pack rat.

In a loft above the garage, I had stored away the sum total of my past in a half-dozen boxes, none of which were labeled. I pulled one randomly, took it through the kitchen to the living room fireplace, built a small fire, fetched a tall glass of stout, and began to rummage.

College English and political science papers, newspaper articles. Team pictures. Love letters from old girlfriends, which everyone saves but never reads. Pictures with friends. And family.

Family. God, look at these. My hockey and football pictures from boarding school. Mom and dad at my graduation. Dad sure was inscrutable, but that smile couldn't hide a father's pride. That man could communicate everything or nothing in the glint of an eye.

Here on a hunting trip to the Eastern Shore of Maryland, sharing a duck blind with Congressman Hughes. At a table at the Robert Morris Inn in Oxford, eating crab stew with our crew. One of us with Senator Howard Baker, the Majority Leader. Playing golf at St. Andrews with Ambassador Hickley-Allen. Look at those smiles. We sure did have fun together.

That rascal! He was the one who instilled this golf thing in me. Gave me the two cut-down clubs when I was seven, but never forced me to play with them. Bought me the new clubs at twelve, when I played from dawn to dusk during those Cape Cod summers. And taught me the rules, the etiquette, the honor of it. He must have known how much I would love it!

Later, on my way to law school, he told me how he left his afternoon classes and went out to Charles River, where he picked up golf games with Judge Irwin Seavey and Professor Caleb Beckwith. "The greatest legal minds of our time," he called them.

After law school when I took my first job on Cape Cod, he counseled me, "Golf is the best business development tool in the world. Play golf with people. Get to know them on the golf course. Beside a duck blind, there is no better place to make a friend."

And I did, because I always took his advice. Everyone did, and we never regretted it.

And then I got elected. During the exuberant celebration at Locke-Ober, after I'd been sworn in by the Governor, I remember what he said. "You'll be a back-bencher from the minority party. Your effectiveness is going to come from friendships. Use your golf game. Play with as many colleagues as you can. Get a reputation as the guy to have in the group. Get their confidence, and do your job well. The business is built on favors, but never do favors for any lobbyist in exchange for anything. Favors are for your colleagues. The lobbyists will understand that."

How right he was. I was practically a celebrity. And not just with the colleagues. Staffers and lobbyists too. A lot of them.

Look at these photos, all these chairmen and vice chairmen and lobbyists and lawyers, cavorting together, smoking their cigars, swilling their beer, waving their dicks. Why the hell did I save all this crap? Vanity. Hubris. Now, it was evidence, for crissakes.

I resisted a momentary urge to toss the photos into the fire. I had a clear conscience so far. No use spoiling it.

By nightfall, I'd built several tall piles of junk in the garage, shed half of my past baggage, and moved all of the photographs into the media center drawers. I briefly considered driving over to the club for dinner, but the wind howled and the rain came in torrents. The fridge was barren, so I took a run up to Cotuit Landing to grab a pizza and a bottle of red wine. I had to change my wet clothes when I got back.

As I was about to eat, the phone rang. I picked it up, but I didn't say anything, just listened.

"Hey Forté."

"I gave at the office." Click.

I settled in for one of the loneliest nights I'd had in my life: eating pizza, drinking a bottle of plonk, packing things, listening to music, and thinking about dead parents, an ex-wife, my reputation, my freedom, and a woman half a continent away.

I drank coffee in the kitchen the next morning, gazing out on the deck where sleet continued to pelt my Weber, when the phone rang.

"Paul, it's Al. You have a minute?"

What kind of question was that? "Of course I do."

"I received the government's response to my document request. The amendment isn't in there."

The sleet was really coming down now, getting heavier. I

could hear it plinking off the grill. "What the hell does that mean, Al?"

"I'm not sure. It could represent an opportunity to have the indictment dismissed, if they're not able to produce the best evidence of your guilt. I'll have to look into this further. It doesn't make any sense that the FBI would leave behind evidence that it had taken the document and then Justice wouldn't produce it. Something screwy is going on."

"What about prosecutorial misconduct? If the FBI signed for it, maybe they gave it to Justice and they withheld it."

"It makes no sense at all, Paul. The document doesn't kill you and it doesn't kill their case. It's just one piece of a puzzle. Committing obstruction of justice over it is just pure stupidity."

A raft of Ruddy ducks floated together in the inlet below, their blue bills dipped down into their chests. "So was the Watergate break-in, Al. That was all about unbridled zealotry too, wasn't it?" I thought of the mysterious phone calls.

Al sighed into the phone and the ducks bobbed. "The FBI just doesn't do this sort of thing."

"Maybe it wasn't the FBI then. Maybe it was someone in the clerk's office. A Kilroy ally."

"Why don't you ask your friend Shakerman to ask around? Maybe we can get a lead and not waste a lot of time. And call me when you're back in town."

"Will do."

Great. They already had me by the balls, now it looked like they're going to fight dirty too.

Shakey's inquiries into the mysterious disappearing amendment yielded nothing beyond the presence of Hartfield's sign-out, which he copied for me. The House clerk's office employs about thirty people. During the six years since I'd left, there'd been some turnover, but not a lot. They were all loyal to the Clerk, and Clerk was loyal to the Speaker.

The Clerk at the time, Bob McGann, was as upright and righteous a citizen as anyone could invent. He'd also retired to Naples two years ago and was in ill health. The current Clerk, Vincent Dunn, was a cagey veteran who'd dye your hair red in your sleep if Flannery told him to. I was going to have to go back to Flannery, or have someone else do it. And even with that, I wasn't supremely confident I could count on him for support on this one.

A golf game only goes so far.

A warm spell hit Boston in early May, and on a Saturday afternoon, I walked around Back Bay watching the season change. I wondered what the hell happened to that amendment and thought about who was going to say what to a jury and tried to convince myself that I really didn't have to worry too much about going to jail. I stopped in to a few cafes for a cold glass of Stella Artois, and some superb calamari at Davio's. The April breeze still held a chill.

When the sun was long gone, I began to head toward The Beehive to see the Duke Robillard show, but an urge came over me and I jumped in a cab instead. It made a u-turn on Columbus, headed over Herald Street and across the Broadway Bridge into Southie. By the time it crossed the bridge, it occurred to me that I really should have called first, but this was a rare act of impulsiveness. The cab cruised up Broadway all the way to Marine Park and took a right on Farragut Street. I looked up at her building and her lights were on. I climbed the steps to the portico and looked at the mailboxes. Jesus, was I nervous.

S. McGonigle—400 stared at me.

I hit the buzzer, and waited. Nothing. I hit it again.

I was about to leave when a voice came over the intercom. "Who is it?" It was Shannon all right.

"Federal agents, we have a warrant to search the premises for bootleg oil paints and Bob Seger CD's," I said in a false baritone. I could hear her chuckle.

"Call my lawyer," she said. "He's at the T."

"I'm sorry to tell you, ma'am, but he's already in custody."

She guffawed at that. "Your timing is pretty good, I just got in this morning," the voice in the speaker said. The big metal and glass door buzzed, and I opened it. "Two floors up and straight ahead," the intercom said.

I ran up the stairs two-at-a-time and peeked in the open door. Shannon stood in the middle of a big open living area. She held a palette and a paintbrush and stared at a huge armoire in the middle of the floor. She wore an oversized white smock, all pocked with paint, torn jeans that showed a lovely patch of creamy thigh, and rubber clogs. Her short black hair was slightly askew, and she had a smudge of burnt sienna on her nose.

She glanced at me and back to the armoire. "What, no bottle of wine? What kind of surprise visitor are you?" On the upper doors of the armoire, she had painted the panels to appear as glass, and inside the glass doors were images of hanging clothing. The first glass drawer below the doors had socks in it, and stuffed in the corner, a package of condoms.

"Nice touch," I said, pointing to them. "Why not just a pocket watch or some reefer?"

She laughed. "Take a look around for a minute while I finish this up."

So I did. The oak floor held no rugs, and the entire outside wall was glass, sixteen feet to the ceiling. Beyond the glass loomed the darkened skyline of Marine Park, Castle Island, and beyond, the scattered lights dotting the Boston Harbor Islands. Flashing lights of airplanes floated across the upper edge, going in and out of Logan. I turned to look back toward the door. Above the entrance hung a catwalk that ran to the sidewall, where a brushed steel spiral staircase met it. In the middle of the clamshell white side, there appeared to be a large window that looked across the street to the neighboring apartment buildings.

I walked over to it. It wasn't a window at all but a large canvas, depicting a window, frame, sill and sash. I couldn't tell if it was a photograph or a painting until I touched it and felt the roughness of the canvas. Through the window, I looked below where children were playing stickball. I could have believed I was looking down on the abutting street, except it was dark now and the daylight in the painting showed summer flora. In the upper left corner of the painting was the end of Marine Park and in the background, the tip of Castle Island. I examined the children in the street below, and discovered that one of them had a fish tail instead of legs. I must have stared at it for five minutes while Shannon finished up her work.

"It's called tromp l'oeil," she said.

"Tromp l'oeil...fool the eye."

"Good for you," she said. "But I leave a little clue, to let you know it's not always as it seems."

I couldn't take my eyes off it. "I'll say."

On the corner of the street scene, holding a bag of groceries and watching the kids play stickball, was a young woman. A young woman with strawberry red hair, who looked remarkably like Stacey.

"The woman in this painting, she looks like a lady I met at a fundraiser for the Speaker last fall. Stacey was her name."

"That would be my sister."

"No foolin'. Small world."

"Small city. Everybody knows everybody, especially in politics."

She took a final look at the doors of the armoire, expelled a satisfied sigh, covered the palette with a piece of cellophane and laid it on a small table.

She smiled at me. "So what brings you here?"

"I was abducted by a rogue cab driver."

"Well, thank him for me next time you see him." I felt like I was going to faint. I swallowed hard, but there was no moisture at all in my mouth.

"Do you want another drink?" she asked.

"Do I look that obvious?"

She snickered. "Your cheeks are flushed."

She walked to a galley kitchen tucked in the left corner and pulled a bottle of white wine from a brushed steel Sub-Zero. She beckoned me to the counter and tossed a corkscrew at me.

"Make yourself useful," she said.

I opened the bottle while she slipped two wine glasses from a hanging rack, and she walked out of the kitchen, saying "follow me" over her shoulder. I followed her across the floor and up the spiral staircase, briefly examining the perfect fit of the jeans ahead of me. At the top of the stairs, I saw a loft bedroom through a slider to the right. She took a fleece pullover from a coat rack and opened a doorway along the near wall.

"Grab something, it's still chilly up here." I did, followed her outside onto a narrow fire escape and shook off a little dizziness during a short climb to the roof.

A wooden catwalk led to a pergola-covered deck. The pergola was draped with dormant wisteria that rose out of huge terra cotta pots. Under the pergola sat two sun-bleached

Adirondack chairs and a terra cotta chiminea. The chairs faced due east, toward Boston Harbor and the airport beyond.

"My word." I gasped at the view. The moonlight cast an inky sheen on the harbor, where tiny red lights blinked above black shadows that slid across the shimmer—water taxis navigating their way in the dark. The airport runway lights across the harbor strobed the approach to airplanes that followed the same spooky path across the sky as they came in to land, one after another.

"You have managed to make a nice Eden for yourself, haven't you?"

"I don't know about Eden, but it sure does beat Savin Hill." She uncorked the wine bottle and filled the two glasses.

I stole one of her Marlboros. We watched a couple of planes come and go from Logan. "Noise isn't too bad," I said after two or three had passed. Shannon was unusually quiet, just gazing at the sky and smoking her cigarette.

"So. What's up?" she asked.

I had no idea. I'd gone there on a whim with no clue what I would say. "Wa'allll," I said with an embarrassed drawl, "I can't get you out of my mind, so I guess I came to swoon."

A quiet moan escaped her, like she had an aching toe. "You're not thinking you want to sleep with me, are you?"

That startled me. "Well, no. I mean, I didn't come over here to get laid, if that's what you meant."

"That's a good thing, buddy. Cuz I know I told you I was falling in love with you, but I'm not ready to let you into my body right now."

"Let me into your body?"

"Yah. You know, fuck me."

"That the way they say 'make love' in Southie?"

"They don't have any saying for that here that I'm aware of."

"Well, that's fine, but I ain't here for that anyway."

"Then we're okay. So what do you need? You wanna talk about your fear of prison?"

"I don't want to think a thing about it. I need to be vulnerable with you without any sex involved."

She looked at me hard, staring through the dark at my face. I could see her eyes through the long, dull beam of the streetlight below. "You're incredibly sexy, but weird."

That killed some tension, and we both smiled. "Maybe that's why I ended up at your door," I said. "You're wearin' some weird yourself."

She threw the empty cigarette pack at my head. "Everybody's got some weird, pal. Everybody."

We sat together in silence, just taking in the night air. The moon hid behind a cloud, but the city lights put a gauzy halo around the skyline. Orion loomed over the roof deck, the sword from his belt dangling above us.

"Come on, we'll go down to *Connah Stoah* and get some more wine and butts," she said. "Although you really should have brought both with you."

"I can only have one inspirational thought at a time."

We left the roof to maraud the streets of South Boston.

Walking down Sixth Street, she slipped this out:

"So tell me about your first sexual experience?"

I glanced at her and stopped. She kept walking, looking back at me, like I was a nut.

"What?" she asked.

"Why you ask a question like that?"

She laughed out loud and continued to walk, giving me a wave, "Come on, let's get to the store before it closes."

I caught up. "Really. What's with the interest?"

She shook her head again. "Buddy boy, I'm tryna get to

know you." She stopped and turned to me. "I'm tryna get to *know* you," grabbing my forearms, looking into my face. "You *know?*"

She turned and ambled down the sidewalk. I started alongside her, and we strode languidly, side by side. "Sorry, Shannon," I said. "I'm not used to this." I put my arm around her shoulder.

"S'all right, Paul," she said, slipping her arm around my waist. "Neither am I. I just think that sex is the defining thing about a relationship, and the way your sexual development occurred tells a lot about you. Once you start screwing someone, it's too late to avoid a broken heart. And I can't afford one of them again. That's all."

"I get it. So, is this mutual disclosure?"

"That would be only fair."

We got some weeds and a couple of bottles of Pinot Gris, a good half-hour after legal closing time. We walked down L Street to the Bath House and up to the beach near Castle Island. We sat on the sand, backs against the seawall.

"So…my first sexual experience, huh?"

"Yah. With another human being, that is," she said, opening the Pinot Gris.

"Funny you should qualify it like that."

She laughed and took a swig from the bottle. "I thought that was a joke."

"Well, I figured. But it's relevant to the experience."

"How so?"

"I was in the fifth grade, and…"

"Fifth grade?"

"Hey! Don't be spookin' me here. These things happen, you know?"

She quieted right down.

"My friend's house next door, it had a gazebo at the top of a bluff in this secluded spot. I used to go over the house when no one was home, take one of his dad's Penthouse magazines, go on up into the gazebo with it. One day I'm up there, jackin' off with the mag and this girl from the neighborhood, Becky Moran, sneaks up behind me and says 'I'll do that for you if you want.'"

"Oh my," Shannon exclaimed.

"Yah, no foolin'. So we said nothing but quickly stripped ourselves naked below the waist and frigged each other raw."

"Wow," she said, gulping.

"Well, it sure gave me something to remember."

"I'll bet."

"But it wasn't all good memory."

"Why not?"

"Because within a few days, this Becky girl and I, we became mortal enemies."

"I understand that," she said immediately.

"You do?"

"Sure," she said, glancing over. "You both had exposed yourselves completely, and yet you had no basis of trust. You were both insecure about trusting the other to keep your dirty secret." She said this as she took a swig from the bottle, corked it and handed it over, all in one fluid movement. "You remember me asking you if you trusted me?"

"I do."

"Remember, or trust me?"

"Both, you twit. So it's your turn."

She got quiet and gazed down at the sand, like she was gathering courage.

"My first sex was being forced to give a blow job to my

brother's friend while my brother was passed out on the couch."

"How old were you?"

"Fifteen." She fell silent again.

"Can I guess that wasn't your preferred initiation?"

She sighed. "I guess not, but what did I know? I grew up in a Catholic family, living in a Catholic town, where the girls were taught at church how dirty sex was and parents avoided eye contact at the mention of the word. If some slug from the neighborhood grabbed my tits and told everybody on the bus about it, my dad gave me a beating cuz I must have been asking for it."

"Your dad beat you?"

She stared more at the lamp. "Not too often." She drank from the bottle. "Often enough."

"You ever had an honest lover?"

She smiled sadly. "Yeah, I did. Gave me my first orgasm. Three of them, actually," smiling.

"Woo-hoo, a three-fer! What happened to him?"

She shrugged. "Went off to college, moved away, lost touch."

"Break your heart?"

"Of course, you moron. But what the hell. You can't be happy without knowing what a broken heart is. Gimme a butt."

I cracked a fresh deck of Reds, lit two and handed her one.

"So, any other traumatic sexual experiences you don't talk about?" she asked.

"Well, at the end of college, I had this girlfriend from Greenwich, Connecticut. Rich girl. A real lady. So the last night we're together before I graduate and leave, we've gone to this fancy French restaurant and had a lot of wine, and smoked some pot, and we're pretty trashed and very horny, so we get back to her place and this is the last time we'll ever make love, you know?"

"How did you know?"

"Just because—we'd agreed, this would be our last night. But this last time, when we're all hot and ready, she turns her back to me."

"She wanted it in the ass?" She could have been one of the guys on the seventh tee at the Port the way she said that.

"She did."

"Well? Did you oblige?"

"I did." I took a swig from the bottle.

"And?"

"Hold your freakin' horses, will ya?"

Shannon sighed. "You're narrating a soft-porn story here, but your timing is a problem."

I laughed and she joined me, both of us feeling the wine.

"Well, I have to tell you this…"

"Tell me anything—just tell me how it came out."

That cracked me up, I don't know why. After I recovered and wiped the tears from my eyes, I told her, "To tell you the truth, at the time it was incredibly erotic, and she sure enjoyed it, which is what was important, I guess, but it upset me after we split up."

"Why?"

"I guess for the same reason the Becky incident upset me. They left scars. Or maybe they're not scars at all, just vivid memories that make you feel dirty and cheap. Or maybe it's just a vestige of my Catholic indoctrination. I mean, it could be me, but I don't think the most romantic way to say goodbye to someone you love is to screw her in the ass."

Shannon laughed softly at that, and fell quiet, staring out across the bay at Columbia Point. "People've been doing that to their friends since the beginning of time. Let's mosey."

I teetered to my feet and pulled Shannon up; we climbed over the wall and headed back toward her pad. "Let's watch the sun rise," I said.

"Let's."

We went back up onto the roof deck. The sky had begun to lighten and the dark shapes beneath the flickering lights began to show definition. We sat in the still silence of the coming dawn. I had never felt so peaceful and safe.

The sounds of morning traffic began below as the gray eastern skyline turned a rusty brown and brightened to tangerine as a sliver of sun peeked over of the tip of Harbor Island. We watched it grow to an amber beach ball. She got up slowly and put her hand out to me. I took it and she pulled me up, and I followed her down the catwalk, to her balcony, and then her bedroom. She turned to me and gave me a lazy, gentle hug.

"Let's lie together and dream for a little," she whispered.

"Let's."

We stripped down to our skivvies like we were siblings at summer camp and laid down on her bed. As she turned on her side away from me, she took my hand, pulling my arm around her, and sandwiched my hand in hers. I spooned her, gave her shoulder a tender kiss, and closed my eyes.

I don't know if I dreamt or not, but I sure felt like I was living one.

Chapter 14
Turning of the Screws

When my eyes opened, the digital clock on Shannon's bedside table said 9:17, and I was alone. I threw on my clothes and tottered down the staircase to an empty room and small note taped to the door:

> *Hi,*
>
> *Didn't have the heart to wake you. Door locks behind you so don't leave anything behind, unless you plan to come back. You do plan to come back, don't you?*
>
> *Shannon*

I drove like a nut across town to my building, did the shower and dress thing and hustled down to the office. By the time I got there, I had a stack of messages waiting for me. One from Rex, another from Al Croston. In the battle of priority, the lawyer wins. I went to the extension line in the conference room, just to be safe.

"Al, it's Paul. What's the good word?"

"I'm afraid there's no good word today, Paul," he said.

"Talk to me."

"The grand jury has just issued a superseding indictment."

"Okay."

"Tax evasion, and another twenty-seven counts of mail fraud."

"Twenty-seven?"

"Let's just say every golf partner you had in six years."

"Even the ones who came to Hyannisport?"

"It seems as though after each of those visits, you had a meal of some sort."

"Naturally. I get it."

"If I had to guess, I would say that Kilroy wants to eradicate the nefarious game of golf from the arsenal of weapons used in the political business."

My heart started pounding against my ribcage—worse than the night before.

"Here's the deal, Paul. I won't sugarcoat it. The lid is blowing off this whole thing. When it does, people start talking. Lobbyists to save their law licenses, legislators to save their pensions. Your relationship with these golfers arose out of your position as a legislator. And whether they asked you or not, you've got dozens of votes in support of the industries they represent. That's all Kilroy may have to show a jury, and I doubt it's enough, but juries are notoriously unpredictable."

"Are you telling me I could go to jail for voting my conscience?"

"The conscience is an ephemeral thing, Paul. It's hard to get a jury to understand a politician with a conscience."

I shrieked, "Jesus Christ Al, all I did was play a few goddamn rounds of golf!"

But of course, that wasn't the point. The gift statute thing was just a civil fine, but there was the federal mail fraud statute. And income tax evasion—failing to report as income the economic value of the free round of golf. In my case, there had been dozens of them, with dozens of patrons. At $150 a round, it could amount to a few thousand dollars of unreported income, and an unpaid tax of a few hundred dollars. It might be ridiculously petty, but as Inspector Javert would have said, the law is the law.

All of this Croston explained to me in the pedantic manner of a white-shoe lawyer.

"Okay, Al. Thanks for everything."

I hung up and sat in the conference room for who knows how long, staring into space. The all-nighter with Shannon and Al's call really put me into a twilight zone; I was having trouble thinking.

Cindy tapped on the door. "You have a phone call on hold."

"Send it in here, please."

She left and a moment later the extension lit.

"Paul Forté," I said.

"Figure at least one month in the can for every round of golf, pal." Click.

I disconnected the phone from its jack and hurled it against the wall. Then I left, walked back to the condo and slept for fifteen hours.

By the time I got out of bed, showered and ate breakfast, the sun shimmered off the Trinity Church steeple and the weatherman predicted low 70s. I grabbed my keys, locked up, jumped in the Saab and hit the highway south toward the Cape.

I soon entered the hamlet of Hyannisport, where the "One Way" signs apply only to drivers of non-indigenous vehicles and the lawns were littered with windsurfers, bicycles, drying jib sails and the occasional empty bottle of gin.

I turned right at the "All Traffic Turn Left" sign, and at the top of the hill, entered the Hyannisport Club parking lot, which has the finest parking lot view in the world, I am quite sure. It looks over the finishing three holes laid across a sweeping open hillside that tumbled down to the Hyannisport marsh. Across the marsh, the quaint homes on gumdrop-shaped Squaw Island jutted out of the treetops. Beyond that, the coastline ran west from Craigville Beach to Wianno and then in the hazy distance, Popponnesset Beach. Out across Nantucket Sound to the south, far off in the distance, you could see a faint glimpse of Chappaquiddick, twenty-five miles in the distance. It is a view that intoxicates any mortal soul, particularly the golfer.

I felt the visceral buzz in my bones and rushed to put on my golf shoes. I headed along the clamshell walkway in front of the clubhouse to the locker room door, where I nearly ran into the exiting club President, Parker Fessenden IV.

"Hello, Parker," I said with the requisite deference. This is what men like Parker expect. Slightly older than me, he had a vast inheritance, rugged good looks, a patrician demeanor and scant intelligence.

"Forté! Well, well," he said. "I've been reading about you."

"Ah well, you know the motto of the press. Never let the truth get in the way of a good story."

Fessenden didn't seem to appreciate my humor. Other members entered the hallway. He nodded toward the Boardroom. "Come in here for a moment, Paul." We entered the small sanctum of the Board's private conference room, and he shut the door. "Have a seat."

"Parker, I'd like to get down to the pro shop and get my name into the lunchtime scramble, if you don't mind."

Parker ignored me. "Paul, some of us are troubled by the publicity that your situation is bringing the club. We're wondering how long this is likely to continue."

Oh boy. "What are you referring to, Parker?" I'd learned well by now that people like Parker prefer the elliptical approach, which allows them the illusion that they do not have to deal with the underbelly of our culture.

Parker shifted. "We're uncomfortable having the name of the club mentioned in connection with a pending criminal trial involving one of its members."

"And what control over it do you think I might have?"

"Well, er…none, Paul. That's the problem."

"So what are you asking me, or telling me?"

He hadn't an answer for that, apparently. Perhaps his mind could not work quickly enough to have anticipated running into me at just this time.

"We would like you to know we are uncomfortable, and expect that you will do…er, you will do what is best to preserve the good name of this club."

"What is best."

"Yes. What is best."

"For this club."

"For this club, to which your membership remains at the discretion of the Board."

These are the defining moments of one's reputation, when, faced with the need to respond to such innuendo, one has mere seconds to weigh the impulse to say what could be said against the repercussion that follows. At this moment, it occurred to me that I ought to tell Parker Fessenden what he deserved to hear. That his inherited fortune was derived from bootlegging, that the fortunes of the other Old Guard entailed abuses of humanity and law untold. That I was hardly the first politician whose proximity to legal peril brought notoriety to the Hyannisport Club, if one is to consider Ted Kennedy's killing of Mary Jo Kopechne or his brother's alliances with Chicago mobsters or Hollywood starlets, etcetera, etcetera.

And I would perhaps have let loose on him with such a tirade. But I had no audience for it. And if one is to crash his plane solo into the deck of an enemy ship, one had better have the satisfaction of knowing he's got a proper cheering section.

Besides, I loved the golf course too goddamn much to get myself kicked out just yet.

"I understand, Parker. Let me say this. I am not going to be tried until well after this season, and between now and then, I don't expect a great deal of publicity during the summer. If it ever gets to a point where the name of the club or its members begins to receive unwanted publicity, I will offer to tender my resignation, with the understanding that I may make my case directly and personally to the Board as to why it should not be accepted."

Parker Fessenden stared at me as I finished this statement, and it was quite clear to me that he was simply trying to understand what I had said to make sure he didn't respond erroneously.

"That is acceptable," he finally said.

"Thank you, Parker." I got up and left him in the conference room.

This exchange had sapped my desire to remain on the property. I walked back to my car and left, trading golf for an afternoon of calamari and gin & tonics at Baxter's Boathouse. On the fifth of the latter, I admitted to myself that I had lied to Parker Fessenden.

I had no intention whatsoever of tendering my resignation, no matter what happened.

Chapter 15
Secrets Revealed, a Spoiled Round

Shannon had run off to Idaho or someplace again, and by this time I'd learned not to guess when she might return or to expect a warning call. More nights than I cared to admit, I drove by Farragut Street, looking for some sign of her return. It was driving me insane, these drawn out periods with no contact.

One day, I wrote her a note and drove over to stuff it into her mailbox. There wasn't a slit in the box and I didn't want to leave my note lying out for a neighbor to snoop, so I was trying to figure out what to do with it.

As I stood on the steps feeling like an idiot, a pick-up truck pulled up in front of the building and double-parked. A big strong guy with dark hair and a smoldering look got out of the driver's side and hoisted a couple of large pieces of luggage from the bed.

Shannon got out of the passenger side, and seeing me, she hesitated, paled and gave a weak "Hey."

The thought flashed in my head that I shouldn't be standing there, maybe he was her goddamn husband or something. Talk about awkward.

"Hey."

"Paul, this is my brother, Brian. Brian, this is Paul Forté."

Brian put the bags down and looked at me. He had huge arms, a bull neck, a massive chest and a flattop crew cut. The guy looked like a weightlifter.

"Hey Brian," I said, and I gave him a good hard handshake and looked him in the eye. "Readville Yard, shop steward, right?"

"Yeah," the man said, wrinkling his brow, frowning. "How'd you know?" Guy was scary tense.

"Your sister Stacey told me a while back."

He looked at Shannon, confused, pointing at me. "He know Stacey, too?"

She shrugged. "He met her once at a fundraiser for Flannery."

"Why'd she tell you that?" he asked, squinting at me.

"Brian, Paul is general counsel of the T. He's okay, Brian. This is all cool."

He looked at her and back at me. "You're the general counsel at the T, huh?"

"Yup, that's what I do."

"You got indicted for golfin'?"

"That's me, Brian."

He looked at his sister. "You sure you're okay?"

"Yeah, Brian, I'm okay. You can take off. I'm fine. Paul's my friend."

He looked at me again. "You take her bags?"

"No problem."

"Okay. You treat her right."

"Just friends, man. Just friends."

He gave me one more look, jumped into his truck and peeled out.

Shannon stood next to her bags on the sidewalk, dead eyes fixed on me, and I couldn't tell what the hell they said. I felt like I had just avoided the subway guy wielding the tuna can lid.

I did a little two-step soft shoe and spread my arms. "Surprise."

"Can you carry the bags for me?" she asked crossly and strode past me to the door, holding it tight-lipped. I cut the performance short and struggled through the door with the two overstuffed bags.

"You take up geology, harvest some rocks on your trip?" I asked, huffing past her. She didn't respond.

We rode up in the elevator in silence, she not even looking at me. She opened the door to her apartment and held it for me. I lugged the bags in and dropped them. She closed the door firmly and threw the bolt.

"Did I say or do something to anger you?"

She stood like a statue with her eyes closed, and after too long, moved. "I'm going to take a quick shower. Give me a minute till you hear the water and bring the bags up for me?"

"Sure."

She turned without a word and went up the stairs. I heard the slider close and then the water began to run. I gave it a minute and hauled the two bags of rocks up the spiral staircase. I went back downstairs and checked the fridge for wine, but it was empty. I thought of walking down to Connah Stoah, but I wasn't sure Shannon would let me back in. So I just loitered.

I examined the tromp l'oeil on the wall again, marveling at the perfect likeness of Stacey, even at such small scale. Then I noticed that in the buildings across the street, there were images of people behind the windows of the apartments. One of them was Shannon's brother. He was standing by a half-open window in a wife-beater tee shirt, looking straight back at me, holding a pair of binoculars. In the next window over, an old woman stood with a walker, hunched over a kitchen table. At the street level, there was a walk-down apartment, with the window at sidewalk level. The window had bars on it. There was an image of a man sitting on a bed, elbows on knees, head bowed.

I looked back at her work area. She had another furniture piece set for work, a sort of French divan, I think it was. It was upholstered in a white canvas or linen of some kind and had been prepped for paint and had the beginnings of sketch marks. Soon I heard Shannon's footsteps as she emerged from her room, and I watched her come down the stairs, stride to me and stop, hands at her sides, shoulders held tensely, eyes fixed on my chest.

"I'm sorry. I'm very, very sorry for going off on you like that. You did nothing wrong, and you didn't deserve that." When she finished, her gaze shifted from my chest to my eyes, remorse behind the taut frown.

"No problem." I gave her a hug, which she returned weakly, and she pushed me back.

"Let's go get something to eat," she said.

"What have you got in mind?"

"Sullivan's."

"What the hell is Sullivan's?"

"It's the hot dog stand across the street at Castle Island."

"Sounds perfect."

We went down to the street and strolled toward Castle Island at a slow pace. She had her hands jammed into her jean pockets and looked at the ground a lot with that frown.

"You must be going crazy, not being able to contact me, not hearing from me for weeks, and I'm not being fair to you."

"Well, I have been a little anxious, tell you the truth, but that scene back there was just plain scary."

She nodded emphatically. "I know, I know." She took her hands out of her pockets and waved them around. "I've got a very complicated family. I wasn't prepared for them to find out that I was seeing a man right now."

"Are you?"

"Am I what?"

"Seeing a man? Who is the bastard? I'll fuck him up."

She slugged me hard in the arm. "You jackass."

I began to feel much better.

We strolled a bit in silence until we got to the park, queued up in the line for a hot dog and kept the talk small until we had our dogs and were sitting in the shade of an elm tree on the lawn. We got comfortable, and I must say, it was a pretty damn good dog. Then she started to let go.

"My brother, Brian? He's insanely protective of me."

"No foolin'."

"I have a lot of secrets I need to share with you."

"You do, huh?"

"I do."

"You want to take them one at a time? Baby steps?"

She picked up a twig and began to crumble it into pieces.

"Brian is the way he is because of something that happened to us a long time ago. When we were growing up in Savin Hill, my mom was having a hard time. Dad kind of turned into an angry drunk and her nerves didn't handle it well. He was beating on all of us, alternately. She got sick with cancer, and I'm sure it was all the worrying.

"I was supposed to be home taking care of her, but I wasn't doing a very good job of it. She needed something and I wasn't there to get it for her. She tried to get up from her bed, but she was too weak, and she fell."

Shannon stopped there, making sawdust of the twig now.

"Was she okay?"

More sawdust. She looked up at me and back down. "She died, Paul."

"No."

"She died, right there on her bedroom floor, alone," she said, now weeping quietly.

"And you blame yourself."

She nodded emphatically as she wiped her runny nose with her bare hand.

"Shannon, you can't do that."

Her weeping halted and she flashed anger, "Paul, I was in my room giving a blow job when she was calling me! A fucking blow job! My boyfriend was with me, the music was up, and I was getting laid!"

The twig was obliterated now and she was pulling grass out of the ground, piling it up.

"Brian came home and found her there on the floor. He called 911 and then came to my room, broke down the door and beat the shit out of Drew. Threw him out of the house, all bloody and half-naked."

"Shannon, you don't have to do this."

"Oh, yes I do. I do have to. You're the first guy I've been attracted to in seventeen years. You need to know this before you get yourself in any deeper…"

"I'm afraid it's too late." I patted her hand. "That was seventeen years ago?"

"Uh-huh. After that, people in the neighborhood told me that my sister was calling me a skank whore. Our mother wasn't gone one month. I confronted her, like 'Stacey, what the fuck,' but she said some vile shit to me, kept coming at me, so in my face I could feel her spit. I closed my fist and punched her front teeth out. She's never said another word to me since."

"You ever ask her to forgive you?"

"For what? Punching her lights out or killing my mother?"

"You didn't kill your mother."

"Tell that to her."

"What about your brother?"

She shook her head slowly. "He blames himself for what happened cuz Drew was his friend."

"I'm sorry, Shannon."

"He's scared away every man that's gotten within ten feet of me. There's not a guy in Southie that'll even buy me a beer at the L Street Grille."

"Good thing."

She looked at me, almost sad, and looked back down. "Yeah…it is…" She looked up at me again, and smiled sweetly. "It is."

"Really?"

"Really, Paul. I was going to let him know about you, I just didn't expect you to show up like that."

"You know, by this point, people in our position usually talk on the phone, like every day. I know we're both a little out of practice, but that's the way it's done, I'm told."

"I hate telephones. I don't even check my answering machine. I'm not even sure how it works."

"See? I didn't know that. That's important information to know."

"Paul, I'm still not ready. I'm terribly afraid. I know I don't act like it, but I am."

Ouch, that hurt, but I wasn't going to crack. "I understand."

"I'm getting there, because you're you. But I'm not there yet." She looked at me, pouting. "I'm sorry."

I flashed her a hundred watt smile. "Are you joking? I've never been happier."

"Are you nuts? You're dealing with one messed up lady from a crazy family."

"Been there…done that. I'm in no hurry myself."

She raised her eyebrows at me. "There's a lot more. But I've had enough for the day."

"Don't sweat it."

"Yeah?"

"Oh, yeah." I winked at her.

"Okay." She smiled and wrinkled her mouth, like she had at Pete's the first time we met.

We got up and began to amble back to her place.

"So your sister doesn't know about me, then."

"No reason to think she does. She's too busy chasing bad guys to care about her brother or sister."

"Chasing bad guys? As a compliance officer at Morgan Stanley?"

She gave me a look, raised her eyebrows and smiled. "That's what she told you? That she's a compliance officer at Morgan?"

"Well, yeah. That isn't what she does?"

She laughed quietly. "No…no, that's not what she does."

I gave her plenty of time to continue, but it seemed she'd decided against it. "Well, what the hell does she do?"

We reached her building, and she stopped on the front step. "Paul, my sister is the deputy director of the public corruption unit at FBI Boston."

"Mother of God…"

"I told you, there's a lot more."

"The suspense is killing me."

"Well, it'll have to kill you a while longer."

"Metaphorically speaking."

"Listen, wait right here, I'll be right back." She ran upstairs and came back in no time.

"I've got some family business I have to take care of right now, and Monday I have to go on another trip. I'll be back in a couple of weeks, and then we'll talk about me."

"Aha, I can't wait."

"In the meantime, I want you to have this." She took my hand and placed a key in it. I looked at the key, and then looked into her eyes, hard. "Use the deck while I'm gone," she shrugged. "Or not."

I gave her a bone-crushing hug and she followed me down to the street. I got in my car and looked in the mirror as I rolled away. She was beaming. I waved, she waved. I drove off and watched her in the rear view mirror, standing in the street with her arms crossed, until she was out of sight.

In the morning of a perfect early summer golf day, I spent a few hours in the office finishing up some business before beginning a vacation weekend I had scheduled months ago. I hadn't taken a day off in four months, and I was a wreck. I planned to leave the office at noon to catch a tee time with three fraternity brothers at Woods Hole Golf Club, a crafty little design by Stiles and Van Cleek.

My job came with eight weeks of paid vacation, but my first assistant begged me not to take it all. "Please. Don't leave for more than a few days. Think of the mischief your absence will invite," he said. He's a former Marine. When a former Marine begs, you have to take heed.

At 11:15 that morning, GM's office sent word that my presence was required at an emergency meeting at two that afternoon. Some sort of crisis involving a bus manufacturing contract. I called the head of bus operations, Mort Stuckey, who was pretty much shitting his pants worrying about what this meeting could be about.

"What's the problem, Mort? Why's this meeting necessary?"

"I don't know what the hell they're talking about," he said. "The contract's going fine."

I summoned the two deputies in charge of labor and contracts, Jimmy Fantozzi and Vinnie Mattarazzo. "Mr. Fantoztic" and "Vinnie the Guinea," I called them. I instructed them to attend the two o'clock meeting, and they looked at me like I was sending them to their own execution.

"You guys look like you've seen a ghost. What's the problem?"

Vinnie said, "We both got called by the GM's office and were told we're not invited."

They looked at each other and back at me.

It took me two seconds to get the picture, and I laughed out loud.

"What's going on?" Jimmy asked.

"I'll tell you what's going on. Cruddy and Fetore are up to their tricks again. I'm telling you to go to that meeting. If they don't want you to attend, that's up to them."

The two of them turned white. I almost passed them my puke bucket.

"Look guys, you got nothing to worry about. This meeting is bullshit. It's manufactured to fuck up my long weekend. If they ask you what the hell you're doing there, throw me under the bus and tell them that I don't know shit about bus contracts." And I kicked them out.

At twelve o'clock sharp, I left my office and took the elevator down to the lobby. As the doors opened, there was Lou Fetore, standing like a menacing guardian.

"Hiya, Lou," I said. "You're waiting for me, aren't you," I asked, wagging my finger at him.

Fetore did his swaggering thing, complete with the tight-lipped grin.

"Hello For-tay," he said. "We'll be seeing you at the two o'clock meeting?"

"No, you won't, Lou," I said, stopping right in front of him, face on.

"This is a crisis management meeting," he said, "This matter requires your immediate and full attention. The Chairman has made it clear that your attendance is mandatory."

I looked down at the brick floor and shuffled my foot, and looked back up at him, smiling. "You ought to be ashamed of yourself, Lou."

"Why's that?"

"You know better than to bring the Chairman into this when he has no idea what you're up to."

He shifted a little and set himself again. "How do you know that?"

"Let's ask him, right now."

He swaggered a bit and put his hands on his hips. "We better see you at two o'clock, that's all I got to say to you."

"At two this afternoon, I will be on the first tee at Woods Hole. You want to see me at two o'clock, that's where you can find me. But if you show up dressed like that, don't be surprised if they have you arrested."

Fetore stared at me and began to shake his head.

I couldn't resist the temptation. "You know, something tells me that if one of us is going to be convicted of a crime, you'll be first." I walked away, leaving him to smirk alone.

That afternoon, I played like shit. I was goddamn furious that those pricks wasted precious time trying to fuck up my golf game. And they did. But I still had fun with my buds and managed to scrape out a 79.

I had a reputation to protect.

The following Monday, I arrived at my desk at six fifteen, fully rejuvenated and relaxed after a long weekend of golf and gin, red wine and lamb chops, and an excellent late show at the Beehive by The Fat City Band.

An envelope sat on my desk, sealed, inside of which I found a handwritten note on Chairman Liguotomo's personal stationery. It read:

> *Paul,*
>
> *Bravo!*
>
> *I admire your courage.*
>
> *You understand that you have two choices: being hated and being disrespected. You have made an honorable choice. Hope your golf game wasn't spoiled too much.*
>
> *Your loyal client*

What a Machiavellian prick.

Chapter 16

Confronting Demons, a Modest Severance and a Missing Link

The following Tuesday at 2:23 in the afternoon, thirty-seven sparkling-new city buses rolled, one after another, into the Broadway bus garage in South Boston. They had left the Texas plant the previous Thursday. While Fetore's little sabotage was exposed, I took a ride up the VFW Parkway to the MBTA's Readville Yard on a little personal business.

I parked my Saab outside a dirty old concrete bunker of a building and walked in through a rust-stained steel door. A dank hallway led me past a string of desolate, dark offices to a gray metal door that opened into a cavernous open garage area about the size of the Superdome. Eight sets of rail tracks entered the building through large hangar doors along the left wall. Running between the tracks were fingers of concrete platforms. It looked like a third world train station. Five of the tracks were empty. Three had subway trains parked at them. No human activity in sight. I followed the platform past the trains to a set of metal stairs that led up to a raised trailer. Aside from the hissing of hydraulics and an idling diesel engine, the only noise came from the trailer. Creedence Clearwater's "Born on the Bayou."

I climbed the staircase toward the music and opened the door. Five men in blue coveralls (none of them dirty) sat around a cheap conference table. They looked dull-witted, laconic. On the table were a dozen beer bottles, a mess of cards and a large pile of ones, fives, tens and twenties. Brian McGonigle sat at the end of the table, tapping his Bud Light bottle in rhythm to the song, a pile of loose bills in front of him. He looked up at me and stopped tapping. The others followed his eyes to me, looked me up and down like they'd never seen a halfway decent suit on a man before.

"Got a sec?" I asked him.

He looked again at his hand, shrugged, tossed them into the middle of the table and got up, walked past the others and out the door, not bothering to invite me to follow. I followed him down the stairs to the platform. He stood with his arms at his sides, shoulders back, chin raised slightly, and bore his eyes into me.

"Sorry to take you away from the game. Looks like you're hot."

"What's this about?"

"I need to talk to you about your sister."

His eyes flashed. "She all right?"

"She's more than all right, Brian. She's great."

"Then why you come to talk to me about her?"

"Because I'm pretty sure she wants to have me around, and I want to know that's going to be okay with you."

"She don't need my permission," he said.

"Oh, whether she needs it or not, Brian, she wants it. And if she wants it, I want it."

His face softened, only a little. "I don't know you."

"I know that. So there's something I want you to do."

He shifted. "I'm listening."

"The union you represent, the Carmen's Local 589?"

"Yeah."

"They've got people all over the T whose job is to know who's who and what's what."

"Yeah, that's right."

"So, I'm suggesting that you ask around."

He shook his head; almost imperceptibly, but I saw it. "We don't have too many friends in that building, way I hear it. You sure you want me to do that?"

"Brian, here's how I see it. I don't want you to have to rely on Shannon's word. You don't know me enough to trust my word. Right?"

"S'poze not."

"You trust your union brother's word?"

"More'n anyone else's."

"So do I."

"That right?"

"Abso-fuckin-lutely, Brian. You have them check me out."

He looked at me long, and I held his look back, until a smile crept into his tight face.

"You're pretty sure of yourself, aren't you, Counselor?"

"You're goddamn right I am, Steward McGonigle."

That dude could hold a stare. But I'd never been so sure of anything in my life, and I was determined to let him know that.

"Better get back to the cards before they cool off."

Mission accomplished.

I was long overdue checking in with the Gov's lawyer, so I called him.

"Hiya Goody. Got a sec?"

"Sure. How are you surviving the onslaught?" he asked.

"Passably. I still have my humor."

"Last thing to go on a guy like you."

"Let me ask you hypothetical."

Oh-oh, another hypothetical. Go ahead."

"Let's say that our hypothetical general counsel thinks that someone might have some information that is liable to compromise one of his individual clients."

"You mean, such as a corporate officer or member of the board?"

"Yes."

"Okay."

"He has no control over whether this is disclosed, and due to his own circumstances, its disclosure could benefit him personally, if it's handled right."

"Does he have any relationship with the discloser?"

I hesitated a moment too long.

"Paul, does he have any role whatsoever in the disclosure of the information?"

"Not directly."

No sound came for a good while. "Okay, let me guess. This hypothetical general counsel, he has provided some sort of public record to someone else who had an interest in seeing if there was anything fishy in it. He has reason to believe his someone else has found the answer."

"That's plausible."

But Goody seemed to have lost his humor. "Did I not explain this to you months ago?"

"I believe you said it was okay to look into it as long as the document wasn't disclosed."

"Well, did this counsel disclose the document or not?"

"What if he just informed someone of its existence and the

someone got it on his own?"

"Goddamnit, Paul, I don't know. But I'll tell you this. Before any of that information is used by this someone else, your general counsel had better resign."

I was afraid he'd say that, but on second thought, realized I wouldn't miss any of those pukes one bit.

First thing the next morning, I called over to the Governor's office to see if he'd see me. He was due in at ten A.M. after his squash match, and had fifteen minutes before his first meeting. Using my very best groveling techniques with Sheila, the appointment secretary, I weaseled my way into that crevice.

I was sitting in the anteroom of the Governor's office suite when he ambled in, looking like a million bucks, except for his wet hair. He waved me to follow him and I did, into his "ceremonial" office. We sat and he got right down to business.

"Are you keeping my friend on the straight and narrow," he asked.

"That's much easier said than done, especially for me."

"Goody mentioned something to me about it. Are you having problems?"

"My problem is that since I am facing a criminal trial, my moral authority to keep them in line is pretty much nil."

The big redhead raised his eyebrows and looked coolly at me, like I had just challenged him to a squash match. "He hasn't said anything to me about not wanting you around."

"That's what worries me. I'm already up to my eyebrows in white-collar crime. I don't need any more. If you'd like to talk to Goody about it, I'll authorize him to—"

"No, no—that won't be necessary," he said, waving it off like it was cigar smoke. "What do you want to do?"

"I want to resign from the T as soon as possible, with a

modest severance."

"Three months?"

"That's more than fair."

He smiled and shook his head gently. "You have no idea how bad a negotiator you are."

"You'd have given me six, right?"

"At least."

"I know. I wouldn't have taken it."

He sat looking at me with a mild, amiable grin. "Paul, you're one of a kind. I wish I'd made you banking commissioner."

I guffawed at that. "Oh no you don't, Guv'nah."

He nodded slowly. "Well, it's a close call, but I suppose you're right. I'll call your boss this afternoon and make sure you're good to go. Effective when?"

"The next Board meeting. They haven't set the date yet, but whatever it is'll be fine."

"I'll take care of it."

"That'd be very much appreciated."

"Say nothing of it—you've earned it." He paused a second. "Say Paul, you mind explaining this golf thing to me?"

"What do you mean? You want to know the details of the criminal case?"

"Oh hell no," he said with another wave of his hand, "that doesn't interest me a bit. I've just never gotten the golf thing. Why people like it so much. Why, for instance, you'd be willing to risk your reputation or career for the opportunities to play golf."

Boy, had I thought about that during the past year, but I hadn't expected to explain it to the Governor of Massachusetts. "It's like this. You hunt?"

"Avidly."

"You fish?"

"Equally so."

"You lie awake at four in the morning, anticipating the coming day? Where you might cast your fly, into which eddy or pool? Which duck blind you will favor based on the wind that morning? How you might configure your decoys?"

"Yes, yes, of course."

"I do the same thing with a golf course. Play every hole from tee to green, in my head."

"You don't say."

"You have an honor code, an ethical construct. You observe those rules, because not to do so destroys the joy of the experience."

"Absolutely."

"And the camaraderie. Your hunting and fishing, you do it essentially alone, but you are with friends. You rely on your own instincts and skill, but it wouldn't be the same without the camaraderie, would it?"

"Exactly," he said, nodding.

I pressed forward on the edge of my chair. "You know, when I am on a golf course, I have two states of mind. The one between shots, and the one for the three seconds during each shot. That three seconds is a Zen moment, a test of my connection with the Q'i of the universe. And when I strike my shot, when it is pure, when it is as true as your shot over dense gorse at the head of a wild boar, it's a sensation we can't explain."

He took this in, eyes narrowed as he looked at me and nodded slowly.

"Tell me this," he said, "aside from your family, the people who you are closest to. The people you would drop everything to help."

"All golf buddies," I said without hesitation.

"I completely understand."

He rose, head still nodding, gave me an emphatic shake of the hand, thanked me profusely for my loyalty and service, and assured me all would be well.

I believed him at that moment.

The telephone rang at six fifteen A.M. I answered it in the kitchen, where I was preparing a chorizo omelet and hash browns.

"Talk to me."

"You read the paper yet?" It was Rex.

"Nope."

"Do, and call me back." Click. People who don't know him think he has no manners.

I flipped the omelet, perfectly, turned off the burner and went down to the front walk to get the Herald. I began to scan the front page and stopped reading. It was time to kill this habit.

Back in the kitchen, I riffled from page to page until I found this:

Federal Prosecutor Increasing Visibility

Rumors of AG campaign swirl

The election of the next Attorney General is nearly two years away, but there appears little doubt that Assistant United States Attorney Bernard Kilroy intends to throw his hat into the ring. Campaign finance records show that for the last reporting period, Kilroy's contributions to Democrats across the state have skyrocketed. Since June of this year, Kilroy and his wife, Virginia Erichetti Kilroy, have together contributed a total of $23,000 to Democratic incumbents in the House and Senate as well as Congressional incumbents and mayors from Pittsfield to Plymouth.

The federal Hatch Act prohibits employees of the Justice Department from soliciting or raising funds and running in partisan elections, but there is no such prohibition on contributing to other campaigns.

Local political operatives queried by the Herald were not surprised by Kilroy's frenetic activity. "The guy has been to every Rotary meeting in the state during the past six months," said one high-profile campaign consultant who requested anonymity. "He may not be campaigning yet, but he might as well be."

I called Rex back. "Very interesting," I said.

"What does an assistant U.S. attorney make?"

"Maybe eighty-five, ninety grand."

"You notice the wife?"

"Could be just a coincidence."

"It's not," Rex answered.

"No?"

"Virginia Erichetti Kilroy is Vincent Erichetti's sister."

"And what does Mrs. Kilroy do for a living?"

"She is an insurance executive at IWO."

"IWO?"

"An international casualty insurance giant."

"What does she do at this IWO place?"

"She's in charge of the surplus lines worldwide."

"Surplus lines as in…"

"Environmental liability."

"Do you think there could possibly be a connection?"

"I am a naturally suspicious person," Rex said. "It's time to look a little closer at the Kilroys' lifestyle."

"Go get 'em, tiger."

Click.

Chapter 17
The Making of Impressionist Art

On a cloudy July afternoon that threatened thunderstorms, while I played in the Cutler Memorial Tournament with three old pals at the incomparable Myopia Hunt Club, my cell phone rang. I didn't hear it, because I never bring my cell phone onto a golf course. This should be a rule enforced with corporal punishment.

When we finished around sunset, I put my clubs in the car, changed my shoes and checked my calls. I saw that I had missed three calls from Al Croston. I didn't listen to the messages.

Instead, I did what any respectable lawyer would do when faced with the prospect of a federal penitentiary. I joined my friends in the clubhouse for several martinis and a sumptuous meal of kidney lamb chops, roasted baby red potatoes with rosemary, and grilled asparagus. With two bottles of 1986 Silver Oak Cab.

Once I milked it of frivolity, I hopped in the car for a slightly tipsy ride back to Boston. I carefully drove in the center lane with the cruise control set on 60 mph, which around the city of Boston guarantees you at least a half-dozen one-finger salutes.

But I wasn't taking any chances. If I'm going to jail, it's going to be sober, in a suit, in the morning.

Reflecting on my possible loss of freedom had a cleansing effect. I realized that I had to put my shit in order, to face the music on solid footing. And not just about my legal problems, either. This epiphany arrived just in time, as I rolled slowly past the Storrow Drive ramp and proceeded straight to South Boston, to the address on Farragut Street where the object of my desire resided. There was a parking space, right in front of her place. That, I thought, was good karma.

I used my key for the very first time, and opened the door to find Shannon standing at her workspace, applying some substance to a piece of antique furniture. A clean canvas drop cloth covered the floor under her. I walked over and examined the furniture. It was a three-step staircase, built for a library, probably. When the middle step was pulled out and lifted, a toilet seat was revealed. She looked up at me like I'd just come back from the corner with milk.

"When are you going to learn about house gifts?"

"Aren't I enough?"

She pondered that without answering, although maybe I heard "Meh."

"That furniture brings new meaning to the term 'stepping in shit,'" I said.

"Not that you needed another example for your resume," she said, smiling as she dabbed at a row of briars circling the rim of the toilet seat. "What's the occasion?"

"There's something I need to tell you," I said, trying to be casual about it.

"Really? What is it?"

"Something I've wanted to tell you for some time." I said, still looking at the commode, examining the wooden seat as she continued to dab away. "Are those thorns you're painting on a toilet seat?"

"Diabolical, isn't it," she said, her eyebrows dancing.

"I'll say. Makes me flinch just looking at it."

She snickered. "Yah, I know. So what's the big news?" She stood, her brush hand tilted back, the other at her waist, like she could have been holding a cocktail glass at Tanglewood, except for the spattered smock and denim capris.

"I have to tell you that I am profoundly and desperately in love with you, and if you don't make love to me right here, right now, I will die." I tried very much to say this as though I was giving a five-day forecast, but I am just not that smooth, so I choked it up a bit. This was a big risk, I realized at that moment, and no sooner had I said it than I feared I might have blundered badly.

She kept her pose, looking like a Nieman Marcus mannequin, except her eyes narrowed, like she was discerning my earnestness and might rate it. Inscrutable. I really thought I might throw up, or perhaps that she would hit me.

Almost imperceptibly, her chin quivered. Then the tremble spread into her lower lip and up to her eyes, and a tremulous whimper escaped from her throat.

"If you don't say something, I'm going to ruin this toilet art of yours."

She tossed her brush on the floor and jumped on me like I was a rope swing at the summer lake, wrapping her legs around my waist, clutching me in a bear hug, burying her face in my neck. And I held her so tight I was afraid I might break her ribs, if she didn't break my back first. At long last, her arms gave out about the same time as my back, and her feet slid to the floor. Her arms came from around my neck, and she grabbed two fistfuls of shirt collar and pull my face close to hers.

"Tell me it's okay," she demanded.

"What's okay?"

"Tell me…" yanking both fists, "it's okay…" tugging again, "to make love to you…" pushing her forehead against mine, "and nobody will die." Her face went back to my neck and her arms around me.

"It's okay. You're safe," I whispered. What else could I say? It was the truth.

She drew her face away from me, hands flat against my chest. "Prove it."

What was a man to do?

If I didn't have such a vivid memory of what lovemaking was about, I might have believed that I'd never had a clue until then. I had the fleeting sense of needing to be cautious, but she quickly cast that to the floor, along with my clothes. She could have been an emergency room nurse, the way she stripped me naked, and without scissors.

Her urgency was frightening and infectious. She didn't have the smock off her shoulders before I fell to my knees and tore at her belt. She rid herself of her smock and tee, took two fistfuls of my hair and pressed my face to her navel. I inhaled her scent with my eyes closed, grasped the waist of her jeans and panties together and looked up at her face for one last look of approval. Her fingers playing with my ears, she beamed a naughty smile and with tears in her eyes whispered a husky "yes," and I pulled them down to the floor in one motion.

As I took in the sight of her full nakedness, my heart welled in my chest and crept into my throat until I couldn't breathe. Even she couldn't have painted an object as beautiful as herself. With my chin on her tummy, I ran my fingers up the backs of her legs and didn't stop until they found the creases of her shoulder blades. She took my face in her hands and with the same beaming smile, she pushed me back and followed, until I lay back on the canvas-covered floor and she hovered over me on her knees. She showed me at once the depth of her tenderness, never once did the smile on her face abate or her eyes leave mine as she brought her face so close to mine that I felt the cilia of her cheek, the warmth of her skin, and then the faint brush of her lips on mine.

She pulled away with a look of mischief. She could see my puzzlement and put a finger to my lips before I could speak. She rose to her feet, and I watched her glide to her supply hutch. She opened the door, reached in, pulled out a plastic bottle, and sauntered back to me with a grin. She slid back down to the floor and laid on her back next to me and she handed me the bottle.

Blue body paint. Edible.

Her smile did not move. Her eyes flashed a look I had not seen in a long time, and she laid her arms at her sides. My task was clear.

I used her belly button as an inkwell first. I dipped one finger and slid it up her tummy line, along her ribs, tracing the soft indentations between each one back and forth until I had reached the bottoms of her breasts. I traced the faded tan lines around them as she watched with amusement and cool murmurs. I refilled the inkwell and dabbed each of her taut nipples and she cooed. I looked at her face as my fingertip circled each one and brushed over them. She watched intently and bit her lower lip, but still her smile persevered. I painted in the outlines so that it appeared she had a bright blue bra, and embroidered it with lip marks.

I had warmed to the task and the well emptied too quickly so I turned up the bottle, intending to squirt a line from her breast plate to her mons, but I squeezed too hard, the cap popped off and as the bottle emptied onto her tummy and dripped over her hips to the canvas, she let out a cackle.

There was only one thing to do. You can't be wasting good body paint. Grinning at her with my blue lips, I smooshed my hand in the puddle and began to spread it over her body with vigor. I painted to her chin, her neck and shoulders, her hips. She wiped her hands in the spill by her sides and slapped them on my back, sending speckles of blue across the canvas. I emptied the rest of the bottle's contents on her tummy, dipped my hand and slipped it down, wide arc around her mons, to her thighs, painting first the tops and then the insides.

This was more than she could take. She pushed me onto my back and rolled over on top of me, intent (apparently) on using her whole body as a paint roller. As she laughed in my messy face and shimmied her breasts against me, she glanced over to her former place and gasped. I followed her eyes to see, on the canvas, a partial imprint of her body—the curved lines of one side of her bottom (which looked curiously like the Yin), her hip and thigh, and a blotch where she had used her elbow and forearm to roll on top of me. A sparkle again ignited in her eyes, she jumped to her feet and skipped to the hutch, revealing on her way the lovely curvature of the line responsible for the imprint (the Yang to her Yin, so to speak), and returned with a bottle in each hand—yellow and red. Like she was channeling Jackson Pollack, she squirted random shots of the two colors on top of the blue-stained canvas.

"Turn over," she commanded. I did, and she gave my back the same treatment. She cast the bottles to the floor and laid back down in the prismatic mess.

"Let's make art."

I was never so compliant in my life.

In what followed, the communication between us was only

what our faces said and our bodies did, the involuntary oohs and ahhs that escape the throats of two lovers in a shared erotic trance, and the greens, purples and oranges that embellished our primary colors. We spontaneously moved together on the canvas as though a divine hand was at work. That glorious moment came upon us with a synchronicity so perfect that I could not tell her shuddering body or soul from my own, and we fused together from head to foot in a technicolor embrace so tight, so full of spiritual release that I feared my heart would burst from my chest.

She might have been on top of me for an hour or ten days—it was not long enough or it was the end of time, I couldn't tell. After eons, she whispered to me, "I think we've made something quite extraordinary."

Of that I was certain.

On her count of three, we scurried off the canvas and raced to the shower. There, we had almost as much fun getting the paint off as we did putting it on. It all started when she soaped me down below and asked, "Mind if I borrow your tool?" All that paint and soap, whipped into a froth made some lovely pastel shades.

Eventually we pulled ourselves out of that euphoric stupor, dried off and dressed, and headed up to the roof deck with a bottle of St. Estephe '85.

It was a sultry night, and a breeze coming off Dorchester Bay rustled through the flourishing wisteria. The canvas umbrella fluttered. We could hear the snap of loose halyards clanging off the aluminum masts all the way from Squantum Point. I opened the wine while she moved the two Adirondacks so they faced seat-to-seat, the armrests touching. I climbed in first, put my legs up on her armrests, then she climbed in and did the same, so we sat facing one another, arms on each others' shins, grinning like fools.

"I'm terribly in love with you." It was the first time she said it, and I'd never heard anything so sweet.

"I'll never forget you saying that."

"I've known for a while."

Her grin faded a moment, and returned stronger. We clinked glasses and toasted. "Thanks for being so patient," she said.

"I have some things of my own going on, you know."

"Uh. Yuh."

"Want to tell me something about your family?"

"You like the timing?"

"I do."

She gazed at me a moment, took a sip, followed it with a deep sigh, and started.

"I told you that my father was an MBTA manager. He was more than that. He was a bagman for Malcolm Fitzgerald, the former Mayor of Boston. He was given the job, they said, because he could be trusted. I and my brother and sister were just kids then, but I know now that they didn't give him the job because they trusted him. They gave it to him because he was too weak to turn it down."

She spoke with her head lying back on her Adirondack, and I could feel her words vibrating through the wood to the back of my own chair.

"I think he was wracked with guilt, being a common crook so he could provide a better life for his family, and it turned him into an angry drunk. My mother tried to control his rages, but she was no match for him.

"My mother was not a strong or brave woman. She was sweet, she had a frail psyche. The worse he got, the worse she did. She withdrew into a shell, and eventually got sick with the cancer."

Shannon delivered all of this with a calm monotone, as though she were reading a bedtime story to a restless child. Her head didn't move, her hands lay still on my legs.

"My father couldn't deal with a sick wife. He was a coward. He abandoned us, left us to deal with her care. That doesn't go over well in a Catholic town. The Fitzgerald machine turned against him, pinned a fare token skimming operation at the Andrew Square station on him. Fitzgerald's people wouldn't even pay for his lawyer. He had some half-wit public defender, they ran circles around him, and he was convicted and sent to Walpole.

"Our state senator, Warren Finnerty, who owed his seat to dad, made sure mom and the three of us were taken care of. Someone—we don't know who—paid the mortgage and the bills and our tuition at St. Katherine's. That's where I was in school when I kill—when mom died.

"I spent sixty days at MacLean Hospital with a nervous breakdown. That's where I started painting, first just for therapy, but I seemed to have a knack for it. Eventually, I went to work at the State House. Finnerty arranged for Brian to get dad's old job at the MBTA. Stacey had graduated from Bridge-water State and went into the FBI trainee program. I kept painting, and worked at the State House while I studied at Mass College of Art.

"My dad had a heart attack and died in prison nine years ago. Between Mom and Dad's death, Brian came unglued, got into drugs and stuff. He's been through a few detox programs. Finnerty made sure his job at the T was safe, and the guys there pretty much look after him, but he's a walking time bomb, and he doesn't want to listen to me or Stacey or anyone else.

"I completed my Masters in Fine Arts while I was still on the State House payroll. That's when I sold those first few paintings. One day I read an article in Esquire about how much money rich people pay for one-of-a-kind things, and I had this idea to paint tromp l'oeil on furniture. I sold my first waterfall-drenched rocking chair for $17,000 to a couple named Von Duyken from Philadelphia. I did a few more pieces and had a lot of cash, and an accountant friend told me I better buy some real estate fast so I had some deductions. So I bought this love nest which we have just defiled," smiling at me like I'd rescued her. She had it the wrong way.

"Thank you," I whispered.

"Thank you for loving me," she whispered back.

I had a million questions, most of which could wait. But there was one I wanted to ask right then.

"Were you in the State House during 1980s when I was there?"

"Yes, I worked for Senator Bovanelli."

I thought about that for a minute.

"It's a good thing I didn't meet you then."

"Why?" she asked.

"Because I'd have turned you into a home wrecker," I said.

She called me a jackass (again), punched me hard on the thigh.

"You know, I'm going to require a lot more sex to get me through my trial."

"Well, then, I think we're off to a good start. How's it looking?"

"Tough," I said.

"More lobbyists lined up behind Mr. Stackhouse?" What a sport.

"Doesn't this worry you?" I asked.

"Of course it worries me. I've just made passionate love to the first adult man I've ever been crazy about. I don't want to lose you. But you're worth taking a chance. I figured when I heard about your exploits with Stackhouse he wasn't the only one."

"Not by a long shot."

I looked out over the harbor and watched a plane coming in over Spectacle Island. She was looking at me hard, with a little smile on her face.

"You can handle this, Paul," she said.

"Can you?" I asked.

She smirked. "Dude, my father died in prison and I let my mother die while I was giving head. I think I can handhold a golf nut. We'll do fine, you and me." And she gave me her grin, patted her tummy and cooed, "I'm all buzzing inside."

I had to laugh. What a lucky bastard I turned out to be, having this woman crawl into my soul before I faced the crucible of my life.

Chapter 18
Battle Plans and Evidence

In the morning, I felt like a million bucks, which was quite an accomplishment for a man in my circumstances.

I left Shannon in bed, spiffed up, checked in at the T for one of my waning days and walked over to Post Office Square for a little skull session with Al. It was time for me to tell him about Bernie's wife.

I went through security in the lobby of One Post Office Square, showing my picture ID as General Counsel of the MBTA. The security guard scowled and waved me through. I rode the elevator to the twenty-sixth floor and popped my ears. The elevator door opened to an oak-floored hallway with a twenty foot Persian runner that led to glass doors emblazoned with the fir-m name, which I will not mention, because they do quite enough self-promotion on their own and I've paid for plenty of it.

The reception area resembled parts of the Gardner Museum. A receptionist sat at a desk that might have been stolen from Louis XVI. She asked my name and invited me to sit on one of the pieces of furniture, which I was always afraid to do. So I stood around and examined the artwork on the walls. I wasn't much of a critic, I admit, but Shannon's stuff beat the hell out of the skid marks on one canvas (if it was indeed canvas). There must be some sort of committee choosing this stuff—that's how big law firms create the illusion of democracy. Anyway, it was pretty obvious why they had to charge $750 an hour.

The receptionist whispered into her phone. Al came out rather quickly and led me to a small conference room that had a breathtaking view of the financial district, Charlestown and Boston Harbor. This is no surprise, because the view from the 26th floor of any building is bound to be impressive. Al had a small file with him that he opened and scanned. There were some sheets of legal pad paper with hen scratching on them and a couple of faxed letters of some sort. He didn't waste any time getting down to business.

"How are you doing," he asked me. What kind of question was that?

"Al, I'm doing great. Believe it or not, I'm doing great. I am ready to start the trial today, if I must, I'm ready. Bring it on, I say."

Al chuckled. I didn't convince him I was on the level. But he didn't know about Shannon. His smile was a little forced, and it quickly melted as his eyes dropped to the pages of hen scratching in front of him.

"Here's the deal," he said, and I settled in to listen to everything, including his freaking breathing pattern. You can tell a lot from those. "He's got twenty-seven lobbyists that admit to having provided you meals, golf or both, here in Massachusetts and in various resort golf destinations in the Northwest hemisphere. I don't know all of the destinations, but I think you might have an idea."

"I certainly do," I said.

"He's spent a lot of effort looking into this golf thing," Al said. "You are the only Republican that shows up more than once or twice." He said it with a perplexity that was foreign to him. "It's inconceivable to me that so many lobbyists would spend so much attention and money on an insignificant member of a very small minority party."

That was my lawyer. A brilliant legal mind, perplexed about something as subtle as the irresistible lure of golf. But I let him go on.

Kilroy had become the zealous standard-bearer for this idea of federalizing the violation of state misdemeanors that related to corruption, and he stood on shaky Constitutional ground. It was one thing to tie the use of the mails to an attempt to induce a public official to do something, or reward him for doing something. But a gray area existed, where there was no evidence of quid pro quo, in a situation where the donor might not have a specific action in mind, but was simply using the gift as a means to develop a sense of camaraderie. A more extravagant way to buy a round, so to speak. The Constitutional weakness was in the vexingly vague language of the federal mail fraud statute that referred to "depriving the citizens of the honest services" of their elected representatives. How do you know what that means? And how do you prove the intent not to be honest?

"The proof of a crime has always required evidence of intent," I said. "The state statute says that the official has to commit an act, it says 'on account of an official act.' If nobody can show an act—other than this stupid Pierce amendment thing—how can there be a crime?"

"The Ethics Commission interprets the word 'act' to mean 'position.' But for your position, you would not have received the gift."

"Well, bully for them, Al, but 'act' means 'act' and 'position' means 'position.' I remember my law of statutory construction pretty well."

"Correct," Al said, "the argument is that a official's conduct—or act—can be inferred simply because of the donor's position, the recipient's position, and the interests that the donor is advancing."

"That seems to make reasonable doubt a pretty high hurdle," I said.

"It does," said Al. "But I think he sees you as an ironic prop for his platform."

"His platform?"

"Yes, his campaign for attorney general is built on anti-corruption."

"So I am a campaign prop."

"In a way, yes." Al said. "He gets to make lobbyist influence an issue without alienating any of the Democrats in the legislature. It's all a big joke to them, at your expense."

I supposed that Al's explanation was the best a rational person could make out of the facts. But I still didn't believe it. We were missing something.

Except for Stuart Pierce and his amendment!

"The one thing that distinguishes you from the others is the sheer number. I mean, forgive me for saying so, but Jesus Christ, it looks like you played with everyone but the Pope."

"I don't believe the Pope plays golf."

"You do have the House Pastor on here."

"He's Episcopalian. Not a bad golfer, Father Tom. He cheats, though."

"You've got to consider the tax evasion problem there," Al said.

I had been thinking about that too. So the Justice Department would take the position that every time someone gets bought a meal and doesn't report the value of it as income, he's committed tax evasion? Every time a vendor pays for a round of golf for his customer, the customer has a tax problem? I'd had more than a few of them down to Hyannisport—reciprocal hospitality, it's called. Let them try to argue the comparative value of Hyannisport versus Pebble Beach. I'll bring goddamn videos with me. This was bullshit.

"Are we certain we've got them all?" Al asked.

I had provided him with at least thirty pages of handwritten notes—a memory dump of every occasion I could remember where I'd been treated to anything more than a cup of coffee. I thought I'd gotten them all, but there were so many. We identified the pool of witnesses, but we couldn't be certain we'd gotten them all. We were pretty sure who'd testified to the grand jury, and Al was in the process of contacting their lawyers to discover what had transpired.

"Aren't I entitled to the transcripts of the grand jury proceeding once I'm indicted?"

"Not in the federal system. You only get the transcripts of witnesses the government intends to call at trial, and we don't discover that until the time for filing the joint pre-trial memorandum."

"So we won't know who's testifying against me until just before the trial?"

"If that."

The idea that a federal prosecutor running for Attorney General would single out a guy like me, when he had a couple dozen members if his own party he could pick on—all of whom must have actually done something significant for their benefactors—was frustrating.

"This Kilroy seems like a bad, bad character."

Al sat back in his chair, frowning. "He's a very intense man. I spent a lot of time in law school with Bernard. We drank frequently—and frequently too much—at the bars in New Haven. When he got drunk, he'd make prank phone calls. Not funny, but cruel."

"What?"

"He'd call old girlfriends or rivals from undergraduate class, tell them a parent had died or their house had blown up. Sick stuff. Sometimes he'd go on a tear about his father. One moment he'd be telling me how powerful he was, and the next he'd be calling him a son of a bitch. My guess is he had trouble measuring up, at least in his own mind."

"It's tough having a father that's larger than life, but the guy sounds unglued." He obviously hadn't lost the knack, but it seemed incomprehensible to me that it would have been *him* making the phone calls to me.

"Seamus Kilroy ran one of the largest private investment firms in the country."

"Seamus? His first name was Seamus?"

"He emigrated from County Armagh, in Northern Ireland."

"Ah. Black Irish. Makes sense. So what was the fall from grace about?"

"He was in line to become Chairman of the SEC, but on the eve of confirmation the President withdrew his nomination. I never heard the details, but I understand after his embarrassment, his firm nudged him aside and eventually forced him out."

"No idea what caused the President to cut him loose?"

"Only rumors."

"'Only rumors.' Listen to you. This is politics, Al. Rumor is the coin of the realm."

Al chuckled. "Yes, of course. What was I thinking?"

"Let me guess," I said. Elder Kilroy's story had a familiar ring to it, if only because it had been repeated so often before him. "He had one formidable political adversary who must have had something on him. Something shaky, or close to the line, but not necessarily criminal. His partners at the investment bank told him they didn't want a bruising confirmation fight. It would 'reflect badly on the firm,' or some bullshit like that."

Al raised his eyebrows. "Very astute, Paul. But the rumors were a little worse than that."

It was my turn to raise eyebrows.

"The chief rumor was that the Senate had trouble acting on the confirmation of a man being investigated by the agency he was nominated to head."

"Well, that would be awkward." Something didn't sound right. "Wait. How could the President put a guy like that forward?"

"There's only one likely possibility, as I see it."

"They thought they had vetted the issue, but they didn't get accurate information?"

Al nodded. "They went ahead thinking that once he became the lead candidate, whoever ran the investigation would get pressure from the top to scuttle it."

I shook my head. "That's a ballsy play, Al. And if the President was aware of it, then I can't see them risking it politically unless they were confident they could quash the investigation."

More nodding from Al. "The guy in charge didn't care about his civil service career. He was incorruptible."

"He had huge balls, you mean."

"Another way of saying it, yes."

"And he had a white knight with some serious juice in the Senate."

"Perhaps that's something to look into."

"Okay. Look, you're costing me a fortune, we're done."

Al walked me to the door. In the reception area, I nodded at the walls. "Tell the head of the art committee I have a local artist he should look into. We can take it off my bill."

I realized in the elevator that if that comment ever got back to Shannon, she'd put a knot on my shoulder.

A still August dawn began to light the bedroom with a rosy glow. I lay in bed and watched Shannon sleep. Her face was serene and smooth, her small mouth slightly ajar, and the terrifying thought occurred to me that she might have died of happiness in her sleep. I could hear a soft breath that reassured me that she was still alive. Good thing, because nothing that beautiful should ever be harmed.

I slipped out of the bed, slid on my jeans and tiptoed out of her room, padded down the stairs and out to the front steps to retrieve the paper. Just below the masthead, front page above the fold:

STACKHOUSE SENTENCING DELAYED

BOSTON – The scheduled sentencing of former lobbyist Raymond Stackhouse was postponed yesterday, as courthouse watchers speculate that U.S. Attorney Bernard Kilroy wants to keep Stackhouse on the hook until after his testimony against former Representative Paul Forté.

Forté, a minority party backbencher from Cape Cod, faces trial next month on dozens of similar charges.

Political wags continue to speculate on what's behind the Justice Department's interest in a legislator who had little to offer Stackhouse, or anyone else, besides his membership at the exclusive Hyannisport Club, which has been home to the Kennedy and Shriver clans since John F. Kennedy played golf there as a young man....

I read this far and realized I was standing outside on the front stoop of a South Boston condo building. It was a long way from Ocean Avenue in Cotuit. I brought the paper to Shannon's kitchen, so she could see it first thing. She'd get a kick out of it.

One thing about stupid people is they have no power of discernment. They see in black and white; they couldn't spell nuance or ambiguity much less define them.

It was obvious when I returned to work this morning that the Governor had spoke to Liguotomo, who had spoken to Fetore and Cruddy. They knew I'd be leaving soon, and the reason was apparent. I might have thought they were waiting for me when I walked into Starbucks that morning.

"Hello For-tay," the big one said, swaggering. "Looks like you guessed wrong."

"What on earth are you talking about, Lou?"

Dim Lou couldn't help himself. "What you said about the first one to be convicted of a crime." He wobbled his head while he spoke, and Cruddy smirked and nodded at his shimmying side.

Hatred sometimes blinds one's judgment. "Are you so sure your conscience is clear, Lou?"

Fetore hesitated, his face blank, and he stole a quick glance at Cruddy, who was equally at sea. "You accusing us of something?" asked Cruddy.

I looked at Cruddy. "Did you know your name rhymes with putty?"

They both reacted like I was speaking Swahili. I might as well have been.

An hour later while sipping an oversugared iced coffee, I got a call from Chester Adkinson, one of our outside counsel in the environmental litigation area. Chester was handling the biggest liability case we had—one that was extremely sensitive politically as well. One of the MBTA's old trolley yards had been transferred to another independent authority, sight unseen, with an indemnification clause that no lawyer in his right mind would have allowed. We promise to hold you harmless, in perpetuity, for whatever, wherever, whenever, blah blah blah. It was too stupid for even a law school exam. Anyway, they discovered forty-nine years later that the property had been used as a subway car graveyard. Twenty-seven orange line subway cars, broken into pieces and buried, along with their asbestos, arsenic, volatile organic compounds and what have you.

This other authority had anticipated at the time using the property for aboveground storage of equipment—a staging area for some nearby construction of a new office building. Plans changed, and they decided to put the office building on this parcel, and when they did the subsurface exploration, the stupidest lawyer in public service could "spot the issue," as they teach you in first year law school.

So, Chester wanted to give me an update, which was fine, but then he hemmed and asked me, "Do you have some sort of liability consultant on retainer?"

"Why do you ask, Chester?"

"Well, if you do, you ought to consider someone with more of a sense of reality."

"Why do you say that," I asked.

"Because the guy you're using is estimating the extent of liability exposure at $200 million, and that would cause a serious problem if it ever were to get out to opposing counsel that we valued the case so extravagantly."

"What is the worst problem we would face if this were to get out?" I asked him.

"Well," he said, "the environmental liability insurance market is pretty much of a frontier. There's a lot of money to be made, and not a lot of expertise in assessing the genuineness of the risk. If a number like this gets out, you'll have a problem getting coverage anywhere in the world. It's such a huge number for one piece of liability, it would pretty much exhaust the entire capacity for the available coverage—even with Lloyds of London and the other surplus lines carriers."

I pondered that for a minute. "You mean, the MBTA might face the liability bare?"

Chester was silent, then, "could be."

I asked Chester who had contacted him, got the information and shooed him off the phone. I then called Rex—or H. Ross Perot did—and told him I was coming right over to visit.

I was at the back stairs, pounding on the door again ten minutes later, and Rachel answered as usual, but she was more demure than before. So was I, to be honest, now that Shannon had evicted everything but the memory of my deceased parents from my capacious heart. But Rache was perfectly sweet and in a minute, Rex and I were in conference.

Nothing I reported from Chester surprised Rex. Just pieces of a puzzle. He told me he'd add a bedroom for me at his new house in Maui. Of course that would be illegal, and I told him so. Just a futon would do, in the pool cabana.

"How much?" I asked.

"Ask one of your insurance buddies to figure the annual commissions on a billion dollars."

I didn't need to ask my buddies. When you talk about a billion dollars, that's when smart people started calling their commissions "basis points" instead of tenths of percentages. Everybody gets rich on a billion dollars worth of insurance coverage—if it can be had.

A billion dollars. And Chester thought $200 million would strain the excess market.

"When will you be ready?" I asked him.

"A couple weeks, I think."

I raised my glass, clinked with him and said, "Here's to greed and stupidity."

"To greed and stupidity," Rex said.

The Board of Directors accepted my resignation and the terms of my severance, both of which had been contained in a terse letter I had hand-delivered to the Chairman's office the week before. There were no speeches or fond farewells. They were well rid of me, they surely thought, and the feeling was mutual.

Before I left the building with my pictures, I stopped into Halsey's office and mentioned, as casually as I could, that he might want to check into the cost of environmental insurance on the construction projects. He showed a bit of interest until I confirmed that the insurance cost was a federal expense. Then he just shrugged and wished me luck. I swore to myself that one day there'd be a revolution of the masses.

Coincidentally, this same day, the Intercontinental Insurance Consortium of Bermuda wired $11 million in insurance commissions to Specialty Risk Agency of Baltimore, Maryland, which then wired $3.67 million to Epsilon Environmental

Consultants of Flagstaff, Arizona. The receipt was confirmed at the Epsilon end by one Hilda Griswold, a plain but efficient middle-aged lady who had been Epsilon's office manager for about ten months.

Rex told me this during my retirement dinner that night.

"How the hell do you get a hold of this information?"

"Hilda's on my payroll too, you idiot."

Chapter 19
Kitchen Prep, Full Disclosure and a Road Trip

I didn't feeling like rolling the dice on the parking in Southie, so I left my Saab on the street in front of my place and jumped in a cab.

"322 Farragut, Southie," I told the swarthy foreigner behind the wheel, "with a stop at Shawmut and Milford on the way."

Massoud—his hack ID said—stopped in front of South End Formaggio, and I ran in for a few essentials. A hefty block of Parmagiana Reggiano, four golden delicious apples, a bottle of Louis Roederer, two packs of Reds. And a scratch ticket, just to see if my luck might change.

After several minutes of Massoud's one-handed, death-defying, molar-jarring driving, I guessed it hadn't changed yet. I got out of the back of the rattletrap cab and gave him his fare and a buck tip. He looked at it contemptuously and muttered something in Pashtun.

"Massoud, my friend, if you wish to receive a larger tip, you must stay off of your cell phone, try to learn English, and stop driving like a maniac. And get rid of that putrid cologne." He sped away without reply.

I climbed the stairs, used my key and, miraculously, saw all the luck I needed. Shannon stood at the prep table in the kitchen, emptying her own bag of goodies more wholesome than my stash of cheese, booze and butts. Fresh linguine, vine ripe tomatoes, olives and a half-duck, already roasted.

I dropped my bag on the table and gave her a big hug. She didn't often wear a skirt, but this one I noticed (actually, it was the legs that attracted my eyes), so I did what any loving man would do. I goosed her.

"Let's celebrate my upcoming criminal trial."

"You have a dark, dark humor that sometimes worries me."

I shrugged. "Ahhhh, what's the point of fretting. The most I'd get is seven to ten, and some of these federal facilities have golf courses."

"If you don't end up at Hanscom I won't come visit you."

"Okay then, better beat the rap."

"That's the spirit," she said, patting me on the back. "Champagne, I see."

"Yes'm," I said, "with Reggiano and golden apples. Make a nice appetizer to the pasta, don't you agree?"

"Let's find out right now. I'm starved."

Shannon's place had become a refuge from sadness or worry. Maybe it had lead walls that repelled bad karma. Maybe it just had Shannon. I cut up apples and cheese and poured champagne. We clinked, sipped and nibbled while I told her about Epsilon Environmental and the MBTA.

"Rex hired this lady, Hilda Griswold, a forensic accountant out of Scottsdale. She worked in the Treasury Department with him fifteen years ago. She used to examine international money transfers to track down drug dealers and IRA gunrunners. Now she specializes on 'inside jobs.' She got herself hired as the office manager at Epsilon, and gained this Erichetti guy's trust. Now she knows everything the guy's up to."

"So what's it all about?"

"He's found an opportunity to make a lot of money in an area of insurance that very few people understand. The laws on liability for environmental contamination are draconian; big organizations like the MBTA have a lot of potentially contaminated property. They're looking for affordable ways to hedge their bets. When you own miles and miles of rail beds where dirty trains had been running since the industrial revolution, those are big bets. Vince's outfit has contrived a way to overestimate the risks, price the coverage and package the program through offshore insurance companies in Bermuda, England and Israel. He set up these 'environmental consulting' entities that put together legitimate-looking reports that wildly overestimated the potential clean-up costs."

"For instance?"

"Take Boston. There's an old rail car dump over in Chelsea the T sold to the MWRA years ago. Epsilon estimated the liability exposure for that site at $200 million, based upon the depth of the dump, the number of cars that might be there, the site's proximity to a public water supply, and the chemicals that might typically have been included in the cars. Asbestos. Toluene. Arsenic. Lead. Mercury. Scary stuff."

"Holy Christ," she said.

"No foolin'. So then Vince negotiates the price for all that coverage with a consortium of insurers, the T pays the premium, and Vince gets an obscene commission."

"What a great scam. You sure he's not from Savin Hill?"

"It gets better. Since Vince knows the insurers are writing more coverage than necessary, he incorporated his own reinsurance company in the Cayman Islands. With that, he creates a second layer of reinsurance to enable the real insurers to offload some of the 'excess risk.' The consortium then pays Erichetti to take on risk that doesn't exist. He gets paid to insure a phantom risk."

"How'd he get into the T?"

"I think the Chairman and his henchmen are involved in the scam."

"Really. How come?"

I poured Shannon some champagne. "I saw the consulting agreement."

"Really." Mouth ajar.

"They've been doing this with all the major transit systems."

"Really."

"Here's the worst part. The insurance cost is covered with federal transportation money."

Shannon's jaw dropped. "They're getting paid with taxpayers' money?"

"Lots and lots of it."

"How much?"

"Rex is guessing around twenty-two million."

"Mother of God! Our tax money?"

"Yup."

"So what's the connection with your case?"

"Vince Erichetti's sister is Kilroy's wife."

"What?"

"And she's in the environmental insurance business."

"Get out of town!"

"On the next train, baby."

She narrowed her eyes. "Is Kilroy involved?"

"We don't know yet."

"What's Rex gonna do with the information?"

"He wants to trade the feds for my prosecution."

"Will that affect his whistleblower reward?"

"Quite possibly, which is why I discouraged him."

Shannon gave me a look as contemptuous as any I had seen on her strikingly beautiful face. "Don't be an idiot."

"What?"

"The guy may have the keys to your freedom in his hand. Make sure he uses them."

"I guess it's up to him, isn't it?"

Shannon leaned against the counter holding her champagne flute and scrutinizing me.

"What?"

"Who are you and what have you done with my lover?"

"What?" I pleaded.

"You sound like you're fighting for a cause beyond merely keeping your ass out of prison."

"Is there nothing worth fighting for here? My honor, my reputation, perhaps?"

"No, not in this particular case."

"Not at all? You think I should be okay with being forever tagged as a dirty ex-pol who slipped out of the noose by ratting out his client?"

"You'll be tagged that way by certain people no matter how this comes out. All I'm saying is that you're better off never going to trial than you are taking a chance on a Boston jury who's just as liable to see you as a spoiled white lawyer who flaunted the law and abused his position."

I was pretty steamed and ready to argue. I guess she saw that on my face, because she set her flute down and came over to me, hooked her fingers into my belt loops and yanked my hips into hers with a hard thump. I tried to resist, but she lowered her eyelids to half-mast, and looked up at me with her sleepy, sexy leer.

"Have I told you how horny champagne makes me?"

"No."

"Do you know how sexy you look in that suit?"

"No."

She stepped away a few feet and looked at me from head to toe. She stopped at my waist, and noticed the effect of her little seduction. Her leer was joined by a dirty grin as she stepped up and ran her hand over the growing bulge, and whispered in my ear, "Let's be careful you don't stain the material."

At that instant, I began to wonder if it was fair that woman-kind had at their disposal such an efficient and ruthless means of ending an argument to their advantage. My effort to weigh the equities in this were soon overrun by the notion of just how ridiculous a man looks with his suit pants and boxers around his ankles and his full-masted erection poking out from under his pinpoint oxford dress shirt.

But Shannon is a resourceful woman, and she distracted me further with a deft raising of skirt and removal of underwear, and we used the prep table for a wholly unintended function which I suspect debilitated the structural soundness of its legs.

After such an experience, it is impossible to eat pasta and duck naked without giggling like a fool, and there is always the sense that the taste is just a little different.

By the time we'd managed to clean up each other and the kitchen, a thunderstorm ruined any plan to use the roof deck, so Shannon showed me a surprise. She walked to an over-stuffed futon mattress, rolled in a tube against the vast window facing the Harbor. She pulled three cloth stays and the futon rolled out into a queen-sized mattress on the floor.

She tossed several throw pillows onto the futon, hit the dimmer switch to a faint glow and instructed me to get wine and an ashtray from the kitchen. When I returned with both, I discovered that she'd slipped out of her robe and laid naked on the futon, ankles crossed, looking out the window at the night sky.

"That picture would make a great album cover."

"Join me."

I shrugged. What's to argue? I dropped my boxers and joined her.

"I discovered one day while painting naked that not having window shades is a gas when you are absolutely certain no one can see in—but there is this insidious thrill I get from the thought that I might be wrong."

"Imagine the delight of all those airplane passengers."

We settled in, just lying back, watching the planes take off and land, alternating flicks of ash into the tray between us.

"So what're you going to do?"

"About what?"

"You don't have a job, you have an expensive lawyer to pay, and defending yourself is a full-time occupation, right?"

"Yup. I have a good six-month cushion."

"I have an idea."

"I'm listening."

"Why don't you move in here with me and rent out the furnished condo?"

I rolled onto my side, facing her. "Are you serious?"

"Why not? You could get at least two grand a month for it, you're here enough as it is, and I travel enough that I won't get sick of you hanging around."

"You think so?"

"Pretty certain of it. I've been thinking about it since our painting party."

"Really?"

"Yeah, I'm certain enough about it that I decided to screw you first and then tell you."

"That why you had a skirt on?"

"Yep."

"You are diabolical."

She stubbed out her butt and moved the ashtray to the side.

"I have something else for you to do." She took my hand, placed it below her tummy and languidly opened her legs.

"Speaking of which, what happened to our canvas?"

"It's at the framer. Please get busy."

Soon the loft echoed again with the sounds of lust.

An office tower is a lonely place on Sunday morning. Even the new associate lawyers eager to earn their embarrassingly high salaries weren't in evidence as I wandered from the elevator through the glass door and back to Al's office. I found him reading the Sunday New York Times, his desk littered with legal pads.

"Did I tell you I'm dating the sister of an FBI agent? Shannon McGonigle is her name. Her sister's name is Stacey. Know her?"

"McGonigle, did you say?" He laid the paper aside.

"Yup."

"I don't believe so. A fellow by that name who worked for Mayor Fitzgerald went to the can for stealing subway tokens."

"Her father."

"I'll be damned. Framed, wasn't he?"

"Quite a knowledge of local political history, Al."

"Who could forget that? Such a tragedy." Al stared at the table for a moment, like he was thinking if he should continue. "How's this lady hold up under pressure?"

"Like a brick, Al. She's got some scars, but she's a goddamn brick."

"Huh. Amazing." More thinking. "Her sister inclined to help her?"

"They don't talk."

"Why not?"

"Dunno," I lied. "Haven't asked."

"Maybe you should. Let's not leave any stone unturned here."

"Speaking of stones, I need to tell you about something."

I hadn't yet mentioned anything to Al about Rex's adventures, because I wasn't eager to let him know about the one-pager I'd slipped to him. So I told him about Epsilon's environmental insurance fraud scheme. Al listened, but with some impatience.

"Why is this relevant?"

"Because Rex is thinking it might come in handy for bargaining."

"Trade you for the Epsilon people."

"The small fish for the big fish."

He raised his eyebrows and frowned in thought. "Environmental insurance..." He stared out the window.

"What're you thinking?"

"Kilroy wrote a law review article during our Yale Law Journal days about liability for environmental contamination. Around the time Congress wrote the Superfund law."

"Is that right? Well, then, the next thing I tell you should be really intriguing."

"What's that?"

"The head of Epsilon is a man named Erichetti. His sister is Kilroy's wife."

"Any connection with her?"

"She's a specialist in the environmental insurance surplus lines market."

"You don't say. Quite a coincidence."

"I don't think it's a coincidence, Al."

Al made a note on his pad, put the butt end of the pen to his lips and looked at me blankly.

"I wonder how he stumbled across this Arizona outfit, Paul," a hint of suspicion in his voice. "They wouldn't happen to have the MBTA as a client, would they?"

"They might, yeah."

"And was this relationship the foundation of your friend's investigation?"

"Might have been."

"Do you realize what you've done?" he asked, as stern as my own father.

"I violated no privilege. The document was a contract between the authority and another party. It was subject to public disclosure."

"That doesn't mean it wasn't confidential. Did that document initiate your friend's investigation?"

"Do I have an obligation to tip off a client that someone's looking at his business activity?"

"Answer my question."

"Doesn't that make me an accessory if he turns out to have been crooked? Besides, I remained willfully ignorant of everything he did until after I had resigned from the MBTA."

"Answer my question."

"Yes."

He sat like a stone for seconds. "Do you have any personal interest whatsoever in your friend's activity?"

"You mean financial? No."

"Other than financial?"

"Like what? Do I feel a personal antipathy toward my client and his minions? Wow, Al, you'd have a hard time governing the attorney-client relationship if you had to disqualify a client because he's a scumbag."

Al shook his head, disgusted. "Why didn't you tell me about this before?"

"Tell you about what?"

"Cut the crap, Paul. In the course of your representation, you saw something fishy. Rather than go to your client and say 'this looks fishy, you must stop it,' you gave the fishy document to a private investigator and played Mickey the Dunce."

"Look Al, I'm not going to fight with you about this. Frankly, if this leads to a choice between being disbarred and being convicted, I'll find a different profession. Besides, if a couple of rogues are involved in a scheme to rip off the Authority that I am supposed to protect, my helping someone else bust them is something I can sleep with. Now the question is, can my pal Rex use his information to help me out or can't he?"

"Well, I'll tell you right now. I will have nothing to do with the use of that information to bargain your own case. You'll have to find someone else to handle that."

I looked at Al with eyebrows raised. "I'm sorry Al, have I offended your sensibilities? Defense of white collar felony crime is appropriate but a lawyer ethics issue is too sketchy for you?"

Al sat back in his chair and took an audible breath. "I will need to have our people do some legal research before we decide how to proceed."

"It sounds to me as though your primary concern is the exposure of your law firm to involvement in the use of unethically obtained confidential information. Does that pretty much describe the problem?"

He shifted in his chair. "Well, yes, I think that's a significant part of my concern."

"Fine, you've got a new client business committee, you don't want to have an internal political problem. So if you want to continue representing me on this case, you can have as many people research the issue as you want. But since it's for your own ass-protecting benefit, you won't be charging me for it."

Al had picked up his pen and doodled on his pad without looking at me. "While we're on the subject…"

"How much?"

He glanced up and back to his pad. "A hundred thousand, cash retainer."

I wouldn't have guessed a penny less, and came prepared. I pulled the mutual fund checkbook out of my back pocket and wrote a check for $50,000. "I'll have the other fifty thousand when you tell me I won't have to hire a second firm to handle the hard work. Otherwise, you can give me the check back and we'll part company."

I extended my hand with the check in it, but Al sat there, looking at it. So I flicked it onto the table and it slid across the mahogany and hit his pad. He sat motionless for way too long.

"Al, what's the problem? My money not as good as a drug dealer's?"

"Listen to me, Paul," jabbing his pen in my direction. "You have precious little righteousness to expend questioning my business judgment or the internal decisions of this law firm. Frankly, I don't care if you've got the ethics of a mobster—some of whom I've represented, by the way—so you won't make any hay wagging your finger at me. My problem with your case is the source of the information you want to use, and whether or not there is any exposure to this law firm if we participate in its use."

I couldn't begrudge him that. "Well, you look into that, and I'll give some thought to taking that piece of the puzzle to someone else."

I got up to leave.

"Paul, I understand that you could be confused that a public document is still subject to the attorney-client privilege. By itself, the idea is counter-intuitive. I will look into whether there is a way for this information to be discovered independently, but I am concerned about the fact that at its inception, it was learned in confidence."

"While you're looking into it, see if the privilege would extend to others."

"Erichetti and Kilroy's wife."

"Yes, them. And remember that Rex is formerly military intelligence. He has contacts you don't want to know about."

Al sat back and fixed his eyes on me, hands folded to his mouth. He hesitated, then spoke, choosing his words carefully. "You're speaking about an area that is outside both my expertise and my comfort zone. I fully realize there are many ways to achieve your objective that are outside the legal arena. Perhaps what would be best is if you rely on me strictly for preparation of a defense to your case, and you can pursue independently whatever other means you find prudent. How does that sound?"

I smiled at Al's taut face. "Let me think about that, and discuss it with Rex. We'll talk again the beginning of next week."

"And you'll bring the other fifty thousand then?"

"Yes, Al. I'll bring the other fifty thousand."

"Enjoy the rest of the weekend."

Easy for him to say.

• • •

I walked out of Al's office building into Post Office Square at a little after noon. I was pretty furious, but I didn't quite know at what. Could I have been wrong? How could any public document be confidential information? If it were so, then would it matter at all that I was no longer employed at the T? The attorney-client confidence follows me after employment. And besides, who was the bad guy here? I was looking into Fetore and Cruddy, not any member of the Board. Was I looking into anything? What the hell was my motivation? Was I protecting the Chairman and the Board members from two rogues? Or was I just engaged in a spiteful exercise to cut the balls off of two guys who I knew were the pit bulls for my primary client?

Oh hell, I don't know what I was looking at or why.

I called Rex's cell phone.

"Hello."

"Rex."

"Where are you?"

"Post Office Square. Where are you?"

"Martha's Vineyard."

"Sounds delightful. We need to talk."

"Come on down. I'll be here until Tuesday."

"You alone?"

"No, Amelia's here too."

"I don't want to intrude."

"Intrude on what? We've been married thirty-one years. Bring your new lady friend. We'll get acquainted."

"What's the address again?"

"Sixty-seven Marsh Road, in Menemsha."

"Okay, I'll call you from Woods Hole when I know what boat I'm on."

"Better get the 6:20. And get me a mixed case of red wine

and a leg of lamb on the mainland before you leave. Prices here are stupid."

"Where the hell am I going to find a leg of lamb on a Sunday?"

"Use your faculties. Four pounds, minimum."

"You've lived in Boston your whole life and you've never been to Martha's Vineyard?"

Shannon responded defensively. "Don't you have to take a boat to get there?"

"Well, it is possible to fly."

She blanched. "I don't much like flying."

"Got a problem with boats?"

She pouted. "Sort of."

I gave her a pep talk. Our first road trip, new friends, get to meet Rex. Cool place on a tidal pond, just two couples, all romantic and everything. I did a good job, even got out the atlas and showed her where the house was.

She eyed me, stern-faced and wrinkle-browed, thinking, and suddenly she brightened.

"Road trip!" she sang.

I discovered that Kennealey's was open till 5:00, and picked up a four-pound leg of lamb, a mixed case of red wines and a carton of Marlboros. I sped back, threw some stuff in a bag and chased Shannon up the spiral stairs to her boudoir and made sure she had plenty of fresh undies in her overnight bag. We were out of there and on the road to Woods Hole in time to catch the 6:20 to Vineyard Haven on the Uncateena ferry.

The big old stinkpot blew its horn and backed off the Woods Hole dock. Our car sat in the ship's bowels and I had successfully coaxed Shannon out of the car and above-decks. Before the ferry cleared the tip of Naushon Island, she was in a deck chair, wrapped in a wool blanket with a ten-ounce cup of Shiraz, and we laid back and watched the village of Woods Hole recede in the long shadows of the late summer day.

That serene view, my predicament, and our current position brought a welling of tears to my eyes, and I sought out Shannon's hand under the blanket. She looked over and guffawed.

"What?"

"You are such a sap," she said.

I couldn't help but smile, too. "Yes," I said. "Aren't you lucky."

"Yes, I am."

I led Shannon to the bow rail as the ferry pulled in to the Vineyard Haven dock. The village's narrow sidewalks bustled with tourists and the streets buzzed with rusty Jeeps and pick-up trucks. I led her back down into the bowels of the boat where the vehicles were packed like sardines. We squeezed into my car and followed the traffic and trucks off the boat and into the streets. A few turns led us out of the town center along North Road toward Menemsha. Twenty minutes later, I turned the car off the pavement and we bumped and rattled down a one-lane dirt road, overgrown Rosa Rugosa brushing both sides of my shitbox Saab. The road turned downhill, revealing the brilliant sun's reflected twin shimmering off of Menemsha Pond.

Shannon ooooh'ed. "That's beautiful."

It was indeed. Almost at the bottom of the hill, I turned sharply into a dirt driveway and gunned the car up a short incline to the side of Rex's island home. The house sat on the side of an open hillside, its enormous deck facing Menemsha Pond. The short staircase to the deck ended by Shannon's door.

I got out of the car into the chilly air.

"What the fuck is that smell," my dainty woman asked.

"Steamers, right out of the mud flats of the pond below."

She looked skeptical.

I led Shannon up the steps onto the deck. Set into the floor at the near corner was a large stone pit filled with a roaring fire. Atop the stone pit, a cast iron grill held a large horse trough filled with boiling water. The center of the deck held a half-dozen weathered Adirondack chairs in a semi-circle around a terra cotta chiminea stove. At the far corner of the deck, another knee-high stone frame rose out of the deck, covered with a black canvas tarp.

"What's that?" Shannon asked.

"Hot tub."

"Damn, these folks know how to live."

The deck ran along the length of the wall of yawning windows that was the house's front. A double center door led inside.

Rex came around the far side of the house with an armful of logs, crossed the deck and dumped the logs at the foot of the pit with a deafening rumble.

Rex met Shannon.

"What's in there," she asked him, nodding to the vat.

"Sea water, seaweed and clams."

"Smells like shit," she said.

"Spoken like an authentic Dorchester native." He looked at me. "Where's my lamb?"

"In the car."

"Let's get everything inside and dress that thing up."

We lugged the wine, food and bags into the house, a modern A-frame with cedar-planked walls, a gaping open living area and kitchen and a stone center-fireplace full of wood that crackled and popped. The wall facing the deck was glass to the roof peak. Rex introduced Shannon to his wife, Amelia, who stepped away from her own vat on the stove to give Shannon a hug.

Rex was all business. "Take your bags up to the guest suite pronto, freshen up if you have to and get back down here. We have work to do."

His wife grimaced at her cantankerous husband. "You're an abysmal host."

I shooed Shannon up the staircase that led to a short balconied hallway overlooking the living room and glass wall.

"Look familiar?"

"It's just like my place. The deck chairs, the stove, the balcony, the wall of glass. Gives me goosebumps."

We threw our stuff in the room and I began to hustle back when Shannon grabbed me and hugged me hard. "I am so happy to be here with you."

I hugged her back. "Worth a little fear of water?"

"Uh-huh."

"You know how you make my heart sing?"

"Uh-huh."

I goosed her and ran from certain retaliation.

Back in the kitchen, Rex handed me a martini in a highball glass. I watched him dress the lamb and offered suggestions while he responded with verb-pronoun combinations.

Shannon kept Amelia's wine glass full and watched her make the base for the chowder while they gabbed. Gary Burton and Chick Corea rode herd over our cacophony and gave synchronous rhythm to our feet and fingers.

Rex prepped the lamb leg and brought it to the pit. We used two steel poles to lift the trough off the fire and lower it to two stone tablets on the deck. He used a paddle strainer to fish the seaweed out and scoop the clams into a bowl, which he handed to me. He then ladled some cooking water into the bowl and ordered me to deliver it to Amelia. When I returned, he had replaced the trough with a steel-rod spit and hand crank contraption.

"What the hell is that thing?"

He looked at me dead-faced. "It's a fucking lamb leg rotator. Shut up and fill my glass." I complied.

I went back and forth from lamb spit to chowder pot. Each time it seemed the ladies got louder, their laughter more unruly. Chick Corea had surrendered to Weather Report.

Shannon, who had professed such disgust at the smell of the steamed clams on our arrival, was now busy pulling the slimy skin off the necks with a studied ruthlessness and flipping the denuded critters into the broth. I stopped to study her technique as she held one close to her face, the tip of her tongue protruding from tight lips. She pinched the wrinkled foreskin with her nails and yanked. She glanced up at me and back to her subject.

"I feel like the mohel at a bris," she said.

When we got to eating, the mood corkscrewed further. As we gabbed, joked and needled, clams were shucked and sucked, chowder slurped. We drenched and gnawed ears of corn. We ravened the lamb leg, along with the roasted fingerlings and grilled asparagus. With each succeeding outburst of laughter, the wine supply dwindled. Rex presided at the end of the table with a dry and taciturn wit; the women were increasingly giddy, an amusing and spontaneous tandem of straight lines and double-entendres. Mirth flowed from a broken spigot. I felt better than an accused criminal should.

When we were all sated, the ladies kicked Rex and me onto the porch and resumed their banter while banging and clanging the kitchen clean, and Rex and I fired up the chiminea and settled into Adirondacks with a couple of Monte Cristo Number Fours. The air was crisp, the fire beat back the chill just in time, and as the clay stove's toasty aura settled over the ring of chairs, Shannon and Amelia joined us with wool blankets and a bottle of Fonseca white port. The silver-dollar moon that loomed on the horizon when dinner began had risen high and shrunk to a dime, but its reflection still shimmered off the pond below.

"Rex, this is just what the doctor ordered," I said.

"I must say, Paul, you're pretty relaxed under the circumstances," Amelia said.

I shrugged. "How else could I be with you all?"

"Let's not dwell on Paul's situation tonight," warned Rex.

"Actually Rex, I'd like to."

"What in the world for?" asked Shannon.

"Because I find myself reviewing the facts of what I've done. I've been charged with a shitload of crimes. I find it hard to believe in my own innocence when a government I want to believe I can trust charges me with a felony. Since my fate will be made by a jury of one's peers, I'd prefer to be judged by people I love and trust. Preferably in an inebriated state."

Rex passed over the white port. "No sense leaving it up to chance then."

I poured myself four fingers and handed it back.

"So what did you do?" Amelia asked.

"I let lobbyists buy me golf and meals and didn't report them."

"How often?"

I pulled on the Monte Cristo. "Serially. Does that matter?"

"Depends. Why did you accept?"

I stared up at the glowing dime to consider. "I accepted the golf because I couldn't say 'no.' Simple."

"Never?" Amelia asked.

"Practically never. I declined a few times. I was sort of a snob about the venue."

"D'you ever do anything in return?"

"Consciously?"

Shannon scoffed. "Consciously. What the hell does that mean? No, unconsciously. How do you do something unconsciously?"

I gave her the look I thought she expected and added a middle finger for good measure.

"I believe you are referring to the metaphysical conscious, not the political conscious," I said with glass aloft, pinky extended, before lowering the glass to my lips for a slow sip, rolling the port with my tongue. I meant this as a spoof of myself, and it was well taken. The loving derision was true, and I laughed with them. It was a deep and guttural laugh.

But the question deserved a proper answer.

"The answer to the question is no, and yes."

"Why no?" Amelia asked.

"Amelia, I am a man who believes in rules. On the golf course, in life. I am a lawyer. I believe in the rule of law. No lobbyist ever asked for anything. Never asked me for a vote on a bill or an amendment. Never asked me to write a letter or help a friend. Never asked me for a goddamn thing."

"Except that Pierce amendment problem," said Rex.

Amelia held up her hand to her husband. "Hold on, we'll get to that. Why yes?"

"Because I feel that regardless of the letter of the law and the absence of improper motive, there were times when some of them may have invited me out of a sense of gratitude."

Amelia peered. "Give me an example."

A half dozen sprang to mind, all pretty much the same sort of thing.

"Some idiot rep from East Bumfuck thinks the unclaimed bottle deposits should go to the state—escheat, it's called. That money is all the nickels that we had to pay so that every liquor store had to accept bottle returns, at no small cost to them. Rep Bumfuck proposes that the state seize the unclaimed deposits—the meager sum of twenty-five million dollars. If the state doesn't take that money, it's used by the retailers to offset the cost of collecting all those goddamn empties and shipping them to the recycle plant. A cost we pay every time we buy a six-pack. Seems only fair, doesn't it? So I know that the package store association is represented by Billy McCarthy, he's had me out to Woodland a half-dozen times. I also know that he's standing outside the door of the House chamber with a bunch of information—facts—about how the recycling program works, and I know that he's not worried about this amendment passing, he's done his job and the result is a foregone conclusion. But I go see Billy, get his sheet full of information, go back into the Chamber, and I go up to the microphone and kick the shit out of the amendment. I give a real Holy Roller speech on the free market and consumers being ripped off and the cost of Joe Sixpack's six-pack. By the end of the speech, I'm calling it 'the beer tax,' and the sponsor is jumping up and objecting and the members are laughing out loud. So the guy's amendment, instead of going down fifty to 110, he only gets thirty-five, because my little performance peeled away fifteen votes. And Billy's amused."

"Why would you do that?"

"I just happened to be sitting in the chamber at the time, and it was the right thing to do. And if I embarrassed idiot reps for proposing idiot things like that, maybe fewer of them would do it. So I did something about it."

"Was that good for another round at Woodland with Billy?"

"Could have been. I dunno. When he invites me, he doesn't say, 'Paul, on account of your magnificent performance on the floor of the House chamber on behalf of our organization, I would like to purchase you a round of golf. He just says, 'hey Paul, you free to play Woodland on Friday,' and I say 'sure, what time.'"

"Any of your hosts ever bring an amendment to you, ask you to carry it on the floor?"

I laughed out loud at that. "Amelia, there is no lobbyist so desperate that he needs me to carry his amendment. A few of them would let me know the amendment was coming up in case I wanted get involved."

She nodded. "So what's this Pierce thing all about?"

I explained my role as delivery boy and how the unknown document had become "the Forté amendment."

Amelia raised her eyebrows and frowned. "That doesn't sound very encouraging."

"No fooling. Now the amendment has disappeared after the FBI made a copy of it."

"What?"

"Yup. No longer exists, except maybe floating around in the Department of Justice, if it hasn't been shredded."

"Jesus Christ, that's serious, Paul." Amelia looked at her husband, who looked exceptionally dour, even for him.

He glanced up and saw her staring at him. "Hey, we're doing what we can. We'll get to the bottom of it."

Amelia steered us to the subject. "Back to the question at hand," she said, smacking Rex on the arm and waving her glass at him for more port.

I was laughing inside. I needed just this, exactly this, to be here at this moment with these people, where I knew I could speak the pure truth and get it back. "Right-oh, Amelia."

"Did you think what you were doing was morally wrong?"

I remembered my answer to Kilroy's question in the grand jury. What an arrogant ass I was.

"Morally, no. I do not believe it was immoral to accept the hospitality of others. I would extend the same hospitality to them, and I had the means. I did not consider it a gift, and they did not offer it as such."

"You think the law intended to allow lobbyists to pick up bar and food tabs indiscriminately?" She held her glass out to Rex again, and he obliged her, then he passed me the rest of the bottle.

I sipped the bottle and cradled it. "I think the law was written by the legislators that way for a reason. People grab checks, Amelia. I can take a bunch of cash out of my pocket and stuff it into Larry the Lobbyist's shirt, insisting that I cannot violate the campaign finance law. Or, I suppose the strict moralist would tell me I should get up and leave. But politics is a people business. I can either assimilate to the culture to get my job done or I can become a pariah."

"What was the dynamic of your relationship with these lobbyists?"

"They invited me because I was a member at a place they wanted access to. Most of the golf I played, I offered a reciprocal at Hyannisport. That's what golfers do. It's an exchange of hospitality. You offer, you accept. It doesn't matter who you are or what you do. Sometime, now or later, you reciprocate. It goes into a big invisible bank of golf favors."

"Are you saying this is a course of conduct with golf club members?"

"It is more than a course of conduct. It is a code."

"And it has nothing to do with the occupation of the members?"

"It has only to do with the individuals involved. You give and get on the basis of who you are, not what you are."

Shannon snickered. "*Who you are.* You think any of my neighbors can get into that game?"

I got up from my chair with the bottle in my hand, standing next to the stove, looking down on my friends.

"Let me ask you," I said, pacing back and forth in front of the stove. "If the rep from Mattapan goes to a community bowling event and wants to bowl a few strings with his constituents, is it a problem if he doesn't insist on reimbursing them in cash? Or is it better that he makes a large contribution to the organization? Better yet, he sponsors the bowl-a-thon with a check from his campaign committee—cost nobody, right? No ethical question involved in that, the guy uses his campaign account to give a hundred voters a free night of bowling. What's not the same? It's fine to allow a rep to buy his votes, as long as he's buying people of modest means? You want to argue class? As long as it's someone who needs help, it's okay? Guy can buy televisions and DVD players for every senior center in his district, with big plaques on the front, 'donated by Representative Jimmy Spazzutollo,' and he's a model of ethics? He shows up with his mini-vans on Election Day, gives the old folks a ride to the polls, feeds them hot cider and egg salad sandwiches, that's the way to do it?"

Shannon settled into silence, staring straight ahead at the pond below.

Amelia shifted in her chair. "There's a difference between campaign activity and the relationship with lobbyists, Paul."

"Yeah, there sure is, Amelia. A rep doesn't need the lobbyist's vote to keep his job. Lobbyists don't keep members in office, and they don't kick 'em out. Voters do. You know what Speaker John McCormack used to say about lobbyists? 'If you can't eat their food, drink their liquor and fuck their women and then vote against them, you don't belong in this place.'"

When I got to the end I realized I was yelling, that my arms were extended and my fingers tight around the neck of the Port bottle. My audience was still as death, staring at me like they were watching the subway man with the tuna lid. Man, I was on the verge of killing that party, which would have been more of a crime than anything I faced in a court of law.

Just at that moment, the music shifted to Bob Marley. Rex pulled himself up and offered his hand to Amelia, and the two of them began to move together to *Stir It Up*. I followed suit, putting my hand out to Shannon, who regarded it suspiciously, scowled at me, and then her scowl melted into an impish snarl, and she took my hand, allowed me to pull her up, and we snuggled close and swayed in the two-four back-beat rhythm. We got lost in the beat and bumped into Rex and Amelia, then we all formed a circle and shucked and jived together like one soul-sated jalopy running on fumes.

Marley faded out, and so did we. Rex shut down the clay stove and we trickled in. Rex shut the lights down, and he and Amelia disappeared into their bedroom in the back. Shannon and I wandered upstairs, cleaned up and got into bed. The clock read 2:27 A.M. and my ears were ringing. We cuddled under the down comforter, her head on my chest. I hoped she heard my heart thumping what I really felt. Grief.

Rex had left the music on. Out of the ceiling speakers at a meek volume we listened to Joni Mitchell singing "I Could Drink a Case of You and Still Be on My Feet." Her assertion applied to us, Shannon assured me, before she disappeared under the covers to prove it.

It just amazes me that things like that happen when they do.

Things got stirring slowly and late at Casa Barkley the next morning. Shannon and I woke up simultaneously in each other's arms. A little bit of warmth spreading might have led to some morning delight if our mouths didn't smell like stale Limburger.

I heard rustling downstairs and soon the smell of brewing coffee was impossible to resist.

Barely noon, we were all seated around the table eating omelets and sipping champagne. A perfect time to discuss criminal business.

"Shannon, can I assume that you are going to be taking part in this effort to keep your roommate out of jail?" Rex has a smooth way of breaking a subject.

"Anything I can do."

Rex asked me, "Have you told her about the other matter?"

"Yes he has," she said. "It's outrageous. How do you use it to benefit Paul?"

Rex gave her his dead face look. "We were wondering if you could help us with your sister."

Shannon sat back and crossed her arms, looking sidelong at Rex, then turned to me.

"Why didn't you ask me this before?"

"You mean when you told me not to be an idiot about using it?"

Oh-oh.

For the very first time I've been in her presence, she was speechless. She stammered and shook her head slowly.

"You...I can't...it's...arrrrrgh," she finally growled, got up from the table, grabbed her sweater and went out the door muttering to herself.

I looked at Rex and he at me. "Didn't think it was that controversial," he said. "You better go do damage containment."

I grabbed a fleece pullover and followed her. She had walked down to the bottom of the lawn and stood by the edge of the pond with her back to the house. I came up behind her and wrapped my arms around her shoulders.

"Someone miscalculated, I guess."

"Big time." She turned to face me. "I told you we haven't spoken in years. Why would you think I could contact her about your problem?"

"I'm not sure I did think that. We were just wondering."

"Well, wonder no more. I can't. I won't. Not even for you." She pinched the shirtsleeves on both of my arms, staring at my chest, leaned forward and thumped her head on my sternum.

"I thought this might be a natural catalyst to break the impasse."

She didn't answer, just rested her head on my chest, then she looked up at me with her screwy eyebrows. "Can't you just go to her without my help? My involvement is not going to help you on this."

I had no reason to think she was wrong. I put my arms around her and rubbed her back. "Not a problem." Maybe we'd get to looking into that one later. Maybe not. I gave her a pat and started to turn, but she pulled my shirtsleeves back and gave me a tough look.

"Hey. I'm sorry. I'm in the game. I just can't do that. Okay?"

I looked in her face and saw something I hadn't seen before. Before, she had divulged her tragedies with a cool, steely grit. But she did not have that now.

I took her face in my hands and bore my eyes into hers. "Sister, if all you can bring yourself to do is paint and fuck, then the rest will take care of itself."

She socked me in the belly for that, and I collapsed, pulling her down with me, feigning mortal injury, and rolled her around in the dewy grass as she squealed in protest.

We finished our cavorting, and lying there on the ground, I shot a look up the hill to the house, where Rex stood on the deck looking down on us.

He smiled and raised his flute.

Chapter 20
Out and About

I walked into Abe & Louie's at about 6:30. It was already crowded with after-work big shots from Hill Holiday, assorted celebrity seekers and aspiring trophy wives. I found Rex where he should have been, sitting alone at the bar.

A bow-tied, clean-cut young man put a napkin down in front of me.

"Sapphire on the rocks with a twist, please."

The young man turned to the bottle library, and finding the Sapphire depleted, he disappeared.

"I got a report back on the Kilroys' financial standing."

"Do tell."

"The Kilroys live in a five thousand square foot house on Marblehead Harbor, assessed at a three million-seven."

"Wow. Mrs. Kilroy must make good money at IWO."

"Oh, she does. But that's not all they own."

"Tell me more."

The bow tie returned with a fresh bottle and went to work.

"They also own a two thousand square foot house on the mountain at Sugarbush. Assessed at a million-three."

Bow tie put a glass in from of me and turned away.

"Excuse me," I said. "This has olives. I asked for a twist."

"I'm sorry, sir, you asked for olives."

I looked at Rex. He cracked a thin smile.

"Well, then, I need to change my mind, because you see, I'm allergic to olives, and if I ever ate them, I would go into an anaphylactic shock and die right here at this bar, in front of all these nice people."

I smiled at the boy, just in case there was any misunderstanding that I might be perturbed. He swept the glass away.

"I'm sorry, sir, it must have been my mistake."

"What's your name?"

"Chip."

"Don't worry about it, Chip. Happens at the best places." I turned back to Rex. "Continue."

"They also own a fifty-six foot Beneteau, moored in front of their house."

"Wow. What's that worth, four or five hundred?"

"Closer to eight-fifty. Plus twenty thousand a year in maintenance."

The bow tie placed my gin in front of me. "On the house, sir."

"Thanks, Chip." Back to Rex. "That it?"

"No."

"Holy smokes. He have a helicopter or something?"

Rex sipped his Beefeaters. "They have one other home."

"Florida? Virgin Islands?" Bastard was making me guess. He shook his head. "Sedona."

"Sedona? Arizona?"

"Yup."

"Don't tell me. Sedona is a stone's throw from Flagstaff."

"Twenty-five miles."

"I'll be goddamned." I sipped my gin and looked over the

dining room. My eyes followed a curvaceous drink server as she carried a tray of drinks to a booth along the back wall.

"Well, what do you know," I said.

"What do I know?"

I nodded toward the booth. "See the people at that back table there?"

"One of them looks familiar. Who are they?"

"One of them is my boss, Liguotomo."

"Which one?"

"The one with the square face and the black hair. The guy next to him is Cruddy."

"Who's the couple opposite them?"

"The guy is Kilroy. I don't know the lady."

"Maybe it's his wife."

"Could be. Let's get the hell out of here." He picked up his glass and held it out. I clinked it.

"To greed and stupidity."

"Greed and stupidity."

Shannon spent the day off at the beach while I lounged under the umbrella on the roof deck.

As luck would have it, Senator Hank Rickenback had a fundraiser scheduled the next week at Anthony's Pier Four. Hank and I had spent fifteen hours a week together in a car. Since he was now the Vice Chairman of Senate Ways and Means, it was a sure thing that most of the lobbying corps would attend.

"Do you realize this is the first time you and I have been to an affair together?" Shannon was slipping on her black cocktail dress.

I stopped what I was doing to watch her. She wiggled it past her hips, slid her arms through the straps and pulled it up over her skimpy black bra.

"You know, when I watch you get dressed, all I want to do is stop you." That made her giggle.

"We'll put that on the to-do list for after, okey-dokey?"

"I suppose I can wait. So you figure you'll know many people at this fundraiser?"

She shrugged, pulling a pair of heels out from under the bed. "I suppose I'll run into someone. It's a small world, and a lot of the old gang never did stray far from the feedbag."

I laughed. "The feedbag. Ain't it the case? A four-day week, twenty paid holidays, and no heavy lifting. I don't know how they could walk away from it."

She pulled a paisley silk shawl out of her closet and met me at the bedroom door. "For most of them, it's the best they can do in life. Feel sorry for them." She smoothed my blue suit coat lapels and straightened my tie. "You're a handsome sonofabitch. Let's go show off."

In the cab ride over to Anthony's, we agreed to a simple strategy. Smile, have a good time. Innocent until proven guilty.

Predictably, the fundraiser was mobbed, Hank being a guy with power. We checked in, handed over my check, declined the nametags and moved toward the bar. Shannon hooked her hand under my arm. Another first, I thought.

"You noticing the double-takes?" I asked her.

"Oh yeah, big time."

"Are those for me or you?"

"A bit of both, I think."

We got ourselves a glass of wine, moved to the perimeter and scanned the room.

"I've been to a hundred fundraisers in this room, and it never changes. Same lousy cheese and crackers. At least it's free."

She laughed. "It's not free, you dope. You paid $500 for it."

"Well, then we'd better get our money's worth."

Most of the people in the room were familiar strangers. People who called you "pal" and asked about "the family" but didn't listen for the answer. A hundred pairs of eyes turned our way for a furtive glimpse and turned back to their business. A small klatch of ladies scurried over to greet Shannon. She introduced me, and they were polite enough, although they had that look that I might suddenly brandish a hunting knife. Weird.

"Go on ahead, I'll catch up," Shannon said, pushing me toward the suits and ties.

I spotted Hank and thought I should warn him I was there. He saw me coming, excused himself from the three men around him and greeted me in the middle of the room.

"Glad you could make it, it's been a long time," he said. He sounded like he meant it well enough.

"Thanks. I left a check at the front. If you'd prefer not to have it, I won't feel bad if you send it back."

He scowled at me. "What the hell are you talking about? I don't care about that. Besides, my seat's as safe as any in the state. We're old friends. I know you. I'm not going to run away from you."

"Thanks, Hank. I appreciate that."

"That Shannon McGonigle you came in with?" he said, grinning.

"You know her?"

"Not really. I just remember her from a while back. She worked on our side, for Finnerty."

"Right."

"Good looking lady."

"Yeah. I'm living with her now. Over in Southie."

"Atta boy." He took his eyes off her and looked at me. "You gonna be okay?"

"I think so. Wondering if any of Kilroy's witnesses

will show up."

"I know Shanley, Harrington and Pierce got called up, they'll be here."

Three who hadn't taken their reciprocal to Hyannisport yet.

"I got no interest in seeing Pierce. The other two around?"

"Not yet, but they will be," he said, with assurance. "Listen, I gotta mingle. I'll ask around. Call me next week."

Frank Shanley, Winchester Country Club. A classic Donald Ross design. Joey Harrington, Worcester. Another Ross. And Stuart Pierce, The Country Club in Brookline, the venue of one of the greatest moments in golf history where, in 1913 an amateur boy named Francis Ouimet beat the two venerable English professionals Ted Ray and Harry Vardon in an eighteen hole playoff to win the U.S. Open. Perhaps my cavorting with Stuart would add to the lore.

Vinnie Duncan caught my eye, waved me over. As I approached, he left the two guys he was with and met me in the middle of the room. Vinnie lobbied for National Grid, another power company. We'd traded rounds a few times. He played to a seven handicap at Belmont, and he loved Hyannisport. Loved it. He greeted me with a smile and we chatted about nothing for a few minutes.

"So," Vinnie said, "I guess you must know I was called to your grand jury."

"Don't worry about it, Vinnie. I had to do the same thing with Stackhouse. The whole world is turned crazy. You do what you have to do. I assume they just wanted to ask you all about our home-and-home practice?"

"Funny you say it that way."

"Why?"

Vinnie looked at me. "When the FBI interviewed me, they asked about your invitations to me. And I explained how I'd been a guest of yours and had lunches and dinners and drinks, all of that."

"I would assume."

"Yeah, well, when they brought me to the grand jury, this Kilroy bird didn't ask me anything about my trips to your place."

"You too, huh?"

"Me too?"

"Yeah, you're nothing special, Vinnie."

"No, huh? He asked me only about the events at Belmont, and just when I thought he'd get into the Hyannisport stuff, he dismissed me."

"That's the motherfucker's M.O."

"No kidding. Now I know what they mean when they talk about how easy it is to indict a ham sandwich."

"Will you be a witness?"

"Got my subpoena two days ago."

"We shouldn't talk then."

"Probably not. Don't worry about me, Paul. I'll look forward to your lawyer's cross."

"Good enough. Listen, Vinnie. You and I, we've got nothing to hide. We traded fair, no gifts, no bullshit. Just honest hospitality, right?"

"Paul, I got no reason to ask. You can't do anything for me."

"And I'm not insulted by that, Vinnie."

"Just the way it is, right?"

"The way it is. Thanks Vinnie."

"Don't mention it, Paul. You're a good guy. I'm sorry for your troubles. Good luck to you."

He gave me the shoulder clap and moved along.

The way it is. The lobbyists I'd swapped rounds with told the same story as Vinnie. They'd disclosed the reciprocity to the

FBI, but were not asked about it at the grand jury. With each successive report, I felt an increasing desire for self-medication, which led me back to the bar several times, until I was both ornery and inebriated.

I hunted Shannon down and whispered in her ear. "You mind if we get out of here?"

I could see the blush on her neck as she said her goodbyes and the ladies leered at me. On the way to the door, we passed within a few yards of where Stuart Pierce stood with a couple of reps. I didn't look at him, and he didn't look at me.

Back at Shannon's place, I ran over and over the event that now represented a real and serious threat to my freedom. The simplest of menial tasks. *Sure, Stuart, I'll deliver it.* Crissakes, I didn't even read the thing. But no one else was allowed in the House chamber besides the court officers and the pages. They wouldn't have delivered it for him—only for a member. That was it. I was screwed.

I lay on the futon, watching the planes float in and out, running these thoughts on a loop. I might have done so until morning, were I not in the company of a consummate professional in the distraction game. The lovely Ms. McGonigle padded in front of me, dropped her black cocktail dress on the floor and made me practice my body searching technique.

I did a damn good job, so she said.

Chapter 21
Laying Bait

For forty-five minutes at the end of an early September workday, I sat on a concrete bench that faced the front door of the entrance to Three Center Plaza, waiting for an individual I had only met once, but I couldn't possibly miss her.

Just as I thought about packing it in, Stacey McGonigle strode out the front door, looked at me without recognition, and continued on her way past me.

"Stacey?"

She stopped and looked again. "Do I know you?"

"Paul Forté? General Counsel, MBTA? Flannery Christmas party, last year?"

"Oh yeah," she said, recognition in her face. "The ex-rep from the Cape."

"Yeah. Amy's prey."

"I'm sorry?" she said, then "Oh, yes," with a hint of embarrassment. She seemed eager to be on her way.

"I'm sorry, Stacey, you must be spooked. I need to talk to you for a few minutes about your sister. Can I buy you a beer? Glass of wine?"

"My sister? You know my sister?"

"I know your sister, and I know your brother, too."

She stood still, peering at me with a mixture of suspicion and amusement.

"You know Shannon *and* Brian, huh?"

"Better than you know."

"Then I most definitely would like to have a drink."

We conducted polite chatter to the door of The Claddagh and took a booth in the back corner. The place clattered with the after-work noise of Guinness and Paddy's lovers. A tiny, dark-haired girl with a nametag came over right away.

"Wot kin I get youse?" said Clodagh.

"Paddy's and Harp," Stacey said.

"Same."

Clodagh from The Claddagh disappeared.

"So how are things at Morgan Stanley?"

She looked at the table, hands laid flat in front of her. "If you know Shannon, then I'm guessing you know I don't work for Morgan Stanley."

"You guess right."

"So is this about Shannon, or me? Or is it about you, Paul?"

"I'm not quite sure. Let's start with Shannon and see where it goes."

"It's bound to be a short conversation."

"No shorter than the ones I've had with her about you."

"What has she told you?"

"That she's responsible for your mother's death and that you two haven't spoken since she knocked your teeth out."

Clodagh dropped off the whiskey and beer.

"So, sounds like she didn't spare the details then."

"Not really. Nice bridge, though."

Stacey blushed and ran her tongue across her front teeth. "Thanks. So as we say in Southie, 'what's it to ya?'"

She raised her whiskey glass, I clinked with her, and we both took a good belt.

"Coimirce Dé ort," she said.

"Sorry?"

"Gaelic for 'may God protect you.'"

"Ah, you're very kind."

She shrugged. "It's a toast. So why are you stalking me?"

"Stacey, Shannon and I are madly in love."

She halted movement. "Really."

"Madly." I locked her eyes so she'd be absolutely certain.

She raised her glass again, and we clinked and finished the first. I caught Clodagh's eye and showed her two fingers and an empty whiskey glass.

"Does Brian know this?"

"Yes he does."

"Really."

"Really."

"How?"

"I told him." I looked at her and gave her a hint of a smile.

She dropped her jaw and looked wide-eyed at me, picked up the beer and took a good slug. "You're a courageous man, Mr. Forté."

I rolled my eyes. "That's what Shannon said when I told her."

"What do you know about her past?"

"Everything."

She raised her eyebrows.

"Why do you tell me this?"

"Because sisters should talk."

"So why don't you tell her to come to me?"

"I'm not asking you to go to her."

"What are you asking?"

"I'm not asking anything. I want to tell you that time changes people, that bad memories should be forgotten and people should move on."

"Well, I've moved on." She took a good sip of whiskey and slugged some Harp. "Do you know what that woman did?"

"Stacey, I know all the details I need to know. I know what she went through, and I know that whatever she did, she deserves to be forgiven."

"So you're saying I should reach out to her?"

"No, I'm not saying you should. I'm saying if you did, you'd find a different person than when you last spoke. She needs you, Stacey. She needs your forgiveness."

She wrinkled her brow and looked at me sideways with an amused scowl.

"What?"

"You're an intriguing guy."

We'd gone to nursing the drinks, which was good. We had a lot to talk about, and I felt loose enough to open my mouth but not too loose to shut it.

"I suppose you know a lot more about me than I do about you."

She laughed at that. "I have nothing to do with your case, and there's nothing I could tell you if I did."

"Fair enough. I'm glad you don't, and I wouldn't ask," I lied.

She grinned. "But?"

"But I want to know about Bernard Kilroy."

She put on the poker look. "What do you want to know about Bernard Kilroy?"

"Whatever you're willing to tell me."

She swirled her whiskey and watched the legs of it drip down the glass.

"Bernard Kilroy has questionable ethics. No one in my office likes to work on his cases."

This was off to a smashing start.

"You luck out on this one?"

She smiled. "I run the unit. I don't do anything on luck."

"What's the rap on him, as far as your people?"

"He makes us look bad."

"How so?"

She looked a little wary now. "Let's just say he's sometimes selective about what he uses."

"So, for instance, if the bureau were to turn over some exculpatory evidence to him, that information might not always make it to defense counsel?"

"We're speaking hypothetically now?"

"Purely hypothetically."

"Hypothetically, that might happen."

"I understand. How do the attorneys who work for him feel about him?"

She sipped her beer and regarded the Guinness coaster in front of her.

"I think some of them are terrified of him. Some despise him. Some think he's a tragic figure."

"A tragic figure?"

Through the elixir of whiskey, I saw the same twisting of eyebrow and mouth as I had seen in Shannon's face that day at Pete's.

"Do you know how much you look like your sister when you do that?"

"Speaking of tragic figures?"

"Now, now, we're through talking about Shannon."

We laughed together, and I felt that magic moment when you know you've turned someone into an ally.

"Kilroy is one of those men whose ambition will be his

destruction. He is singularly focused on his objective, but a lot of us think he lacks the moral anchor to guide himself between the rocks."

"An example of unbridled hubris?"

She raised her eyebrows and twirled a cocktail straw. "Not an ordinary example, I'm afraid."

"I heard he had a tough father."

"His father was a very bad man. Very powerful, and ruthless. Very well connected politically."

"I heard about his background."

"You know he was President Bush's Yale roommate?"

"Something like that."

"Skull and Bones, too."

"Naturally. Did Bernard make it in too?"

"Of course."

"Is the old man still around?"

Stacey shifted, twirling the coaster. "No. He died a while ago." She had more to say, it seemed.

"Something controversial?"

"I'm not sure," she said.

"For an FBI agent, you're a lousy liar."

Her eyes flashed at me. "This is none of my business. I only know what I heard."

I'd gotten plenty out of her without trying. I could have let it go and looked it all up. But no. "I guess I could do a little research. Big shot like that, I'm sure it's in the public record."

She shifted again. "He killed himself."

"Really."

"In his New York townhouse, right before it was to be seized by the IRS."

"That's making quite a statement. What was his problem?"

"Some sort of political scandal, I think."

"Well, I'll be doing my best not to emulate him then. Wouldn't be fair to Shannon."

Stacey looked at her watch. "So listen, I've got a yoga class to get to. Is there anything else you'd like to ask me?"

"Why does he hate being called 'Bernie'?"

Again with the shifting. "I think that's where the 'tragic figure' thing comes from."

"Okay, so. What? His mother named him for Bert and Ernie?"

She blinked. "No. His mother called him Bernie."

"So what?"

"His father berated her for it. Then he used the name to ridicule his own son. After the mother died."

I gulped. "His father teased him for his mother's pet name?"

"Yes."

"After she'd died?"

"Yes."

We were both still.

"Any more questions, or have you heard enough?"

"Yeah, one more. What does Kilroy's wife do?"

Stacey's face froze for a split second before assuming its casual mien. "I have no idea," she said. She gathered her things and began to stand. "I really need to get going, Paul. Sorry to be rude, but my yoga class is essential to my well-being. I hope you understand."

"Of course. I practically kidnapped you anyway. Thanks for your time and company." I stood and put my hand out.

She gave it a sturdy shake and paused, still holding it. "I'll give some thought to your suggestion about Shannon."

"That would be lovely. Thanks."

"Goodbye, Paul. And good luck with your situation." She turned, strode to the door and disappeared.

My *situation*. Reminded me of the White House "Situation Room." Where the President deals with things like nuclear threats and terrorist attacks.

I love most euphemisms. That one, not so much.

Rex and I got together in his office.

"So Kilroy's father committed suicide, eh?"

"Apparently."

"Then you understand you're dealing with no ordinary sociopath."

"I understand."

"So let's make sure we get him before he gets you."

"Well, hurry the fuck up, will you? My trial starts, like, yesterday."

Hilda had recorded Cruddy making a half-dozen trips to Flagstaff, all occurring within a few days after Epsilon had received large wire transfers from their insurance company clients, including IWO Risk. She confirmed that the Kilroys were not listed as shareholders or members of Epsilon in the company's annual reports to the Arizona Secretary of State. Nor were Fetore, Cruddy or Liguotomo.

So why was Cruddy making regular trips to Flagstaff, visiting an office he had no business in?

"Who are the shareholders of Epsilon?"

According to Hilda, Epsilon was a limited liability company registered in Arizona, and besides Erichetti and his wife, the only other member of the company was Premier Investment Management, Ltd., a company registered in the Cayman Islands. When distributions were made after premium funds were received, a corresponding wire transfer was made to an account in the Caymans in the name of Premier, and a large withdrawal of "petty cash."

"We've got to find out the shareholders of this Premier group."

Rex was not sanguine. "That is not going to be easy, even with my prodigious skills and international contacts. The Cayman Island corporate and banking laws virtually guarantee anonymity."

"So how do you crack that?"

Rex reached for his glass and took a slow sip of scotch, swirled it around in his mouth and swallowed. "We're going to need some luck."

"Swell."

Chaos reigned at Abe & Louie's. The Sox were hosting the Yankees, the Jets were in town for Monday Night Football, and it seemed that the whole world was adorned in sports attire. People were imbued with adrenalin and alcohol.

Rex and I perched on our regular barstools, at the curve on the end, looking across the floor at the rabble. They looked like ants carrying red and green crumbs. Our bartender friend, with whom we were on a first-name basis, brought us our third martini.

"What's going on with Hilda? Tell her to hustle, will ya? We need the goods on Bernie."

"I'm well aware of your schedule, knucklehead. The poor lady is watching like a hawk."

A pair of redheaded twins in their mid-twenties and matching red cocktail dresses walked past.

"Speaking of watching like a hawk." I looked past redhead number two and saw the purpose of our visit walk in.

Cory Fitzpatrick shuffled through the throng toward us, dressed like a news reporter. Amidst all the revelers, he looked like a street bum crashing a society function. He reached our corner, perspiring and huffing. I introduced him to Rex and got Chip's attention.

"Bud Light, please," he said to Chip.

Rex and I looked at one another, and Cory shrugged. "Hey, I'm thirsty, what can I say?"

Rex and I figured we'd draft Cory onto the team, so I had Shannon call him and set this up. We had to do something to try to flush the peacock out of the bush, and nothing would do that like a piece of political gossip appearing in a well-read publication. Rex had been up to something in Washington, but he hadn't told me what.

We chatted about the Sox and Pats enough to break the ice with Cory again, and we told him enough about my upcoming trial to make him think that he had fresh (but not necessarily true) information, and then Rex went into his pocket, came out with a folded piece of paper and handed it to Cory.

Cory opened it, inspected it and handed it to me.

It was a correspondence from the Federal Transit Administration to the Chairman of the MBTA, notifying him that the FTA had opened an audit pertaining to the use of federal transit funds to pay for environmental liability insurance. It requested that the MBTA begin to assemble all relevant procurement documents, correspondence with any providers of environmental insurance services or products and make its Chief Financial Officer available within thirty days for inquiry.

"Fellas, I don't want to sound stupid, but what does this mean to me?"

"It means that Bernie Kilroy's life is beginning to unravel, Cory. Do you care to play a leading role in that event?" Good old Rex.

Cory responded appropriately. "Fuck, yeah."

We spent two more martinis filling Cory in. The Federal Transit Administration had somehow become aware of a significant spike in project costs from several transit agencies involved in environmental remediation work. The MBTA was, coincidentally, one of them. The vendor for the MBTA was an Arizona firm called Epsilon-something-something. The MBTA had spent millions on insurance during the past year. We played it pretty cagey, I thought.

"That's all very interesting," Cory said, "but what's it got to do with Kilroy?"

"His wife is in the business," Rex told him, matter-of-fact about it.

Cory's whole body went erect, like he'd had a shot of adrenaline.

"No shit. What's her name? Virginia? Virginia E-something Kilroy?"

"Erichetti."

"Yah, Erichetti. Like the pasta," Cory said.

"Like the pasta?" I asked.

"Yah, orichiette."

"Never heard of it. What's it look like?"

"Like little yarmulkes."

"Yarmulkes, eh? Oy!" That was the gin talking.

"So what does she do?" Cory said, now reaching into his pocket for the pad and pen.

Rex filled him in on the IWO insurance group and her role in the surplus lines market.

"Plus," I said, "Kilroy himself wrote a law review article on that very subject. Very authoritative."

Rex told him to check the corporate ownership of Epsilon. Cory asked why, but Rex wanted to make him go back to the paper and ask for resources. He would need his editors, if he wanted to find what we couldn't show him. Besides, editors get nervous when reporters are handed gift-wrapped packages.

"What do you want me to do?" he said after completing his note taking.

We wanted a tight little blurb in the Boston Phoenix reporting on the FTA audit of the MBTA and mentioning Epsilon and the lovely Mrs. Erichetti. "And get your editor to send you to Arizona."

"There's still no direct tie to Kilroy. I don't know if they'll go for it."

"That's why you have to get to Arizona, Cory. I thought you said your publisher has a beef with the guy." Rex's stolid, no bullshit mien was deadly.

"Okay, I'll give it a shot," he said, shrugging.

"Now, Cory, do you want to stop working and drink with us, or should we tell you to get lost?"

"You ever known a reporter that passed up a free drink?"

Cory stuck around, and we had a good old time until we started calling Chip "the motherfuckinchipster," when he shut us off.

The boy had judgment.

The Boston Phoenix came out this morning. The front page looked like this:

Feds Audit Transit Program Tied to Attorney General Hopeful

I couldn't have thought of a better headline myself, and neither could Rex. He even laughed as he read it over his eggs at the Hungry Eye on Court Street.

The Federal Transit Administration has opened an audit of the MBTA's unusually high expenditures for environmental insurance on federally funded projects. The notification came via letter from FTA Administrator Frederick Penjada to General Manager John Halsey. Sources said the expenses are related to the MBTA's consulting contract with Epsilon Environmental Consulting, an Arizona company, and complex insurance products purchased through a division of IWO Risk Management managed by Virginia Erichetti, the wife of Attorney General-hopeful Bernard Kilroy.

"Cory's got some juice there at the Phoenix, don't you think?" I asked Rex.

He stared at the story, looking rather smug. "I don't know if he does or not. He hasn't gone to Arizona yet."

We ate our eggs and sausage and stared at the headline.

"Say, I forgot to ask you. How'd you get the FTA to send that letter?"

"Trade secret."

"Bullshit. Tell me."

Rex continued to tend to his breakfast, flicking some of the home fries to the side to get to the eggs. The fork's clinking stopped. "I have a friend in the DOT inspector general's office. That's where I started my qui tam. I give them enough information to begin an inquiry, and it acts as a placeholder for my claim."

"But the FTA audit is a different procedure."

He looked at me like I was stupid—something he'd been doing more of lately. "My friend had the FTA initiate it. At my request. The idea is to get all of the information from the transit agencies cooperatively first. Aside from the T, all of the others are probably clueless to what's going on." He held a forkful of sausage above the plate, waving it for emphasis like a short-order conductor.

"So you think this'll do it," I asked.

"Let me ask you something. If you were Vince Erichetti, and you saw this article, what would you do?"

"Buy a shredder?"

I believe that remark restored Rex's faith in me.

Chapter 22
Gamesmanship, Like Father Like Son

I knew the jury selection process was tedious and arcane, but when you're the one who's being tried, it is excruciating. You just sit and sit and sit while nothing happens around you and then you hear "All rise!" and the judge marches in and you sit again and then ordinary people are summoned, one by one, and the judge asks each one a series of questions, the last of which is "is there any reason in your mind that you believe prevents you from performing the task of a juror in a fair and impartial manner?" And that person says "no," but you really never know.

From Al's point of view, it boiled down to two things. He'd try to exclude people with connections to law enforcement, and Kilroy would try to exclude golfers and friends and family of politicians. What's the mystery in that?

Judge Wheeler wouldn't permit Kilroy's blanket exclusion of golfers, however.

"Counsel, you may have read a different Constitution than I did, but we do not exclude people from a jury based upon their preference for recreation."

Barred from asking prospective jurors about their golfing

habits, Kilroy resorted to exercising his peremptory challenges based upon whether the prospect was dressed in any sort of golf attire. This had the salutary effect of excluding a number of black males in polo shirts and polyester slacks. Al was prepared to use his own peremptories on them after learning from me that at least one of the clubs I had frequented still utilized a surfeit of black caddies.

All in all, it took them three days of procedure, spread over ten days, to get a panel of twelve jurors and three alternates. Each day, when I met Al in the lobby outside the courtroom, he looked my sorry ass over and said, "You look perfect."

He was a *sonofabitch*, but he was *my* sonofabitch.

Tomorrow promptly at ten o'clock in the morning, Judge Charles Wheeler would call in the jury of fifteen people, instruct them about how things work, and then he would invite Bernard Kilroy to give an opening statement. What I imagined vividly as a perversion of that opening statement ran through my head on a closed loop from about noon on, and by about two in the morning, I'd been spinning like a top in bed for four hours, annoying Shannon to beat the band.

I slid out of bed and went down to the futon, rolled it out in front of the window and grabbed the throw pillows and puff from the couch. I lay on my back and watched the stars move across the purple-black sky. I thought about Mom and Dad, and about Kate. I thought about the times I'd spent on the golf course that brought me to this point. I tried hard to think about sex, so maybe I could get some sleep, but it didn't work. In a waking trance, I heard the soft padding of feet on wood, and Shannon's naked body suddenly appeared in a silhouetted apparition between the window and me.

"There's only one way you're going to get any sleep, and I

aim to make it happen."

The black shadow began to sink.

"Do you think the flush will leave my cheeks before the jury sees me?"

I sat at the defendant's table with Al. Behind me on the benches of the spectator area I spotted Cory Fitzgerald in the corner, notepad ready. He nodded. Stuart Pierce sat in the front row on the center aisle. The government's "star witness." He looked like he was about to puke.

A few seats down, Frank Shanley and Joe Harrington sat together. That's two thousand dollars an hour down the drain. They looked like they were at a funeral. I hoped they were not. None of them anxious to make eye contact, but a curt nod and fleeting grin perhaps. Kilroy's first three witnesses. Probably a couple dozen rounds with them, all told.

On the bench behind them sat Hank Rickenback, who I hadn't seen since his fundraiser. He gave me a wink and I slinked over to the bar. He stepped up and shook my hand.

"Just thought I'd show up for a little moral support."

"Thanks, Hank, I appreciate it. Enjoy the show."

After I sat back down, I wondered where this exterior of calm was coming from. Dad, probably. Then the door opened and the "All Rise!" came, and I got weak in the legs again.

Wheeler bounded up the steps to the bench and got right down to business. He instructed the marshal to bring in the jurors, and the marshal opened a side door next to the jury box.

Fifteen people shuffled in. A few late middle-aged white women, a couple of Hispanic men looking like they came off the day labor line. Three men, ethnicity uncertain, in middle-grade business suits that didn't fit them well. Two young black guys, dressed like students. Three older black women in house frocks with bus-sized handbags. And three thirty-something guys, Italian-looking, like they just took a break from bocce.

I looked over at Kilroy. The smarmy bastard beamed a fake smile, making eye contact with each one of them. He can't win that game against me, I thought.

Judge Wheeler got them all acclimated and clued in, and before long, he turned to Kilroy. "Mr. Kilroy, your opening statement, please."

He rose slowly, buttoned his blue pinstripe suit jacket, snapped the shoulders tight and turned to face the jury box.

"Good morning, ladies and gentlemen, my name is Bernard Kilroy. I am the United States Attorney for the District of Massachusetts. I am appointed by the President of the United States to enforce the laws of the federal government, civil and criminal," turning to sneer at me, "against those whose disrespect for the Rule of Law jeopardizes the very democracy we enjoy.

"In a few moments, you will begin to hear evidence in the case against Mr. Paul Forté here. Mr. Forté is accused of tax evasion, conspiracy and mail fraud. Those are very serious charges. I take them seriously, and you should too. You are being asked to take away this man's liberty, after all. It is only fair that you be convinced of his guilt before you do that."

I turned sideways to watch Kilroy in front of the jury. I made a point of not looking at the jurors, but just focused on Kilroy. I knew some of them would look my way. I glanced toward the back corner of the courtroom. Since I'd come in, three new spectators had arrived. Gina Gianferrante, Frank Dawkins and Will Hartfield. They sat together with their arms folded in front of them. Interesting that they'd be there. Why?

Shannon sat next to Hartfield. She smiled and winked, and my stomach fluttered.

"You will hear evidence that Mr. Forté made a routine practice of soliciting and accepting gifts in the form of free golfing privileges from a roster of paid lobbyists so long you'll wonder why he's not on the pro golf circuit. In exchange for these gifts, you will learn, Mr. Forté exercised his duties as an elected official by voting with his lobbyist friends one hundred percent of the time. One hundred percent of the time."

He paused to let that sink in, and I felt fifteen pairs of eyes glaring at me. I fixed my eyes on that prick and shook my head, disgusted.

"You will soon hear from one witness in particular, who will describe how on at least one occasion, Mr. Forté sponsored an amendment to a banking bill worth millions of dollars to the lobbyist's client."

The very sight of that fraud made my blood boil. The mendacious bastard was probably figuring out how he could throw his wife under the bus and continue his campaign plans, all the while painting this grand tableau of Paul Forté, The Poster Boy of the Political Corrupt to fifteen unlucky people and the world at large. Yet on he went.

"Four hundred sixteen, ladies and gentlemen. That is the number counts to the indictment, each describing how this defendant willfully and premeditatedly broke the law while he strolled the fairways of the world's most opulent private country clubs."

If I didn't know he was talking about me, I'd have been outraged. Knowing he was made me apoplectic. He continued, mentioning the lobbyists, the country clubs, the dates and times, and then the purported "official acts" I was supposed to have done in exchange for these "free gifts." Not once did he mention that the men sitting in the back of the room, subpoenaed by the United States government to testify against me, would step forward and affirm that Paul Forté has reciprocated their hospitality at his own club, that they never once asked me for so much as one vote for any of their interests or clients. Pierce's delivery boy charge was the worst of it, but I just had to hope that no juror with an ounce of intelligence would buy it.

The more he talked, the more furious I grew. Ten months of my life spent lying awake in bed worrying about my freedom, my reputation, my father's name. Ten months I could have been paying attention to Shannon, to Kate, to the memory of my deceased parents. Instead, this public servant—appointed by the President of the United States! he tells us—marshals the resources of the federal government my taxes helped pay for, and abuses them to further his career. Fuck. Him.

I lost track of his calumnies while my emotions roiled. My ears hissed with rage as my eyes watched the pantomime of this rancid charlatan. He posed and feinted the truth like it was a plaything with no intrinsic meaning. I'd have my day. I'd have my day! When his words finally ceased to have meaning and the cadence quit, I heard the welcome voice of Judge Wheeler.

"Mr. Croston has chosen to withhold his opening statement until the beginning of his case. Call your first witness, Mr. Kilroy."

"The government calls Joseph Harrington," Kilroy announced.

Harrington rose from a back corner of the benches and shuffled toward the bar. Joey was a big redheaded Irishman, a decent fifteen at Winchester. He lobbied for Boston Edison, whose plant occupied part of the Southie neighborhood where he grew up. He was a young looking 50 or so, and his navy pinstripe hung like it was made for him.

I turned and whispered to Al, "Leaving Pierce to last, you think?" Al nodded.

Harrington lumbered through the gate and walked with an ex-B.C. lineman's limp to the witness stand. Watching him raise his hand and swear to tell the truth, I wondered if he'd ever done it before.

Kilroy strode to a spot on the carpet equidistant to both the jury and the witness.

"Mr. Harrington, please state your name and address for the record."

He leaned toward the microphone and bumped it with his lips as he answered.

Judge Wheeler interrupted. "Mr. Harrington, there's no need to lean forward, the microphone will adjust automatically to your voice level."

Harrington blushed. "Thank you, Judge." He sat back and folded his hands in his lap.

"What is your occupation at the moment?"

"I am the chief legislative counsel for Boston Edison."

"And was that your occupation between July, 1987 and October, 1990?"

"Yes, it was."

"And at that time, were you a registered legislative agent?"

"Yes."

Kilroy led Harrington through the facts that described the nature of his job. Foundation stuff.

"Mr. Harrington, are you familiar with the defendant in this case?"

"Yes I am."

"And in what context did you meet him, if you remember?"

"I met him at a reception at Anthony's in January of 1985."

"What was the nature of this reception?"

"It was a reception to welcome the new members of the House that were elected in the fall."

"And did you come to learn at that reception that Mr. Forté was one of those members?"

"Yes."

"A Republican, from Cape Cod?"

"Yes, the second Barnstable district."

"What else did you learn about Mr. Forté at the time?"

"That he was a member of the Government Regulations Committee."

"And did that information have any significance to you?"

"Yes, it did."

"What was that, Mr. Harrington?"

"The Government Regulations Committee is responsible for the majority of legislation that affects Boston Edison."

"Did there come a time when you learned something else about Mr. Forté?"

"Yes, the following summer."

"And what did you learn?"

"That he had a two handicap at Hyannisport."

"Was that information significant to you in any way?"

"Definitely."

"In what way?"

"Well, in two ways. First, I am always interested in people within my business sphere who play golf at a high level. Second, Hyannisport is one of the best golf courses in the world." He hesitated. "In my opinion," he added, like he thought Kilroy would accuse him of lying under oath.

Al rose from his seat. "Your Honor, Mr. Forté will stipulate to the witness's expertise on that matter." Demure laughter rippled through the courtroom. I counted four members of the jury among them.

"No need, counselor, the Court takes judicial notice of the fact," said Judge Wheeler. Scattered laughter ensued, including one guffaw from the jury box.

Kilroy stifled a scowl. "Getting back to the trial, Mr. Harrington. As a result of what you learned about Mr. Forté on that night, what, if any, plan did you make?"

Harrington shrugged as though it were a stupid question. "I made it a point to watch how he responded to the legislation that interested Boston Edison, and I resolved to get him on the golf course at the soonest opportunity."

Kilroy faced the jury while Harrington answered, and raised his eyebrows for them. *You see what we're dealing with*, he was saying to them. I didn't notice any of them nodding in agreement. He kept his eyes on the jury while he asked the next question. "And how did he... *respond*, as you put it, to the legislation that interested you?"

Harrington waved a hand. "Well, he was a Republican, so I would have anticipated that he'd be supportive, and he was."

"He supported the Boston Edison position in his voting record?"

"Objection," Al said, rising to his feet.

"Mr. Croston?"

"Your Honor, I submit that Mr. Forté's voting record, by itself, is irrelevant to the prosecution's case."

Wheeler held up both hands and Al halted. "I'll see counsel at sidebar, please."

Al and Kilroy headed to the left of Wheeler's bench. Al stopped halfway there, turned, and waved me to follow. I met them at the side of the bench as Wheeler asked Al to continue.

"The statute requires that the legislator perform an 'act,' and I submit that the exercise of voting is not an act, it is speech under the First Amendment. If Mr. Kilroy submits that voting is an 'act' and therefore constitutes an element of the crime my client is charged with, I would like a ruling on that so that I may bring the issue to the First Circuit on an interlocutory appeal right now."

"Mr. Kilroy?"

"Your Honor," he began, "Mr. Croston's argument might carry water if this was a state prosecution under the gift statute, but these are federal charges under the mail fraud statute, and no such 'act' is necessary. Even if it were, Mr. Forté's vote is achieved by means of the pressing of a button, green for yes, red for no. That is a physical act."

"Do you not agree that under the federal statute a 'quid pro quo' is required?"

"Oh yes, your Honor, I agree with that."

"Are you suggesting that a legislator who votes his conscience, not at the specific request of a lobbyist, has violated a criminal statute if he thereafter accepts a meal from the beneficiary of that vote?"

"If any part of the lobbyist's motive in buying that meal is to reward that legislator, yes."

Wheeler cocked his head, and his forehead wrinkled as he frowned. "Well, Mr. Kilroy, I seriously doubt you'll get that instruction from me when it's time to charge the jury. Mr. Croston, for the purpose of your objection, I'm going to allow Mr. Kilroy to have his question, and to follow his line. Step back, please."

Al and I returned to our table.

Wheeler raised his voice and spoke to the jurors. "I am overruling Mr. Croston's objection and will allow Mr. Kilroy to question the witness regarding Mr. Forté's voting. But I want the jury to understand that how Mr. Forté votes on legislative matters, or what he might have said in debate on the floor of the House, is only evidence, and may or may not be relevant to any element of the crime with which he is charged. And in that regard, the witness's motive is not necessarily relevant either. Proceed, Mr. Kilroy."

"Thank you, your Honor." He gave the jury a smug nod before turning back to Harrington.

"Jesus Christ," I whispered into Al's ear.

He placed his hand on my arm and whispered into my ear. "Shut up. No reactions the jury can see." He scribbled something on his pad and tilted it my way. *Poker face*, it said.

"Mr. Harrington, I asked you previously if you would review the legislative matters in which you were engaged during the years of your familiarity with Mr. Forté. Have you done that?"

"Yes, I have."

"Let's go through them, shall we?"

"If I must," Harrington said.

Kilroy then led Harrington through a laundry list of legislative issues. Stranded cost recovery. Rate setting. Eminent domain. Easements. Local zoning exemption. Environmental permitting. Blah blah blah.

After each issue was identified, Kilroy asked, "And how did Mr. Forté vote on that issue?"

"Mr. Forté voted against that amendment."

"Was that the vote Boston Edison advocated?"

Harrington's "Yes, it was" response was repeated, ad nauseam. Literally. He was killing me. My head began to spin slowly, ears ringing and I felt the cold clamminess that precedes the old barfo. Then two words crept into my ears.

"Nothing further."

Kilroy was done. The reeling stopped. I took a few deep breaths. Al slid a water glass to me. I picked it up and it shivered in my hand.

"Mr. Croston, cross-examine?"

Al jumped out of his seat. "Good morning, Mr. Harrington." He walked to the end of our table closest to the jury box.

"Good morning, Mr. Croston."

"How long have you been a registered lobbyist?" he said, casually leaning a hand on the end of the table.

"Seventeen years."

"All for Boston Edison?"

"No, sir. I started out at an independent lobbying firm, representing insurance, real estate, some racing and casino interests. I went to Edison nine years ago."

"Nine years ago. So you'd just begun with them when Mr. Forté started his career."

"That's right."

"You were both 'rookies' in your respective positions, then."

"You might say that."

"But you weren't a rookie when it came to counting votes, I bet."

"No, sir, I was very much a veteran at that," Harrington said with a faint chuckle.

They might have been sitting on two bar stools at Pete's.

"Do the terms 'saved,' 'savable' and 'lost' have any meaning to you?"

I watched the jury. They shared a singular attention to Harrington.

"Oh sure. 'Saved' is the term used to describe those members whom you can count on to be with you all the time. 'Lost' applies to those who are always against you. 'Savable' applies to those on the fence. The ones we would spend the bulk of our effort on."

"Did Mr. Forté belong to one group or another?"

"Mr. Forté was firmly in the 'saved' group. We could pretty

much count on him no matter what."

I looked at the jury again. A number of them looked genuinely puzzled, like they were wondering why my lawyer was reinforcing the fact that I was in the bag.

"No matter what, eh?"

"No matter what. He was a reliable supporter of the industry point of view."

"So you didn't have to curry favor with him then."

"Not at all."

"In fact, the golf you played with him, the meals you ate with him—none of them were for the purpose of obtaining his support or to reward him for his past support, were they?"

"Objection!" Kilroy hollered. "I'd ask the Court not to permit Mr. Croston to supply the witness's testimony."

Wheeler looked over the top of his half-rims again, eyebrows jumping. "Mr. Kilroy, this is cross-examination. He's *your witness*. Mr. Croston is permitted to lead him."

"Your Honor, Mr. Harrington is a reluctant witness. He's testifying under limited immunity, and he is unquestionably sympathetic to the defendant. I'd ask that Mr. Croston be instructed not to lead the witness with language that goes to the heart of the witness's intentions with respect to the gifts."

Wheeler removed his glasses, looked down at his gavel on the bench, gave an almost imperceptible shake of his head. "Mr. Kilroy, I am aware that this witness was also on the defense list. But he's *your witness*. If you were so unsure about his testimony, then perhaps you should have left it to Mr. Croston to call him. But that is hindsight at the moment. To use a golf metaphor, you're out of bounds and you get no mulligan, counselor. Objection overruled."

Al turned tight-lipped toward the witness. As he was about to ask his next question, Wheeler interrupted him.

"By the way, in case it isn't clear, absent a marked difference in the circumstances, that will be my same position toward any witness that is present on both the prosecution and the defense lists, Mr. Kilroy."

Any man in my position would have had trouble with Al's *poker face* instruction at that point. I scribbled a note for him. *You're my sonofabitch.* I looked at the jury, and it could have been my imagination, but it seemed like a few of them were scowling at Kilroy.

"Mr. Croston, you may proceed."

Al asked him again if his intentions were to either persuade or reward me.

Harrington said, "Not in the least."

"So why did you play golf and socialize with him so frequently, if it wasn't necessary?"

Harrington looked perplexed and shrugged again. "He's a scratch golfer, he tells great jokes, he's very entertaining." He looked at the jury and shrugged once more. "He's just a good guy. I don't know what else to say."

"No more questions, your Honor." Al returned to his seat. I felt like socking him in the arm.

"Mr. Kilroy, redirect?"

Kilroy charged out of his seat to a spot five feet from Harrington's perch. "Mr. Harrington, if Mr. Forté were never a member of the House of Representatives, would you ever have known who he was?"

"Objection," Al said in a tone of annoyed amusement.

"Sustained."

"I'll rephrase. Mr. Harrington, your relationship with Mr. Forté—it arose out of his position as a House member, correct?"

"Correct."

"And as you sit here today, you can't say that if he hadn't

been a member of the House, you'd have met him otherwise."

"I can't say that I would or I wouldn't."

"Thank you." Kilroy returned to his table.

Judge Wheeler looked at Al.

"Nothing further, your Honor."

"You may be excused, Mr. Harrington. There is the possibility that Mr. Croston will want to call you as a witness when it is his turn, so please do not move to Bali in the next six months without letting the Court know. Until that time, you are still under subpoena as a witness in this case."

"Yes, your Honor."

Wheeler held his gavel in both hands. "Counsel, I am told by my clerk here that I a number of emergency matters have arisen that I must address in another courtroom, so we will have to suspend for the moment. We will resume the trial a week from Thursday at 9:00 A.M. sharp. Until then," he said, turning to the jury, "you are dismissed to return to your respective lives, but remember my admonishments at the outset. Do not discuss this case with anyone, and do not read any newspaper accounts or watch any television news accounts. Do we understand?"

The jurors nodded in unison.

"Okay then, court is in recess until Thursday, September sixteenth at nine A.M. I'm dismissing the jury now, but I would ask counsel and the defendant to remain for a moment."

The jurors filed out of the jury box and disappeared through the side door. When the door closed, Wheeler looked down at us.

"Now then. During our pre-trial conference, I expressed my desire to have counsel review the expected testimony of each of the common witnesses and, when possible, stipulate to their testimony, so that we have a chance of completing this trial before the end of the decade. Judging from the experience of this witness, I gather that you've found this not possible, Mr. Kilroy?"

"Your Honor, I believe it is absolutely necessary for this jury to gain the full effect of the sheer multitude of lobbyists who have spent money on Mr. Forté. I believe that filing written stipulations of their testimony will not fairly characterize the nature of the crimes committed."

"Alleged crimes," Al said. Kilroy gave him a blank stare.

"If you insist on this, Mr. Kilroy, then we'll all understand now that there will be no more objections to Mr. Croston's leading questions. Despite how you care to characterize Mr. Forté's relationships with them, they're still prosecution witnesses, and Mr. Croston is entitled to be as aggressive as he wishes. Are we in agreement?"

Kilroy spoke with a tight reserve. "I will be circumspect in my objections to Mr. Croston's crosses."

"Thank you. One more thing." Wheeler hefted the gavel in his hand and spun it, catching the hammerhead in his other hand. "I say again that Mr. Kilroy will not enjoy a jury instruction from me that either Mr. Forté's voting record, or his statements made during debate on the floor of the House, singly or in combination, constitute evidence of a quid for the quo. So Mr. Kilroy, I understand that your parading of many witnesses to emphasize Mr. Forté's weakness for golf is designed to influence the jury, and while I find it distasteful, you are certainly allowed to do it. Just be damn sure you remember this when it comes time for your closing argument. Any attempt to characterize those events as parts of a crime will be dealt with. If you doubt me on this, then I invite you to appeal my ruling to the First Circuit now, and we can all save ourselves a lot of fighting later. Do you want to do that now, Mr. Kilroy?"

"No, your Honor, but I do reserve the right to appeal the instruction if the jury finds against the government on that issue."

"Fair enough."

"Fair enough, Mr. Croston?"

"Fair enough, Judge."

"See you next week," he said, and he turned, bounded down the steps and through the door and was gone.

I sat as Al and Kilroy gathered their piles of papers and stuffed them into their oversized litigation briefcases. Al kept shooting glances intermittently at Kilroy, who ignored us assiduously. It was comical, how uptight the man was.

"The offer to stipulate remains open, Bernard," Al said casually.

Kilroy didn't break pace or look up. "No thank you," he muttered.

"Let's go, Paul." Al clipped his briefcase shut and turned to leave.

I got out of my chair and began to follow Al, Kilroy still fussing about, obviously waiting for us to clear the room before he exited. I couldn't help myself.

"Bernie, Al and I are going out for some osso buco, if you'd like to join us."

I imagined I could hear his veins popping as I left.

Chapter 23
An Old Ally, Shredders and a Crack

I used the week off to accomplish a small matter of personal business.

The Norumbega Skilled Nursing Facility was built twenty years ago on the grounds of the old Norumbega Amusement Park, off Route 30 by the Pike. I rode the roller coaster there as a child. Dad had fished in Lake Norumbega as a young boy. Now, where I once rode an open-air train car around the same lake that my father fished, a sprawling nursing home took care of the elderly infirm, Sidney M. Hartfield among them.

It had been easy enough to find him, and no more difficult to decide that I would not ask Agent Hartfield for permission to visit. Even if he'd wanted to say yes, he oughtn't. Asking him was itself an imposition. Better to ask for forgiveness than permission. I just left a message with the staff director that Charlie Forté's son wanted to say hello to Sidney Hartfied, and two days later I was on my way to visit him at cocktail hour.

Sid Hartfield had the look of a man who'd taken some serious punches in his life but wasn't bruised inside in the slightest. He was in his late eighties and looked it. Wisps of white hair askew atop his gaunt, withered face, he met me at the front desk in a wheelchair pushed by someone else, something he didn't seem too pleased about. Still, his body might have been weak behind his tartan robe, but his blue eyes blazed out of their gray-ringed sockets, and they announced the presence of a man whose spirit and mind were indomitable.

"Mr. Forté! Christ, you are the spitting image of your father!" This he blared, oblivious to the otherwise dour atmosphere of the lobby. The desk nurse shushed him, albeit with a smile.

I shook his hand. Frail as he looked, his grip was a vice, and he held it long.

He turned to speak behind him and said, "Molly, get lost. Mr. Forté will push me. We'll be down at the pub room when it's time to get me for dinner."

Poor Molly retreated, Mr. Hartfield pointed me to "go that way," and I rolled my new friend along a corridor until he stuck his left arm out like we were in traffic, and I turned him into a small room that did indeed look like a pub, but there were no bartenders or patrons. And no booze in sight.

Mr. Hartfield reached into his robe pocket and produced a key, handed it to me and directed me to a small locker against the wall, in which I found a half-gallon of Dewars scotch, a quart of club soda and two crystal highball glasses.

"There's ice behind the bar," he said, winking. "But make mine light, I like it to last."

I got busy, made us a pair of tall ones, and in a minute we had the place to ourselves.

"Where's the rest of the happy hour crowd?"

Mr. Hartfield frowned and shook his head in disgust. "This place is dead—no pun intended. I've tried a million ways to get people going, but I've got nothing to work with." He nodded over to his locker. "There are two dozen lockers on that wall.

You know how many have liquor in 'em? One. You know how depressing that is?"

"Very, I'd imagine."

He waved his hand. "Bah, I wouldn't want to drink with most of them anyway. I get visitors, we have the place to ourselves. I almost prefer it." He raised his glass toward me. "Here's to your father, God rest his soul."

We clinked and drank.

"You knew him well enough, your son tells me?"

Mr. Hartfield held his glass and scrutinized at me. "How much do you want to know?"

A curious question, I thought. What son doesn't want to know as much about his deceased father as he can learn?

"You know things about my father that you think I wouldn't want to know?"

The old man shook his head. "Not in the least, I assure you. Everything I know about your father is unqualifiedly positive. I loved the man. Revered him. And while I appreciate your coming to visit me just because of your father, that's not all you're here for, is it?" With that he turned one eyebrow down and winked.

"No, it's not."

"Well, let's get that out of the way. You tell me why you're here."

I told him about my indictment, how I'd found the story about Kilroy's father intriguing and wondered if the world were so small. I also told him I was curious if his son knew.

"I never told Will anything about it."

"Why not?"

"Since Will was a teen, he was determined to be in the FBI," he said, pausing to wet his lips with the glass, "so I felt that teaching him the hard art of keeping your trap shut was important. If I got in the habit of telling him about my work, he might get the idea that it was okay—and it's not. In his line of work, it could get him killed." The eyebrow went up again, he raised his glass with another wink and wet his lips again. He wasn't kidding—he'd make that weak scotch and soda last a long time. "I didn't want him to be worrying about me while he was in school, and I haven't told him about Bernard Kilroy's father because I didn't want him to develop a personal animosity against him."

"Why did you say anything at all to him about my father?"

He nodded slowly and swirled his glass. "Because it is important for a man to give his son living examples to follow—other than himself, of course."

I took a moment to fight the tennis ball in my throat.

Mr. Hartfield sat still in his chair and looked me in the eye, swirling his glass again. "Paul, I'm going to tell you a story that very few people know. That's why you're here, isn't it?"

"Yes, it is."

"Okay then. Sit back and listen.

"When I was the chief of the enforcement division of the SEC, it was the early nineteen-sixties, many of the big investment firms were teetering on the verge of bankruptcy, and the New York Stock Exchange was doing very little to regulate its own members. At the time, your father represented members of the regional stock exchanges in Boston, Philadelphia and Chicago. By themselves, they couldn't participate in stock issues above a certain size. He had devised a way for them to band together legally to promote bigger issues. I know it was legal because he cleared it with me first. This put them in competition with the Big Board. They charged a much lower commission, and some of the New York members didn't like it. It made them look greedy—which they were."

Mr. Hartfield paused for a breather and a lip-wetter. He put his glass back carefully, reclined and placed his hands together at their fingertips, staring down, and gathered himself to continue.

"A few of the big shots from New York decided to do something about it. They began a series of whispering campaigns and complaints to my office that accused your father's clients, and your father himself, of securities fraud. As soon as the first few so-called complaints became public, a couple more would come in, and soon, there was a drip-drip-drip of bad press. After months of this, the regional exchange members began to cower. They had trouble with new business, and some of their clients began to drift back to the New York Exchange." He paused again for a wetter and a breath.

"I can guess what's coming."

"I'll bet you can," he said, setting the glass down. He began to continue when a fat old man in a graying red beard and striped pajamas waddled in.

"A little early to be drinking, isn't it, Sidney?"

"Go to hell, you nosy old bastard."

The man gave Hartfield the finger and moved on.

Sidney's eyes followed the man, and he shook his head. "I gotta get the hell out of this place." He reached for a sip and continued. "Mind you, when these complaints first began to arrive, I was duty bound to pursue them, and I did. That's how I began to really know your father. I brought an enforcement action against one of his clients, and based upon some of the information that had been supplied to us, I suggested to him that I would settle the case by allowing the client to remain in business, if their chief executive agreed to a lifetime ban from the securities business. You know what your father said to me?"

"What?"

Sidney leaned forward, his eyebrows arched high atop his furrowed forehead. "Right there in my own conference room, with my staff and his client sitting right there, your dad looked down the length of the table and he said, 'fuck you, Sidney.'" His eyes sparkled and his face glowed, grinning ear to ear. "I'll never forget it. We were dumbstruck—all of us, especially your dad's client, who must have feared he'd be taken out in leg irons."

"What'd you do?"

"I sat there with a stupid look on my face for a good long while. I'd been the head of enforcement for fifteen years, no one had ever said such a thing to me. 'Fuck you, Sidney.' I tell you, what a steel-balled sonofabitch. And then before I could think of anything to say, your dad leaned forward on the table, and he began to talk, in a cross manner. He lectured me and my staff for a good twenty minutes."

"What'd he say?"

Sidney waved his hand in a circle. "Not one of us moved while he spoke. He was furious that we'd accepted the accusations of these 'white shoe shylocks from Manhattan,' he called them. Accused them of disseminating false information about their competitors for the purpose of unfair competition. Conspiracy to commit investment fraud. Violations of the Clayton Act. Market manipulation. Price fixing. Racketeering. And then he said that if we pursued our threat to ban his client, we'd spend the next decade litigating." His animated display had taken the wind out of him, but his joy was indelible.

"How'd it turn out?"

Sidney's face changed, no hint of the amusement left. "Your father was one hundred percent right."

"He was?"

Sidney nodded. "Little of the information in the complaints

was legitimate. It was an insidious and cynical campaign to put the competition out of business. And I do believe that most, if not all, of your dad's clients would have folded rather than take the heat. And I would have destroyed the careers of some good men if he had allowed it. But he didn't flinch."

"What became of the New Yorkers?"

"Ah, you see, that's where the story begins." He handed me his glass. "Make yourself another and top me off with some ice and a wee splash, would you?"

I did as I was told while he continued.

"I pursued a few of the sources, and discovered that the campaign began on the top floors of the two biggest investment banks in New York. Although your father's clients were just as happy to move on, he wasn't. He told me if I dropped it he'd go to court himself.

"This was just after the 1968 election. Nixon was lining up candidates to take over the SEC chairmanship, and it was a matter of great interest to anyone in the business, more so than usual, because of the state of the industry. There was a list of three or four candidates, with one frontrunner."

"Seamus Kilroy," I said.

Sidney nodded. "Yes, Seamus Kilroy. I went to the outgoing SEC chairman—my boss—and told him my concern, that Kilroy's candidacy was a grave risk because of his involvement with this campaign. His reaction was beautiful," he said, shaking his head and wincing at the memory.

"What was it?"

"He put both of his hands up, shook his head and said 'I don't want to hear it. That's someone else's problem. I'm not getting involved.'"

"Profiles in courage."

He nodded his head.

"So what did you do?"

"I went to the Justice Department and briefed the Attorney General. His first question was 'who else knows about this.' As soon as he said that, I knew I had a problem. His last words to me were 'we'll take it from here.'"

"Oh-oh."

"You ain't kidding, brother. Oh-oh doesn't begin to say it."

"Then what?"

"Then I called your father," he said, like it was a stupid question.

"What for?"

"What for? To hire him, of course! Think about it. I was a career man. If Kilroy became my boss, I'd have to keep my head down and go to work every day not knowing what kind of crap was going on, and what'll happen if I learn about it. I wasn't going to live like that. I had to keep that guy from being confirmed by the Senate. Your father was the only guy in the city I could trust." Sidney sank back in his chair and put his hand to his forehead. He'd put his drink down, and wasn't showing any interest in picking it up.

"Am I wearing you out?"

He came alive at the suggestion. "Hell no," he exclaimed with a flash in his eyes, but just as quickly simmered back. "I haven't told this story before, you know. It brings back much pain and anger, but also the feeling of triumph we felt, your dad and I.

"He didn't ask for any retainer, or even ask if I could afford him. He just told me to make a copy of everything I had assembled on the matter and bring the copies to his office. It was against policy to do that, but I understood that it's better to be asking for forgiveness than permission when your own ass is on the line."

"That sounds familiar."

He didn't pause to find out why. "So I went to his office, figuring I'd be working hand-in-glove with him in devising a plan. He took the files, poured me a cocktail from his wet bar, and we had a nice leisurely chat. A few of his partners wandered in, we had some more cocktails, and then we all went out to dinner at The Bagatelle. Three hours and several bottles of French wine later, we left the restaurant, and I asked him what else he needed. He said," now leaning forward with two fingers pinched together in front of his face, "'I need you to go back to work, say nothing to anyone and let me take care of it.'"

He stared at me, waiting. I thought I got it, but perhaps I missed something. I shrugged.

Sidney raised his shoulders and spread his arms. "He wouldn't let me get into the arena! Of course," he said, waving his arm, "I realized he was just protecting me. He had no way to know how it would turn out—yet—and he didn't want me to be identified with him, in case he lost and I'd end up out in the street."

"Do you know what he did?" I asked.

He burst into a laugh. "Yes, I know what he did. He went up to the Hill. He visited a handful of Senators and three days later, the President announced he'd withdrawn the nomination. At the same time, he went to the Attorney General and told him that his clients had instructed him to draft a class action against the United States of America and him personally for violating their Constitutional right to due process and equal protection by ignoring prima facie evidence of corruption, and that if the Attorney General didn't take action, he would make public the evidence of misconduct that the SEC has amassed and he had ignored."

"Wow," I said, with a welling inside of me of both glee and

sadness. Old Sidney's memory certainly was sharpening.

"Didn't the Attorney General ask him where he got the files?"

Sidney slapped the table hard and laughed again.

"You're a chip off the old block, Forté. Just as sharp as your father. Let me ask you," he said, moving closer again, lowering his voice over the table. "What do you think he said?" He was grinning fiercely.

"He said 'I stole them.'"

"Right! God damn it, you're right! How did you know?"

"Wild guess."

"Bullshit, Forté. You have his instincts. Tell me why you'd have done the same."

I had to laugh at that. "I don't know that I would have, but I'm guessing that he knew the Attorney General was trying to find out if you—or someone inside the SEC—were involved. Dad never said he represented you, or that he had the files, he just said they'd be made public. If he said anything that suggested he didn't personally have them, or even refused to answer, the Attorney General would have suspected you were involved. Dad would decide to bluff, tell the AG he had stolen them, keeping you in the clear and making the AG do what he'd have to do, which he wouldn't ever do, because you can't play Russian roulette with a fully loaded gun."

Sidney listened to this with a placid smile, his keen blue eyes fixed on me. I finished my wild guess, and he nodded almost imperceptibly. "Exactly."

"So Dad played out his hand, which forced the AG to make a deal with Kilroy to get out of the business or have his career and reputation destroyed."

"That's right."

"And you got the credit for it on paper."

His whole face flinched downward. "Oh no, no, no. Not in the least."

"No?"

"Hell no! I was finished there." He paused a moment and shrugged. "Of course, I was anyway. You don't go through something like that and survive it in your same skin. When you come out the other end, both you and the place you're in are different. I knew that when we were having cocktails in your dad's office."

"So what happened to you?"

"The day the nomination was withdrawn, I joined your dad and some of his partners for another three-hour dinner. It was a real celebration, and let me tell you, your father and his friends knew how to celebrate. There was a real sense of satisfaction that we'd gone to war against some really bad people and prevailed. Of course, it was bittersweet for me, because I realized my career was over, and I didn't know what I'd do yet.

"Toward the end of the party, a fella arrived to join us. Your dad had kept a chair open between us, and he invited this fella to sit. Your dad poured him a glass of champagne, ordered another bottle, and introduced me to the man. His name was Bobby Cagnina, and he was the chief operating officer of Bear Stearns. I knew his name but had never met him. He says to Cagnina, 'Bobby, say hello to Sidney Hartfield, your new Senior Vice President of Compliance.'" As the old man uttered the last word, he choked up and tears grew in his eyes. "I spent the next fifteen years at the Bear and made more money than I'd ever dreamed of." The tears rolled down the old man's craggy face, and he wiped them away with the palms of his hands.

I sat as still as a scarecrow, watching the emotion roll over the man, but the welling inside me expanded too. I envied him, to have known my father that way, to witness him in that arena. Something I could only learn second hand.

"Did you get to spend any social time with him—other than the dinners—or was it all work related?"

The question resuscitated his spirit. "Oh hell," he said, "Your father loved his fun. Until I left the SEC, it was all business. He needed to protect the record. But once I left, we did all kinds of crazy things. We probably ate in every restaurant in Manhattan. I went to two Super Bowls with him and your mother. The America's Cup in Australia. We toured the wine country in France. Went to the British Open one year. He and your mother really knew how to travel. They were having a ball." He fell quiet and still. "I'm so sorry you lost them that way."

"Ya, well..." Ya well. Well what? What do I say to that, I thought. I'm sorry you had more fun with them than I had time to? "I just wish I had more time with them."

"Of course you do. But you don't get a choice. It's either you regret all the times you missed or you regret having to watch them fail slowly in front of you. There comes a point where we all regret the way it's coming to an end. I sure didn't pick being in this place as my dream point of departure."

Molly poked her head around the doorway. "Mr. Hartfield, time for dinner."

"I'll be right along, Molly." He gave her a wave. "She's a good young lady. I'm lucky I have her." He looked down at his lap for a moment. "Paul, I'm going to make a guess at something. I'm going to guess that it's not so much that you miss your father or the time you never had with him."

"What do you think?"

"I think you feel that you missed the chance to know that you measured up in his eyes."

"I'd be lying if I denied that."

"I don't blame you. Your father was a great man. A great man. There are few who live to achieve his stature—not just professionally, but in every respect. His intelligence. His loyalty. His generosity. His morals. His courage. His devotion to his wife and to you. Every man goes through life comparing himself to his father. He can't help it. And because of who he was, I'm quite certain that you aspire to be as much like him as you are capable of. And that is admirable, but it's a fool's errand. Remember your father. See in yourself what was in him. And be proud of who you are. He sure was."

"He was?"

"He most certainly was. He boasted about you all the time."

"I'm finding that hard to accept under present circumstances, Mr. Hartfield."

He dismissed that with a wave. "Bullshit. You think your father wouldn't be proud of how you've handled yourself? Bullshit."

"I'm thinking of the fact that I got myself into a jam in the first place."

"More bullshit, Paul. Your case is bullshit, just like the case Seamus Kilroy made against your father. You can't stop a corrupt man from doing what he's going to do. You were just unlucky you got in his way. Now deal with Kilroy the same way your father dealt with his father. The same way your father would have you do. I see more of him in you than you can imagine."

"I'd like to know how he'd deal with one particular detail. It seems a certain document has disappeared."

Sidney's eyes lit. "Oh?"

I told him about the missing amendment and its conspicuous absence from our discovery requests. He furrowed his forehead and frowned.

"That is troubling. Like father like son, one supposes…"

Molly poked her head in. "Mr. Hartfield…"

"All right, all right, come get me if you must." He raised his empty glass to me. "Thank you for visiting, Paul. You've brought back some wonderful memories."

Molly took our glasses behind the bar and washed them out.

"Your son doesn't know I was coming to see you."

"I have no reason to think he'd disapprove," he said, winking. "Come back again if you like. I don't get enough intellectual stimulation here, as you might imagine."

"I'll make a point of it."

Molly released the brakes on Sidney's wheelchair, turned him and headed toward the hallway. I followed them to the door and shook his hand one last time.

Rex and I sat in his office entertaining Johnny Walker, while I told him about Sidney's story. "That bastard is doing the same thing to me as his father tried to do to my father, and it's going to come out the same way, mark my words."

Rex began to respond to my vow when Hilda Griswold's call came in. Rex put her on the speaker.

"Hello Mr. Barkley, Hilda here." She really did sound like a Hilda.

"Hello Hilda, how are things in Flagstaff?"

"Well, the evenings are quite cool, but I'm sure you're not asking about the weather."

"No ma'am. What have you got to report?"

"A young man from Boston came to the office today asking for Mr. Erichetti. A reporter named Fitzpatrick. He waited quite a while."

"Did he see him?"

"Technically, they met, yes."

"What happened?

"Mr. Erichetti threw him out of the office. Physically."

I made a note to buy Cory a case of Bud Light.

"What else, Hilda?" Rex asked.

"Well, sir, there is a great deal of activity here. We seem to be preparing for a move. We're packing up all the office files. And this morning, an office equipment vendor delivered a large shredder to the comptroller's office."

"How's Mr. Erichetti's frame of mind?"

"Well, sir, I'd have to say that he is...a bit tense."

"Tense."

"Yes, sir. Everybody is a bit...tense."

"Do we need to worry about the shredder?"

"No, sir. I've been here seven months now. I've sent you just about everything you need."

"Not everything, Hilda."

"Oh yes, sir, everything. I've found what you're looking for. It's on its way."

Rex's eyebrows went up and he looked my way. "What is 'it,' Hilda?"

"A check endorsement. Mr. Kilroy endorsed the back of the last distribution check to Premier."

Rex looked at me with his eyebrows up to his hairline. "You are prescient, young man."

It was the first time I ever saw Rex Barkley smile.

"Sooner or later, even the smart ones make a mistake."

Rex reclined in his leather office chair, shoes perched on his walnut desk, staring at the document he held in the fingers of his right hand. On it were photocopies of the front and back of a check in the amount of $367,500. The front showed that the check was drawn on the account of Epsilon Environmental Consulting, LLC, payable to Premier Investment Management, Ltd. The back showed a special endorsement that read "pay to the order of Safe Harbor Ventures, Inc." with a signature that, although nearly indecipherable, looked to be that of a person whose first name began with "B" and last name began with "K" and ended with "y." It was deposited in an account at the Warren Savings Bank, Warren, Vermont, and cleared through a "Cayman Int'l Bk" with an international routing number printed below it.

This was indeed an exhilarating development, with my trial approaching. But I couldn't afford to be too optimistic. "I don't know, Rex. These are clever people. There could be a perfectly plausible explanation for this."

"Yeah, but there isn't. Safe Harbor's on the title to their boat." He picked a document off the top of a pile and passed it to me. A record of incorporation for Safe Harbor Ventures, Inc. from the Delaware Secretary of State Corporations Division. It showed two members—Bernard Kilroy and Virginia E. Kilroy.

I handed the two documents back to Rex, and he placed the copies back on the top of the pile, put a fat elastic around it, slipped the package into a manila envelope, put the envelope into a satchel and patted the satchel.

"I'll go see your friends Hartfield and McGonigle. You go make sure Shannon is well fed."

"Brilliant idea," I said.

I walked into Shannon's with a bag full of Peking duck, moo shu pork and enough rice for a Chinese New Year. I'd thought that, and the two bottles of Riesling, would thrill Shannon, but she seemed engrossed in her latest project—a bathroom door with faux glass and a naked child in the tub—and more than a little distracted.

"Up for more duck? Last time it seemed to be fun."

She reacted with a coolness I'd not seen before. "Maybe in a while." She went back to dabbing at the tub. "There's a message on my machine for you."

Oho. "You feeling a little weird, me getting phone calls at your place now?"

"It's 'our' place, Paul. And no." She paused. "Well, yes. Just listen to the message, you'll see, maybe."

I walked to the table, studied the answering machine, tapped a few buttons that did nothing, muttered a few expletives. Shannon grumbled, strode over with a painty sponge in her fingers and punched one button, with more gusto than necessary.

Kate's voice burbled out. "Hi, um… Paul? Hi, it's Kate. I'm sorry to leave this at your, uh… new place, but I called your old number and your message there left this number. So. Anyway… I have something important to talk to you about and… oh shit, Paul, could you just call me as soon as possible?"

I looked at Shannon while the machine clicked and beeped. She looked back, dead face, dull eyes. "See?" she asked, and an eyebrow crept toward the ceiling.

"I see." I was frozen in my spot, really wanting to take duck out of a bag or open wine—anything but pick up the phone.

Shannon's face unfroze. "I'll get the food out of the bags. You'd better call her, hadn't you?" She walked coolly past me to the bags on the prep table and began to rip them open like they were phone books.

I dialed the number Kate left, thinking *why don't I already know it*, and her sleepy voice answered.

"Kate."

"Hi Paul! Thanks for calling back."

"Did I wake you?"

"Don't worry about it. It's nice to hear from you." She sounded sluggish.

"What's going on?"

She didn't respond right away, but I felt that she was struggling. It was in the nature of the silence and no little noises. Then I did hear some irregular breathing, and that was not part of the old scene. She never, ever cried on the phone.

"Kate, if you need me, I'm here." I eyed Shannon. Her movements halted for a split second, her eyes anywhere but at me.

"Are you sure? You don't know what I need."

"I don't care what you need, Kate. If you need me, I'm here." I heard a muffled whimper and might have joined her if I'd had just one Sapphire already. Shannon's bag ripping made a racket.

"Can I come right out and say it? I'll come right out and say it. You remember how you've always been telling me how you worry about me worrying? About how it isn't healthy to worry all the time and—"

"Yes, yes, Kate. Come on honey. Just tell me. What is the problem?" Shannon's head snapped at the "honey."

"I have cancer."

I heard it before she said it. I heard it before she sucked the breath in to push it out over her tongue.

"Tell me."

She breathed in deeply several times, like she was getting up the gumption. "I have an aggressive form of cancer. The prognosis is not good, but I have some appointments at Mass General for some tests, and…" She halted. "Oh Christ, Paul, who am I fooling. I just don't want to *die alone*."

I couldn't process this information, or give her the reply that I wanted, quickly enough. Silence is liable to be misunderstood, especially by one who has the designation of "ex" anything. But she did not misunderstand me; she didn't say it, but I didn't doubt it either.

"I'll take care of it."

Silence on the phone while Shannon shoveled food onto plates.

"Kate?"

"Yes, Paul."

"Is that okay? Can I do that for you?"

"Yes. Yes, Paul. You're wonderful." I don't know for sure that she was crying, because I heard no evidence of it. But that's what intuition is for. Sometimes you just know.

"I'll call you tomorrow. We'll come down and get you."

"Okay, Paul. Bye. Thank you."

"Bye Kate."

Shannon had halted her food preparation and stood by the prep table, hands glued to her hips.

"Kate has some health problems and needs a place to stay in Boston while she gets some tests at Mass General."

"What kind of health problems?"

"Cancer."

She stood as still as I did.

"She doesn't want to *die alone*, she said." The last word squeezed out of my throat and I began to sob.

Shannon didn't move at first. Then her arms fidgeted, she scratched her forehead, fiddled with one of the spring rolls on the table. Then she just let out a big sigh, strode over to me, took my shoulders in her hands, and said, "Let it out."

So I did.

• • •

It takes a special kind of woman to make tender love to a man under those circumstances. A cynic might suspect that she was just laying claim to her property, but I chose to believe that she was just giving me the sweet balm she knew I needed. Right or wrong, it didn't matter. Another cynic might say she was just fucking the sadness out of me, and there'd be a good deal of truth to that. Whatever her purpose, it worked.

We'd showered, returned to the kitchen, and warmed up and ate the moo shu in an awkward silence. I didn't know what was on her mind now that the sex was done.

I stared at her, watching something going on in that curious brain of hers. Then her brow furrowed and her lips pursed. "She'll stay at your place."

"With whom?" I realized what a dumb question it was, but the damage was done.

"You idiot. You're staying there, with her, until whenever. So will I." She picked up her dish and mine and brought them to the sink. "As long as she's here and needs us, we'll be giving her as much help as she needs," she said to the dishes and she rinsed them.

"You and I, huh?"

She shrugged. "I suppose so."

"She doesn't have anyone else, you know."

Her shoulders slunk as she turned to me. "I know she doesn't have anyone else. So we do what has to be done, and you'll let me help because you're a little preoccupied right now."

I walked up behind her and slipped my arms around her. "I want to hug you."

She snickered. "Don't push your luck."

Shannon rented a minivan the next day and we drove it down to Providence to Kate's place. I had tried to convince

Shannon not to come, but she wasn't hearing it.

"Listen, dickhead. I don't care if she's your ex-wife. I know how you feel about her, and she's family. So quit being a pussy and let's go do what we have to do."

I just love that woman.

We had a quiet ride down, save for the Muddy Waters CD. I think we were both wondering about the weirdness of meeting. At least I was. But the two of them embarrassed me with their kissy-kissy. It was really something, like they'd been having an affair behind my back.

We packed up the stuff Kate wanted to bring and put the rest in storage. Before we hit the road back, Kate directed me to an Italian deli and we got subs and chips and gnocchi for the ride.

"What the hell's with the gnocchi?" I asked Shannon.

"I love gnocchi."

"What's to love about gnocchi? It's bland and squishy."

"I love gnocchi, too," from Kate in the back seat.

"Since when? Five years we were married, how many times you ever order gnocchi?" I looked at Kate in the rear view mirror. She had a mischievous glint in her eye, but her color was chalky and she looked drained.

"I was a stealth gnocchi lover."

Shannon giggled. "Me too. I ate mine in the closet."

"I've been hijacked by closet gnocchi fanatics."

Boston was a fifty-minute ride from Providence, but it seems like ten. Shannon and Kate gabbed like sorority sisters. I couldn't get a word in edgewise. Once, Shannon fed me a bit of gnocchi from a plastic fork as I drove, and in the rear view mirror I caught Kate smiling.

We got to my place by late afternoon and unloaded Kate's things. Shannon and I brought them up the stairs while Kate lay on my couch with her shoes off, looking like she needed a nap. Shannon was ready to run out and leave us alone, but Kate asked for a break, so we left her there on the couch and went out to shop for some food.

"What do you think?" I asked her.

Shannon's face had been a study in cheerfulness and energy. But it dropped in response. "First of all, I have no idea how you could let that woman get away," drooping her head and shaking it.

"That's not what I meant."

She stopped on the sidewalk and turned to me. "You want the truth? I'll tell you the truth, Paul. Your ex-wife is on death's door. I can see it in her skin, I can hear it in her voice. I know what to look for. I've seen it before. She's dying."

"Aren't you subtle."

"Paul, there's a time for subtlety and this ain't it. You need to know this. Your ex-wife is dying. I know the timing sucks and you've got your own world of problems right now, but this isn't going to wait. She needs us. All in. Are you all in, Paul?" There was anger in her face. But not a furious anger. It was the anger that is evoked when the exigencies of life deal you more than you can handle and you suck it up and beat your chest and put on the game face and say "bring it on."

It was the same anger I felt when I heard Bernie Kilroy's opening statement.

"Bring it on," I said.

Shannon's phone rang at an ungodly early hour. No good comes from that. Sure enough, it was my lawyer, angry with me again.

"Good morning, Al." I took the phone from her bedroom and wandered down the stairs to the kitchen.

"I got a call from Will Hartfield just now."

"Will? You mean Agent Hartfield?"

"He identified himself as Will. He called me to ask permission to meet with you. Alone."

"Really."

"Paul, what the hell are you up to?"

"What am I up to?"

"Yes, Paul. What are you up to? Why is the FBI case agent asking me if he can meet with you alone?"

"Probably because we agreed that you're handling the legal defense and I'm handling the 'other strategy.'"

I heard Al sigh into the phone. "What are you doing talking to Will Hartfield's father?"

Aha.

"He and my father were old friends. Agent Hartfield told me that. I thought I'd go visit him and see if he could tell me any stories about my father."

"I'm not buying that, Paul. What are you up to?"

"You sure you're not better off not knowing?"

"I'm not sure of anything anymore."

"Okay, but if I tell you, I'll have to kill you."

"Knock it off, Paul."

"Sidney Hartfield was the SEC whistleblower. And my father was the white knight."

After I explained what my father had done for Mr. Sidney Hartfield, my lawyer felt more comfortable about my meeting with my case agent alone. More comfortable, but not ecstatic. And I had not—and would not—tell him about the package Rex had delivered to him.

Al spent the next hour fretting over the parameters of my visit, drafting something with "the government shall not discuss, inquire, or otherwise refer to," followed by a growing laundry list of people, places and things. I kept telling him to relax, it doesn't matter what Hartfield says, I'm not going to fall into that trap. This was the usual patter between criminal lawyer and client, I presumed, although under usual circumstances, it is idiotic to talk to a federal agent without a lawyer present. Under usual circumstances.

Shannon and I had worked out our schedules so that Kate was never alone.

I took Kate to Dana-Farber for tests and sat with her when the oncologist gave her the bleak news. Nothing could be done that offered any hope and wouldn't ravage what was left of her health with chemicals and radiation. She held my hand when he delivered this death sentence, and there wasn't a quiver in her fingers. It was as though she was already prepared for it.

"That option doesn't appeal to me, doctor," she said, and she looked at me and asked, "Will you take me to dinner?"

That night, Shannon had a gallery show, so I got some take-out from a Japanese restaurant and served Kate in bed. She loved sushi, and even though she didn't have much of an appetite, she managed to make a good dent in the hamachi and anago. She pushed her plate away and sighed.

"I'm happy that you've found a woman like Shannon. She knows how to talk to you."

"What do you mean?"

She looked at me with sad eyes and a smile. "I didn't know how to talk to you."

"And I didn't know how to listen."

"Do you know why I withdrew from you?"

"No, but I'm sure it was my fault."

"It was and it wasn't. Do you know the old joke about how

to tell when a politician is lying?"

"His lips are moving?"

"That's the one."

"What about it?"

"It's more true than some people think." She reached out and took my hand, and I let her.

"Do you think I lied to you?"

She paused, choosing her words. "When you were in your role, you lied incessantly. I watched you. Not big lies, but a thousand little ones. And you did it effortlessly. I don't think you even realized it. At least, you didn't show it."

"I don't think I lied to you, Kate."

She smiled. "Did you ever go off to play golf and tell me you were doing something else?" She had a glint in her eye as she squeezed my hand.

"Yes, I did that." Oh, I sure did.

"More than once?"

"Now that I think about it, many times."

"See? You didn't even think about it. It came naturally."

"Why didn't you say something about it?"

"Because you weren't trying to hurt me. You had your reason for not telling me the truth. It wasn't malicious, just cowardly. But after a while, I couldn't bear thinking about what else you might lie to me about."

"You just let it eat away at you." Our hands were caressing now.

"I'm afraid that's the way I am." She quickened her caressing and gave a reassuring pat.

"I was never unfaithful to you, Kate."

She put her other hand on mine. "I believe you, now. Because we're no longer together. I know you're here with me because you want to be."

"You know I still love you, don't you?"

A demure giggle escaped her. "I suppose I do. At least, in the way I need to be loved right now."

I didn't need to ask. "I do. Absolutely. We're here for you. Whatever you need." When I heard my voice say "we," I flinched, and she caught it, and giggled again.

"Don't be silly, Paul. I know how in love with her you are."

"Yeah?"

"Yes. And she with you, too. You're naturals."

"Does it make you happy?"

"It does."

"Yeah?"

"Yeah. It does." She had a look of serenity, an acceptance of something that had to be more than her ex-husband finding a new lover. I watched her face with its now closed eyes and the up-curled lips of her smile dissipated and the brow furrowed and her eyes turned crinkled.

"Pain?"

Her tears ran as she nodded.

I fetched her morphine from the side table, poured her water, put the pills in her hand.

"I think we might want to push up the hospice people, sweetheart," she said, doing her best to turn a smile.

Within two days, we had someone else helping us, twenty-four seven. Bridey, a lovely older Irish woman from Chicago with a charming brogue, a mouth like a sailor and a repertoire of stories that rivaled Finley Peter Dunn. She was also a nurse who was an ace at setting Kate's IV drip and making sure the little push button thing never left her palm.

Kate used it well.

• • •

I'd seen so many movies with this sort of scene—the clandestine meeting with the spook. Usually it's a CIA guy wearing a narrow tie and a fedora, or maybe a fez and a fake mustache. So I was intrigued to learn they did indeed happen in real life. Or mine, anyway.

My instructions were simple. Take the Blue Line to Wood Island, go to the top row of the ball field bleachers facing Logan. I'd picked up a bag of peanuts from the pushcart dude at Government Center, so I really looked the part. And the youth soccer league was in full swing, with lots of high-pitched screaming and taunting to drown out even the most sensitive surveillance tools.

I arrived ten minutes early, and waited twenty-five. During this time, I scrutinized every adult male coming and going from the bleachers, searching for a disguise, an odd hat, an unnatural movement. No one stuck out.

"Howyadoin'?" said the voice of a guy sitting ten feet away and one bench down. He wore a Red Sox cap, which sure didn't stick out, cheap sunglasses, a black leather jacket, faded jeans and high-top Keds. He looked like a guy who'd been fired from his hawking job at Fenway. I never saw him arrive, and it took me a good long time to realize the voice was Hartfield's.

"Jesus Christ," I said. "How do you guys *do* that?"

He stood and moved down so I was over his right shoulder.

"Peanut?" I asked, sticking the bag out. He shook his head.

I'd looked forward to seeing Agent Hartfield, oddly unconcerned that he might be angry at me for visiting his father. If the old man had told his son about my visit, he might have said why, which couldn't have hurt me. I found it hard to believe that Will Hartfield didn't know about Seamus Kilroy. How many Wall Street titans put a gun in their mouths?

But what the hell? Why would an FBI agent in Boston notice a story like that from years before? One thing I had to remember was not to give him any clue about my involvement with Rex's package.

"My father says he had a bang up time during your visit."

"Will—"

"Don't worry about it."

"Don't worry about it?"

"That's right." Below, a scrum of kids fought over the ball. Will clapped his hand and cupped them around his mouth. "Way to go, Mikey!" he hollered, glancing back and pointing down toward the field. "My Little Brother."

"Little brother?"

Will smirked over his shoulder. "Not 'little brother,' Little Brother. From the program, you know? Big Brothers and Big Sisters?"

"Oh." Then I noticed that Mikey was as black as a moonless sky. What an idiot. "So Will, why are we here?"

Hartfield sat, looking at his hands cupped between his knees. "Do you have any idea how much we have in common?"

"It's bizarre, I know."

"You don't know. You might think you do, but you don't."

"Look, Will. I didn't go to your father looking to position you or pressure you or—"

"Quiet."

"Huh?"

"Shut up. Just listen to me for a minute." He slid back and leaned his elbows and back against the bench next to me. He looked straight ahead and his mouth moved very little while he spoke.

"Okay."

"I went to visit my father yesterday with the same objective I've had for the past twenty-five years. To get him to tell me stories about the things that he did that made his life what it's been. I expected to fail, again, as I have all that time. But he doesn't have much time left, and I figure one day before he goes, he'll decide it's time. So imagine my surprise when he tells me you visited him, and then he tells me the story of your dad and him and Kilroy's father."

"You didn't know about Kilroy's father?"

"Gimme some peanuts."

I handed him the bag and he spilled out a handful.

"I didn't know about Seamus Kilroy or either of our fathers' roles in it. Or what your father did for mine. But I'll tell you one thing I do know, at this moment."

"What's that," I asked.

"I now know why Bernie Kilroy is prosecuting you." He couldn't hide the contempt rumbling inside him.

Well, that's nice and all, but hello? Still, I could tell from his face that he wasn't just angry about it. He was vein-popping furious.

"I didn't take this job to help a federal prosecutor settle an old score."

"I appreciate that, Will, but your job is pretty much over, isn't it? I mean, don't take this the wrong way, but you can't do any more harm, can you?"

He glanced sideways and smirked.

"Can you?" I asked.

"Not to *you*," he said. I guessed he was looking at me behind those shades. He looked back at the soccer game and slid his hand into a jacket pocket. It pulled out a small manila envelope, placed it on the floorboard and slid it over to my foot.

"That's your amendment."

"Really."

"Yup."

"I don't get it."

"For a lawyer, you're pretty stupid."

"Sorry, man, I don't know much about sabotage, subterfuge, duplicity, that sort of stuff."

He chuckled. "You didn't get that document in your discovery, did you?"

"No, we didn't."

"Well, I handed it over to them."

"You did, eh?"

"I did." He looked over. "As I should have."

"Of course."

"Of course." He watched the field. "And I signed the document out at the Clerk's office, so that there would be a record of that."

"As you needn't have."

"No. I have no obligation to leave a trail. And Kilroy doesn't know I did."

"He doesn't?"

"Well, *we* didn't tell him I did."

I thought about that. "Wow."

"So you think you and your lawyer can figure out what to do with that?"

"I think so, but isn't that going to cause you some issues?"

He laughed out loud. "If you end up subpoenaing me, I suppose it will. But that's what I have to do. And you know what you have to do. Now you can leave and let me watch Mikey play soccer."

"Alright then." I reached down, picked up the envelope and pocketed it. "Thanks a million, Will." I stood and began to leave.

"Hey," he said. I looked back. "If you happen to get caught with that document between here and the street—"

"I stole it." Jesus, it felt great to say that.

"One more thing."

"Name it."

"Tell your girlfriend to call her sister."

"Will do!"

I skipped down the bleacher stairs with my hand clasped to the envelope, leaving Will to root for his Little Brother, Mikey.

I went back to Al's office and tossed the envelope onto his desk. He opened the envelope and examined the paper.

"Well, lookey here," he said.

"That's awful colloquial for you, Al."

"Isn't it? So what's the story?"

I told Al the story.

"So what do you think?" he asked.

"I think that when Will found the amendment, he left a trail on purpose."

"In case something happened to it on the way to the court-house."

"Yeah. Just what Stacey hinted. Then when Sidney told Will our history, Will decided it was time to repay an old debt."

Al stared at the document with a tight frown. "You realize if we call him to testify, he'll lose his job."

"I've given that some thought."

"And?"

"Like father, like son."

Chapter 24

The Phone Doesn't Ring, a Continuing Parade, and Driving Fear

Another day, another cocktail hour at Abe & Louie's, another stellar performance by our friend, Chip. He'd perfected the twist over the Sapphire, and once even flicked an olive at me, having been reassured that I was no more allergic to olives than gin.

Rex and I clinked over a plate of raw oysters. "To recalcitrant bureaucrats," he said.

We drank deeper than we ought.

"What the hell's taking them so long, Rex? This is driving me berserk."

He shook his head, eyebrows at their height. "I'm stumped. I can't even get a phone call returned."

"I wish I knew what it meant."

"Could mean nothing. Your pal Will did his job, maybe passed the documents off to Washington. He may be just as in the dark as we are."

"Yah, well, the trial proceeds apace. We're running out of goddamn time. I'm ready to buy a fresh toothbrush, for crissakes."

"Quit complaining and drink up."

I did. "Hilda move on from Epsilon, did she?"

"Yup. Made a clean escape without raising one eyebrow. I might have to hire the lady."

"Will you give her a cut of your qui tam award?"

He glared at me. "Why would I do that? Fee for services, baby."

"You're a cheap prick, Barkley. There'll be plenty to go around."

He relented. "You may be right. I might use it to lure her to my team. We'll see."

"If our public servants don't move fast, the only way I'll see is on closed circuit television."

"Be quiet and have some oysters."

"The government calls Stuart Pierce."

A school vacation week and an emergency stent procedure on Judge Wheeler had delayed this day long enough. Even though it had given the feds more time to look into Rex's package, their continuing silence was excruciating. I was sick of sleepless nights in which Pierce's imagined testimony ran through my head until the gray light of dawn arrived. And Shannon was ready to pitch me onto the futon for good. It was time to find out which team Stuart was batting for.

Stuart rose from a corner seat and his lanky frame glided through the gate toward the witness stand. His hawk eyes bore straight ahead until, passing our table, he turned his head and gave me a subtle nod.

"Nice suit," I whispered to Al.

Stuart raised his hand on command, took his oath and settled into the witness chair like it had been made for him. He looked comfortable, crossed his legs, even. All eyes were on him, but he didn't seem to care.

Kilroy got the preliminaries out of the way, then got right down to business.

"Mr. Pierce, directing your attention to the time period of late March of that year, did you have some legislative business at the House of Representatives?"

"I did. The Interstate Banking legislation."

"And what was your interest in that?"

"I represent a small group of state-chartered banks whose tax status would have been adversely affected by some of the provisions."

"What did you plan to do about it?"

"I'd prepared an amendment to the bill, discussed the amendment with the Chairman of the committee, and arranged to have it attached to the legislation when it came onto the House floor."

Kilroy paused and smiled. "So, in other words, you arranged to have the law revised to suit your clients."

"Yes, that's right."

"How did you accomplish the delivery of that amendment?"

"I asked Paul Forté to do it."

"Do what?"

"Deliver the amendment to the House Clerk for reading."

"Why Mr. Forté?"

"Because he was a friend of mine, and he was a member of the Banking Committee."

"Why not a member of the majority party? The Chairman or the Vice-chairman?"

Pierce gave a languid shrug. "Paul was the first guy to walk by."

"Walk by?"

"Yes. I stood in the hallway outside the members' entrance

to the House Chamber, waiting for the first appropriate member to ask, and he came by first."

"Just happened to be random chance?"

"I suppose."

"But you wouldn't have asked any member who happened to walk by, would you?"

"No. That's what I meant by 'appropriate.'"

"What made Mr. Forté 'appropriate?'"

"He was a member of the committee, and I was friendly with him."

"How did you become friendly with him, Mr. Pierce?"

"On the golf course."

"On whose golf course?"

"Mine."

"Where is that, Mr. Pierce?"

"The Country Club of Brookline, and Kittansett, in Marion."

Kilroy stepped to the jury box and placed both hands on the wooden railing. "Could you describe the first club for us, Mr. Pierce?" he asked, with a subtle tone of derision.

Pierce answered evenly. "It is an old, private club with a golf course that is well thought of."

"Is the club open to all?"

"Hardly."

"Explain."

"It is a very exclusive club. Very hard to join."

"Are there any *African-American* or *Hispanic* members?" Kilroy, still in front of the jurors, tilted his head to the side.

Al rose. "Objection, Your Honor. I fail to see what the Country Club of Brookline's membership policy has to do with the charges against Mr. Forté."

"Sustained."

Kilroy wheeled around to face Pierce. "Well, could Mr. Forté join?"

"Objection."

"Sustained," Wheeler said again. "Mr. Kilroy, let's move on to something pertinent, shall we?"

A few of the black jurors frowned. One crossed her arms below her ample bosom.

"Mr. Pierce, did Mr. Forté play golf at The Country Club of Brookline as your guest?"

"Yes."

"How many times?"

"I don't know exactly, but I'd guess around a dozen."

"Did he pay his greens fees?"

"No."

"What are the guest fees for golf at The Country Club of Brookline?"

"A hundred twenty-five dollars."

"Did he pay his caddy fees?"

"No."

"How much there?"

"Seventy-five, with tip."

"Did you have lunch?"

"Yes."

"Did he pay for his lunch?"

"No."

"Did you have cocktails afterward?"

"Sometimes."

"Did he pay for his cocktails?"

"No."

Kilroy repeated this obnoxious routine for Kittansett, with the same result. He wheeled toward the jury for his final flourish. "So help me with my math, Mr. Pierce, all told, is it fair to say that the value of the entertainment Mr. Forté received from you would exceed two thousand dollars?"

"I think that's fair to say."

"And did some or all of these golf outings occur before you gave him your amendment to deliver to the House Clerk?"

"Most, if not all."

"Thank you," Kilroy said. He glanced at Al. "Your witness."

With a face that betrayed no emotion, Pierce leaned forward, picked up a glass of water from the dais he sat behind and took a slow draught as Al approached him.

"Good morning, Mr. Pierce."

"Good morning, Mr. Croston."

"We haven't spoken before this moment, have we?"

"No, sir, we have not."

"I haven't 'prepared' you in any way, have I?"

"Absolutely not."

"Okay then. This amendment of yours. You haven't been able to locate a copy of it, I presume?"

"I'm afraid not. It's been several years. Once it becomes recorded in the House Journal, I have no need for a hard copy."

"And you said that you had previously discussed it with the legislative leaders, correct?"

"Correct."

"And shared copies with them, yes?"

"Yes, or with their staff."

"And you wouldn't have any reason to go around and retrieve those copies."

"Not at all."

"And you say that the day you stood outside the chamber with your amendment, you had already received word from the leadership that your amendment was going to be accepted, correct?"

"Yes."

"So you weren't looking for a sponsor, per se, for the amendment when you approached Mr. Forté."

"No."

"Did you already have a sponsor lined up?"

Pierce adjusted himself, turning more toward the jury. "Well, yes. But his name wasn't on the amendment."

"Please explain that statement, Mr. Pierce."

Pierce turned so that he was facing the jury as directly as his seat allowed. "Routinely, when I or another lobbyist wishes to have an amendment considered by the House, it is drafted in such a form that the sponsor's name is blank. Every amendment begins in the same fashion. It will say 'Mr. Pierce of Westfield moves that the bill be amended...' for instance. When we don't know in advance who the sponsor is going to be, we leave blanks for the name and the town."

"And that's how your amendment was drafted?"

"Yes."

Al put on a confused look. "But Mr. Pierce, you indicated that the Speaker and the Committee Chairman had already authorized your amendment to be accepted. Why wouldn't you put either of their names?"

"That's just the way it's done. My understanding is that the floor leaders like to be in charge of who gets credit for what."

"Or doesn't?"

"Or doesn't. There is certainly business done that a representative might not want to be identified with."

"Why not, Mr. Pierce?"

Pierce smiled. "Well, Mr. Croston, I'm afraid you'll have to ask them that question. I've been a lobbyist for thirty-seven years and I've got no better understanding of a politician's thinking now than I did when I began."

"Fair enough. So Mr. Pierce. There you are, standing outside the House chamber with your amendment in your suit jacket. It states 'Mr. BLANK of BLANK moves that the bill be amended, right?'"

"Yes."

"Is it in an envelope?"

"No."

"Folded?"

"Yes, in thirds."

"Okay, so it's folded in thirds. Print on the outside or inside?"

"I don't recall."

"Who are you waiting for?"

Pierce shrugged. "The first House member I can ask to deliver it to the Speaker's rostrum."

"So if the Chairman or Vice-chairman had walked by?"

"Absolutely."

"You would have said, 'Hey Mr. Chairman, here's that amendment we were talking about,' and he'd have said what?"

"I assume he'd have taken it without pause and said, 'I'll take care of it.'"

"But Mr. Forté happened to be the first guy by."

"Yes, that's right."

"Lucky for him, eh?"

He shrugged again. "Things have a strange way of happening."

Al moved toward the jury box. "Let's talk about golf for a moment. When you first hosted Mr. Forté at The Country Club, did he offer to pay for his expenses?"

"Not in so many words, no. But that would be highly unusual."

"For a politician, you mean?"

"No, for anyone."

"Could you explain?"

Pierce shifted casually and waved his thin hand toward the jury. "Well, that's just not how it's done."

"How is it done, Mr. Pierce?"

"It would be considered rude for a golf guest to offer to pay for his round. Especially in this case, where the guest was a member of another private club. In Paul's case, being a member of Hyannisport, he responded to my hospitality by extending an offer of his own, which is the tradition."

"So he invited you to Hyannisport, by which you understood he was returning your hospitality?"

"Exactly."

"But you never took him up on it, did you?" Al would not leave this line of cross to Kilroy to sabotage. Pierce's face broke into a broad smile, the first I'd seen of it since our last outing.

"No, not yet. Not that I never will, but I consider the invitation still open."

"Did Mr. Forté ever express an opinion on your failure to visit Hyannisport?"

"Frequently. In fact, it was the subject of routine ribbing on his part. He accused me of being allergic to Kennedy turf."

"Was he correct in that accusation?"

"Somewhat, I suppose. I come from deep Brahmin roots. My ancestors' disdain for Irish immigrants is an albatross around my neck, especially in my business. But truthfully, it had more to do with my dislike of driving."

"You didn't care to drive to Cape Cod to play golf?"

"I don't care to drive anywhere I don't absolutely have to."

"Fair enough. Let's return to the delivery of this amendment. So Mr. Forté walks by, and you say what?"

"I say hello, we chat briefly, and I ask him if he'll deliver the paper to the rostrum."

"Well, do you say, 'here is an amendment,' or do you say 'here is a piece of paper,' or 'a note' or 'a message?'"

"I don't recall specifically referring to it in any particular manner."

"So you could have simply said, 'Could you give *this* to the Speaker?'"

"I could have."

"And if it had been folded print-side in, he wouldn't have known what he was delivering, isn't that so?"

Kilroy jumped up. "Objection! Speculation."

Al didn't wait for Wheeler to rule. "I'll rephrase, your Honor. Mr. Pierce, was there anything said by Mr. Forté, or any action by him that you witnessed, that would cause you to believe that he knew what he was delivering?"

Kilroy rose again, slower this time. "Objection."

"Overruled. He is permitted to give his impression of events he witnessed."

Kilroy dropped into his seat as Pierce leaned forward toward the microphone. "No."

"So you have no idea, as you sit here today, if Mr. Forté knew what he was delivering to the rostrum?"

"I do not."

"Nothing further, your Honor." Al returned to his seat without looking at Pierce or the jury.

"Re-direct, Mr. Kilroy?"

Kilroy jumped out of his chair and practically charged at Pierce. "Mr. Pierce, you say you never went to Hyannisport because you," looking down at a legal pad, "'don't care to drive anywhere I don't absolutely have to.' Do you remember saying that?"

"I certainly hope so. I just said it."

"How far is the Kittansett Club from Boston?"

"It's a little under an hour's drive."

"How do you explain your frequent trips to Kittansett with Mr. Forté?"

Pierce smiled languidly. "I am a creature of habit, Mr. Kilroy. The car practically drives itself there."

Kilroy smirked at the jury. "Nothing further."

Judge Wheeler looked at Al. He shook his head. "Mr. Pierce, you are excused," Wheeler said.

Stuart rose languidly from the witness chair and glided past the jury. He turned his head slightly toward them and gave that same subtle nod that he had given me. Their eyes were trained on his face, I could see, but I couldn't get any read from them. They could have been fascinated or repulsed. And like me, they could have had no idea what to make of his testimony.

As Judge Wheeler dismissed the jury, and they, then Kilroy, filed out of the courtroom, I sat in my chair and reflected on the irony of the story Pierce had just told. Was I just some clueless dolt, like Bags or Bobo, stumbling through another legislative day, picking up his per diem, doing a friend a favor, performing the menial task of delivering a piece of paper like a page? Or was I engaged in a criminal act? As much as I tried to convince myself that no reasonable jury could look upon me as a felon, I could not shake the persistent dread that I had no idea who those people were, they had no idea who I was, and they might not ever appreciate my devotion to the rules.

Of one thing I was certain. I was going to need Shannon's help getting to sleep again.

Chapter 25
Christmas Reprise and Inconsolable Grief

With the death of my ex-wife looming, the idea of another three-week delay in my trial was maddening, and I didn't hold out much hope of evading my usual Christmas slump. But I turned out to be wrong.

A few days back, Shannon snuck off, bought a small tree and set it up in front of the fireplace. She and Kate decorated it with popcorn and cranberry strings and blinking colored lights.

I broke away from the criminal defense business and went on a spree through the Copley Place stores, where I spent a stupid amount of money on frilly things that women like to wear in close company, and a few good books too, just for show. I even paid extra for fancy wrapping. I watched the frumpy church ladies cutting and taping when I remembered my sojourn to Chinatown and the doctor's diagnosis. I decided he was wrong. I did not have a weak heart. I had reason to have a broken heart, but that was different. And a year had passed. I'd been feeling sorry for myself, and it was long past time to cut the crap.

One of the ladies looked up at me. "You seem to have gotten a lot of pleasure out of buying these gifts, judging from the look on your face."

"I have indeed."

"A special someone, is my guess."

"Don't take this the wrong way, but a special two people."

Another of them raised her eyebrows, eyes wide. "I hope one of them is your sister."

I took the packages from them, put a twenty-dollar bill in their glass jar, and winked.

"I'll have to leave it to your imagination," I said, winking. They tittered.

On the way back to my place, I grabbed some cheese puffs and pâté at the gourmet deli, and I felt happy walking into my place bearing gifts and goodies. The girls were cozy on the couch, sharing a blanket, their serene faces reflecting the blinks of the bulbs on the tree. They cooed when they saw the gifts but couldn't twist my arm about opening them right away.

We sat together, listening to Nat King Cole, eating the hors d'oeuvres, sipping Champagne, and trading memories of Christmases past. More than once I fought back the tennis ball—but it was not one of sadness, or at least, not that I could tell. Shannon served up some duck and pasta, she and I trading a knowing glance.

After we cleaned up, Shannon announced she had a surprise and left the apartment. I sat with Kate on the couch, neither one of us with any inkling of what the nutty lady was up to. Soon we heard Shannon's footsteps coming up the stairs along with her labored breathing and grunting. She bumped the door open and struggled in, carrying in her arms a three-wheeled vehicle, which she promptly wrestled to its open position. It was a rugged tricycle wheelchair, designed for cross-country, with large treaded bicycle tires and handlebars equipped with brakes.

"Let's go for a spin," she said, eyebrows raised and hundred-watt smile stretched across her face.

I looked at Kate. She stared at the contraption, mouth agape, eyes wide. "I don't know if I have the strength," she finally said with a look of worry.

"I'll carry you down and up," I said. "All you have to do is sit, for crissakes."

"Do we have enough blankets?"

Shannon went to the closet and removed enough wool and mohair to make all of Boston sneeze.

Kate looked up at us and set her jaw. "Let's do it. I haven't been out of this shit hole in a month," she said with a twinkle.

Shannon and I together helped Kate don layer upon layer. A cashmere sweater. A down vest. A nylon shell. Snow pants. A Puffy white fur hat. By the time we were done with her, she looked like the Michelin Man.

"Get me out of here before I die of heat prostration." The lady was feeling her old self!

Shannon took the trike and the blankets down ahead of us, and I picked Kate off the couch. Even with all of the layers, she weighed nothing. She shrieked in my ear several times as I lumbered down, once bringing me to laughter so badly I had to stop and warn her. When we'd gotten out to the sidewalk, Shannon had the blankets spread across the seat. I laid Kate down in the seat, she wiggled to get herself comfy, and we wrapped her in blankets, tucking in the edges around her.

She giggled and looked up at us. "Mush," she said.

The night was calm and dry, no snow on the ground, and the going was easy. I pushed the cycle, Shannon walked alongside Kate ahead of me, and the two gabbed away. With her back to me, I couldn't hear Kate's words, but I could tell from the timbre and tone of her voice that she was happy, and

Shannon's face affirmed it. We strolled down Dartmouth Street toward Copley Square. The trees lining the sidewalk were strung with white lights. The road was empty, and the voices of the ladies echoed off the buildings, giddy and animated.

We walked under the bright marquis of the Fairmont Copley Hotel, where a tall doorman in resplendent topcoat with gold epaulets tipped his hat and returned the girls' smiles. I heard Kate giggle.

"I love a man in uniform," she said to him.

"Whose line was that, Katherine Hepburn?" I asked.

"Pippi Longstocking."

The fellow nodded at me, smiling, as though he had any freaking idea how lucky a guy I was.

We crossed into Copley Square and stopped to rest (at least, I stopped pushing Kate and Shannon had no choice) at a bench in the middle of the plaza. We faced the resplendent facade of Trinity Church, with its Romanesque redstone pillars and arched windows, their rich and intricate stained glass ignited by the interior lights. Through the open center doors, the sound of that same magnificent organ that had evoked my misery a year ago then began to flow—the rapturous "Joyful, Joyful." It rounded to the end of the first verse, and began again from the top.

"Joyful, Joyful Lord, we adore Thee," Kate sang out, meekly at first, "God of glory, Lord of love, hearts unfold like flowers before Thee, hail Thee as the sun above..." She smiled at Shannon and me, and as we joined in, her voice swelled.

"Melt the clouds of sin and sadness, drive the dark of doubt away, giver of immortal gladness, fill us with the light of day," we harmonized feebly across the near-deserted plaza.

On we went through succeeding verses, Shannon now twirling about, head flung back, belting the tune at the sky, prompting Kate to laughter as she tried to sing through the absurd display. The tennis ball caught in my throat again as I listened to them holler the last verse, Shannon now gesturing to passing cabs like she was auditioning for Broadway.

Our chorale performance took its toll on Kate. She announced that she'd had enough, so we walked back, quieter than before, but no less enchanted, I thought. When we got to the building and I stooped to pick Kate out of the carriage, I could see from her face that she had indeed been exhausted by the adventure. We got her upstairs and into bed, and she might have dropped right off to sleep, but she asked us to stay. Shannon climbed onto the bed and lay next to her. Kate looked at me, patting the empty side, so I obliged, and the three of us lay together, saying nothing.

I could only guess what was going through their heads. Perhaps we were all thinking the exact same thing, but I chose to believe that we fell asleep at the exact same moment.

Christmas had regained its luster, even against the backdrop of the maddeningly protracted ordeal of my trial.

Shannon left me alone at home, so I had time for my secret errand.

I took a document from a manila envelope. I made a copy of it, then whited-out all identifying pencil markings. In the blank space after the word "By" in the first line, I wrote MR. KILROY in block letters. In the blank space after the word "of" I wrote MARBLEHEAD. I folded the document, put it in a plain white envelope, taped it shut, addressed the envelope, put a stamp on it, and walked it down to the General Delivery slot in front of the South Boston Postal Annex.

That would test the man's blood pressure.

• • •

I carried my post-holiday exuberance into Rex's office Monday morning and proceeded to rant at him. Surely, all of his important Washington contacts had gotten together and agreed that Rex was washed up. Out to pasture. Off his game. What the hell kind of PI can package evidence of direct involvement in a massive fraud by one of the Justice Department's top people and fail to get a phone call returned? It's a good thing Rex's humor is stronger than his jab, or I'd have ended up at Mass General, and deserved it too. I was one big walking pain in the ass.

After he accepted my third apology and accepted my lunch offer, we left his office and walked out to the reception area, where Rachel huddled on the telephone. She put her hand over the receiver. "Paul, your friend Shannon is on the phone." I didn't like the look on her face, and stepped over to the courtesy line at the reception lounge.

"What's up? We're on our way to lunch. Care to join us?"

"Kate isn't doing well. I don't know whether to call an ambulance or what."

"She didn't want that."

"I know, but it's so hard."

"Is she conscious?"

"Yeah, she's conscious, but she's in an awful lot of pain. The morphine isn't doing much."

"I'll be right home." I hung up and looked at Rex. "Afraid you'll have to eat alone. I've got other business."

"Understood. We're praying for her," he said with a grave look. "I'll call you later."

Rachel began to cry as I ran out.

I hit the Boylston Street sidewalk in a trot and didn't stop, cleared Copley Place without a pause for traffic, turned onto

Columbus Ave, took the steps of my building two-by-two, keyed the door, ran past the elevator and covered four flights of stairs. When I got to the top, I was huffing.

Shannon had left the door ajar, and she must have heard me clambering up the stairs because she met me at the door with a look that I thought told me I was too late. She didn't stop to hug me or say a word. She just took my hand and pulled me down the hallway to Kate's bedroom and right to her side.

Her eyes were closed, beads of perspiration on her forehead. Her face was gaunt and pale, but even the emaciation could not hide the beauty of its lines, like a skeleton angel. Her arm had shades of purple around the IV, and it was frail, the skin withered and loose. Still, there was a natural beauty to her that reminded me of the first time I'd met her, almost twenty years before. When I sat at her side, and Shannon at her other side, she stirred, opened her eyes, and smiled wanly. I leaned down and kissed her forehead.

"You've come to see me off." It wasn't a question.

"Don't say that."

"No, you have. It's time to go."

"We don't want you to go yet. We've just begun to have fun."

Her face sagged to a weak smile. "My time has come, Paul." She said it so matter-of-factly, but with a glint in her eye, like she was anticipating something special. "You've both been so wonderful. I love you and I'll miss you." Her face brightened. "Do you know that Shannon is my soul mate?"

I looked at Shannon. "She is?"

"Yes," she said, turning to Shannon and taking her hand, too. "She's the artist in me but with your spirit of adventure. She is who I wanted to be but couldn't."

Her smile beamed, she closed her eyes as tears rolled off

their corners into her wispy hair. Her hands, bony and pallid, held their grip on ours. She opened her eyes again, smile persevering.

"I was always afraid that you would never find what you were looking for. I was afraid that your unhappiness was something you couldn't solve by finding the right woman. I was sad for you. But not any more." She squeezed Shannon's hand and raised it up. It must have taken so much of her strength. "Shannon, thank you for taking care of me. Please know how happy you've made me. I love you both."

Her hand fell to the bed again, still holding Shannon, and she closed her eyes.

"Joyful, joyful," she whispered, and her smile remained until every little crease of anguish and joy on her face relaxed into a visage of perfect peace.

At that moment, I thought about how empty I'd felt since Mom and Dad had died. I had thought it was because they left me so far away and I had no warning that the end was coming, no chance to help them, or even to say goodbye. I'd received a call from some dull-sounding lady at the U.S. Embassy, dropped what I was doing and flown to Dublin to claim their bodies and attend to the excruciating bureaucracy of arranging for the transport of "the bodies" homeward. But they were already long gone. You are not given the chance to prepare for death, I had learned, or thought so. You are not given the chance to learn how to react to it. It just comes at you, and you try to summon some inner strength to cope with the profound loss. But no matter how you deal with it, no matter what resolve or strength you might muster, deep within you cannot help but feel a vacuity so vast that you wonder how it fits inside your soul and leaves room for anything else. It's a black hole that is everything and nothing.

Now I sat at the bedside of the person to whom my vow had been broken, not because of infidelity or spite or hatred or alienation, but because she felt she wasn't strong enough to be my co-pilot, that she wasn't right for the journey she knew I was made for. Yet here she lay, even in death, holding onto both of us, having faced the end with a grace and power that made me feel tiny and weak. And I thought that there is no more relief in being close by when death takes those you love, except to know that they might have died with the comfort of having some control over the details.

We held Kate's hands and watched her, for how long I don't know, but in the stillness I heard our sobs, the siren of a passing ambulance and the voices of children from the street.

Shannon rose, passed behind me on her way to the door, caressing my shoulder as she did, and left me alone with Kate. I told her how sorry I was to have failed her, how enriched my life had been for knowing her, how humbled I was that she would ask to be here with us, and how awed I was by her strength and pride in the way she faced death. I told her we would meet again, and then she would be the one to lead me on adventures and become exasperated by my hesitancy and doubt. I told her her spirit would always be a part of me, and Shannon too, and we would honor her in our lives and see that she lived on in us. And then I asked God to watch over her spirit and bring her elation in Heaven.

It was the second time in five years I had prayed and meant it.

I woke up at eleven A.M. in the same position as I'd gone to bed. Shannon was long gone, the apartment was silent. I padded down to the kitchen for coffee and found the Globe on the table, folded over to the front of the obituary page, with this at the top:

Katherine Swan Forté, 35;
artist and interior designer

Katherine Swan Forté, a fine arts master whose quirky sculptures and edgy paintings were popular in regional contemporary art museums, died Friday at her Boston home after a brief illness. She was thirty-five.

Born Katherine Annabelle Swan, Ms. Forté grew up in Noank, Conn., the only daughter of sailing legend Theodore Swan and Yale literature professor Marguerite (Faxon) Swan. She attended the Rosemary Hall School in Wallingford, Conn., where she was captain of the women's field hockey team. Ms. Swan went to University of New Hampshire on an athletic scholarship and captained the 1980 varsity team to a NCAA championship victory over Maryland in which she scored the final goal (her third) with seconds left.

After college, Ms. Swan moved to Boston to pursue a Masters in Fine Arts at the Museum School. In Boston, she met and married Paul G. Forté of Washington, D.C. While at the Museum School, Ms. Forté earned acclaim for her quirky sculptures made from wood, metal, glass and household detritus. Her most famous piece, entitled "Raptor," was a ten foot long bird of prey with eyes of glass doorknobs, a beak of twin scythe blades and breast coloring achieved with six thousand green, blue and white thumbtacks.

The Fortés divorced in 1992 and Ms. Forté moved to Providence, R.I. where she earned a name in the interior design field. An aggressive form of cancer struck her last year. She moved back to Boston to be with her ex-husband, who was with her when she passed away quietly in their home.

Funeral services will be private. In lieu of flowers, donations may be made in her name to the Dana-Farber Cancer Institute.

I poured myself some coffee and brought the paper over to the window. I was reading the obit through my tears, for the fourth time, when I glanced over to the far wall and noticed that Shannon's painting was not in its place, but had been moved onto her easel in the middle of the room. I went over to examine it. One of the windows in the painting, on the top floor, had been changed. There'd been a frail older woman standing with her walker before. She had been replaced by a young lady, reclined in her bed, propped on pillows. The hair and the shape of the face were unmistakable. It was Kate.

Shannon opened the door and walked in as I looked at the painting. I was slack-jawed. She put a bag of pastries down and came to me. She stood beside me and we held each other while we admired her work.

"You are something."

"It's not done yet. I still have some details on the face."

"But I can tell."

"I guess if you can, then it's okay."

We stared some more. "The old lady who got erased?"

"My mom," her voice dropping in pitch.

I rubbed her back. "That all done now?"

She turned into me and buried her face in my chest. "It'll never be all done. But it's done."

"Good." I felt that welling of excruciating joy growing inside again. It was a feeling that had become a regular visitor lately. "That was quite an obituary, darling."

She sighed into my chest. "I hoped you'd like it." She looked up at me. "D'you think Kate would have?"

"She loves it. I asked. She said you did good."

"She gave me permission."

I hugged her hard and spied the bag. "What's in the bag?"

"Apple Chaussons."

"Let's eat 'em."

That was but a brief lull in our storm of emotions. We knew what was to come, we didn't know how it would turn out. We only knew we had each other and a pretty good idea that would be enough.

Judge Wheeler was exceedingly sympathetic to me, and postponed the scheduled beginning of my defense until the next week. Shannon and I spent our time moping around in a daze. I had a big hole in my heart, and that could be under-stood—if not by the usual divorcee. But Shannon was incon-solable. For nights on end, we lay in bed while I hugged her as she cried until she fell asleep. And on those nights when I could sleep myself, I would be awakened by her sniffling and shud-dering. That woman loved Kate as much as I did, but I suspect-ed she was crying for her mother as well.

At the same time, while I tossed and turned, I found my thoughts of Kate interrupted persistently by an all-consuming hatred of Bernie Kilroy that bordered on violent. At times I had to fight off images of punching him in the face. Once, I dreamt of burying my elbow in his eye socket, shattering his lacrimal bone, standing over him, urinating on him while he suffered. The vividness of it shocked me awake, and I was ashamed that such a vile thing had outranked Kate in my subconscious.

Even more persistent, though, was the nocturnal nail-biting and abject despair over the continuing silence from the FBI about Rex's handiwork. My persecutor was a despicable, hypocritical, ruthless scoundrel! We'd delivered his stinking carcass on a silver platter!

The fix must be in. I was doomed.

I fully expected that when next week arrived and I put on my sensible gray suit with the not-too-fancy tie and slightly scuffed shoes, I would still be woozy from lack of sleep and feeling as vacant as Shea Stadium during the World Series.

I could only hope the jury would feel better about me than the Mets' fans do about them.

Chapter 26
A Hail Mary Pass, an Incompletion and Sudden Death

At the end of the prosecution's case, every defense lawyer files a Motion for Directed Verdict. Every one. It is an argument that says that, considering all of the evidence the prosecution has produced, no reasonable jury can convict on the law. It's a Hail Mary pass, and it is almost never caught.

While Shannon and I spent the week blubbering, Al worked his fingers to the bone, producing one of those legal briefs that no one but a judge or an insomniac would read. Since it happened to pertain to my freedom, I read it with great interest, and I appreciated why he charges $750 an hour. It was righteous, it was accurate, it was written with inescapable logic and supported by clear and compelling case law. Before Al proceeded with my defense, he and Kilroy both argued the motion orally to Judge Wheeler, out of the jury's presence. Wheeler listened to both, questioned them with stunningly precise recall of testimony that was now months old, and when the lawyers had shot all of their ammo, he took it under advisement—an annoying legal idiom for "I'll decide later."

The jury was summoned. It had been so long since I'd seen

them, some appeared to have aged, or were at least tired of having to return to this courtroom week after week. I was relieved to have at least that in common with them.

When they were settled, Judge Wheeler explained that it was our turn now, and that they would hear Al's opening statement, which was not evidence, but argument, and so forth.

"Mr. Croston, you may proceed."

Al rose and buttoned his suit coat as he began speaking. He thanked the jury for their patience, promised them an efficient defense and hoped to have them home with their families by the end of the week. What a nice guy, they must have thought.

While he spoke at length about the volumes of testimony Kilroy had subjected them to, I looked at the table in front of his seat, and noticed the two documents we'd been holding onto these months. The "nuclear option," we'd begun to call it. The last hope. Life saver. Pick a shopworn idiom. I glanced over my shoulder at Will, who sat next to Shannon in the back row. (Where was Stacey?) I knew I didn't have the same ability to save his career that my father had with Sidney. I thought about Rex's exhaustive efforts to uncover the whole insurance scam, how much it had cost him, what he was giving up, and that it had come to nothing. A fortune, vanished in the bureaucratic maze of the agency we ought have been able to trust the most. I couldn't let Al play another high face card and get trumped again.

"You've heard volumes of testimony about golf games and dinners. It is a lifestyle many of you might resent, or perhaps aspire to. But Paul Forté is not on trial because of his lifestyle…"

Oh yes he was, I thought. It *was* a lifestyle, ignoring the small "technicalities" of the laws that separate the honest from the corrupt. He *was* a scofflaw, habitually flouting what he knew were minor laws, because he convinced himself of something convenient and nice. Why, those laws don't apply to him!

"He did nothing in exchange for the unconditional generosity of his friends…"

Didn't he? Was the ardency of his debating or the conviction of his vote utterly devoid of any sympathy to or affinity for his "friends?" His "friends" whom he had so seldom seen since the end of his legislative career? Who was he fooling?

"A simple game of golf…"

On a piece of hallowed ground.

"Food and drink…"

Osso buco and Romanee Conti!

"And for all of this testimony, you will note the absence of any direct evidence, not a single original document that proves beyond a reasonable doubt that Paul Forté knowingly offered an amendment at the request of Stuart Pierce. Why?" Al joined his hands like a supplicant and walked to the railing of the jury box. Plaintively, he asked them, "Why did not the government in this case present for your inspection the actual amendment that he allegedly delivered to the House rostrum, as Mr. Kilroy wants you to believe? Where is this evil amendment? Where's the smoking gun?"

I looked at Kilroy. He had both of his hands planted on the table, poised to pounce up and object.

"I'll tell you why!" Al raised a hand, finger pointing at the ceiling. He turned from the jury and strode briskly back to the table. He reached for one of the documents. "Because the document that would prove his case—"

"Objection! Objection! I object!" Kilroy's face puffed out and flushed crimson. "Improper argument! Unfair surprise!" he sputtered. "I demand a mistrial! I demand Mr. Croston be sanctioned!"

The jurors gawked at Kilroy. Wheeler tapped his gavel lightly." "Calm down, Mr. Kilroy. What is your objection? Mr. Croston is permitted to refer to evidence he intends to introduce, as long as he introduces it—eventually."

"But he doesn't. He can't—" Kilroy caught himself, paused, then, turning quiet and grave, started again. "I believe, your Honor, that Mr. Croston is in possession of fraudulent evidence and intends to use it in this Court."

Kilroy's voice had a rhythm and cadence to it that stunned me. The courtroom fell eerily silent. My mind raced, the picture in front of me like it was on a screen, the edges blurry. I feared for a brief moment that I was having a stroke. It must have been the pure adrenaline combination of fear, anger, hatred and that most basic instinct of survival.

Then the stillness was broken, and with it, Kilroy turned toward the gallery. I followed his gaze and saw Stacey McGonigle walking toward the bar. I glanced at Shannon, who now wore a fierce grin. Menacing. What the hell was going on?

Kilroy turned to the judge, incredulous. "Your honor, I'm in the middle of an objection."

Judge Wheeler was inscrutable. "Hold your horses there, Mr. Kilroy." He looked at Stacey, who'd halted at the bar. "What business do you bring before the Court?"

Kilroy protested. "Your Honor, we're in the middle of a trial here."

"That's right, Mr. Kilroy, and it's my trial. And I have this gavel here." He held it up for all to see. He turned his attention to Stacey. "Please step forward and identify yourself."

Stacey stepped through the bar gate and came to the side of our table. "Your Honor, my name is Stacey McGonigle. I am the Agent in Charge of the Public Corruption Unit of the

Federal Bureau of Investigation. I am here on official business."

"State your business," Judge Wheeler said.

I looked at Al. He watched as though he had written the script for the entire thing.

"Your Honor, I am here to place Bernard Kilroy under arrest."

I looked at Kilroy as the audience gasped. His jaw dropped as his face turned beet red. "That's the most outrageous thing I've ever heard!" He turned and moved toward the bench.

"Stay where you are, Mr. Kilroy. Do *not* approach this bench."

Kilroy froze, looking like he'd been stricken. "Your Honor, I demand to see that warrant. I want to know what judge signed that warrant," his voice a quavering shout.

Judge Wheeler was impassive. "I signed the warrant."

Kilroy turned from red to white. He looked from Wheeler to Stacey to the jury, now with his palms up, hands at his sides like a dazed supplicant. The jurors' mouths were as agape as his. "Ms. McGonigle, you may take Mr. Kilroy into custody."

Stacey looked back at the corner and Frank Dawkins stepped forward with Will Hartfield. The courtroom was so quiet, I could hear the soft soles of three pairs of shoes pad across the carpet. As they passed our table, Will winked at me.

Dawkins took out his handcuffs. As they jingled, Stacey held up her warrant to Kilroy's face and her voice filled the room.

"Bernard Kilroy, you are under arrest for mail fraud, conspiracy, theft of public property, racketeering, tax fraud, and criminal violations of the civil rights statute."

Bernie looked at it, but I doubt that he saw a word on the page.

Dawkins reached him. "Please turn around, sir."

Kilroy looked up from the warrant and saw the handcuffs. "Are those necessary," he squeaked, his dignity in tatters.

"Yes, they are, sir. No exceptions for rank or office." Dawkins maintained utter professionalism. I could tell he enjoyed his job, though. He flashed me a quick glance and grinned.

Kilroy turned around and put his hands behind him. I looked at Wheeler. Still inscrutable. The jurors mouths agog. Al, solemn and stoic, staring straight ahead. Gina, Rickenback, Shanley, Harrington and Pierce, all of them—in fact everyone in the gallery—catatonic as the cuffs riffled around Kilroys wrists. Reporters with pens not moving.

The metallic scratch of the handcuffs ratcheting signaled to all that murmuring was permitted. But not for long. Dawkins and Hartfield began to lead Kilroy to the jailevator—the same one I had taken! As Dawkins opened the door and ushered Kilroy into the cell, the murmur grew to a din until Wheeler's gavel rapped the oak sound block a half dozen times. The crowd grew quiet again. I think all souls were eager to know how such a farcical scene could continue.

Wheeler spoke. "Is there someone in the Courtroom with authority to speak for the United States in this matter?"

From somewhere, I hadn't noticed her before, appeared the lady who'd been gutted at my arraignment. "Frances Holloway, for the United States, your Honor."

"Yes, Ms. Holloway. What is your desire?"

"In the interests of justice, your Honor, the United States moves to dismiss all charges, with prejudice."

The courtroom erupted. Gallery. Jury. Marshals. Wheeler hammered his gavel until the block jumped in the air. He shouted, "Does the defense object?"

Al jumped to his feet. "No objection!"

"Case dismissed, with prejudice," Wheeler hollered above

the din. "The jury is dismissed! Court is adjourned!" He rapped the gavel one last time and charged off the bench, disappearing into his secret lair as the crowd erupted.

What happened next came in vague and incoherent snippets. I looked at Al and he looked back stone-faced, until the slightest squiggle of a grin appeared in one corner of his mouth. He clapped me on the shoulder, said "congratulations," and slipped into a crack in the crowd that was now surrounding me, despite the best efforts of the two marshals to keep them at bay.

I remained in my chair, still stunned and looking up into the faces that shouted and prodded and slapped my head and shoulders. Reporters shoved microphones toward me and hollered many questions at once. I heard them all but didn't hear a word they said.

Eventually, they were dispersed from the courtroom by a phalanx of marshals that had appeared from somewhere. Still sitting, I looked toward the door. Shannon and Stacey stood at the bar, hugging and swaying, oblivious to me. And Gina Gianferrante, standing to the side, looking at me with a grin the size of Rhode Island, waving some piece of paper and hopping up and down. I looked at the table and saw the two documents still sitting on the table. I turned them over. They were flyers for the courthouse deli.

I jumped up and turned, but Al was long gone. Gina broke through the bar and approached me with her gift. It was a check for the return of the deposit on the bond fee. Five grand, payable to yours truly. I gave her a kiss and shooed her out.

I opened the gate of the bar and put my arms around the two sisters. It turned into a three-way hug-a-thon. I was going to get some serious nose goop on the sensible suit I was wearing, but I had money for dry cleaning now.

· · ·

Rex and I had traded our two catbird seats at the corner of the Abe & Louie's bar for the best table in the house—a grand elliptical booth of black leather perched above the open floor of the main dining room. The table sat six, but we'd crammed two more in. Rex and Amelia. Stacey, Shannon and Sidney and Will Hartfield. And Al.

Barely more than a week had passed since the event that the national news had unimaginatively dubbed The Greatest Show on Earth. Artist renderings of the courtroom scene, starting with Stacey's approach to the bar and ending with Judge Wheeler's final crack of the gavel, had been flashed on the national news for days. Newsreel footage of a dazed Kilroy being placed into a black sedan by men with FBI on their jackets was picked up in syndication by the television news specials and the Sunday morning talk shows. I'd done a dozen interviews and turned down three times that many. Charlie Gibson interviewed me, for crissakes. He was an okay guy. Some guy named Matt Lauer called eleven times until I finally got through to him. "Unless you're Barbara Walters, you're no one."

That did the trick.

Shannon had put this soirée together. I agreed to it on the condition that Sidney Hartfield attended. Shannon called Stacey. Stacey talked to Will. Will called Norumbega. Many general releases and disclaimers were signed, and there was an ambulance idling out front and a RN sitting at the bar drinking seven-dollar Perriers. But we got it done, and Sidney was having the time of his life.

We all were. Champagne glasses and platters of tuna Carpaccio, calamari and oysters filled the table. There were veal chops and lobsters Thermidor on the way, along with a couple of Oregon Pinot Noirs and Cortons Charlemagnes. Sidney sat in his wheelchair between Will and me.

"I can't believe the two of you are sitting in public with me," I said to the two feds.

Stacey whispered to her sister and left Will to respond. "As an official matter, the Kilroy case is not being handled by the Boston office. It's been a joint operation between Washington and Phoenix for more than a year. Kilroy just happened to be in our jurisdiction when we got the word that the indictment had come down."

"You've known Kilroy was involved for that long?"

"Not at all. We—they—never had any reason to think he was involved. They knew about Erichetti's insurance operation, which they'd discovered while monitoring offshore banking transactions. They knew nothing of the Kilroys' involvement until Rex fed them his information a few months ago."

"You guys sure took your sweet time."

Will looked sheepish. "Understand, when we're about to take down a man of his rank, we need to get a very high level of approval."

I picked up a bread roll and flung it at him. The passing waitress was horrified.

Sidney leaned over toward me. "Paul, you're a chip off the old block." He gestured to the spread on the table. "I feel like I'm sitting at The Bagatelle with your Old Man. He couldn't have done it any better."

I reached around Sidney's back, grabbed Will's shoulder and pulled him in to share my reply. "Sidney, your son is a chip off your block too. Will, why did you give me that document?"

Sidney answered for him. "I told him to."

Will corrected him. "He asked me to help. Besides, Stacey asked me to give you consideration."

"Consideration. Hey Stacey, what the hell is consideration?" The wine was at work.

Stacey turned away from her sister. "I meant that he should take into account that you weren't a jackass."

Everyone laughed, none harder than Sidney. He gestured to his son to pour him more champagne, but Will shut him off.

Stacey resumed. "What I meant was, when you came to see me to stick up for Shannon, it made me wonder which side I was on. We have discretion, Paul. Sometimes the line between right and wrong isn't that clear."

"You knew more about my case than you let on, didn't you?"

"Not really. When I met you at Biba—that was pure coincidence, by the way—I knew who you were. I had no idea that Kilroy had you in his sights until he widened the investigation. And we certainly didn't know anything about the connection between your father and his, until Sidney here told us."

I looked at Sidney. "You old dog, you."

Sidney snickered. "It's been a long time since I've been in the game, Paul. But I remember how it's played."

There was something not quite right, though. "Hold the phone. I can understand why Sidney's revelation would have meaning to Will, but as an official matter, why would it be significant?"

"It had meaning to me on two levels, Paul. First, there was the obvious coincidence of our fathers. But you have to understand something. Like I told you before, we don't pick and choose the cases we investigate. We question Justice's decisions all the time, inside the family. But no one ever understood why Kilroy came after you."

"Because he called him 'Bernie,'" Al offered. That got a chuckle.

"You're half right, Al," said Will. "We always thought the case against Stackhouse was a crap shoot. The statute is so vague. So when he came after Paul, we began to think that he'd flipped his lid. I remember when I first got this case, I interviewed two people. They both said the same thing. 'Paul had us down to Hyannisport.' I play golf. I know how it works. I told Kilroy, 'there's nothing there.' He stared at me and said 'keep digging.' When we realized he was stacking the case against Paul in the grand jury, we knew he was a rogue. But we didn't know what motivated him."

"What difference does it make?" I asked him. "Who cares why he did what he did?"

Will got serious. "The prosecutorial power of the federal government is not for settling scores. You have constitutional rights. We're supposed to protect them, not shred them."

I remembered the two documents on the table. "What did you think when Al here began to refer to the failure to produce the amendment and then walked back toward the table?"

Will put his arm around his father. "I thought nothing of it, Paul."

I looked at Al, but he was Mr. Pokerface. I wouldn't ruin that for him.

"Well, I hope I can thank all of you meaningfully at some point, but I'll start by picking up this tab."

"The hell you will, Paul," said Sidney.

"Bullshit."

"Bullshit nothing. Your father never let me pick up a tab, even when I was at the Bear. You'll have to fight me for it." Will laughed, and Sidney turned on him. "Don't you laugh at me, boy. I'm still compos mentis. You bust my balls and I'll disinherit you."

That brought the whole table to a cacophony, but Will

looked a little nervous that maybe this was too much excitement for his father. I caught his eye and gave him a nod.

"So what happens to my old friends at the T?"

Neither Will nor Stacey moved to answer.

"Hey, come on. Rex and I have a lot of personal investment in this. What's gonna happen to Cruddy and Fetore?"

"We can't talk about that, Paul," said Stacey.

"It's ongoing," added Will.

"I'll bet Liguotomo was better at hiding his involvement than Kilroy."

More silence from the feds. Al said, "You needn't worry about the public document you passed along to Rex." It seemed that everyone was interested in their plates.

"All righty then."

That seemed to exhaust the shoptalk, and just in time, because the veal chops and lobster arrived, and we turned our attention to the food and more frivolous matters. There were many toasts, which went from maudlin to ridiculous. Occasionally, one or another person of consequence stopped by the table to congratulate me or just to say hello to Al or Stacey or Rex. An older man in a dark suit came over to Sidney, recognizing him from his Bear Stearns days. Sidney introduced me to the man. His name was Walter Fauntleroy and he was the managing partner of Fauntleroy, Cadwallader and Cheetham.

"Yes, Forté! I knew your father well." He gave me his card, encouraged me to call him, bade his goodbyes and moved on.

"You should call him," Sidney said. "Your father helped him out a long time ago. He's got a very successful firm."

"I'll consider it. Thanks, Sidney." I said it, but only to be polite.

He suddenly looked very tired, and informed Will and us that it was time to go. He gave me a pat on the back and said "see you around," the others gave him a warm goodbye, and Will took him off to the wheelchair van.

He'd started a wave, apparently, as Al and then Rex and Amelia peeled away, leaving me sitting between Shannon and Stacey on the big leather bench, looking out over the thinning dinner and drinks crowd. I was mentally and emotionally exhausted and more than half-drunk. And I felt great. Who wouldn't, sitting between two of the most beautiful women in the world?

When our banter was reduced to silly one-liners and giggling, I called the waiter over and asked for the check.

"It's been taken care of, sir."

Sidney, that ol' buzzard.

Summer 1995

At the crack of dawn, Shannon and I hit the road in a very large camper. We drove it to Toronto, where we stopped to ride to the top of the CN tower, dine at Opus and make furious love in a luxury suite at The Hazelton Hotel.

We drove into Michigan and up to Mackinaw City, across the Straits of Mackinac into St. Ignace, Canada, and on to Sault Ste. Marie. There, we chartered a boat with a captain who took us to the middle of Lake Superior and threw chum in the water to show us lake sturgeon the size of canoes.

Then we picked up the Trans-Canada Highway to Whitefish Bay into Lake Superior Provincial Park and farther on, Pukashwa National Park. In both of these locations, we eschewed the comfort of our camper to slather ourselves in DEET, swim naked in the frigid clarity of running streams and get naughty on their cool and slippery rocks.

Later at the Prince Arthur Waterfront Hotel in Thunder Bay,

Ontario, we amused the staff and patrons alike with our strange Boston accents (I put mine on) and half-drunken revelry at the hotel bar. West from there, we hit the wilderness in earnest, passing through towns with odd names like Winnipeg, Moose Jaw and Medicine Hat.

We reached the heart of the Canadian Rockies in Banff where we stayed at the breathtaking Fairmont Hotel. Shannon accompanied me as I attempted to play golf on their fabulous Banff Springs course, just the two of us in a golf cart. The views were vertiginous and one fairway climbed hard against a precipitous thousand-foot rock face. It exhilarated Shannon to a state of arousal, and there on the edge of the thirteenth fairway in a stand of scotch pines, we used the golf cart for our own erotic pleasure, while a quartet of regally antlered caribou passed by, nonplussed.

In British Columbia we stopped at Kamloops, a crusty old gold rush town on the Thompson River, where Shannon became the object of desire for every man without a dance at Cactus Jack's Saloon. Thence , headed due south through Vancouver into the Pacific Northwest United States of America. We hugged the Pacific coastline like it was a dying sister, following Route 101 from Aberdeen, Washington, all the way to Redwood National Park. It was a dizzying ride of breathless vistas and rests at seaside beach parking lots where aged hippies warned us against the lure of the surf, and pot smoke was whipped away by the relentless Pacific winds.

In the tiny town of Legett, California, we left the Redwood Highway on a hair-raising snake of a ride through the mountains, where our rolling palace crossed the center line at every hairpin turn, to the Shoreline Highway, Route 1, which brought us through the loony city of San Francisco, and eventually, to the Monterrey Peninsula and Carmel-by-the-Sea.

There, I and my wife unloaded our belongings into a cozy three-bedroom bungalow in Pescadoro Canyon, hard by the Pebble Beach Golf Links. She will paint and I will insinuate myself into the membership of Pebble Beach and Cypress Point, two of the most stunning golf courses in the world.

Of course, there is always the possibility that we will change our plan, or that in the course of determining said plan, we will have a difference of opinion. In that case, I will be slugged on the shoulder or pelted with an empty Marlboro box, and I will wallow in the knowledge that I am the luckiest man alive.

The End

Epilogue

Before we said goodbye to Boston, Shannon and I held a small ceremony at the Trinity Church. We did spring for the organist, the same one from Christmas past. Stacey was Maid of Honor and her brother Brian was Best Man. And honestly, it was a sweet time, and I love my in-laws.

While Shannon and I were settling in Carmel, I followed developments in *United States of America vs. Bernard Kilroy* with interest. True to character, Kilroy professed his innocence with a sanctimoniousness that I suspect he inherited from his father. Shannon passed along a report from Stacey that Kilroy's wife had left him and was trying to cut a deal; he was attempting to ban her testimony based upon the spousal privilege, and she was arguing that they were never legally married. In the meantime, the feds had seized their houses in Arizona, Vermont, Marblehead and Nantucket, and their yacht in Palm Beach. His political plans were put on indefinite hold.

Liguotomo tried to cut a deal for himself, but that fell apart when he insisted that it had to include a waiver of all state criminal charges. He had trouble selling that to the new state Attorney General. He fired four lawyers in the process and is now representing himself. Too bad Bernie Kilroy wasn't the A.G. at the time. What goes around comes around.

As soon as Kilroy was arrested, Lou Fetore approached the prosecutor and offered his testimony against Liguotomo and Kilroy in exchange for total immunity. Unfortunately for Fetore, Rex had already provided everything Lou could have offered them, plus more, including some long-range blow-up photos of Fetore coming out of a motel room with Erichetti's wife. That must have made for an awkward family get-together.

Cruddy made it as far as Morocco before he was detained at the request of the U.S. State Department. He was on his way to Lebanon, and stopped in Rabat under the erroneous belief that Morocco had no extradition treaty with the U.S. Turns out it was Algeria, not Morocco. Oops. The State Department is in no hurry to extradite him, and the Justice Department isn't pushing. Say hello to our Moroccan friends, Mikey. Don't drop the soap.

Sidney Michael Hartfield passed away in his sleep at the Norumbega Skilled Nursing Facility on July sixteenth, his ninety-third birthday. He was discovered by his devoted nurse-aid, Molly, who reported that he had a smile on his face.

Stacey McGonigle left the Federal Bureau of Investigation on maternity leave in the fall of 1996. She gave birth to healthy twins named Sidney and Shannon Hartfield. She works part time for Data Quest Investigations and gets along quite well with Rachel.

Rex Barkley is our landlord, although he seems to be uninterested in collecting rent. He and I are talking about opening a California office of Data Quest. When he gets around to leaving his new home on Kahului Bay, Maui.

I'm not holding my breath.

Acknowledgments

It has been so long since the beginning of this journey, I hardly have room to fit all of the people who've helped me along the way, so I'll have to arbitrage a little bit.

I begin with a big debt of gratitude to John Hudspith, who discovered my very first chapters on youwriteon.org in the Spring of 2008. He brought me over to The Bookshed to join a small community of writers who flogged me mercilessly and lovingly until I could write. Patty DeLois, Danny Gillan, Gillian Hamer, Jo Reed, Lorraine Mace, Jill Marsh, Sheila Bugler, Liz Miller, Dan Holloway and others. There is nothing more valuable than honest criticism from people who know what they're doing.

I made so many dear friends during the crazy days at Authonomy, when Small Fish grew into a novel. I have to single out the fabulous beta readers who gave so much time and input to its development—Oliver Corlett, Maria Bustillos, Kate Kasserman, Jason Riley, Philippa Fioretti, Tony Barker, Christy Jordan, Marcella O'Connor, Suzanne O'Leary. But no one was a better beta reader than my local friend Michael Strahm, whose input before the last and final rewrite produced some elegant adjustments. Most especially, I want to thank Robb Grindstaff, who I met on Authonomy, drank many beers with, and now refer to with pride as "my editor."

Then there is my pal Russ Bubas—the real, live Rex Barkley; and Frank Dawkins, an Assistant U.S. Marshal at the John Joseph Moakley Courthouse; and John Foley and Gail Marcinkiewicz of the Boston office of the FBI. Those folks gave me tours I'll never forget. And thanks to Attorney Jim Bolan for his counsel in the area of legal ethics. And of course, my old schoolmate Dean Rohrer, for his work on the superb book cover.

Finally, there is my fabulous agent, Christine Witthohn, and her husband, Jeff Mehalic, who read this manuscript and had confidence that it would sell to a traditional publisher, just as the publishing business was tanking, and then encouraged me to self-publish it. They are members of my team, hopefully for a long, long time.

About the Author

Pete Morin has been a trial attorney, a politician, a bureaucrat, a lobbyist, and a witness (voluntary and subpoenaed) to countless outrages. He combines them all in this debut novel.

Pete's short fiction has appeared in *NEEDLE, A Magazine of Noir, Words With Jam, 100 Stories for Haiti*, and *Words to Music*. He published many of them in a collection titled *Uneasy Living*.

When he is not writing crime fiction or legal mumbo jumbo, Pete plays blues guitar in Boston bars, enjoys the beach, food and wine with his wife, Elizabeth, and their two adult children, and on rare occasion, punches a fade wedge to a tight pin surrounded by sand or water. He lives in a money pit on the seacoast south of Boston, in an area once known as the Irish Riviera.

Pete is represented by Christine Witthohn of Book Cents Literary Agency.

Also by Pete Morin

Giving It Away (free short story)
Uneasy Living (short story collection)

Please enjoy a sneak preview of Pete's newest novel

Law & Disorder

Chapter One

In my considerable experience, drug dealers are more likely to die a violent death than get hit by a bus. So, when I was summoned to Ernesto Chula's party house on Long River shortly after 11:00 P.M. on a Saturday night, finding him with a hole in his chest the size of a Thanksgiving turkey was no surprise.

The cause of my anxiety was not the grisly murder, but the mountains of evidence that a party had been in progress when Ernesto met his untidy demise. That raised the practical certainty that his usual party guests would eventually be identified. Professional acquaintances of mine, you might say. People who shouldn't have been anywhere near the place.

But I am a homicide detective. If the evidence happens to ruin someone I know, that's their problem. I leave the politics to someone else. At that moment, the someone else was the first man I saw when I entered the house. District Attorney Frank Falvey.

"Hello Marty," Falvey said. His ponderous bulk stood inside the open front door as he looked in the middle of a sunken living room, hands jammed in his suit pants pockets as though he were waiting for a bus in the cold, eyes cast downward, a frown buried deep in his jowls.

"Evening, Frank." On the living room floor lay Chula's blood-soaked body. "Mr. Chula looks like he's not feeling well."

I stood in the stoop and shook Falvey's outstretched hand. We looked down at the body.

"He seems to have a bad case of heartburn," Falvey said.

"Better not spend any more time inside, Frank. You might leave some hair behind."

"God knows I'm losing enough of it," he said. "Don't worry, Marty. I didn't touch anything."

"Better still, don't go further than where you are."

I slipped on my booties and gloves and stepped down into the living room to the body.

The hirsute corpse lay on its back, naked except for a paisley silk robe, open. The face staring up at the ceiling, still holding a hint of surprise. A gaping hole in his sternum spread outward in the indiscriminate pattern of a shotgun blast. The shot had taken away part of his chin and throat. Black and red pockmarks from scattershot dappled his jaw, shoulders, chest and stomach. I crouched down for a closer look.

"Looks like a twelve gauge," I said. A mass of shot, concentrated just below the windpipe, had opened a hole that bared the esophagus.

"From five feet, you don't need a lot of gauge."

I observed the blood spatter on the carpet to the sides of the body and on the front door frame and wall. A few feet from the body, two unopened Champagne bottles lay askew. "Looks like he got it when he opened the door."

"Beats me, Marty. That's your job." Falvey took a hand from his pocket and tugged his necktie loose.

"What brings you here tonight," I asked him. "Isn't this job left up one of your crack assistants?"

Falvey's hands returned to his pockets. "They're all on the Vineyard for the weekend. I was eating veal at Urano's when I got the page. All I got left are juniors, and I didn't want them to lose their prosecutorial zeal, exposing them to this mayhem."

"Four assistant DA's away together. Two men, two women. I dunno, Frank, sounds like a sexual harassment nightmare waiting to happen."

Falvey chuckled and shrugged, but he didn't seem too amused. "They're all consenting adults."

"I could argue over both the noun and the adjective," I said.

"It's just a figure of speech." Falvey looked around like it had been years since he'd been to a crime scene and wasn't happy to be breaking his streak.

"Yeah, figure of speech." I surveyed the room. White plush carpet (except for the blood stains). Sleek contemporary furniture, all black. The kind that looks good but is impossible to sit in. Glass coffee table, side tables with Oriental lamps. All of the tables littered with beer bottles and cocktail glasses, some of them half-empty, and ashtrays piled high with smoking detritus. "Where the hell's crime scene control?"

"I sent the patrolman home when I got here."

Just like Falvey to ignore protocol, if he even knew it.

"There's a shit load of evidence here," I said.

"Your people are on their way."

"My people? You mean our people, don't you?"

Falvey shook his head. "It's not a done deal yet, Marty. You've still got your crime lab. If it closes, I'll make sure Billups and Moses are okay."

I wasn't going to take that to the bank. "What about me?"

"You made your own bed, Marty. I've done what I can for you already."

"And I am eternally grateful."

Marty fidgeted. If he stuck around any longer, he'd be tempted to start wandering around, and I'd have to get official and tell him he was contaminating the scene. "You plan to stick around?" I asked.

"Tell you the truth, the smell of death gives me indigestion."

"Sure it isn't Urano's veal?"

"Nah, Urano's veal is like butter." He jingled the change in his pocket. "You mind if I scram?"

"I don't mind. You'll just be getting in the way anyway."

"I'll just let you guys do your job," the DA said as he stepped out the front door.

I doubted that, but it didn't do any good to say so.

Made in the USA
Charleston, SC
21 November 2011